CW01457786

The Midnight Factory

THE
Midnight
Factory

Book One *of*
The Shimmerfall Trilogy

Russell Luyt

FLARETAIL
PRESS™

© 2025 Russell Luyt
All rights reserved. No part of this publication may be reproduced,
stored in a retrieval system, or transmitted in any form or by any means
—electronic, mechanical, photocopying, recording or otherwise
—without prior written permission of the copyright owner.

This is a work of fiction. Names, characters, places and incidents
are the product of the author's imagination or are used fictitiously.
Any resemblance to actual persons, living or dead, events,
or locales is entirely coincidental.

ISBN (Hardcover): 979-10-979129-2-5
ISBN (Paperback): 979-10-979129-1-8
ISBN (eBook): 979-10-979129-0-1
ISBN (Audiobook): 979-10-979129-3-2

First Edition
Rights: Worldwide

Published independently under the Flaretail Press imprint.
Flaretail Press is a registered trademark in the European Union
and the United Kingdom. ™ used in other jurisdictions.

Book design: Adam Hay Studio, UK
Copy editing: Nicola Hodgson

Mentions légales (France) :
Tous droits de traduction, de reproduction et
d'adaptation réservés pour tous pays.
Dépôt légal : octobre 2025
Imprimé en France par Amazon KDP et IngramSpark
selon le lieu d'exécution de la commande.

www.shimmerfall.net

For Heidrun

I

'Did you see the hanging?'

It was dark, and he narrowed his eyes in the glare of the strobe lights behind her. He paused, drawing vapour into his lungs before exhaling a rehearsed suspension. 'Don't think so.' His voice was flat.

Anouk considered him for a moment. What was it with dealers? 'Her head fucking came off, mate. It's not like you could have missed it,' she said through clenched teeth, swallowing the last word as her throat tightened. Tears gathered in her eyes. Why had she brought it up? Maybe to make conversation. No—the guilt. It just wouldn't let go.

The dealer leant back, his head lightly touching the wall behind him. Someone had scrawled a cock and pair of balls where it came to rest. They stuck out from behind his left ear. 'Sweet-Cheeks, I don't do politics. You want the shimmer or not?'

Dickhead. People like him lived in a twilight world, and it dimmed their senses. Obscured by shadow and substance, so they didn't have to feel anymore. The distaste was etched on her face.

He continued. 'Look, we all do what we do to get by. You came to me?

'Yeah, sure.' She tasted her own hypocrisy as she slipped him cash from her palm. The notes wore worn and no longer in official circulation. A small paper packet glided from his hand to hers in its place.

Anouk turned, eyes lowered. She twisted her body around a mirror-clad pillar and caught a blurred glimpse of her own reflection. A crack running down the centre distorted her image, and she momentarily imagined the two faces staring at her. The music seemed louder now, mingling amongst a throbbing mass of bodies. Bursts of light exposed momentary gaps for her to exploit as she made her way towards her companions. They sat at a small table on the far side of the basement. She accidentally kicked a bottle lying in her path, which went spinning between moving feet. Anouk reached the table and slid down next to a young woman. They were both dressed in black. It was not an uncommon colour to wear among their kind. The woman was barely twenty. She grudgingly slouched along the bench to make space. Anouk didn't notice. 'You have it?' The words slurred together.

'It doesn't work as well with alcohol. It would be an arsing waste on you,' Anouk said.

'Didn't hear you complain when I gave you my share of the cash,' the woman responded.

Anouk suppressed the rising tide of irritation. It was just the withdrawal. *God, I can be such a bitch.* Rookie mistake to team up with a stranger hanging around at the entrance, but she and Jimmy needed the money, and the woman was rattling badly. She was an easy target and had agreed to pay well above her fair share. 'Jeez, I need a sprit,' Anouk said aloud.

'Pass it over then,' Anouk's friend sitting opposite said.

His sandy-blond hair was visible as a silhouette in the flashing light. Although she couldn't see his face, she knew it was kind. Troubled beyond his years, but kind. His hand moved across the table in anticipation, trembling. Anouk reached down into her pocket and slipped her fingers in to retrieve the packet she had placed there a few minutes before. Her jeans were too tight, and she raised herself slightly above the seat to reach further down. She pulled the packet out between two fingers and deposited it into his outstretched hand. 'Jimmy?'

'Yes?'

Anouk leant furtively towards him. Her movements were exaggerated, hinting at a more playful past. He leant forwards too.

'Jimmy, remember: all that glitters is not gold,' she whispered into his ear.

He said nothing. But as Anouk pulled away, settling back beside the young woman, she imagined an old smile on his lips. They had shared that joke ever since their first sprit of shimmer together. It was a rare moment of honest recognition. It made her feel normal again, in control—or at least provided the illusion.

Jimmy worked swiftly. He placed and opened a small clear bottle with a pipette on the table in front of him. He came prepared. It was three-quarters full with a simple saline solution. He tore the corner of the packet deftly apart with his teeth, and, despite his unsteady hand, he carefully emptied the contents into the bottle. It was too dark to see, but Anouk knew well the look of shimmer crystals settling, like glitter. He closed the bottle and held it tight in the palm of his hand.

'Good thing it's bloody hot in here. Should dissolve quicker.' He meant this as reassurance. It had been a long while—at least since the previous evening—since any of the three had had a fix. The next track played; the opening ambient chords were unmistakable, followed by hardcore beats.

Kiss me dead, baby, you're my inclination
Kill me softly, baby, I'm your dedication

Okay, so it was vintage. But who didn't love it? A bit of electronic dance. Her dad would be pleased. She stopped there. Thinking of her father just before spritting up. *What the fuck.* She shook her head.

You're my today-future, bittersweet tomorrow
You're my every hour, panic-sown sorrow

Jimmy's voice brought her back to the present. 'All done. Who'll do the honours?'

'You first, Jimmy. No worries. The brewer gets to taste his brew,' Anouk said.

Jimmy nodded his gratitude, and, after a brief shake of the bottle, unscrewed the pipette. Pinching and releasing the top, he pulled it out and raised it towards his head, tilted back. His hand was still trembling. The first drop missed the corner of his eye and rolled down his cheek as though it were a tear.

I'm the one hurting, every minute hour
I'm the cause-victim, tasting life so sour

'Well, that's a waste!' the moody young woman grumbled.

'Shut it! Here, Jimmy, let's give you a hand.' Anouk rose and moved to sit beside him. She took the bottle and the pipette, then gently wiped the glistening trail from his cheek with the back of her hand. She loved him. Not a lover's love: the tender love of friends who know each other deeply. Close friends through their reflected past—both alone in an unforgiving world. She placed the bottle on the sticky table, withdrew the now-full pipette, steadied Jimmy's head by supporting his chin, then softly squeezed the rubber end. One drop fell to the corner of his eye, lingered for a moment, then dissolved under his eyelid.

'Oh God!' Jimmy sighed as he melted into the backrest. 'Thank you, shimmer, glimmer, shine,' he intoned, reciting the drug's street names.

Anouk followed the ritual next. She held her breath as the drop fell and then, after the familiar slight sting of the saline solution and a rush of shooting warm light, all was good. She glided effortlessly under the drug's spell—into shimmerfall—that moment of bliss when all earthly worries melted away.

You're my master, hated, foul obsessed, enchanted
I'm in thrall, subjected, wrecked, possessed, disgusted

But bliss was a fragile thing...

2

'Pig! Cunt!' the young woman screamed, spittle congealing at either side of her mouth. Senior Superintendent Jerome P. Kilgore of the Bureau for Virtue stared passively back, facing her, red jackets holding her arms at either side. His gaunt features expressed a mix of blunt indifference and distaste.

He considered the woman coldly, puffing out his hollow cheeks. She appeared to be in her early twenties. Her dark shoulder-length hair fell over her face, but not enough to hide the pink and aggravated whites of her eyes. *How curious*, Kilgore mused. *A lively spritter?*

As if reading his mind, a bearded red jacket to the woman's left responded, 'She's been drinking. Dulls the effect.'

'Aah,' Kilgore drawled. 'So, you enjoy a little bit of everything, do you?' The corners of his thin lips curled upward. The young woman did not respond, stiffening her body in anticipation. Kilgore paused. He scanned the surrounding hall. He hated underground shithole clubs like this. They stank of sweat; of people. They made him feel unclean. 'Unfortunately, you are not much good to me in your current state.' He turned his attention

6

to the red jackets. 'Process her for holding; we can decide what to do with her once her manners have improved.'

'Yes, sir,' the red jacket to her left responded, bowing gratuitously. He led the young woman, who staggered as she turned, to a group of already assembled detainees in one corner. They stood under an old exit sign above a door, the curtain already pulled to one side. It shone red and mockingly flickered on and off.

'Oh, and officer...' Kilgore trailed.

'Yes, sir?' the fawning man said.

'In my experience, manners are best taught.' He smiled joylessly. He then focused his dispassionate attention on the young woman's two companions. One was a lanky young man with unkempt hair. His eyes were pale blue-grey but stained with the betraying pink surrounds of shimmer. 'Also of no immediate use to me like that,' Kilgore said to an attendant red jacket, and with a perfunctory wave of his hand indicated the same group of detainees to which they had led the woman. The young man, as if in a daze, compliantly followed the red jacket.

'Jimmy?' someone whispered.

Kilgore fixed upon the remaining youngster. 'Pardon me?' he hissed.

'Jimmy?' she whispered again, only slightly louder. She had taken shimmer. The whites of her eyes were pink—evidence enough. But she was not drunk. Something about the young man moved her beyond stupor.

Kilgore's annoyance stirred again. He ground his teeth. Clearly, this trip would be trouble. Pickings were not new. People surely understood the order of play; the rules? Had his authority escaped notice? He stroked his badge of office. Regarding the woman who dared speak, he considered how best to impress these simple truths upon all present. She stared ahead, in a

7

daze. Without warning, and with practised effort, he swung a backhanded blow to the side of her face.

The young woman was of medium height but slender. The weight of the blow lifted her to her toes, as if a ballerina, before she sank to the floor. Kilgore felt a familiar tightening in his groin: cruelty and desire fused in youth, repressed then, but now fully claimed. He placed his hands in his pockets and re-arranged himself to avoid an obvious bulge. He did this unconsciously, much like breathing. A thin rivulet of blood and clear mucus worked its way down from her nose, over her parted lips, to drip from her chin onto the floor. Slowly, she pulled herself to a sitting position and raised her head with blurred eyes.

Kilgore regarded her. The blow had thrown greasy hair from her face, shimmer playing in her eyes; they seemed to leak as he traced the blood flowing down her face. He was wondering, then pulled himself from reverie. 'Another stoned spritter, same group as before.'

'Excuse me. I mean, pardon me, sir?' Another unsolicited voice appeared.

Kilgore looked up, seeking the person to whom it belonged. His irritation had not yet subsided and now rose even quicker. The collar of his shirt felt tighter. His eyes closed as he steeled himself. 'Yeess?' he whistled, mouth barely moving.

'She's one of ours, sir. She's a dealer. With all due respect, sir.' The voice belonged to a tall man. He had stubble a few days old that matched his uncurated appearance. Kilgore recognised his mixed ancestry. The man walked tentatively forwards. His hesitancy seemed out of character for someone who might otherwise hold himself confidently.

'Yours? One of yours? A dealer?' Kilgore sneered. 'Pray tell then, why is she lying like a degenerate on the floor? Dealers deal drugs, rather than devour them, do they not?'

'Ah, sir, it's sort of a business perk,' the man responded, a twinkle daring to appear in his eye. The assembled red jackets sniggered. Kilgore did not laugh. The man continued, 'We find it a helpful motivator—paying extra in shimmer—a kind of bonus incentive and loyalty programme wrapped up in one.' Gaining some of his characteristic confidence back, 'We have great employee retention and...'

'That's enough,' Kilgore snapped. He regarded the man again. Hopefully not for much longer. 'Fine, come and drag her skinny arse back. But...' now addressing the officer attending the group of gathered dealers, '...make damn sure you scan her in before we leave, just to check.'

'Consider it done, sir,' the red jacket said.

'Right, I think we're done here for now. Take that lot and load them up,' Kilgore said, pointing to the half dozen dazed club-goers, including Jimmy. He'd hoped for better pickings, but this haul met the quota. 'That lot...' he now pointed to a third group of shimmer-free employees and clientele, '...scan them in, check credentials, and then they're at liberty to bugger off. Same with the four dealers.'

Kilgore turned to go, but hesitated. He looked down at the young woman sunk on the floor. The blood had stopped flowing and was now coagulating in globules. Pity. She was pretty, even for a degenerate. Such striking dark auburn hair. She reminded him of his daughter.

3

Anouk's head ached. She perched on a bar stool. Her feet were resting on the lower crossbar but kept slipping off. Her jacket was hanging on the stool's backrest.

'Here, take this,' a man said. 'It will help level you out. It will also help with the headache.'

She reached out, peering through slitted eyes, groping towards the voice's general direction. The light felt unbearable. Her fingertips touched a palm and a pill resting in its centre. With difficulty, she picked it up and manipulated it onto her tongue. She swallowed, but it stuck in place as though on a flytrap.

The rim of a glass rested against her lower lip.

'Swallow. Just a sip.'

Gingerly, she sipped. The pill escaped and pursued cool water down her throat. It felt soothing. She sipped again.

'Thank you,' Anouk murmured.

'That was quite a whack you took,' the voice said. 'Lucky all that shimmer you sprit hasn't left too much of your brain. Not much to lose, eh?' It wasn't a funny joke, but it wasn't malicious.

'What did you give me?'

'Dexedrine,' the voice said. 'Good thing one of my customers is a doctor. Keeps me in steady supply.'

Oh bollocks. She recognised that voice. Anouk risked increased light, opening her eyes a fraction. Pain pierced her forehead, and she couldn't see his face clearly. It was like looking through a set of unadjusted and moving binoculars. Vomit threatened to work its way upward.

'Whatever you do, don't throw up on me,' the man said.

'Aidan?' she ventured.

'That's it, Dimples. Didn't know you knew my name. I thought I was only Master Shimmer to you...'

'You are. You were, I mean...' Anouk slurred, touching her cheek. It had swollen, and she could feel caked blood under her nose as she tentatively wriggled it. It had been ages since anyone had mentioned her dimples.

'Keep your hair on,' Aidan laughed, 'I know what I am.'

'What happened?'

'Kilgore. As always, a butt-clenchingly awful guest. Never invite that man for tea,' Aidan said.

Anouk was confused. Her head still hurt. 'Tea?'

'No, not tea, fool!' Aidan raised an eyebrow. 'He was here for pickings. You know the Bureau rounds up a few spritters now and then...'

'Yeah, sorry, of course,' Anouk interrupted, feeling daft. He didn't need to finish his sentence. Everyone knew that getting taken by the Bureau was a one-way ticket. 'Just not with it yet,' she confessed.

'Anyway,' Aidan continued, 'they round up a few spritters like your lame boyfriend Jimmy...'

'Jimmy? What? Holy crap! Why, I mean, where? Where did they take him?' Anouk spluttered. Her heart leapt, and a hot flush rushed up her back, across her neck and head. A ringing sound buzzed in her ears.

'Sweetheart, if you let me finish, you might...'

Anouk felt a drop of sweat run lazily from her armpit down her side. 'Might what? Where the hell did they take him? Where?' It was a futile question borne only out of panic. Where? There were rumours, of course. Whispers in the shadows and behind closed doors. None were good.

Aidan hesitated. Anouk's reaction had taken him by surprise.

One of his two companions appeared by his side. Anouk's vision was clearing. The Dexedrine was kicking in. It was another young woman. 'Cuz, we've got to go. Party's over. They want us out,' she said. 'Look, Anouk. It is Anouk, right?'

Anouk nodded.

'I feel you, I do, but some serious shit went down here tonight. Aidan saved your ass. And we went out on a limb...'

Anouk was struggling to take it in. She pushed her shoulders down, trying to relax. 'Saved me, what?' she said, with a wrinkled brow.

Aidan winced. 'Yeah, I might have said you were a dealer...'

'A dealer? What!' Anouk blurted.

Aidan's face lost animation. 'Okay, okay, let's stop the gibber.' He raised his index finger. 'First of all, honey bunch, we're all,' he said, showing his companions, 'we're all not too keen on "a dealer, WHAT" description.' His voice climbed several octaves higher on the 'what'. 'And second, it cost me two packs of shimmer to bribe the red jacket who scanned you so he would keep walking.' Aidan looked like he wanted to say more but settled for crossing his arms.

Anouk consciously slowed her breathing and felt her anxiety lessening. The ringing in her ears subsided. She took a sip of water to ease her dry mouth and scanned her surroundings. The hall was bright now. The music had stopped. Reality switched on, and the comforting alternative of shimmer vanished. The mundane and the depressing had taken its place. A few remaining employees were uncommittedly mopping spillage from that night. It looked like alcohol. At least it lacked any revealing chunks.

'I'm sorry.' She drooped in her seat.

The table clattered as someone righted it from its side. The club's clientele had obviously left in a hurry. Anouk pictured the red jackets' encouraging blows as they left. Those who had not successfully got away were scanned, fined and sent on their way, thankful for mercy. It was only the spritters among them who interested the red jackets.

'You know what, all's peachy. We're fine. But it's been a tough night,' Aidan said. There was a brief silence. 'You alright to walk?' He got up and moved to her side. Surprisingly gently, he placed one hand on her back and the other on her elbow and aided her to her feet. As Anouk regained her balance, his companion gathered her jacket from the stool's backrest.

The three crossed the dance floor, still littered with bottles, towards a flickering exit sign. Aidan's remaining companion, a genial looking young man, had hovered out of sight during their exchange. He stayed behind, talking earnestly to what looked like the barman, who had a shaved head. A tattoo of three arrows, slanting diagonally downward, was just visible below one ear above his jawline. It looked familiar. Anouk's gaze caught his attention. He turn his back to her, screening his conversation, and casually rested a hand over his tattoo.

They reached the door, which rested slightly ajar. The push bar looked broken and hung limply in its brackets, perhaps because of the red jackets' visit or the clientele's subsequent eagerness to leave. Aidan shoved it open with his shoulder and, with his hand still on Anouk's back, steered her to a flight of outdoor steps climbing to the street. The handrail was moist, and Anouk could feel flaking paint beneath her hand as she ascended. As always, the pavement was damp, but it seemed not to have rained. The night sky was out, the air cool and fresh against the stale indoors. 'You going to be alright?' Aidan asked. He was quite a lot taller than Anouk, so she had to look up towards him. She felt steadier now.

'Yeah,' she said, 'think so.' But something still nagged her. 'Why did they let us go? The red jackets? Kilgore? It doesn't make sense. You're dealers, right?' She added hurriedly, 'And that's totally cool by me.' Grateful to Aidan, she avoided riling him again so soon.

He grinned. 'Let's just say we have an arrangement. A *business* arrangement.' He tilted his head in mock thought. 'Although I'll wager there's nothing that skinny sack of shit Kilgore would like to do more than string me up and cut my nuts off.'

Aidan's companion snorted. 'Like he could ever find them,' she scoffed, nudging him.

'Oi, steady now, Fred!' Aidan playfully snatched Anouk's jacket from the woman's hands, holding it for a moment, then handing it back to its rightful owner.

'Cheers,' Anouk said, taking the jacket. 'That makes sense, but it's also... Why...' she faltered, trying to find the words, 'Why did you cover for me?'

Aidan mulled the question over. 'I saw the hanging this morning too,' he admitted. 'It's not something you can forget in a hurry, right?'

Anouk gave a small nod. She couldn't meet his gaze. She had looked away from many obscenities. Yet not everything was easy to ignore.

Aidan changed the subject. 'Watch out for the patrols,

especially the Free Fliers.' He was referring to unscheduled patrols of red jackets that roamed randomly during curfew and were difficult to expect. 'It's unusually bright tonight.' He paused, admiring the sky. 'You stay safe, Dimples.'

Anouk put on her jacket. She winced as the collar brushed her cheek. With one final glance at the pair, their faces indistinguishable, but their forms haloed in nightlight, she said, 'Thank you,' and made her way across the narrow street to the warehouse opposite. She turned back. They were gone.

———◎———

They were there. Anouk could sense it. Free Fliers parked on the leeward side of an apartment block. Worse than the usual red jackets, they were signed and paid-up Pary members—State instruments of terror. The moon half shone over the apartment block's flat roof, casting a night shadow over the utility vehicle and most of the road running alongside. The contours of floodlights emerged on the roof of the vehicle's cab. No one was visible inside, but their watchful presence filled the air with static.

She crouched at the edge of a shuttered and barren corner shop, which lay across the road from the vehicle. It was almost dawn. She could backtrack for ten minutes and take an alternative route, it was risky. Darkness was her friend.

Her breathing was rapid. A twirl of condensing breath escaped her mouth and drifted around the corner from where she hid. It hung there for a moment and then dissipated, but still blushed betrayingly in the moonlight before fleeing. She sucked in her breath.

The vehicle's floodlights ignited. Anouk's heart jumped. Had she been seen? Its diesel engine rumbled to life. She pushed deeper into the wall. Rough pointing between the bricks grazed her bruised face. Angles of shadow and light shifted across surfaces as the vehicle pulled out onto the road. Anouk glanced around the corner just as the vehicle passed. The rhythmic beating of the engine and slapping of wet tyres were out of place in the silence. Three red jackets were visible in the cab. They had not seen her. A tingling relief swept through her body as the tension in her muscles eased.

As the sound of the vehicle receded, Anouk rose to her feet. One knee cracked in complaint at its awkward angle. She rounded the corner cautiously onto the road. Small streams of water tracked her progress down towards the next intersection, where she bore left. The water carried on straight, taking a different route. A gully encouraged its course, carved into the asphalt through years of unrelenting rain.

Anouk rested for a few seconds, deciding on the best path. She contemplated the gully. At least the coastal defences were still holding. It was one thing to live in constant wet, another entirely to live under the sea.

The stream on the road rested on the far side of the intersection. It pooled around a stop sign before welling over a modest rise and continuing its journey. The sign, leaning a few degrees to one side, was daubed with familiar white sketching within its 'O'. These resembled continents of the Earth. She half-smiled at the memory of her dad.

Anouk carried on, turning left again down a cobbled alleyway. A few Elizabethan timber-framed houses hung claustrophobically above her head. Once the street had been a popular market with tiny shops selling a mixture of tourist memorabilia and oddities. As a young child, she had loved an umbrella store where each umbrella handle resembled a weird and wonderful animal; some had coloured feathers, others had gleaming scales. She reached the end of the alley and emerged onto a square, but was eclipsed by the night shadow of a protruding window from above.

The old woman's body remained. Red jackets had strung her up by one ankle after the hanging because of her decapitation. The other leg dangled in an impossible position, at ninety degrees to her torso, bent at the knee and barefoot. The street lamp in front of the Corn Exchange was ornate. At its base, blood had pooled below the stump of her neck and covered most of the lost shoe. Its laces peered out like the sails of a sinking ship. The head was gone. A haunted-looking dog stood hungry, licking the edges of blood where it settled.

Anouk expected it, but the horror was still too much. An involuntary moan seeped from her throat. She was there when it happened. She walked closer, but kept to the square's margins, and remembered the old woman's dignity; a dignity from a past period that now seemed distant. The woman had failed to show respect at the morning flag raising outside the Exchange. Red jackets had intervened, insisting that she stand still during the daily ceremonial. When she did not, an officer had struck her to the ground. Yet, at over eighty, she had found the strength to rise. He struck again, and once more, she rose. Nobody helped. Nobody came to her aid. *Not even me*, Anouk considered. The tears that she had fought earlier in the evening now ran freely down her face. She gritted her teeth and squeezed her eyes shut, willing the tears away as a gasp of remorse escaped her.

She peered at what remained of the old woman. They had tasked a red jacket—a recruit judging by his age—with placing the noose over her head. As if transfixed by shock, he had struggled to raise his arms. The old lady had reassured him, with a steady voice and compassionate eyes, 'It's fine, lad, it's fine. You go on then,' as she lowered her head to assume his burden. And now what remained of her hung like a bled chicken. A floral skirt draped over chest and arms. Sinewy legs and oversized underwear exposed. Where was her dignity now?

'God save New Albion,' Anouk muttered. The dog had slunk away as she approached. It stood looking at her from a safe distance. It disappeared into the remaining darkness, carrying its complicity with it. Anouk followed.

———◍———

Dawn was breaking as Anouk reached her home. Even the veiled trade in shimmer had gone to bed. The ethereal white hue of the easterly horizon was visible between two buildings. Home was a former council estate, an apartment block of grey concrete. It had seen better days twenty years ago. It had received no attention since. She climbed two flights of metal stairs, taking two at a time, then stopped at the first door on the right. No. 20 Jervis Gardens. No gardens here, that's for bloody sure: the closest thing to a garden was in the plastic house sign attached alongside the front door, where the number '20' sat surrounded by bright yellow flowering calendula. Her mother's painted addition.

Anouk recovered a key from behind it, slotted it in and tried to turn it. It was stiff, and she had to jiggle it before it caught and the latch dropped. She pushed the door gradually open, and entered. It was cold inside even though it was still late summer. The sour smell of old cigarette smoke clung to the air. Anouk could hear her mother snoring. She hadn't made it to her bedroom again. Anouk rolled her eyes. Sleeping on the sofa was a strange habit for someone so very particular about everything.

The apartment was small. Her mother was asleep in the kitchen-living space. A door leading to a toilet, basin and shower lay opposite the front door. The other rooms were two small singles. Anouk turned the handle of her bedroom and prodded.

The thin plywood door opened harder than she had intended. It banged on the chest of drawers behind. Her mother's snoring hiccupped before returning to a steady rhythm. Anouk moved forwards and closed the door behind her, sliding the latch into place. She moved her fingers up the wall flanking the door, located the light switch, and brushed it on. A light bulb flickered into dim glow.

She hated her room. She had never liked it. All things little girls were supposed to like adorned the walls. Pink and purples, lace and frills, baby unicorns. It was a temple of birthday presents she had received from her mother for as long as she could recall. Every birthday she would open her present and look excited, placing the gift in her room in a show of enthusiasm. And not once, not a single time, even into her teenage years, had her mother deviated from this script—her vision of girls.

Anouk unzipped her jacket, patting her pockets for stray items. A hard bump revealed itself on the right-hand side. She fumbled at the pocket's rim before sliding her hand in to recover the item. She raised it and recognised it like an old friend. It was a small amber bottle and pipette. Its colour distinguished it from the one used earlier in the evening, and someone had wrapped it in a small note. She unwound this to find a neat string of handwritten words.

Thought you might need this, Dimples? Stay off the streets. Don't buy for a couple of days.

The someone had signed with 'A'.

Anouk risked a smile. She placed the bottle on her bedside table, toeing her boots off and leaving them where they lay. She shrugged her jacket off and dropped it on top of the boots. Collapsing onto her unmade bed, she stared at the ceiling. It had an arch of glow-in-the-dark star stickers spreading from one corner to the other. She fingered the bottle beside her.

Jimmy came to mind. *Oh, Jimmy.* Her brief smile was now gone in a flood of anguish. As she unscrewed the bottle, filled the pipette, and brought it to one eye, the memory of him overwhelmed her—she was curled in pain on the floor, in the squalor of a drug den. Yet he held her tight. Protecting and forgiving despite all she had said, all she had done. Where she had been selfish, he was giving. From the outside, Anouk led. She was bold and brash. But in truth, she was alone and frightened. She relied on Jimmy more than she cared to admit.

The eye on the bruised side of her face had red tendrils of burst capillaries radiating from its corner. These merged with watercolour pink from the evening's recreational activities. The eye was painful, so she used the other. The drop fell; she replaced the pipette and raised the bottle just before the light and warmth of shimmerfall overcame her. *Shimmer, glimmer, shine... Jimmy...*

4

The junior officer picked at his teeth while his colleagues herded the seven detainees towards the parked van. 'You going to help out, mate?' one called.

'Yeah, suppose.' He lethargically kicked a straggler into a semi-trot to catch up with the other detainees. The mouthy young lady from the club was first in line at the rear of the van. His colleague, a red jacket like him, although with a bushy beard, was still holding her arm to ensure compliance. The van's double doors swung open from the inside, revealing a third red jacket and, behind him, a row of wooden benches on each side.

'Go on, get yourself in,' the bearded red jacket said, sharply pushing the woman forwards.

'No, no, no. Not too hasty, governor,' the junior officer crooned. It was the most energetic he had been all night. 'She's in the front with us,' he winked.

His fellow red jacket raised a bushy eyebrow.

'You heard what the Senior Superintendent said. We're to teach her a lesson, we are.'

His colleague gave him a tired look. He grabbed the young

woman again by the shirt sleeve and pulled her aside. She glared at him and muttered something under her breath. He slapped the top of her head, leaving her hair in a bird's comb. Now motivated, the junior officer marshalled the remaining detainees into the rear of the van.

Jimmy shuffled last towards the van's rear. The shackles on his wrists and the afterglow of shimmer encumbered his walk. He placed an unsteady foot on the stepwell. His knees were jittery. He hoisted himself up and thrust his shackled wrists forwards for balance. But the weight of his body proved too much. His knees gave way. A brush of steel told him that his chin narrowly missed the bumper. Stomach churning, his fall ended with a sharp jerk as his handcuffs looped over the towbar. A bolt of pain tore through his shoulders as they flexed upward to arrest his collapse. He wheezed, his nose hanging inches from the ground. A splatter of saliva marked his abrupt stop. The junior officer moved to close the doors.

'What do you think you're doing?' His colleague said, squatting just inside the van.

He frowned in confusion. 'We're done. I'm closing the doors. We're off.'

'And this one?' His bearded associate pointed down at Jimmy.

'We've loaded him up. He'll get there. What's all the fuss about?'

'The fuss, my good ol' buddy, my good ol' pal, is that pickings weren't too great tonight, were they?' Without waiting for a response, the red jacket from the van went on. 'And as much as you like fun and games, we had better get these,' he said, showing the detainees seated behind him, 'back to Kilgore in one piece, promptish.'

The junior officer shook his head and sighed. 'Really?' he

asked, hoisting Jimmy up. 'Get in. And don't balls it up again.'

Jimmy clambered awkwardly but successfully into the van, with a tug of help from the red jacket inside. The doors slammed shut behind him. He heard muffled speaking as he stood with his neck bent and pressed against the unlined metal roof. The red jacket in the van had pivoted, still squatting, to face him and snapped his fingers pointing forwards. Jimmy shuffled past the legs and feet of his fellow detainees to take a seat on the right-hand bench. He swayed as the occupants settled into the cab. Doors thumped closed, and he sat down just as the van lurched forwards. He hit his head on the reinforced glass window that separated the rear from the cab.

The bearded red jacket was in the driving seat. He was burly and short. He looked comical. Not tall enough to reach the foot pedals. The young woman was sitting in the centre, sandwiched between him and the junior officer. 'Hey!' the junior officer said. 'You missed the turning there,' indicating backwards with a jerk of his head.

'Not taking that route: too many potholes.'

'Fair enough, fair enough. Motorway then?' he chirped. His colleague didn't answer. They sat in silence. 'Perhaps a few tunes?' the junior officer proposed. His colleague began replying, then realised the question was aimed elsewhere. The junior officer had rotated slightly to his right and now sat grinning salaciously at the young woman. 'No, yes? Yes, no?' He moved his thumbs up and down at his chest, correspondingly imitating happy and sad faces.

'Oh, just get on with it,' the bearded man sighed, as he turned onto the slip road towards the motorway. It was curfew and empty. He congratulated himself on his savvy decision to take this route. The bright headlights tapped on and, after an initial stammer when changing gears, he forcefully sped up.

'Go, Cowboy!' the junior officer hollered in a caricatured American accent. He leant back, pretending to be thrown into the seat, and grabbed the woman on her thigh. He hurled his head back and howled.

The woman moved quickly. She grabbed the middle finger of his hand with surprising dexterity for someone handcuffed. 'Lick my arse!' She forced it backwards with an audible crack. He discharged a high-pitched screech, wrenching his hand free, and gawked in panic at his skewed finger.

'What the bleeding hell!' the bearded man bellowed as the van swerved in response to his startled pull. The junior officer whimpered, still staring at his finger. With his left arm outstretched, the driver grasped a fistful of the woman's dark hair and slammed her head against the glass window behind. She remained there, stunned. 'What in Christ's name were you thinking!' the bearded man roared.

'I-I,' the junior officer stuttered, 'I didn't do anything. The crazy bitch just broke my finger...'

'That's enough then! No more! We're finished for the night. No more messing around.'

'Sod that! This,' he spluttered, holding his twisted and trembling finger aloft towards the driver, 'deserves something extra!' His jaw jutted forwards with a snarl on his face. With his healthy hand, he clawed his trouser zip open, inching it down in quick stabs. He then grabbed at the young woman, taking hold of her right ear and a clump of surrounding hair, and pulled her down towards his crotch. She twisted, but his grip was firm.

She screamed in frustration and shrieked for the young man she'd met earlier that night, 'Jimmy! Jimmy!' Then she sank her teeth into his leg.

Moments earlier, Jimmy, oblivious to the chaos unfolding just a few feet away, rocked from the movement of the van. His eyes acclimatised to his surroundings. A single light shone diffusely from the middle of the roof. Although small, it resembled a bulkhead light, encased in a galvanised steel cage. With his hands cuffed, Jimmy imagined being cramped in the bowels of an old slave galley. The effect of the shimmer he had taken earlier that night was dissipating. His discomfort told him so. Three fellow detainees sat along the bench in front of him. They were unmistakably spritters. Their haggard and pale faces stared into nowhere. Degenerates? He could understand how easy it might be to see them as debauched, not fully human. Yet Jimmy saw beyond this. They were desperate, frightened and alone. He turned his head to his left and searched the faces of his fellow detainees, expecting to find Anouk's familiar and reassuring presence. With alarm, he saw she was not among them.

Jimmy knelt on one knee, looking at the detainees beside him. There were two men. They had positioned themselves to allow their hands to cup surreptitiously, one pair over another, at their shared sides. They were scared too.

Jimmy's agitation must have shown. 'Steady, son,' an older red jacket said, leaning forwards from a seated position at the end of Jimmy's row. 'Back you get.'

Jimmy moved back, but his eyes darted from place to place in the hollow hope of finding Anouk in some hidden corner. And then, through the shared window leading to the cab, he made out three people. Two were unquestionably red jackets. Even in the shrouded light, their maroon clothing was visible. And between them sat a smaller figure with both dark hair and clothes. *Anouk!* Relief flooded to settle his sharp breathing.

The gears faltered as they slid from fourth into fifth. Both rows of detainees synchronously swayed, shoulder to shoulder, towards the rear doors as the vehicle gathered speed. The red jacket at the end of Jimmy's row grunted as he elbowed a detainee from him. The sound of light rain was just perceptible against the van's thin steel side panels. It was calming, and Jimmy closed his eyes. Why was Anouk taken to the front? Perhaps more space? The rain beat more heavily. Muted conversation drifted from the cab. Unexpectedly, a dog howled from within, followed by a high-pitched squeal. Someone chastised the hidden animal for some wrongdoing. He peered down the bench, seeking to gauge the red jacket's response.

There was no chance to see. Without warning, the vehicle veered. The sudden movement flung the detainees seated in front of Jimmy forwards. One lost her balance altogether and landed, face first, against the panel between the two men seated beside him. Cursing, the red jacket stood crouched. With both hands he plied her back to her seat while, simultaneously, someone's head cracked against the glass partition between the cab and the rear. Jimmy hadn't seen whose head it was. He was trying to regain a steady position in his seat. His handcuffs made it difficult. Shouting issued from the cab. One voice was deep and angry; the other higher and hysterical. Then: a woman's voice, his name. She cried out twice in desperation. 'Anouk!' he called back in panic, rising from his seat. Another shriek followed. This was long and painful.

Without warning, the van pitched and rolled. Jimmy found himself in mid-air. Legs and arms hung intertwined, hair floating as though underwater. Then, nothing.

A void.

'Quick! Get up, get out!' a voice urged. An insistent hand shook his shoulder. He opened his eyes. It was all blurred. His senses were tangled and unhurried. With the imagined sound of rushing water, his eyes focused. A woman's face lay in front of him. Her broken nose almost touched his. He first supposed the voice belonged to her. Her inexpressive features betrayed the truth. She was dead. He recognised her as the detainee who had hit the panel hard when the vehicle first swerved. Whether she died then, or later, he didn't know.

Jimmy took stock of where his limbs lay. Tentative movements suggested they were all in working order. He felt winded, though. He was lying face down and pushed himself upright with his arms. When he arched his back, breathing became more difficult, and the pain in his chest worsened.

'Easy now.' A hand patted his back awkwardly, offering ineffectual help. It belonged to the man who had sat beside him. An improvised tourniquet slowed the flow of blood from a gash on his thigh. His friend hovered nervously behind, licking to moisten his dry and chapped lips. Only the red jacket remained in the rear with them. His one leg was cruelly misshapen and wound like a bent coat hanger around a semi-detached bench. He was unconscious, but a rising and falling chest showed he was still alive. 'We've got to go. Now!' The man plucked at the pullover on Jimmy's shoulder.

'The others?' Jimmy asked as his breathing habituated.

'They've gone. They've left. Only you and us now. Come on, get up quickish now,' the man exhorted. He clasped Jimmy's hands with one of his and with the other twisted a key to open Jimmy's handcuffs. With a click, the first cuff slid off, then the second.

As Jimmy scrabbled over the dead woman to follow both men out, he asked, 'Where did you get the key?'

'That one.' The second man pointed back to the motionless red jacket.

It was then that Jimmy remembered Anouk. '!' Panic once again rose in him.

'What?' both men asked in alarmed unison.

Jimmy didn't answer in his haste. The vehicle lay on its side. He was at its doors on all fours and swung his legs around and rotated into a seated position. He slid over a limp door, ducking under the other, which hung from above, and rose with a wobble. In a thin drizzle, he hurriedly made his way to the front of the vehicle. His fingers marked out the exposed axle to guide him in the murky pre-dawn. As he rounded the two front tyres, the cause of the accident was unambiguous. The vehicle had hit a deer.

'It's still alive,' the first man observed with detachment. He had limped after Jimmy and was signalling towards the animal. With heaving breaths, blood bubbled from its nose. If it could see them, it gave no sign out of its already clouding eyes. Jimmy worked his way further around and then gasped. The driver had broken his neck. His head lay to one side, several vertebrae bulging tellingly. The male passenger sat upright, even though the van lay on its side. He wasn't wearing a seat belt, but the deer's hoof had impaled his chest, and he lay motionless too. Jimmy then identified a smaller figure. It lay bunched at the driver's side. The force of the collision and the animal's weight had crushed her head.

Jimmy's wail was long and mournful. As the sun's infant rays spread to the tops of the first trees, he folded to his knees. He bowed his head and let his arms hang lifelessly at his side, sobbing.

Time slipped past him unnoticed.

The sun had risen, and the drizzling had ceased. There was a promise of warmth. The remaining two captives had long gone, and the deer was no longer breathing. Jimmy had not moved since kneeling. He felt numb. A robin appeared, but he was unaware of it. It bobbed and hopped close to his one hand, seeking, it seemed, to deliver an important message. After three short tutting calls, it flew to perch on the uppermost front tyre, where it observed him for a short while. Then, after a series of sharp peaking sounds, it flew off, content in the delivery of its missive.

A beseeching 'Hello?' roused Jimmy's consciousness. 'Hello, is anyone there?' The imploring voice again. With disinterest, Jimmy unfolded his back. His joints complained as he took to his feet. He kept his gaze down, unwilling to relive the scene in front of him. With stiff, hobbled steps, he returned to the rear of the van, from where the pleading was emanating.

The injured red jacket lay as before, but now alert. He looked up. Jimmy stared impassively back, the surrounding death draping him like a shroud. The red jacket sagged under his stare. He tried again, frowning. 'Some help, please?' His leg had continued to swell, pressing against the bench in which it lodged and causing him pain.

'Help?' Jimmy repeated absently. He didn't move.

'Yes, help. My leg. It's broken, stuck.' His voice was strained.

Jimmy regarded the red jacket. He felt nothing for him. No anger. No hate. Just apathy. He studied his face. Wrinkles criss-crossed his brow as deep fissures. His tan came from spending most of his time outside. He was older than most red jackets; his greying hair was short and neatly cut. But it was his laugh lines that gave Jimmy pause for thought. In those lines, he saw a thousand smiles engraved. He saw humour, happiness and humanity. He saw all the things that they tried most to destroy—a shared sameness.

Jimmy couldn't leave him exposed. Help would arrive, but for how long he couldn't guess. He crawled back into the van and settled alongside the red jacket, studying his misshapen leg. It had broken between two wooden bench legs. He placed one foot on the furthest leg and, weaving his fingers between the nearest bench leg and the man's contorted appendage, took firm hold of it.

The man flinched at his touch. 'Is that a good idea?' he said, looking unnerved. Jimmy didn't hesitate; he pushed as hard as he could muster with his leg and pulled back his arm with the aid of his upper body. Both wooden bench legs parted astonishingly easily. The red jacket keened in pain. Jimmy ignored this. The man's leg had probably already prised them apart as it broke. Jimmy positioned himself on his knees and, gripping at each armpit, stop-start dragged him past the dead woman towards the open door. Leaving the man lying on his back, Jimmy righted himself to a sitting position. He dangled his legs to rest on the inclined door and panted from the exertion.

They coexisted in silence for a few minutes. The motorway lay hushed. The curfew must still be in effect.

'Where are we?' the red jacket asked. He had rearranged himself into a seated position in grunted spurts. The man's back now rested against the inside roof of the overturned van, both legs splayed to his front, the broken leg bent at the knee and below it.

'Motorway,' Jimmy responded.

'Well, that explains it,' the red jacket proffered. He received no response and so continued. 'Don't usually take the motorway. Dangerous. Too much wildlife out during the night these days, since curfew began at least.'

No shit. 'A deer,' Jimmy said out loud in explanation.

'Oh,' said the man, nodding in understanding. 'Motorway also explains why my colleagues aren't swarming over the place like flies on a turd. They're most likely wondering where the hell we've got to.' As he said this, he reached into his top jacket pocket and pulled out a pack of cigarettes. The red jacket brushed the top open with the palm of his hand and pinched a lighter out with two fingers. Deftly, he held this under his baby finger and then retrieved a cigarette. Dropping the pack onto his lap, he placed a cigarette between his lips. He then struck the lighter to flame, brought it to the cigarette, and drew a slow breath in until it glowed. Holding it pinched between his thumb and forefinger, he leant forwards with a wince and offered it to Jimmy with a tap on the shoulder.

Jimmy half-turned his head in response. 'That's old-school,' he reacted, taking the scene in. 'Only know one other person who smokes,' he said, thinking of Anouk's mother. His voice trailed off at the thought. The red jacket sensed his distress.

'Go on, take it,' he urged. 'Would like to say it's healthy for you, but...'.

Jimmy had never smoked; he hadn't taken to vaping either. What the hell. He took the cigarette from the red jacket. Turning to face the road, and out of habit, he flicked it absentmindedly as he would a pipette of shimmer to rid it of residual bubbles. He then placed it to his lips and took a tentative breath in. Smoke only entered the top of his throat, and he didn't cough.

'There you go, you're a natural!' the red jacket extolled. Jimmy's second attempt led to unpleasant hacking. 'Well, okay, maybe a little practice then?' He grinned through his pain. They sat in silence for a few more minutes. The red jacket had lit a cigarette of his own, and both men released pensive plumes while pre-occupied in thought. 'Hadn't you better be off?' the red jacket said, breaking the quiet.

'Off? Where?'

The red jacket tilted his head. 'Away. Some place safe. My lot will be here soon. It won't take them forever. It's not worth being captured alive. Not where they're taking you, anyways.'

Jimmy turned to face the red jacket. 'Why do you do it?' he asked simply.

The red jacket's face fell. It was expressionless. 'The Bureau?'

'Yes. The Bureau.'

The red jacket paused, looking beyond Jimmy to some imagined past, where he lingered for a few seconds. 'Hope,' he said. 'I had no hope. Nothing worthwhile left in this life.'

Jimmy considered this. He knew what it was to live without hope. He had found his answer in shimmer. Yet the drug was nothing but fool's gold. It bought him only temporary escape. It helped no one.

'But you're too young to be giving up, son,' the red jacket said, refocusing on Jimmy. 'Come on now. You're not like me. I've done some damn awful things,' he confessed with haunted eyes. 'But we've got to believe in something better? There must be something better? Maybe hope's still out there?' he said almost pleadingly.

Something moved in Jimmy. He hadn't felt this for years, perhaps not since shimmer. He wasn't too different from the red jacket—they had both searched for hope in the wrong place. Jimmy nodded, shuffled through the door, and got up. He threw what remained of the cigarette on the ground, extinguished it with a twist of his foot, and turned. The red jacket looked up at him, and he looked down.

'Good luck, son,' the red jacket said.

Jimmy scanned his immediate surroundings. Without looking

back, he crossed the road and walked along the verge where tufts of grass fought to dislodge the asphalt.

Kilgore listened on his mobile phone as the officer confirmed the location. 'Yes, sir. On the motorway,' the officer repeated. He hung up his mobile and, as he moved to fasten his seatbelt, he kicked the passenger seat in front of him. The force knocked its occupant, a red jacket, forwards, but he knew better than to comment. His colleague, the driver, risked a sidelong glance in his direction and widened his eyes as if to say, *Oh, crap, this can't be good!*

'The motorway, Junction 12,' Kilgore snapped. He had omitted asking the officer for a cargo report. The spritters had bloody well all be in perfect functioning condition. They were already struggling to meet the quota this month. Kilgore loathed missing targets. It spoke of incompetence. Not his incompetence, but the useless red jackets. A conversation with the Chief Superintendent played out in his mind. He hated that smug face. Kilgore would objectively explain the difficulty he was having in recruiting people of ability, especially under current labour shortages, when the Chief Superintendent would cut him off and say something supercilious such as, 'You know the saying, Kilgore: "A bad worker blames his tools" and all that.' He wanted to twist her tits. Worst of all, word had it that the Undersecretary for Industry, or at least the assistant, had called to schedule a tour of operations. *Couldn't be coming at a worse time.* He scowled.

'How long?' Kilgore asked. 'It's past Junction 12.'

'Not long, sir. One or two minutes. We were close.' The driver glanced in the rearview mirror.

This nettled Kilgore. 'Not sodding close enough!'

'Yes, sir. My apologies,' the driver responded. He had no intention of serving himself up as a sacrificial lamb to Kilgore's ire.

The car passed an old farmhouse in the distance. It must have been abandoned even before the Great Change. Broken windows displayed their jagged teeth, and the roof slumped perilously to one side. The car slowed, and Kilgore stirred to locate their destination. The motorway was clear, having been closed to all traffic. Between the two front seats and rearview mirror, he could make out a Bureau transport van. It was lying on its side with the lower rear door flung open. A paramedic vehicle was already on-site, as was another squad of red jackets. The latter had arrived in a second van, anticipating that they would move the detainees. If there were paramedics, his cargo couldn't be dead. *What's the point of a paramedic for dead spritters?* Kilgore reasoned hopefully.

The car came to a standstill, and the red jacket in the front seat launched to open Kilgore's door. The squad leader from the newly arrived group of red jackets was at the door when Kilgore emerged. 'Not great news, sir, I'm afraid. Two squaddies dead, two spritters dead and five escaped. Only one squaddie survived, but injured, sir.' He was pleased to have completed his part for now.

As his anger overflowed, a familiar sensation overtook Kilgore. He was stepping outside his body—an interested observer looking in. 'Fuuck!' He grabbed the passenger door handle and slammed the door shut. 'Fuck! Fuck! Fuck!' he repeated, on each occasion opening and slamming the door again. On the fourth occasion, its glass shattered. Kilgore stood panting, looking at his work. His thin fringe, ordinarily slicked back, hung in his face. With one final 'fuck!', he kicked at the door's centre, leaving a large dent in the otherwise gleaming black paintwork. With shaking hands, and in a single movement, he smoothed his thin hair up to its usual position. The outside observer had left. He was increasingly himself again.

With a pleasant and disconcertingly placid smile, he turned to the squad leader, who had taken several steps back since he last spoke. 'Would you be so good as to show me to our surviving colleague,' Kilgore hummed.

The squad leader led the way to the rear of the overturned van. 'Mind your head, sir,' he said, showing within. Kilgore stooped below a hanging door, then crouched to achieve a better look. The occupants heard the performance outside and expected his arrival. A motionless woman lay to Kilgore's right. Bluish-purple discolouration had progressed across her exposed arms. Handcuffed hands lay at her side. Her eyes were open, and her teeth were slightly visible through an exposed grimace. She had evidently died a few hours before. To his left, a red jacket sat beside a bench that had ripped from its fixings. It had had its legs pulled to the sides and outward. An attendant paramedic hunkered beside the man's injured leg. Both waited expectantly for him to talk. Kilgore gesticulated with a swipe of his finger, showing that the paramedic should move aside. She did so quickly and without question, sliding further back on her buttocks. He slithered to take her place alongside the red jacket. He settled into place, pulled down on both lapels to arrange his jacket, and cleared his throat with a delicate cough. 'Pardon me.' He dabbed his mouth with three fingers. He then hesitated.

Kilgore scrutinised a cigarette butt lying close to the red jacket's hand and began. 'Mm, quite a little mess here.' It wasn't a question. The red jacket didn't answer. There was another pause. 'Your colleagues are in the front?' The red jacket nodded 'yes. 'Ah, with the other spritter, I presume? A woman, no doubt?'

The red jacket nodded again. 'I see, I see,' Kilgore trilled. 'And you,' indicating the red jacket with a sidewards inclination of his head without looking at him, 'all broken up in the back of the van.'

It also wasn't a question, but the red jacket responded. 'Yes, sir. Accident, sir. A deer.'

'Mm.' Kilgore studied his surroundings. 'Tell me, officer, why did you not call the accident in?'

'My leg, sir. It's in a right state. I couldn't move,' he said, tilting his head towards the semi-detached bench. 'It snapped just like a twig.'

Kilgore smiled. He placed a tender hand on the red jacket's injured leg. 'Help me?' He tightened his grip on its lumped surface. 'How is it you know of the deer then?' The red jacket gasped, but Kilgore continued. 'I am also just ever so slightly confused about how you pulled apart those bench legs in your terribly weakened state.' He tightened his grip further.

The red jacket groaned more loudly now—his lie uncovered. He sought to correct himself. 'You're right, I'm sorry, it's all blurred.' His voice wavered.

'Ah,' Kilgore intoned in mock cheer, lightening his grip somewhat. 'Go on?'

'They needed the keys, you see, for the cuffs,' the red jacket gulped. 'Couldn't get them unless they moved me,' he said, out of air, pointing to his trouser pocket.

Kilgore reapplied pressure, but harder now. The red jacket let out a cry of anguish. The paramedic watched on. It wasn't the first time she'd fixed Kilgore's handiwork. 'That all makes perfect sense,' Kilgore began again, 'apart from one tiny thing.' He waited a moment for dramatic effect. 'Do you usually take a break to smoke with a spritter?' Kilgore had just spotted the dead cigarette lying beside the collapsed rear door. He was looking inquisitively at it. 'I rather imagine that it was not you who extinguished that?' He rotated his hand deeper into the red jacket's flesh. The tormented sound issuing from the red jacket made the paramedic flinch.

'No, no! You don't understand...'

'But I do,' Kilgore interrupted soothingly.

'He...' the red jacket's voice trembled, 'He was just a youngster.' Kilgore now released his hand entirely, and the red jacket sighed, slumping forwards. As Kilgore reached into his jacket, the pickings from the previous night returned to mind. 'Lanky fellow. Mousey light hair?'

'Yes, that's the one,' the red jacket responded in an exhausted tone.

Why is it the vulnerable puppy-dog look that encourages people to get into trouble? Kilgore pondered as he removed his pistol from his jacket. He placed it on the man's forehead, slid the safety back, and pulled the trigger.

A ringing settled in Kilgore's ears. He turned to look distantly at the paramedic. She had sprung backwards in surprise. It wasn't the red jacket's jellied brain and blood, which dribbled from the van's roof behind his shattered head, that had startled her. It was the speed with which it had happened. Kilgore knew as much from her response. The scene was all too common. She sighed and packed up her kit.

Kilgore sat still, now calmly facing forwards. He balanced the pistol with both hands on his lap, reflecting. The cold steel pressed against his palms. Its weight always surprised him. Distractedly, he lifted it by its roughened grip to his nose, and sniffed once along its barrel. He liked the sulphuric smell. It mixed enticingly with a hint of heated metal. He moved down the collapsed door and re-emerged into the open. He felt better now; more purposeful.

'Right!' The assembled red jackets appeared anxious but moved closer. 'We've got five spritters on the run,' he said. And then, with slow and deliberate emphasis, 'I want them all, every last one, so help me God.'

The red jackets sped into action. A few of them loaded the salvaged remains of the deer into the van as they prepared to leave. Their salaries didn't stretch far.

Kilgore beckoned to the ranking squad leader. He immediately made his way over. 'There's a lanky bloke, one of the spritters. I want him in particular. Make sure he's found.' *Something about him seems to inspire others to misbehave,* he contemplated. He thought back to the now-dead red jacket and Anouk calling out his name at the pickings. 'Puppy-dog,' he repeated.

'Sorry, sir?' the squad leader asked. He had not heard Kilgore.

'Nothing,' Kilgore said with a wave of his hand.

'Sir, just one thing.' The squad leader spoke before Kilgore's irritation rose. 'Thought you would want to know.'

'What?'

'It's just come through, been confirmed. The Governing Council has ratified Decree 1833.'

Kilgore felt elated at the news. They might make their quota after all.

5

The uncommon touch of warmth on her face coaxed her to prise her eyes open. Soft late-afternoon sunlight glinted as the curtains stirred.

Anouk had slept deeply, waking once to sprit, without noticing the surrounding room. She moved from her side onto her back and dared to open her eyes further. They were dry. The sound of children playing outside and a nearby dove cooing felt otherworldly.

She stared at the glow-in-the-dark stickers on her ceiling and remembered. Jimmy. Where was he? As if prompted, the sun hid behind gathering clouds, and the dove flapped away. An adult called for the children, and their laughter ceased. Anouk sank into her bedding, and mechanically reached for the bottle of shimmer on the bedside table.

A gentle rapping on the door interrupted, and she left her arm hanging over the bed. She lifted her head an inch from her pillow and croaked, 'Yes?'

'It's me, darling. Mummy.'

Anouk imagined her mother, hands pressed palms down

on the door, and an ear placed between them. Her voice was revolting. Her mother spoke in a syrupy and soft tone regardless of what, when and to whom she was speaking. It was a learned voice, one that implored, *I'm so small and helpless, please don't hurt me.*

Anouk placed her arm back alongside her body and lowered her head again. 'What do you want, Janice?'

'Oh, thank goodness you're there, darling. I was starting to worry.'

Had she ever felt fondly towards Janice? Perhaps when she was very young. When her dad and sister were still around. Maybe...

'I'm fine, Mother. There's no need to get your knickers in a knot.'

There was a brief hiatus. Anouk was lifting her arm again when another gentle rap on the door stopped her. 'Yes?'

'Mummy has made you breakfast. It's a rather late breakfast, but it's a special treat. I managed to get bacon.'

'Bloody hell, bacon!' She couldn't recall the last time she'd had bacon, and the thought made her stomach rumble. You had to hand it to the manipulative cow; she knew how to get what she wanted.

Anouk rolled to her side and sat up. Lightheaded, she steadied herself before getting to her feet, stepping over the jacket she had deposited on the floor that morning. It took her two attempts to slide the door latch from its catch. When she opened the door, her mother retreated, as if she had always been a step further away.

Her mother was shorter than her. She stood facing the door, hands clasped in front of her, legs neatly together. Although Janice had been born decades later, she resembled a 1950s housewife; someone you might find smiling inanely in an old home product advertisement. She cut her once-blonde hair into a simple bob, its corners at her chin curling upward. The baby-blue pinafore she wore over a pink poodle skirt-dress had a floating cloud print. She had painstakingly applied her makeup, with matching and perfectly lined pink lipstick.

Anouk looked down. 'Why are you wearing heels?'

'Oh, goodness gracious me!' Her mother ignored her question, covering her mouth in exaggerated shock. 'What on earth has happened to your face?'

Anouk touched her swollen cheek—the Senior Superintendent's gift from the night before.

'It's nothing.' Anouk shrugged.

'Well, young lady, it doesn't look like nothing to me.' Her mother stepped forwards and reached towards her.

Anouk ducked and moved from her touch.

'It's alright, Mother. I'm fine.' Anouk raised her hands.

There was a moment of silence.

'You had better at least clean it up before you eat.' Lips pursed, her mother pointed down the hallway.

Anouk curved around her mother and entered the shower room. She was thankful that the door was slightly ajar, aiding a swift getaway. She closed it behind her. Her mother's footsteps click-clacked as she entered the kitchen-living room.

'Oh, and in answer to your question'—a frying pan clanged in the sink—'I am wearing heels because that's what ladies do, my dear.'

From the emphasis that she placed on the 'do, my dear', she intended this as a lesson in etiquette.

Anouk gazed in the mirror. 'Gross,' she murmured. She could hardly recognise herself. Her hair, once enviable with waves, was an oily and untidy mass. The wolf cut trim that she'd once sported was unrecognisable. Her cheek was blue and raised with split skin. It looked like a piece of exotic but overripe fruit. She gave it a gentle prod. She turned the hot water tap on and waited for the water to heat. It didn't. Growing impatient, she tentatively splashed her face and washed the larger patches of grime away with soap on her fingertips. The dried blood under her nose and on her chin dissolved in the water, dripped into the sink and joined a clockwise whirlpool down the plug.

'That'll do,' she said, turning her head from side to side in the mirror.

Anouk opened the toilet lid by reaching down behind her. She unbuttoned and pushed her jeans and underwear down, then sat with a sigh. She waited for the urine to flow. *It stinks*, she marvelled. She reached for a hand towel and wiped her face dry. Dirty streaks stained its white surface. 'Blast,' she murmured, stuffing it back in the ring on the wall. She wiped herself, rose, pulled up her underwear and trousers, and buttoned her jeans— omitting to flush the toilet containing a dark yellow pool.

She turned the tap on, let water spatter over her hands, and then turned it off. Anouk wiped them dry on her T-shirt and rolled her shoulders to ease the discomfort of her bra digging under her breasts. *Seriously.* She readjusted them. What was the point of wearing those? It sure as hell wasn't for her benefit.

She could smell the bacon. With a sigh, Anouk clanged the bathroom door open and padded in well-used socks towards the rich smell of cooking; the food scent grew stronger with every step. She said nothing, just pulling out a chair and sitting down. She felt entitled to. It was her money that paid for the bacon, no matter how or where it came from. She pushed the thought from her mind.

Anouk ate in silence. Her mother sat in a chair beside her at a small round table. She mulled Janice over as she shovelled scrambled eggs into her mouth from a mint-green dinner plate from Wood & Sons. The older woman had positioned herself away from the table. She sat with one leg crossed neatly over the other. She held a burning cigarette at her side, kept her back straight, and rested one hand in her lap. The cigarette smouldered, unsmoked. Ash had built up, teetering, ready to fall.

Her mother tried to make conversation. 'I've been watching the most charming re-run on the telly recently. *Fawlty Towers*. Do you remember it?' She raised the cigarette, tapping it against the ashtray sitting on the neighbouring kitchen counter, before drawing in a lungful of smoke.

'No,' Anouk lied. They had watched it as a family when they were still all together. A column of smoke seeped from her mother's mouth as she tilted her head upward.

'It's been quite enjoyable, I must say,' her mother continued. 'They just don't make them like they used to…'

'They don't make them at all. Unless you're a masochist and tune into State TV. Is that your thing, Mummy?'

'Really, Anouk Scarlett Walker!' She found additional length in her neck, straightening it further. She took a theatrical breath in and composed herself. 'It would just be nice to have you around a little more, that's all.' Her self-pity was palpable. 'And there's nothing wrong with our TV. NABC is a little boring perhaps, but very informative, very helpful. How else would we know of the dangers of degenerates?'

Anouk snorted. Weak coffee exited her nostrils and landed over stacked toast on the table.

'That's quite disgusting, young lady!' Standing, Janice dabbed identifiable splodges of coffee off the table with a napkin. 'If only you could have been more like your sister.' She recognised her mistake too late.

Anouk's temper flared instantly. 'My sister!' she said in a raised voice, accentuating the 'my'. 'My sister, who left with my father, because of *you*.' She spat the last word, knocking food off her plate with a gesticulating hand.

'Now, now, dear.' Her mother attempted to defuse the situation. 'Your sister didn't leave me,' she said. 'Your father kidnapped her and you. If it weren't for those nice boys...'

'Red jackets!' Anouk bit in.

'Yes, those nice young men from the Bureau,' her mother said. 'Well, you would be gone too. And where would that have got you? You're already a mess!'

Anouk fumed, her face flushed. 'If I'm a mess, it's because of you!' She quivered with anger. 'Father left because he saw you for what you are—a fascist! A vile collaborator.'

All sweetness deserted her mother. Her scowling face was contorted and harsh. 'Your father was a criminal, a traitor,' she brayed. 'They should have strung him from a lamppost when they had the chance. I should have reported him sooner!'

'You reported him?' Anouk repeated in shock. She leant back in her seat, reeling from the revelation.

'Of course I reported him; he was one of them! An agitator, mixing with terrorists. He was a degenerate, like you and like that...' her mother snapped her fingers rapidly together as if trying to remember, 'that, that friend of yours... James,' she said triumphantly, producing a faux giggle. Her slitted eyes studied Anouk. 'Red eyes. Lazy, sitting with your legs apart. You're a drugged slut!' she finished, hurling the last insult.

'That's right, Janice,' Anouk said more calmly but with hurt. 'That's your oldest daughter, not your precious second. A drugged slut! I take a little shimmer to numb the pain. Some cock to tell my body it's not dead already.' She lingered, shaking her head almost imperceptibly. 'So, go on, report me.'

Her mother collected herself. She regained her customary perpendicular pose. 'I have.'

The silence that followed was hollow but brief. She didn't know why her mother had reported her that day and not another. Perhaps it had been the final straw. Or random pique. Either way, Anouk didn't plan to hang around to find out.

———◎———

The backpack was full as Anouk squeezed a pullover into it. 'God dammit,' she grunted, putting a socked foot over the top and pressing down to zip it.

Janice was in the kitchen-living room, serenely tidying the half-eaten meal. She placed an old vinyl of 'Mister Sandman' on. It spun on her prized antique turntable, and she hummed. The record's crackling surface noise added a sense of urgency.

Anouk unfurled her boots from beneath her jacket. She loosened the laces, slipped them on, and pushed her feet in. The laces remained untied. She grabbed her jacket and backpack but stopped. She snatched the amber bottle of shimmer from her bedside table and stuffed it into its original pocket.

Her mother appeared at the kitchen-living room door as Anouk came from the bedroom. 'Are you leaving, dear?' she asked in a saccharine voice. The needle had stuck on the turntable, and the chorus was playing in a loop, beckoning listeners to sleep. 'I hope you enjoyed your breakfast?' She smiled, cocking her head to the side.

'Should I consider it my last meal, Janice?' Anouk asked.

'Why, dear, whatever do you mean?'

Anouk took her confusion as ridicule. She opened her mouth to reply, as always. But then she caught herself. She understood. Her mother was not well. She lived in an imaginary world. One more simple and innocent. It was a world where truth was self-evident and naivety celebrated. *Sleep... sleep... sleep...* The stuck chorus repeated hypnotically in the background.

For years, Anouk had hated her mother. But the woman before her was no monster. She was a broken cog caught in the State's apparatus. Anouk held no love for her, although she no longer hated her either. She was the object of intense pity and sadness. 'The meal was very thoughtful. Thank you.'

Her mother swelled with delight. 'Oh, I am so pleased that you liked it,' she purred. 'Will you be visiting again soon?'

Anouk searched for a response when a loud knock came from the front door that made them both jump.

'Hello. Hello? Mrs Walker? It's the Bureau,' a woman's voice said from outside. Anouk felt an urge to run. But where to? She knew the apartment offered no escape. Even if she could jump two storeys to the ground, the windows had security bars.

Her mother bustled past her to the door. 'I'm coming, officers,' she sang as she turned the Yale lock and swung the door open.

Two red jackets stood waiting. 'Good afternoon, ma'am,' a woman said. She was in front of the door. The other red jacket was behind her, to the side. 'We received a call?' Her eyes darted towards Anouk.

'Oh, yes,' her mother said, remembering. 'Do come in. Will you have some tea? I baked a wonderful lemon drizzle cake earlier today. Perhaps a slice?'

'Ah, thank you, ma'am, but no. We need to head off. Just the girl, if you will?' the red jacket said.

'Anouk,' her mother corrected. Her smile faded.

'Ah, yes. Yes, the girl Anouk,' the red jacket said. She furrowed her brow. 'You did call?'

Anouk surprised herself. She stepped protectively forwards before her mother could answer, forcing her back into the small corridor. She slung the backpack to her front, then turned around with both hands behind her back to facilitate scanning of the microchip in her wrist and handcuffing. Anouk looked at her mother. Her face suggested she had remembered requesting the Bureau's visit. It was riven.

'No need,' the red jacket said, guiding Anouk. 'You're not going anywhere in a hurry. Well, we'll be off now, ma'am.' She looked past Anouk to her mother. 'Thank you for your service.' She nodded. Anouk moved to follow her.

A small voice brought them to a halt. 'I'm sorry,' her mother whispered, 'I had no choice.'

Anouk paused. She reached into her jacket pocket and pulled out the amber bottle of shimmer. She placed it on the letter shelf by the door. 'We all have a choice, Mum.' She then walked through the open front door with the red jackets.

———◎———

Anouk and her escort descended the rusted metal stairs. She scanned the familiar surroundings for an escape route. There weren't any. The transport van was a few yards from the exterior stairs. A circular golden serpent leered out from the side of the vehicle. The Bureau's image of the snake biting its tail, with the words 'For Higher Virtue' printed below, chilled her to the bone. She reached the last step and scanned up towards the windows above the driveway. Most were empty. A few had curious onlookers. Anouk didn't recognise the majority. Mr Cooke, who lived two doors down from her mother, stood on his walkway. He clasped his hands, white-knuckled, along its rail. The concern on his tired face was obvious. He moved his head slightly from side to side, warning against a futile escape. This touched Anouk. She held a soft spot for him. As a younger girl, until a few years ago, she had playfully left him a Valentine's card every February, writing 'Your secret admirer' and signing her name 'Anouk'.

Someone yelled 'degenerate' from an open window that slammed shut afterward. The shout came from someone unseen. Anouk looked upward. As the evening settled, and dark clouds swam across the sky, a storm was gathering.

'In you get.' One of the red jackets opened a sliding side door. 'Oh, and you can leave that with me.' She reached for the backpack. Anouk hesitated. The red jacket read her defiance and stepped forwards. Anouk forced down the urge to shove the woman aside and run. Fortune had stacked the deck against her. She begrudgingly handed the backpack to the woman as she placed her foot on a side step below the door. With a push, she boosted herself into the closest row of seats. The red jacket followed and nudged Anouk along. Her companion slid the door shut with a thud, then moved to the front passenger seat.

It was unusual for two women to be dispatched to detain her. 'Aren't you lot meant to travel with a male entourage?' Anouk intended to be provocative. It was standard practice for female red jackets to pair with a male colleague. But she felt peevish. 'What of your feminine virtue? What would you do if this were besmirched!'

The van's engine came to life. The driver's dark eyes were visible in the rearview mirror for a split second, beneath a legionnaire cap. He gradually pulled out of the estate's driveway and onto the public road. *Ah, there's the obligatory male. Stylish,* she sarcastically considered, as she eyeballed the cap's hanging side extension. 'Loser,' she mumbled. The sun was hardly ever harsh enough to merit wearing one.

The red jacket sitting beside Anouk unzipped her backpack. 'Despite what you think, you're not much of a flight risk. Just a rude little girl.'

The backpack's flap now hung open, exposing a bulging pullover. 'Here.' The red jacket removed and dropped it onto Anouk's knees so that she could delve deeper.

'Do you damn mind!' There was no point, but Anouk said it anyway. The red jacket's description of her as 'a little girl' had stung. There was no answer. The red jacket continued scrapping around until she tipped the entire contents onto the seat to her right. 'Jeez,' Anouk said. But the red jacket still didn't respond as she pawed through the scattered items.

'There's nothing here?' She glanced up at her companions sitting at the front of the vehicle.

'Try her jacket, Rachel,' the driver suggested. His voice was deep and familiar.

'Eat me! You're not taking my jacket.'

The red jacket put her hand out in response and held it there. A silver bracelet hung from her wrist. A charm, a small ring intersected by two parallel lines, swayed as if trying to hypnotise. She stared unflinchingly at Anouk for a long moment. Anouk's mouth dried. She held the woman's gaze but blinked, feeling foolish and childlike. Chastened, she slid the jacket off her shoulders and passed it to the woman.

Anouk faced forwards, embarrassed. Another Bureau transport van was approaching. Its headlights flashed in greeting as it passed. The driver of Anouk's vehicle raised his hand in recognition. 'Guess we know where they're heading.'

'Found it, Ann' the red jacket called Rachel said, as she produced a miniature pen drive from the left jacket pocket. Since the Change, technological innovation seemed to travel in reverse. Old technology, such as pen drives, was in high demand.

The red jacket in the front passenger seat swung her head around to look. She smiled. 'Not too shabby, not too shabby. And this one...?' Ann flicked her head towards Anouk.

'I have no idea what that is! No jokes, I've never seen that before!' Anouk's heart pounded.

They ignored Anouk's protestations. 'Yeah, no use doing it here,' the driver said. 'No time. She comes with us, and we deal with it later. Properly.'

'Are you sure?' Rachel asked. 'Probably much simpler to get rid of her now? Mother will be seriously pissed off otherwise.'

Self-preservation coursed through Anouk's mind. 'He's right. You don't want to cut corners. Follow procedure. A stitch in time, you know.' She tried to stall.

The two-way radio mounted on the dashboard crackled into life. Anouk caught a few codes—10-59 and 10-33—among the chatter. But nothing made much sense to her. The red jackets, however, listened closely and seemed to follow. The crackling talk stopped with a 10-4.

'Time's up,' the driver said, almost immediately turning down a side street. 'Got further than we thought, though.' His colleagues removed their jackets. They peeled these off, tossed them aside, and revealed ordinary gear beneath.

Her escort were not who they seemed. *But who*, Anouk considered in confusion. The storm that threatened earlier was about to break. A few large droplets splashed as a prelude on the windscreen.

The van stopped abruptly, then reversed into an alcove under a disused railway bridge. The bridge crossed the adjacent storm drain channel.

'Out, out!' The woman beside Anouk flung the side door open and urged her colleagues to exit—needlessly; they were already moving, unbuckled. Anouk remained seated, frozen. 'Move it!' the woman commanded. Anouk started towards the door, then hesitated. She snatched her backpack and rammed her belongings inside. 'Leave it! Not important.' The woman was now outside. Flustered, Anouk dropped the backpack, grabbed her jacket, and followed to stand under the alcove. They then walked beyond its protection.

A cold draught descended on Anouk as she stepped into the open. The air pressure had dropped, heralding the coming of rain. Droplets were now gathered into a steady shower as she scanned around. She was at an abandoned Victorian industrial site. The derelict redbrick pottery loomed overhead, its brickwork stained a sooty black that bore witness to its long history of manufacture. Majestic in its time. She stared up at its high walls and through shattered glass windows. Despite night having fallen, she made out its smokestack disappearing into the haze. A heavy drop hit her bruised cheek. It didn't hurt, but pulled her attention back.

The driver yanked shut a pair of heavily corroded gates that pivoted from either side of the alcove. Although he'd remembered to remove his jacket, he had forgotten to take his cap off. Perhaps it gave some comfort from the rain; still, he lowered his head, opened the side door, and stepped into the pottery. His colleagues made their way to the door and, one by one, stole themselves into its gloom.

Anouk wavered. Few options presented themselves. She needed to find Jimmy. But where to start? Rain now fell heavily, soaking through her clothes. The man's voice echoed from a hollow space. 'If you want answers, you'll have to follow.'

The last few words faded as he walked deeper into its unseen interior. It wasn't in her nature to follow; she hated being told what to do. This time, her gut urged her to follow. With trepidation, she entered the unknown.

They walked quietly across the workshop floor. The rain drummed on the corrugated metal roofing high above them. Water dripped, and the smell of used machinery oil lingered as a testament to an industrial past. The path was unclear. Anouk followed behind the closest person. She couldn't tell who was who in the darkness. They walked confidently. The route was familiar to them.

A distant thwapping sound made her companions stop. Anouk walked into the closest person. She stumbled backwards, but there was no reaction. 'Shhh!' the other woman said. And then, recognising the sound: 'Helicopter.'

The thwapping increased into a loud rumble as a helicopter roared overhead. Its searchlight caused momentary shards of illumination to cascade through weathered holes in the roof. Then the sound of air displacement between the rotor blades evaporated into the distance.

'Phew, all good,' the woman said. 'If that was for us, they don't have a clue where we are. Let's keep moving.' The group continued again in the dark. They had walked a distance of several football fields. Through contrasting shades of deep grey walls, horizontals and arches loomed. They passed through adjoining workshops. Concrete covered the ground, leaving it level.

'Why would they care so much about me? Why send a helicopter?' The words slipped out of Anouk's mouth.

The man chortled in amusement. His outline stooped below an unseen obstacle.

'What's so funny?' She didn't see anything amusing.

'The fact,' Rachel said, 'that you think they might send a helicopter looking for you.' She ducked under what now appeared to be old machinery. 'You're right; you're not that important.' The words fell like a slap. For the second time, Anouk felt like a self-indulged child. She bent below the low overhanging object. Her uncharacteristic silence hinted at her discomfort. The other woman, seeking to ease the clear tension, said, 'More likely some civil disorder because of the latest Decree.'

The man came to a stop. 'Okay, we're here.' He was speaking to Anouk. The others already knew their way. 'This is the last tricky bit before we get to the other side.'

'Other side?' Anouk asked in puzzlement.

He either ignored or didn't hear her question. 'The red jackets patrol on foot here. They're quiet and shoot on sight. You get spotted, you're as good as dead.' He let this settle in. 'When we get out,' he tapped on the door in front of him. 'Follow close behind. If anyone gets separated... well, you're on your own.'

Again, Anouk wondered who they were, but as before, a pressing concern pushed the question aside. Damn, she couldn't see the bleeding door, let alone follow anyone. The man eased the door open, just enough for dim light to slip in. His body slank around the corner like a cat, shadowed closely by his two companions. Anouk trailed after them into a narrow street. Disused industrial brick buildings rose on either side. The rain had slowed to a trickle and afforded little cover for the noise of their falling feet. She skirted puddles but splashed clumsily compared to the others.

They continued down the long street, occasionally passing an intersection between buildings. At each point on the same side of the road, barricades from the skeletons of extinct cars and battered shopping trolleys had been erected. All the windows and doors on the same boundary were boarded and nailed shut with salvaged timber. None of the barricades were manned, and many seemed in a poor state of repair, with clear paths running through some of the makeshift fortifications.

The man slowed and nimbly crossed to the other side of the

road, skipping a large pool of water. He came to stand alongside a door. His companions clustered at his side, and Anouk tagged behind. The door appeared boarded similarly to all the others. He knocked on it in a beat of three, two, one and then a final four. The door frame, boarding and fixings were all part of a single structure that swung open together. They were an illusion. Her three companions didn't need an invitation. They moved within, as did she.

The door closed behind them, plunging their surrounds from murkiness into pitch darkness. 'No problems tonight?' a hoarse voice asked. Footsteps shuffled, and a young man with a wide smile drew open a thick curtain. His voice didn't match his boyish face. 'Welcome back,' he mouthed, ushering them into what resembled an erstwhile warehouse. In place of boxes and crates were tens of small groups of people huddled together for warmth; adults and children alike. A few people meandered from group to group, distributing blankets and what looked like hot drinks or soup.

'What is this place?' Anouk examined her surroundings.

'Best way to describe it is, I guess, a temporary emergency shelter for refugees,' the other young woman in the group said. 'Until noon today, this was all but empty.' She wore a hunting knife, sheathed at her belt. It seemed out of place on someone so amiable.

Anouk experienced a creeping feeling of déjà vu. She was reliving her confusion of the previous evening at the club. 'But I don't understand what's going on. What emergency? What happened at midday?'

'I've already told you,' the woman who had sat next to her in the van said. 'Decree 1833. It was rubber-stamped today.' She rolled her eyes.

'I've never heard of the Decree.' Anouk's cheeks flushed.

Current affairs weren't her strength; her mind was ordinarily elsewhere.

'It means,' the man said, turning around and removing his red legionnaire cap, 'that they've extended the definition of who counts as an undesirable. It means spritting degenerates like you are no longer on their own.' His eyes sparkled.

'Aidan! Are you kidding me!'

'Hello, Dimples. Miss me?'

6

Jimmy spotted a gnarled gap in the hedgerow that ran alongside the motorway. The hawthorn trunks that formed the field boundary were thick, but the plants appeared unhealthy, their roots growing in boggy runoff from the road.

He shinnied down a steep bank, but slipped and fell on his rear before sliding down the final few yards. His feet and lower legs disappeared as he came to a stop. The smell of stagnant water and rotting detritus made him gag, and he reached for a nearby branch to pull himself out of the mud, but a thorn embedded itself between two fingers.

'Blast.' Jimmy shook his hand free and sucked at a small drop of blood as it oozed to the surface. Bending down, he studied the gap. He considered climbing back up the bank to search for a better place to traverse the hedge. But the bank appeared as difficult a task, if not more so, than the tight and thorny gap.

Jimmy pushed up his pullover sleeves and warily placed his hands and arms into the mud. As he crawled, the oily film on the mud's surface coalesced around his forearms.

He reached the gap and curved his head and neck through,

moving his arms forwards and arching his body. But a thorn caught between his shoulder blades, prompting him to pitch downward.

Jimmy lifted the hand towards the pain, but as it sucked from the mud, something sliced deeply into his wrist. He gasped and tried to move his arm, but barbed wire drove under his flesh and clung there.

He kept his back down to ensure the thorn didn't work its way in further and crept his other hand to the barb in his wrist.

Removing it felt like pulling out a fishhook. His abdomen stiffened and ached as he strove to free himself. The muscles in his jaw twitched as his skin tore, the barb releasing its grip.

He raised his arm. A lump of distorted tissue showed beneath glutinous muck, which mixed with discharging blood.

He kept his injured arm above the sludge and coiled the rest of his body through the gap. One knee struck the submerged wire, and the other came to rest on top of it. Fortunately, neither encountered another barb.

Tufts of grass provided Jimmy with sufficient grip to leverage himself from the ditch. With one hand pulling the grass and both his feet thrusting at the slippery verge, he touched down on drier ground, and he rolled onto his back. With his hurt wrist resting on his chest, he lay still as his heart rate steadied.

An ant made an exploratory sojourn into one ear from the grass beside him. Jimmy sat upright and swiped to dislodge it. This did the trick. The ant fell onto the back of his hand. He placed it flat on the ground, from where the insect journeyed onto a blade of grass and rootled for cover.

Jimmy examined his wrist again. A gouge was visible above a small existing scar. It stung unpleasantly. He had to clean it.

He got to his feet using one arm and pushed himself up. His sneakers squished as he inspected his surroundings. The hedge and motorway lay behind him. The field that spanned before him rose to a coppice of birch trees some distance away. Still holding his arm at a right angle, he hastened towards the trees.

The morning had grown warmer, and despite his discomfort and an omnipresent awareness of being hunted down, Jimmy soaked in the rare feeling of sunlight on his face. No one had worked the encircling field in many years, and wildflowers had reclaimed the soil. The increase in annual rain, while blighting food crops, was much loved by the grasses that grew tall and healthy towards the sun. Mud fell from Jimmy's trousers as he wandered through the knee-high greenery. Others had come this way before. Lost souls drifting across the meadow, pausing on a threshold before moving onward. The grasses susurrated as he swept through, the tips of his fingers gliding over their silky florets. Timeless poppies watched his progress.

Jimmy walked until he reached the foot of the hill, just as it inclined, and he found a small stream with clear flowing water. He needed to stop. He reached behind with his left arm, pulled his jumper over his head, then shook it off. Carefully, he edged his injured right arm through the remaining sleeve, and let the garment drop to the ground. He lowered himself onto his stomach. The grass was soft and slightly damp but comfortable. He chose a gravelled spot the stream had washed clean and laid his wrist under the cold flowing water. He shuddered. It smarted at first, but the sharp pain faded to a dull throb. He peered down his arm—filthy. Sweat spread dirt across his skin in mottled watermarks. *What have I become?* He felt an urge to strip naked and cleanse himself of filth and more. But he knew the motorway was not far behind him. He didn't have the luxury of time.

Tenderly washing over his wound, he brushed water over a raw piece of flapping tissue. Serrated edges of skin floated independently at the sides of the larger piece as the bleeding started again. It would need stitches. The bleeding was lighter than before. Coils of blood wound their way upward and then drifted downstream, caught by the gentle current. When most of the visible mud was gone, he lifted his arm from the water. He scooped clean water from upstream and drank until quenched. Then, sitting up with his shoes in the stream, he allowed the mud to wash off as he searched for a potential bandage.

Jimmy recognised the broad leaf of a dock plant peering out from under some higher grass. He leant over and plucked it, remembering his aunt telling him once of its antiseptic properties. Crushing it with his healthy hand to release its sap, he wrapped it over the wound. He then tucked the leaf stalk under its blade, twisted a few tougher-looking stalks of grass free from their roots, and tied them around the makeshift bandage. Checking that his work was secure, with the aid of his teeth, he pulled slightly on the end of each stalk. He then got to his feet, clutching his pullover. As he kicked water from his sneakers, he knotted the pullover around his waist. He crossed the stream's clear water and resumed his path up the hill.

Jimmy reached the tree line and gazed back at where he'd come from. The overturned van was visible in the distance. Jimmy judged it to be one mile away. He had jogged further up the motorway before entering the field than he had realised. Beyond the van, he could see two vehicles approaching from the city's direction. They were still a way off. One had red emergency lights flashing. He was pleased. The red jacket would soon receive medical attention. As he turned to continue under the shade of the birches, Jimmy smiled. He imagined the red jacket leaning back, helping himself to another cigarette.

Now panting from exertion, Jimmy reached the top of the hill. He leaned against the smooth trunk of a tree, hidden among its hanging leaves and dappled shade, and gazed down. This was a place of memory: present, future and past. He first observed the accident scene. The vehicles had reached the van, and people were milling around. From his higher vantage point, he made out an old farmhouse beyond, and further on the horizon, the city. He distinguished a few landmarks. The half-destroyed and often charred remains of the old industrial quarter survived as a scar. Leaden clouds had accumulated over the city. They cast shadows, spilling over its boundaries and into the surrounding countryside. Rain was coming, and the sun's brief respite would soon flee before it.

Jimmy hoisted himself up. It was beautiful up there. But he couldn't stay. He crested the hill, leaving the accident scene and city behind. As he picked his way down through dense undergrowth, he thought back to the bleak remains of the industrial quarter. His aunt, he had been told, had died there. He was a child, and she was all that he had. The gut-wrenching despair that he had felt was still palpable. Tears still came unbidden.

It had happened during what propagandists called the Great Change. An alliance of disparate groups from civil society had staged national protests against a better-organised and influential group of ultra-nationalists known as the Blood Martyrs. It was a trap. The Unity Marches, as they were called, played into the hands of the Martyrs. They claimed disorder and anarchy, and with the unspoken consent and active aid of the State security forces, brutally re-secured 'law and order. It amounted to a massacre. Few large towns or cities escaped. Within days, resistance crumbled. And his aunt was dead.

Jimmy thought of Anouk with a pang of grief. Her father had joined the Marches. While his aunt had played an active role in environmental politics, Anouk's father was a key leader in an anti-fascist movement. Jimmy had resented Anouk after his aunt's death. He was angry and jealous. He was bitter that she still had her father and that he had nobody. Then Anouk lost her dad as well. He had inexplicably left with her younger sister, deserting Anouk and her mother. Jimmy and Anouk had found each other. And they found shimmer. The rest—history.

Jimmy broke free of the undergrowth and came upon another open field that had been cultivated over the summer. An old abandoned farmhouse lay across from it. He examined his surrounds, left the trees, and walked into the wheat. Its stalks were dead. The ears of wheat hung limply. They should have been harvested weeks ago. Jimmy picked one. His hands shook as his body metabolised the last traces of shimmer. His wrist also throbbed. He knew his craving for shimmer would begin soon. Mildew covered the wheat. The ear lay light in his hand. Heavy rain had battered many of the grains to rot on the ground. Droplets fell from the sky.

———— ◎ ————

Dusk had given way to night. The rain was pounding on the luxury black saloon's roof. The passenger window wound down a crack.

'We have at least one escaped spritter in there, sir.' The red jacket was standing in the rain, speaking to the window crack and holding a coat ineffectually over his head. 'We were inspecting the property, looking through that window.' He pointed to the place alongside the front door. 'And we saw them, sir.'

'Them?' Kilgore probed. 'I thought you said you were unsure how many there are?'

The red jacket hesitated. He didn't understand Kilgore's question. He got it. 'No, sir, not people. Eyes, sir. Saw them, red as the devil's, staring out at me! His eyes.'

Kilgore regarded the squad leader. *Not another dimwit.* He sighed. 'And have you decided on your course of action? How do you intend to retrieve our cargo?'

'Getting suited up now, sir,' the red jacket said. 'We'll be going in shortly. Shouldn't be a problem. Just taking the necessary protective precautions.'

The old farmhouse was the one visible from the motorway that morning. 'It can't be more than two miles from the accident site.' *What sort of lazy, useless imbecile takes shelter so close to the scene of his escape?* Kilgore berated himself—the answer was obvious. A degenerate, of course.

'Why enter the property? It is a wholly unnecessary risk to expose your men to, Squad Leader. Just think of those wild, mad eyes. In fact, I've heard that spritters, under the influence, are quite capable of eviscerating a man with a swing of their claw...' He corrected himself. 'I mean, hand.' Kilgore reclined languidly in his seat, waiting for a response. The man reminded Kilgore of himself as a little boy—weak and pathetic.

The squad leader stared down, fidgeting with his sleeve. 'Um, I see, yes.' He shifted his eyes uncertainly from side to side. 'Eh, what would you suggest, sir?'

'Well, it's not for me to say, Squad Leader. I anticipate a man of your position to come to a swift determination.' Kilgore stifled a laugh. 'But,' he continued just as the man opened his mouth in reply, 'since you ask, my advice would be to allow him, her or them to come to you. Why trouble yourself?'

The red jacket nodded along, staring at the wet ground, but said nothing. Kilgore waited. Still nothing. 'Squad Leader?'

'Yes, sir. That sounds sensible, sir!' The red jacket continued to stare at the sodden ground.

'Squad Leader!' Kilgore said in mock exasperation. 'You do

have some idea of how to wheedle this fellow out, don't you?'

'Um, no, sir.' The red jacket forced a nervous smile.

'Aah. I see. I must say, Squad Leader, I would have hoped for more. But in the absence...' he said, while spreading out his hands, 'Let's see.' Kilgore tapped his mouth with one finger. 'You chaps do still carry extra emergency fuel in the back of your vans, don't you?'

The red jacket snapped his face up, pleased with the solution. 'Yes, sir. A twenty-litre jerrycan as standard.' He moved and then stopped. 'The rain, sir. Surely...'

Kilgore cut in. 'Let's not let a little rain spoil a perfect opportunity for a barbecue?' He waved the red jacket away with a brush of his hand.

Pleased with his dismissal, the red jacket ran to his colleagues and issued instructions. Kilgore observed the house's front door from the comfort of his heated seat. The passenger headrest obscured his view. 'Driver, be a splendid fellow, would you, and move the car parallel with the house. I'm struggling to see out of my window.' He was tapping this with a long fingernail.

'Yes, sir. That's no hassle, sir.' The saloon reversed in a backwards arc and then moved slightly forwards to position Kilgore's side window in line with the front door. Kilgore did not extend his thanks but sat patiently.

Red jackets hurried in the rain. They sourced two full jerrycans of fuel and set about splattering the noxious liquid over the front door and surrounding porch. Skirting to either side, they heavily doused all exposed wood. Window frames, fascias and soffits dripped, as frantic movement was visible within the house through what remained of the curtains.

The rain had reduced to a trickle as red jackets stood back from the house. A group clustered together, drawing odds on the likelihood of any spritters appearing. The squad leader moved forwards, seeking authorisation to continue. A head appeared above the vehicle's roof. 'The Senior Superintendent says you're good to continue,' the driver called, and then disappeared from view again. The squad leader drew a matchbox from his trouser pocket, removed a single match, and struck it. It caught, but he held it cupped for a few seconds to ensure that it burned bright. He then flicked it towards the front door.

Flames leapt up instantly. The ballooning heat forced the squad leader to retreat as a blue and orange conflagration swept along the sides of the house and under its eaves. Red jackets stationed themselves at each corner of the house to block any getaway. The fire consumed the old building at speed, leaving onlookers captivated. Kilgore's face was visible through the car window. The flames reflected his gaunt and detached features. His black eyes remained cold except in their mirroring the cavorting flames.

One side of the roof, which was already partially collapsed because of age, gave way with a spark-filled crash. Flames thrashed from broken window panes to join those burning on the roof. Kilgore yawned. At the expense of his precious cargo, he had hoped for more of a show. At the least, a flaming body, arms flailing, would've been entertaining.

The front door swung violently open. Two men stumbled out of the inferno. They had covered their faces with the fronts of their tops, but their wheezing and coughing were still distinct through the din of the crackling blaze. One man catapulted off the open porch and came to land at the feet of the squad leader. The second also stumbled down its steps but maintained his balance. Spectators observed dumbfounded, apart from the wagering red jackets, who soon began haggling over their change in fortune, settling bets. The standing man stooped to help his partner to rise. His movement was limited. The gash on his thigh gaped raw. Smoke-stained, and still spluttering, they took each other in a tight embrace and spoke intimate words. The red jackets circled closer.

Disgusting, Kilgore thought, *two degenerates in foreplay.* 'That's enough!' he snarled, emerging from the comfort of the car. 'Get those two pitiful specimens into the transport, along with the other two we already rounded up. And Squad Leader, have the dogs arrived yet?'

They were baying and close. It was just before dawn. Jimmy first heard the dogs several hours ago. At first, he wasn't certain they were dogs at all. Now their excited yapping was unmistakable.

It had stopped raining. He had entered another wooded area at dusk, and it had been impossible to navigate a path through the trees. The ground was uneven in the watery darkness. He stumbled, whipped by branches, and nearly succumbed to fatigue. But through a strange grace, drug-withdrawal-induced anxiety had spurred him on. He felt ill. He had vomited twice—a throatful of bitter bile. His stomach was empty. Yet the nausea continued.

He clutched his swollen wrist. It was hot, and the pain around the wound had intensified. The improvised bandage had dropped off. He stopped for breath. His breathing was fast, and his heart beat in his ears. He stood straight, rested his hands on his hips, and sized up his surroundings. He felt dizzy. The trees blurred and swirled for an instant before popping back into focus. It all appeared the same to him. Was he running in circles? Panic mounted to a frenetic spiral of shadows. Cold perspiration ran down his back. Then, through his disorientation, running water called to him. It was calming.

He staggered on, pushed a branch aside, and entered a clearing. The dogs sounded even closer now, and he heard calling voices. He closed his eyes and tried to locate the sound of flowing water again. It lay straight ahead, so he ploughed forwards, exhausted.

He nearly fell into the fast-flowing river. Its banks lay alongside the woodland. Only the sound gave it away. Clouds obscured the little light that might have hinted at the river's size. The water was dark, and mist hung cloyingly above its surface. But the rushing and purling of water implied that it was large. Just as Jimmy prepared to enter the river over its unsure bank, he saw a small sandy beach. It was conspicuous as light grey and was near where he stood. He hugged trees with his one healthy arm and made his way downstream. His feet slid on wet rounded rocks, loosening and wobbling a few as he went. With a crunch, his shoes met wet sand. At the far side of the beach, a few metres away, lay what seemed to be a rowing boat. It was drawn up onto higher ground.

The baying of dogs was upon him. Torch lights moved and flashed between the trees, while haranguing shouts reverberated. Jimmy clawed through the sand to the boat's bow, found the keel, and braced his shoulder against it. Moaning with effort, he shoved the boat inch by inch through the scraping sand until the stern encountered water. He heaved and shunted again. The current propelled the boat backwards and downstream. Falling on all fours, Jimmy lunged for a frayed rope that was trailing the boat. This was tied to a cleat on its side. As the current took hold of the boat, it pulled Jimmy upright and into the water. Now waist-deep and struggling to stand, he reached the side of the boat. With failing strength, he hoisted and kicked himself over the side and fell with a raw thud between two benches. Oars clattered to the sides.

The current swept up the boat and launched it downstream. It bounced jarringly on a half-submerged boulder before twisting around and hurtling into the darkness. Jimmy glanced back at the sandy beach. He fancied he saw the apparition of a boatman standing on the shore, sternly watching him flee. The dogs reached the sandy beach at that moment. The apparition was gone. They sniffed the ground, wagged their tails and howled into the night.

———◇———

Jimmy roused hours later. The sun had risen but struggled to make itself known behind the clouds. He lay on his back, scissored between benches, legs on one, head on the other. Mist clung to the riverbanks as the boat cradled in a bed of reeds. He couldn't remember falling asleep—perhaps he had been unconscious. It was cold. Shivering, he raised his wrist. It was dreadful. The skin around the wound was red and inflamed. It had receded to expose meaty tissue below. The swelling pulsed with heat, and red streaks had made their way up his arm.

Jimmy's healthy arm lay behind his back in a pool of water that had collected at the bottom of the boat. Listlessly, he brought wet fingers to his mouth and sucked on them to ease the dryness. His swollen tongue stuck to his palate. It loosened as the moisture softened his gluey saliva. His muscles ached, and a cramp tightened in his lower abdomen, causing him to moan.

Pink Himalayan balsam was growing among the reeds. A mild breeze rattled their pods. They popped faintly, seeds propelling outward. The breeze stroked his clammy forehead, and he shivered again. A shadowy apparition loomed over him. The boatman had come to be paid. He would not wait forever. Jimmy closed his eyes.

Days had passed, and Kilgore sat comfortably in his office at the Bureau. His daughter came to mind. It wasn't fatherly love—never—but she intrigued him. An object of curious study, nothing more. Through her, he had honed his ability to perform empathetic-like behaviour. He didn't bother to do this sort of thing with subordinates, but it had proved jolly helpful in navigating relationships with his superiors. Just little things. Nothing particularly onerous. *Funny, it seemed to go such a long way.*

'Father?'

Kilgore snapped out of his thoughts. He was sitting at his office desk. It was a grey and unremarkable space, furnished in a utilitarian fashion. A young woman was standing behind a filing cabinet, holding a brown folder in one hand.

'Yes, pet?' he replied, curling his lips back in a practised smile.

'The accident?' She held the folder slightly up. 'The one on the motorway, the one a few days ago?'

'Yes.' Kilgore nodded. Since finishing school the previous year, his daughter had worked part time in his office as a junior assistant. He enjoyed having her around—to keep a close eye on her.

'Do I file it under "case closed"?'

Annoyance flashed across Kilgore's face. It had been two full days since the dogs lost the remaining spritter's scent at the river, and there had been no progress since. There was much to do for the Undersecretary's visit, and the last thing he needed was a loose end.

'Sorry, Father, was that another stupid question?' the young woman asked, lowering her head.

Kilgore was about to reply in the affirmative, but suppressed the impulse. 'No, Jessica. I was just thinking about something else. Go ahead and file it under "case open".' He specified a second cabinet across the room. Jessica let out a slow and silent breath as she crossed to the designated cabinet. She opened it and started rifling through the alphabetised suspension files.

Kilgore watched her work. She wore a pencil skirt and blouse that fit the curves of her body. Her blonde hair fell between her shoulders in a tidy ponytail. He traced the ponytail down her back and to the contours of her hips, across her buttocks. They were round but firm. Kilgore experienced a pleasurable tingling of excitement. His daughter turned. He pretended to read.

'Will that be all?' Without waiting for a response, she continued, 'If so, I'll ask Marge in Accounts if she needs any help.'

Kilgore surveyed his office for additional tasks when his mobile phone rang. It was loud, and he had set it to play New Albion's national anthem. He waited a verse into the melody before taking a call. It demonstrated to those within earshot his fervent national loyalty. He held the phone to his ear. 'Kilgore here.'

'This is Gamma Squad Leader, sir. Just calling in to report,' a woman's voice crackled over the line.

'Yes, yes. What is it, Squad Leader?'

'We've found him. The last spritter, sir. A member of the public found him alongside the river and called it in.'

'That's fantastic news!' Kilgore leaned back in his seat. 'I love patriots,' he mouthed to Jessica. He meant a compliant citizen. 'When can we expect you?'

'Not long, sir. We're just entering the Bureau's underground parking. No more than two to three minu…'

The signal cut. Still holding his phone, Kilgore punched into the air with a scrawny arm. 'You can get that folder out again, my pet,' he declared with a satisfied smirk on his face. 'Case closed!' He slammed his hand flat on the desk.

'The escaped spritter?'

'Indeed, it is!' Kilgore got to his feet. 'The last wretched...' he corrected himself. 'Last living wretched degenerate from that cargo. I wanted this one in particular,' he said, wagging his bony finger. 'He is a troublemaker. I can smell it.' He finished by tapping his nose.

'Can I come, Father? Come to see him being brought in?'

Kilgore crossed his arms, and Jessica persisted. 'It's just that you always describe them—degenerates—as so disgusting. Repulsive. I'd like to see one up close for myself.'

Kilgore considered the request. 'Well, I suppose it won't do you any harm.' He rationalised further. 'It might be good for you to see one, in the flesh, if only to know what we're up against.' He walked around his desk to stand in front of Jessica and plucked her cheek. 'Aren't you a curious little thing, eh? As long as curiosity doesn't kill the cat...'

'No, Father. Of course not. Thank you. Had we better make our way to the holding cells then?' Jessica was already heading for the office door.

'Aren't you forgetting something?' Kilgore patted his lips with his index finger. 'Daddy would like a kiss.'

She pecked his cheek and swirled in giddy excitement. 'Oh, goody, what a treat. Thank you, Daddy.'

Kilgore leered at her. Then, taking her arm in his, he led the way out through the office door.

They turned right onto a long corridor. 'Morning, Kilgore,' a man dressed in a well-cut suit said as he walked past.

'I'll morning you, you self-righteous shit,' Kilgore said under his breath. Only Jessica heard this. She giggled in amusement.

They continued walking until they came to an elevator. The doors were open, so they bustled in.

'Going down,' its existing occupant, a sombre grey-haired woman, asked.

'Yes please, Mòrag,' Jessica responded, 'The basement.' By mistake, Mòrag had already pressed the basement button along with the first floor, and they travelled down in silence. Piped music sought to create a soothing mood. The elevator missed the first stop, and its door slid open with a ping at the basement. They exited and turned left along another long corridor. The grey-haired woman remained, returning to the higher floor. They came to a door with a black sign engraved 'holding' in white letters. Kilgore twisted the handle and swept into the adjoining room with Jessica following in his wake.

Jimmy lay on his side in the centre of the room with two red jackets standing over him in distracted conversation. Three holding cells made of a thick steel frame and security mesh lined the far end of the room. Jimmy was unconscious. His breathing was shallow, fast and rasping. He was pale, and the rich smell of faeces filled the room. Jessica covered her mouth in a gag reflex.

'What in the sweet name of God is this!' Kilgore's eyes were wide and angry as he studied Jimmy. The red jackets sprang to attention. 'I told you I wanted this one alive!' He gave Jimmy a hard nudge with his foot so that he rolled over motionless onto his back. His head rotated upward and fell back to loll at the side. 'And he's rotten,' Kilgore scowled, pressing the pointed toe of his black polished shoe onto Jimmy's wrist. It erupted with pus that splattered across the floor, some of which landed between the laces of his shoe. This infuriated Kilgore further. He kicked Jimmy in his side. Jessica squeaked.

The red jackets stood speechless until the woman who had spoken to Kilgore on the phone volunteered. 'Yes, apologies, sir, we found him like this. Looks like he's septic,' she ventured a diagnosis.

'He's a fucking dead man, that's what he is!' Kilgore hovered, glowering for a while. The conversation had no mileage—he sought to wrap it up. 'Take him outside and finish him.' He turned to leave but stopped. 'And don't waste a bullet.' Pointing towards the red jacket's baton that was attached to her belt, he ordered: 'Use that.'

7

'You son of a bitch.' Anouk moved menacingly towards Aidan. 'You set me up!'

Aidan blinked. 'Whoa, now! Take it easy, tiger.' He put his hands up, taking a cautionary step back.

'What did you put in my pocket, Aidan! Don't bullshit.' Anouk fixed him with a stare. She advanced, and Aidan stepped back onto the toes of one of his companions.

'Ouch.' The woman laughed and pushed him forwards. 'You're on your own with this one, mate.' She grinned, glancing at their other companion, who shrugged.

'It was just something to keep you going,' he protested. 'Thought you would be pleased!'

'No, not the shimmer. I warned you, don't bullshit!' Anouk was now within arm's reach of him. He bit his lip. 'The other pocket. What did you put in the other pocket, you tosser!' she said.

'Oh, that.' He avoided her gaze. At least half the truth—he'd have to give her that. 'Okay, okay. Fine, relax.' He moved his hands up and down. 'I may have put a pen drive in your other pocket when we were outside the club.'

'May have!' She grabbed at Aidan's chest, but he sidestepped. Their squabble caught the attention of the scattered groups of refugees. They watched with concern. An infant cried at the abrupt uproar. It curbed Anouk's rising temper.

'Okay, true, I put it in your pocket. Had to, had no choice! Kilgore was onto us.'

'So it was a sham, your helping me out that night in the club by telling Kilgore I was a dealer?' Anouk lifted her chin, eyes narrowing. 'You just wanted to get rid of something that you nicked!'

'No, that's not right.' Aidan smiled, but it faded fast. 'It-it was afterwards, when I bribed the red jacket to turn a blind eye to you. He tipped us off about Kilgore then. They were planning a surprise search.'

'He's telling the truth.' The voice came from behind Anouk. She swung around. Aidan's female companion from that night at the club had just approached. Anouk recognised her easy walk and good-natured demeanour. 'What's up, cuz?' She flicked her head upward, greeting Aidan.

'Er, good, good.' Aidan let his hands fall to his sides, defeated. 'You remember Frederica, don't you?' he asked Anouk. He waved, introducing them. 'Anouk, Fred. Fred, Anouk.'

'Hello, properly.' Fred smiled, extending a hand to Anouk. 'It's Fred, just Fred.' She stared daggers at Aidan for revealing her full name—she hated it. They shook hands. 'The red jacket tipped us off after Aidan helped you. Kilgore was on to us. When we left you in the street and went the other way, he was waiting with his thugs.'

'Okay.' Anouk raised an eyebrow. 'Waiting, but why?' She glanced between Fred and Aidan.

'Because of this?' the woman who had retrieved the pen drive from Anouk's jacket suggested. She held it up then handed it to

Aidan. She studied him for a second longer than necessary and blushed, casting a sour look at Anouk.

'Could be that, Rachel,' Fred said to the woman. 'But my guess is that Kilgore suspected us of being more than just dealers and wanted to rub us down. Problem was, if he found us with that,' showing the pen drive in Aidan's hand, 'we would be goners.' Fred made a cutting motion with a finger across her throat. 'Lucky for you, though,' she said, turning to Anouk, 'Aidan thought on his feet. Kilgore asked where you were. Aidan told him you were finishing off the night back at the club, spritting up.'

'Yes, indeed, I did.' Aidan lifted his chest with his shoulders back, pleased to have been both saved by Fred and made to look smooth.

Anouk nodded and processed the information. 'So let me get this right: Aidan bailed me out of trouble by calling me a dealer. He then got me back into trouble by putting something dodgy into my pocket. And then you guys,' she said, indicating Aidan and his two companions, 'rock up and abduct me?'

'Kind of,' Aidan said, slumping again. 'We obviously needed the pen drive...'

'Obviously,' Anouk interrupted, folding her arms.

Aidan soldiered on. 'And so, we contacted our ol' red jacket informant friend to track you down, find out where you live.'

Anouk frowned. 'So now you're stalking me?' she asked.

Fred came to Aidan's rescue again. 'The red jacket informed us that a collaborator had reported you. They were on their way to pick you up. This lot,' gesturing to the others, 'had to get to you first. The pen drive's important to us.'

'AND it cost me another pack of shimmer getting your address from our informant,' Aidan said.

Anouk seemed not to have heard, and instead answered Fred,

'Yes, it was my mother. She was the collaborator.'

'Ouch.' Fred winced. She placed a comforting hand on Anouk's shoulder. 'Sorry to hear that. That's a...'

'It's okay,' Anouk cut in, 'she isn't well.' But her mother's betrayal still hurt. The group stood in silence, awkward glances shifting between them. They had all had similar experiences. New Albion was unkind to trusting relationships.

Aidan broke the silence. 'Control is complete when even the ones who are meant to care for you don't see the problem,' he said almost inaudibly.

A cold draught blew through the warehouse. Anouk shuddered. 'Guess I owe you all a thank you then.' She shifted her weight from one foot to the other.

'Guess you do,' the woman called Rachel replied. Anouk recognised her as the woman who had ransacked her backpack. 'Luckily, it's not the first time that we've had to dress up as clowns, impersonating red jackets.' She spoke to Fred. 'You and Aidan better take her to Mother. Ann and I,' she signalled to the remaining woman, sporting the hunting knife, 'will stay here a bit to help out.'

'Sounds like a plan, Rachel,' Fred said. 'We'll catch up once you're back?'

'No problem,' Rachel said. She and Ann went to the person handing out blankets to the refugees. They had assumed many similar mannerisms. Ann flung an arm around Rachel's shoulders. She was the more easy-going, yet had developed an odd habit of looking over her shoulder.

Turning to Anouk and Aidan, Fred said, 'Better be off then. It's getting late.' She led the way across the old warehouse to what appeared to be a loading bay. It was open to the outside, and the familiar smell of chilly air wafted through. They walked the near-deserted streets of the old industrial quarter, passing scuttling inhabitants who raised silent hands or nodded in greeting. On the outside, people had learnt to mind their own business. There were consequences for caring.

The industrial quarter was partly destroyed. Shattered rubble lay everywhere. It had been piled and pushed to the sides of streets. The quarter was essentially quarantined from the larger city, voluntarily by residents and through red jacket patrols.

'Well, we're here,' Fred said. They had entered a characterless rectangular office block. The building's precast concrete panels and brick cladding failed to integrate it into its original Victorian surroundings. They walked across the entrance area. Guards were stationed outside double doors at the far end but they moved aside when Fred and Aidan approached. Fred pushed the doors inward and Aidan and Anouk followed her to enter into a large dimly lit room. It had once been a conference venue, but now it had little in the way of furniture apart from a few chairs and a long table at its front. The remaining chairs were stacked along the sides.

'You two stay here while I have a word, alright?'

Aidan nodded, and Fred walked to the group around the table. A few bulbs, strung unprofessionally from the ceiling, illuminated it.

'Who are they?' Anouk asked Aidan.

'They're the people who get to decide whether you stay with us at HQ.' Standing next to her, he gave her a quick sideway look. 'So behave. Be nice.'

Anouk was about to protest but knew it was true. *I can be a right rude git when I want to be.* Fred reached the table and stood beside to a tall, middle-aged woman. She planted a peck on the woman's cheek, and they spoke for a few minutes, glancing up periodically towards Anouk and Aidan.

'And that. Who's that?' Anouk asked, meaning the woman

with whom Fred was conferring.

'That's Mother,' Aidan said. 'Fred's wife. You genuinely don't want to mess with her.' He made a whistling sound from between his teeth.

'*Mother?*' Anouk didn't take her eyes off the conversation.

Aidan seemed baffled for a moment and then understood. 'Oh yes, Mother. Sorry. Mother is her codename.' He was so accustomed to the name that it didn't strike him as unusual anymore.

At that moment, Fred motioned for Aidan to join them. 'Oh no,' Aidan groaned—a schoolboy about to receive a bollocking. 'I was hoping to avoid having to talk. Wasn't supposed to bring you here. Bugger. Here goes nothing, then.' Without looking back, he instructed, 'And be good.'

Aidan sauntered over the worn nylon carpet. It was a show; the stiffness in his walk betrayed his unease. Aidan was now talking to Mother; Fred listened. He pulled the pen drive out of his trouser pocket and handed it to her. Mother turned it over appreciatively in her hand. They spoke for a few minutes more, again glancing towards Anouk. This unsettled her, and she shifted. Mother was unhappy with Aidan. It wasn't her posture that gave it away; it was his. He was taller than Mother but crouched in submission as a wolf pack member might do to an asserting alpha.

Aidan returned, dashing away from Mother. 'So there's good news and there's bad news,' he said, waiting for Anouk to indicate which she preferred to hear first.

Anouk fidgeted with her jacket buttons. 'I think I'll start with the good news.'

'The good news is that they'll let you stay,' he declared, forcing a smile.

She snorted. 'That's the good news? I get to stay in this

shithole!' Anouk said this loudly, then moderated her voice. 'Sweet mother of Jesus, Aidan! If that's the good news, do I want to hear the bad news?'

Aidan cringed in anticipation. 'The bad news,' he went on, 'is that they want you clean.'

'That's a bit harsh! I know I need a bath, but do I really smell as wicked as all that?'

'No, Dimples,' his voice softened, 'they need you straight, off the drugs, no more shimmer.'

Anouk didn't respond.

'It's the rules, you see. No spritters at HQ. They think you'd be a liability.'

Her eyes fixed on her feet. She struggled with the words. 'That's okay, Aidan. I am a liability.' A weight lifted. 'And to be honest, when we left my home this afternoon, I already knew.' She looked him in the eye. 'It's time.'

'It's cold turkey, you understand? There's no easy ride with this, Anouk. You get that, right?' Aidan said. 'It's immediate, and it's unpleasant. I should know.'

Anouk lifted shaking hands towards Aidan. Shimmer withdrawal was setting in. 'No better time than the present.' She tried to sound brave; it was now or never. Besides, she couldn't hope to find Jimmy if she was still spritting.

———— ◎ ————

Aidan led Anouk up several flights of stairs in the vacant office block. Dust covered everything, suggesting that the workplaces had been unused for many years. People had gone busily about their business, then they vanished. The signs of a vibrant past life were everywhere. Framed family photos and dried-out mugs on desks, half-written notes on whiteboards, and calendars with entries all ceasing on the same date. Ordinary life had ended on a single day.

'Here you go,' Aidan said, unlocking and opening a door to a narrow room.

Anouk peered in as he stepped aside. It had probably once been a stationery cupboard. It was empty apart from a mattress on the floor, a jug of water, a cup alongside, and a commode in the corner. The room was painted a sickly off-yellow. A small slit window lay on an exterior-facing wall. It might let some light in during the day, but it was far too small to squeeze a body through.

'Too narrow. Don't even consider it,' Aidan warned.

Anouk swallowed hard. The door hadn't closed yet, and she felt claustrophobic. She checked the urge to run. 'Well, well, you know how to treat a lady, Aidan.'

Aidan smiled. 'You'll do just fine,' he said.

Anouk flushed and touched her greasy hair. 'Aidan?'

'Yes,' he said.

'Why do you keep doing it?'

'Doing what?'

'Looking out for me. Getting me out of scrapes?'

Aidan paused but chose not to answer. 'I'll be checking in on you. I'm afraid we both drew the short straw on that. Stay strong, Dimples.' He closed the door gently behind him. A key turned in the lock.

As if a dam wall had given way, Anouk could contain her anxiety no longer. She sat down on the mattress, her heart pounding, short of breath. She clasped her head with shaking hands and rocked back and forth. Alone again. How often did this need to happen? The jug of water sat before her. She was neither thirsty nor hungry. Despite having not slept for hours, she was not tired. She fell to her side in the foetal position, hugging her body for reassurance. She stared at the yellow wall facing her as the sun rose behind the clouds for a new day.

———— ◎ ————

'Just admit it: you fancy her,' Rachel said.

'So what if he does, Rachel,' Fred intervened. 'She's not bad looking, if she had a solid scrubbing down. And apart from her temper, there's a spark in her.'

'Come on! She's nothing more than a childish drug addict.'

Aidan listened to the conversation as if it didn't concern him. He raised a piece of soup-soaked bread to his mouth and munched on it. They were sitting in the mess hall, the previous office canteen, at a long shared table. Fred and Rachel continued arguing until he voiced an opinion. 'Guilt,' he said, offering a half-truth. 'I feel guilty; that's why I'm helping Anouk.'

Fred and Rachel came to a stop. They hadn't expected him to say anything.

'That's nonsense!'

Fred agreed with Rachel but didn't say so.

'Is it?' Aidan asked. 'What sacrifices have we all made for this place?' He spread his arms wide. Fred leant back. Before she could draw a false conclusion, he continued, 'And willingly so, without a doubt. But—and this is the rub—how many sacrifices have we made on behalf of others?'

'Where're you going with this, cuz?' Fred asked.

'Well, here's the thing.' Aidan leant forwards slightly. 'I did what I was asked. I sold drugs. A lot of them. And people paid the price for that. People like Anouk. Guilt.' He shrugged, sitting back and taking another bite of soupy bread.

Fred and Rachel exchanged a look—the debate was over.

'How's the patient doing?' Fred asked, changing tack. 'It's

been three days, right?' She scooped a spoonful of soup from an enamelled metal bowl.

'Yeah, I think...' Aidan tried counting the days. 'She's already passed the insomnia, so at least she's sleeping. But the nausea and vomiting were gruesome. And don't get me started on the anger issues! God almighty, that woman is vicious.' He lifted his shirt sleeve to show deep scratch marks on his arm.

Rachel scrunched up her face in distaste. 'I hope it's worth it. Better be good in bed, that's all I'm saying. Not that I can see what the attraction is!'

'Ah, bleeding hell! I give up,' Aidan said.

Fred laughed, stifling it behind a hand.

'I'll leave you to the rest of your lunch. Besides, I've got to take the vomiting zombie something to eat and drink.' He got up with his tray.

'See you later, Loverboy!' Rachel called as he went to deposit the tray on the clearing trolley.

Fred viewed her with a raised eyebrow.

'What?' Rachel said.

'You know what!'

Aidan collected a new tray, bowl, spoon and mug. At the steel serving counter, he slopped soup into the bowl, poured a little water into the mug, and tore a chunk of bread off an already mangled-looking loaf. *Better hope that the soup has cooled by the time I get up there*, he considered. *I'm not having another hot meal thrown at me.* He crossed the mess hall's vinyl floor towards the exit. Rachel followed his movements with narrowed eyes and a frown. He wished she'd lighten up. She had given him an earful when he volunteered to join the team to extract Anouk:

'Anouk, this, Dimples that. Damn! And now you want to go off and rescue her! You're a pillock, Aidan. Can't you just see...' She had thundered off and had been in a strop ever since.

The elevator was out of order, so he climbed the familiar three flights of stairs, and pushed open a fire door into a corridor. He made his way down, passing office working spaces, until he came to a white door and knocked. 'Anouk, are you decent?'

There was no answer. He was about to knock again when Anouk grumbled, 'Define decent?'

Aidan smiled. At least her sense of humour was returning. He balanced the tray, turned the key, and pushed the handle down. Anouk looked wretched. Her nose and eyes had stopped running, but the constant stream of mucus had left her lip raw and inflamed. Her clothes had dried, but days of excessive sweating had left them stained. It did not smell pleasant in the room.

'How are you feeling?' Aidan asked, setting the tray beside her. She didn't look bad-tempered today, and his shoulders relaxed. The remains of a vegetable stew had dried where she had thrown it against the wall.

'If you mean, do I still feel like the world is against me and you're here to end my life, then yes, much better, thank you,' Anouk replied in a clipped voice. Aidan was about to say something positive when she continued, 'But if you mean, do my guts feel like they're being torn out of my arse and I'm about to shit in my pants, then no, thank you very much.'

Charming. Perhaps Rachel had a point. Aidan noticed she was shivering. 'I know this is awful, I really do.' He took a step closer. 'But you're about halfway through. Hang in there.'

Anouk groaned, 'I wish I were dead.'

'No, you don't, Dimples. No, you don't.' He helped her to lie down and covered her with a crumpled blanket lying at her feet.

'I feel so tired,' she murmured, then closed her eyes. Aidan collected a few snot-glued toilet paper tissues strewn on the floor and dropped them into the well-used commode. Carrying it in one hand, he left Anouk sleeping.

Several days had passed when Anouk pulled herself onto tiptoes and peered out the narrow window. It was daytime, but she didn't know when. This was a blessing. Her addiction had clear timing rituals of morning and evening. Not knowing the time eased the anticipation. It was likely morning; Aidan hadn't yet visited with food. There was not much to see. A narrow street with a building's brick wall in front. Closer to street level was a crude mural. It comprised three interlinked rings. Within each was a symbol. Only one was familiar: the Earth occupied the centre ring. It appeared often as the converted 'O' in stop signs, sandwiched between the 'S.T.' and 'P.' It signified 'Save the Planet'. The other two symbols were unplaceable, but familiar. The one on the left ring comprised three arrows slanting horizontally downward. The one on the right looked very much like a mathematical equal sign. She stared at the mural, and her mind wandered to Jimmy. He was never far from her thoughts. Where was he? Was he alive?

There was a knock at the door. Anouk speedily retreated from the window. She did her best to smooth her hair. 'Yes?'

'Are you alright for me to come in?' It was Aidan's familiar and welcome voice.

'Sure.' Anouk tried to steady her tone. Her trousers were hanging loose, having lost a lot of weight in a short space of time—she pulled them up.

The key turned reassuringly, and the door swung open to reveal Aidan. He had a cheerful grin on his face. 'Big day today!' He entered, holding a pile of folded items. 'How are you feeling?'

'Okay.' Anouk assessed both body and mind. 'I'm a bit tired maybe and feeling a tad down now and then. But otherwise, good.' She surprised herself.

'That's it! Knew you'd pull through.' Aidan held a victory fist forwards.

She smiled, feeling shy. 'I'm sorry you had to deal with this.' The filthy room, the splattered commode. 'I'm amazed you can even bear to be near me.' She peered down.

'Look at me,' Aidan requested.

Anouk met his gaze. She could feel herself blushing.

'There's no shame in it, Dimples. Someone did it for me. And it was my turn, that's all. And believe it or not, I was even worse behaved than you.' He chuckled.

The shattered mug lay where Anouk had launched it at Aidan a few days ago. 'Can't believe that!' Guilt and shame nestled under her skin. In the afterglow of shimmer, they lingered as a constant reminder of her past.

'But you owe me,' he said.

'What?' Her eyes widened. 'Go on then. But be kind.'

'A bath!' He passed her the folded items—a towel, clothes and various cleansing accessories. 'I'm not going to lie, you stink!'

Anouk laughed for the first time in memory, dimples showing beneath smeared cheeks. 'I'm totally onboard with that!'

Aidan followed Anouk into her new world, along the corridor and down the stairs. They'd clean the room later. Anouk recognised the stairs from a week earlier, but her surroundings felt far less foreboding now. They reached the ground floor. Ahead stood two side-swinging doors, each with glass panes at the top. 'That's the mess hall. My favourite place.' Aidan stressed this by rubbing his stomach. 'But you're down this way.' He guided Anouk around the foot of the stairs to a short corridor. 'This is my cousin's favourite place. The old office shower ablutions. It's a miracle that she isn't hogging them right now!'

'Your cousin?' Anouk said in surprise.

'Yes, you've met her. Fred, remember?' Aidan said.

'But…'

'But, but… go on,' he pressed.

Anouk's mouth opened and then closed.

'Is it,' Aidan hazarded a guess, 'that you can't understand how a black bloke like me has a white girl like her as a cousin?' His face was stern, but his eyes sparkled.

'No, I mean…' Anouk stammered, pressing her lips together.

Aidan burst out laughing.

'I don't see what's so funny,' she said.

'Your face—it's priceless,' he spluttered, then guffawed again.

'Take your time,' Anouk said, now feeling less embarrassed and much more irritated.

'It's fine, it's fine.' He held back further laughter and wiped moisture from his eyes. 'Everyone asks the same question; it's just that you looked particularly uncomfortable.' He laughed again.

'It's hilarious, I can see. Side-splittingly funny.' Deadpan, she put her hands on her hips and waited for Aidan to finish.

Aidan pulled himself together. 'No, seriously, it's okay.' He grinned. 'It's a perfectly reasonable question. You see, my mum and dad were—are—South African. She's black and he's white. They came over here when that sort of thing wasn't too common there. Thought it would be less judgmental here. Guess that backfired, eh?'

'And so Fred is—?'

'Oh yes, sorry.' Aidan picked up the thread of his story. 'Fred is my father's sister's daughter. My aunt's daughter, my cousin.' He paused while thinking. 'But acts more like a big sister. Likes to take care of me. Thinks she's in charge.'

The lineage untangled in Anouk's head. 'Okay, that makes sense then,' she said, turning to walk towards the only door in the corridor. And then she stopped. 'I have another question;

it's kind of been nagging me over the last day or two.' Aidan nodded she should continue. 'As you know, I've had a few days to think.' He nodded again with a half-smile. 'You said there had been a decree. That they had expanded the definition of what counts as undesirable?'

'That's correct,' Aidan said.

'And you said that spritting degenerates like me are no longer on our own?' Aidan nodded again. 'Well, I don't understand?'

'It's simple. You know that some people were designated as undesirable several years ago. First illegal immigrants, then so-called degenerates like drug addicts,' he said. Anouk appeared uncomfortable. 'And members of the LGBTQ+ community?' She nodded. 'That gave the red jackets the right to arrest you, take you away.' She nodded again. 'So, there're just more of us now. Anyone who is an immigrant, up to first-generation immigrants.'

'But that's crazy! There must be thousands and thousands of citizens who are first-generation immigrants!'

'Yes, there are. But let's face it, "immigrant" has never meant "white immigrants", has it?' Aidan considered for a moment. 'Apart from a few notable exceptions, it's always been code for people who don't look the same as you. White people, that is. People like me, who don't have strange translucent skin,' he said, tapping his forearm. 'So, basically, you're not alone anymore, Dimples. You've got me.' This filled Anouk with warmth.

'Anyway, time for that bath, I think,' Aidan changed the subject. He showed her the shower room door. 'Oh, and leave your dirty clothes in the bag that I've left in there. It's definitely time to say goodbye to them.' Departing, he added, 'See you in the mess hall when you're done.'

Aidan's footsteps receded as Anouk twisted the lock. Stripping naked, she dumped her clothes alongside the plastic bag Aidan had left, and turned the shower taps on. Wriggling her fingertips under the cascading water, she waited for it to warm, then stepped in. It was exquisite. The hot water gushed across her head, over her shoulders and down her back. Steam swathed around her and condensed to trickle onto white square tiles. With the tip of her finger, she wrote her name on the misted glass shower screen. Anouk Scarlett Walker. And then again: Anouk Scarlett Walker. It was then, as the water carried the muck and indignity from her body, that she was reborn. She had been given another chance. *Aidan has given me another chance.* And she would not mess it up.

She had lost count of how many times she'd washed her hair. It took quite a while to comb the knots out with conditioner. Her skin was pink from using the nail brush to loosen stubborn dirt. She stepped out of the shower and dried herself with the provided towel, and pulled on the comfortable clothes left for her. Underwear, socks, T-shirt, hoodie, jeans and sneakers. They fit well. She found accessories tucked into the clean towel; brushed and flossed her teeth. Her gums bled a little in protest at the novelty. After combing her hair one last time, she tidied the shower room. Placing her repugnant old clothing into the bag, she went to find Aidan.

—————◎—————

Aidan, Rachel and Ann were sitting at a table together, sharing stories of their exploits that increased in outrageous detail at each telling, when Anouk approached. They didn't react at first. 'Can I join you?' she asked.

'Good God.' She was lovely. Aidan gawked at her, his mouth

hanging open. Her clothes were loose but suggested a slender body. Her dark auburn hair shone and fell in waves to her shoulders. Although a fading bruise was still visible on her cheek, her face was alive. Her nose was flecked with light freckles, and her keen green eyes sparkled as she waited for an invitation to sit.

'Close your mouth. You're embarrassing yourself,' Rachel said.

But Aidan hadn't heard her. He got up awkwardly. 'Of course, sit, sit down.' He showed Anouk the seat beside him.

Without planning to, Anouk leant over and kissed Aidan genially on the cheek. 'Thank you.'

Rachel got up. 'I think I'm going to get sick in my mouth!' She kicked the bench she was sitting on backwards, strutting off and joining others at the table a short distance away.

'Don't mind her,' Ann said, looking over her shoulder. It was the other woman who had rescued Anouk on the night she arrived in the quarter. She was still wearing the menacing hunting knife. Strung to her belt, its sheathed tip rested on the bench beside her. She followed Anouk's stare. 'Oh, don't worry about this.' She tapped the knife with one finger. 'It was my older brother's before…' She didn't finish the sentence. 'I don't think we've actually been introduced, Anouk?' She offered her hand. 'I'm Ann.' The familiar symbol of the Earth in a circle was embroidered on the shoulder of her jacket.

'Hello, Ann. Pleased to meet you, um, again.' Anouk accepted her hand.

'The clothes look like they fit?' Ann appraised them thoroughly. 'Fred told me you had to ditch your backpack.'

'I presume that I've got you to thank for them?'

Ann smiled and nodded.

'Well, thank you, Ann, they're great.'

'No worries. I guessed you were about my size, and we asked

around for contributions,' Ann said. 'You'll find that people look out for each other here.'

Aidan had stopped gawking. 'You took quite a while. We thought you might have bolted,' he said.

'Not before I eat.'

A full plate of pasta with tomato sauce sat beside Aidan's arm. 'Oh, that's for you.' He pushed the plate along the table with cutlery. 'Sorry, it may be a little cold.'

But Anouk was already eating.

8

Jessica stood alongside a busy road. She shivered as she gazed at the Bureau, an art deco building that was once a museum of postmodern art. Its grey stucco façade now rose to cower and subdue. She studied the entrance doors—their sturdy black iron frames with bottom panels interspersed with polished chrome studs. Zigzagging geometric lines of iron intersected to form patterned windows—prison bars—and engraved glass rested between the shapes of iron. On either side of the doors climbed two tall columns. Someone had replaced its low-relief panels— botanicals interwoven around native bird species—erasing the building's identity just as he sought to erase hers. Instead, writhing bodies in purgatorial torment supported people standing above. She was among them—the wretched—and her father tormented her from above. Her eyes wandered further up as the human figures developed—built square, healthy, purposeful and firm. She wished she were one of them, free from his control, so brave and strong. Atop each column was a figure resembling Britannica, recast as the man Albion, borne on the shoulders of those below. Escape was an illusion after all; futile under his watchful presence. He held a shield depicting the circular serpent Ouroboros, and in place of a trident, he grasped a bolt of lightning. Between the columns hung a banner flag over the entrance. The Union Jack still displayed its pattern, but only in red and white. A dominant red expressed harmony among the Kingdom's nations. It demanded unity and loyalty to the political forebears of the State—the Blood Martyrs. She complied, crossing the road in quiet subservience.

The holding cells sat in the building's sweating bowels. Jimmy lay motionless on the floor. He could have been mistaken for dead if it weren't for his raised pink and mottled skin.

'Oh, let me keep him, Daddy! I saved that rat from drowning the other day, and it made a full recovery. I even released it into the garden,' Jessica said. 'It was so very sweet to see it scurry away.'

'He's a lot bigger than a rat, Jessica.' Kilgore appeared unconvinced. 'Even if he recovered—and that's a big if—he'd need to be processed like the rest of them. This one,' he nudged Jimmy with his foot, 'is not only rotten, he's also dangerous.'

'Daddy, please. You know how much I like to pretend nurse. And this degenerate looks like a challenge.' Jessica wrinkled her nose and threw Jimmy an aversive look. 'Give me one of your people to help out? And then I should be safe.'

Kilgore considered the costs versus benefits. His quota for arrests was still short despite the recent decree. 'He can only use the old stock of antibiotics we have in the emergency sickbay. If they don't work, then tough! Agreed?'

Jessica skipped up and down in giddy excitement. 'Oh, that's wonderful, Daddy! Thank you so much. You are spoiling me today.' She stepped forwards and flung her arms around Kilgore.

'That's fine.' He patted Jessica on the bottom before she peeled away. 'Just remember, though: don't get too fond of your new pet. We'll either end up putting him down or sending him on. And infections like his rarely respond to antibiotics these days, so don't get your hopes up.'

He turned to the squad leader who stood above Jimmy. 'You'll be helping with the degenerate. Do as she asks.' He pointed sharply towards Jessica.

The squad leader bristled. Kilgore meant it as an affront. He should have asked the squad leader to order the squaddie beside her. She hesitated.

'Is that clear?' His lips curled upward.

'Perfectly clear, sir,' the squad leader said, standing at attention.

'Good. I'll leave you two girls to tidy up then.' Kilgore spoke to the other red jacket. 'You're dismissed. Go off and join your squad. Tell them the Squad Leader is presently, um, occupied as a nurse.'

The red jacket gave a spiteful smile. 'Yes, sir.' He opened the door for Kilgore as he was leaving.

Kilgore reached the door and half-turned to Jessica. 'And when you are done here, princess, perhaps you can come to my office and say thank you properly.' He then left for the elevator with the red jacket scurrying behind.

The door closed behind Kilgore.

I detest that man! Bilious at the thought of his touch, his bad breath and clammy hands—hating him but fearing him. Jessica would do what she had to, to be safe. She banned further thought. 'Apologies, I didn't mean to create work for you.'

'Er, that's okay, ma'am. Just tell me what you need me to do?' The red jacket glanced hesitantly around. Jessica's change of demeanour unsettled her.

'I think if you can help me move him to that cell, that would be a good start?'

'Can do,' the squad leader said, recovering. She moved to the nearest side cell and entered a number into the touchpad. With a click, the gate swung open. 'Will you be caring for him yourself, ma'am?'

'Yes.'

'Well, then you'll need the code. It's 24-12-99.'

'24-12-99,' Jessica repeated. She rubbed her chin. 'But won't you be staying in the cell block to keep an eye on him?'

'No need, no need,' the red jacket said, pointing to a camera angling down from the room's corner. 'They are monitored 24/7. If there are any problems, someone will be here in half a minute. There's nothing to be concerned about, ma'am. If you need any assistance, push this button.' She showed an intercom alongside the door to the corridor. 'Help will arrive.'

Jessica nodded, and the red jacket walked over and gripped Jimmy under his arms. Jessica took hold of his ankles and they dragged him across the floor, through the open gate, and into the cell. The red jacket counted to three. They both heaved and flung him onto a single bunk alongside the cell wall. Jimmy fell harder than Jessica expected. His weight dragged her over, and she caught herself with a hand on the wall.

The red jacket straightened. 'Will there be anything else at this moment, ma'am?'

'Yes, if you don't mind. I'd appreciate it if you could pop over to the sickbay. Ask the duty nurse to provide a trolley of supplies for a severe laceration. And ignore what my father said. He will require intravenous therapy. So, tell them he has acute sepsis and will need a broad-spectrum fifth-generation antibiotic.' Jessica knew that calling it a sickbay was a misnomer. Terrorist attacks had risen markedly over the last few years, and the sickbay served as a standby centre for emergency triage. She'd been called to lend a hand more than once and had picked up a good working knowledge of emergency medicine.

The red jacket appeared uneasy. 'Ma'am, I'm not certain that I'm comfortable in asking for that—anything other than specified by the Senior Superintendent.'

Jessica pointed to Jimmy 'He definitely won't be able to swallow a pill. Besides, my father wouldn't know the difference between one antibiotic and another if they hit him in his face. I promise that if it comes up, I'll say that I got confused which was which.'

The red jacket was not a trusting person, but she sensed Jessica's integrity. 'Alright, then. And anything else while I'm at it?'

Jessica gave a grateful smile. 'That's kind, thank you. Perhaps something to clean him with and a hospital gown?'

'Will do, ma'am.'

The red jacket left Jessica sitting on the floor, with her legs curled together by her side, leaning towards the bunk and staring at Jimmy in concern.

———————◉———————

Jessica's care of Jimmy continued unabated for days. It gave her a sense of purpose and value. It had drawn her away from her father's attentive orbit, for which she was grateful. But she now waited apprehensively outside her father's office door. Her stomach churned. He had summoned her, and she waited for an invitation to enter after knocking.

Jimmy was in the basement, with a cannula in his arm. It had been a week since his arrival, and although his recovery was dubious at first, he had responded far better than she had hoped to antibiotics. His fever had subsided quickly, and despite clear signs of severe sepsis, he had not progressed to septic shock. He was weak and slept for much of each day. She was trying to get him to eat, despite his appetite not having returned.

'Come in,' her father called in a singsong voice. It sounded strange, ominous. Twisting a tarnished brass handle, she pushed the door open. Kilgore sat behind an imposing desk, trying to occupy physical space. He reminded her of a preening cockerel. 'Come, come, my cherub.' He beckoned her in. 'You remember Chief Superintendent Moran, don't you?' He gestured towards a woman in her late fifties, smartly attired and serious.

The Chief Superintendent rose politely to her feet. 'Jessica, how nice to see you.' She took Jessica's hand in hers. Moran was always aloof and business-like, but Jessica had never experienced the overt malice in her that was common among other Bureau employees. 'I hear from your father you have been doing wonderful things here at the Bureau? Perhaps a budding career?'

'Thank you, Chief Superintendent, that's kind of you to say, but I wouldn't want to presume...'

'She's a chip off the old block,' Kilgore interrupted.

'Let her finish, Jerome,' Moran said. 'What is it with men that they feel it so often necessary to finish sentences for women?' She asked Jessica but directed the question at Kilgore. Before Kilgore could answer, she continued, 'You look so grown-up since the last time I saw you. So beautiful. You are well, I hope? Your father, I presume, is treating you with respect?' She said this pointedly, still holding Jessica's hand in hers.

Kilgore coughed, suggesting that they get down to business.

'Are you in a hurry, Kilgore?' She released Jessica's hand and took her seat again. 'Or are you just uncomfortable?'

'Neither, Hilary, I...'

'Chief Superintendent, if you will.'

Heat flushed Kilgore's face. There was a pause.

'You may continue,' Moran offered.

'Apologies, and thank you.' Kilgore spoke with a tight smile. 'Jessica, please sit down.' He showed her to a second chair opposite Moran, who still glared at him. He lowered his eyes in forced deference and looked towards Jessica. His tone took on an air of normality. 'The Chief Superintendent and I were just about to agree the itinerary for the Undersecretary of State's visit. Would you be so kind as to take notes?'

'Of course, Father,' Jessica said, sitting down. She leant forwards to retrieve a notepad and pencil from the usual place on Kilgore's desk. He laid them in an obsessively neat vertical row. She waited for them to continue. As they spoke, she recorded the discussion in shorthand. She had done this for many years during her school holidays and was now adept. Her mind wandered back to Jimmy.

He was so thin and fragile when she first undressed him. He seemed like a newborn chick. But as she wiped him clean with wet flannels, he had regained consciousness and opened his eyes. His troubled but kind blue-grey eyes looked up at her. She was reflected in them. All their shared pain and their common decency. And she felt something—a profound something that she couldn't quite describe. Protective, perhaps? Maybe her care of him was a way to show she was different, that she had feeling and goodness in her? No, it was more than that—a need for connection beyond fear. She felt foolish even thinking about it.

'It's agreed then,' Moran said, standing to leave.

'Yes, I think the visit will be a great success. I am certain the Undersecretary will be very pleased with my... our progress.' Kilgore corrected himself mid-flow. To recover from his faux pas, he added quickly, 'Perhaps you would like to view the spritter that Jessica has brought back from the dead?'

'Yes, *our* good progress indeed.' Chief Superintendent didn't miss a beat, laying stress on the 'our'. 'And yes, I think I would enjoy seeing Jessica's handiwork for myself. Thank you for the suggestion, Kilgore.'

Kilgore's face plainly revealed his disappointment. 'Super, marvellous. Jessica, please show the good Chief Superintendent the way.' He rose, pointing encouragingly towards the door, hoping to rid himself of his guest.

Jessica led the way down the corridor to the elevator. They stood squashed in awkward silence, staring forwards, as the elevator doors closed and it trundled down. A fluorescent tube of light flickered the moment they entered the cell block. It fizzed and clicked. The sight of Jimmy lying prone in his cage, under the stuttering light, made Jessica uneasy. She rubbed her sweating hands together, noticed, and pulled them apart.

'Here we are, Chief Superintendent, the holding cells,' Jessica said when her father and Moran were in the room. 'As you can see, they are rarely in use. Our processing of undesirables is increasingly efficient.'

'Yes, I see,' Moran said.

'There are occasions, however, when we do need to hold one or two for a longer period.' She flicked her head towards Jimmy. 'Most spritters, for example, experience drug withdrawal in a shivering stupor. They can be moved on. But sometimes they get a little feisty and end up in here for a few days to calm down.'

'Yes, that makes sense. But tell me specifically about this one,' Moran asked, moving closer to the cell and peering in through the wire mesh. She observed Jimmy as though he were a zoo animal. He remained on his back but returned her quizzical look. 'His eyes aren't pink and, I must say, there is a certain defiance in them.'

'That's correct, Chief Superintendent. This spritter has come clean. He's now off shimmer. But he caused us some difficulty. He did a runner once he was caught. It took quite some time to bring him to heel,' Kilgore said.

Moran frowned. 'Why keep him alive then?' She observed the intravenous drip. 'He also seems to be costing us a small fortune in medical supplies. I am not convinced the Undersecretary will approve.'

'I couldn't agree more,' Kilgore said. He almost added 'for once', but thought better of it. 'There was some debate concerning the cost-benefit of keeping him alive. Our calculation was, I admit, marginal either way. But given the ambitious quota for this quarter, we felt it justified the additional expense in this instance.'

'Alright, Kilgore. On this rare occasion only. But I am surprised. I never pegged you for the soft sort. Or maybe this is more a case of a father indulging his daughter's whims?' Moran inclined her head, looking at Jessica.

Kilgore spread his hands as if to imply, 'what else could I do?'

'Fine, fine. We all have weaknesses.'

Kilgore gave Jessica an appraising leer as Moran spoke, his eyes pausing an instant at the cleavage of her V-neck sweater. Jessica drew the sweater higher. Moran noticed, and her body tensed, but she did nothing to challenge Kilgore.

'Ensure that this is all tidied up before the Undersecretary's visit. And make certain,' Moran said, pointing to the flickering tube, 'that is fixed. We need a tight ship for the visit, Kilgore. Don't let us down.' Her last sentence carried an unequivocal threat.

'Of course, Chief Superintendent.' Kilgore genuflected, and Moran ignored the irony. 'The assessor is scheduled to visit early next week to process another expected tranche of undesirables.' Kilgore pointed to Jimmy. 'We'll add him to the list.'

Jessica's heart stopped.

'Yes, do that,' Moran said.

———————◎———————

The day of the assessor's visit arrived. He was a short man: a stereotypic optometrist. Almost bald, but with a trimmed border of hair. His glasses were round and black-rimmed, and he wore a full dark blue suit with a matching waistcoat. He was waiting for Jimmy on an adjustable stool, clipboard in hand, beside a large device. Jimmy entered with a red jacket supporting him. His ribs still hurt from where Kilgore had kicked him.

The optometrist raised his head as the two entered and took in the scene. 'This is unusual,' he said, looking between Jimmy and the red jacket.

'He was unsteady by himself. I had no choice,' the red jacket said, shrugging. 'Where do you want him?'

'Just sit him down on that stool.'

The optometrist went back to scribbling on a document attached to his clipboard. The red jacket deposited Jimmy roughly and left. Jimmy examined his surroundings. The room was box-like and nine square yards, painted matte white and surrounded on two sides by waist-high white storage cupboards. Neatly arranged instruments and supplies lined the steel countertop. A small round sink was in one corner.

'Good afternoon,' the man said, looking up from his clipboard. 'Do you speak E-n-g-l-i-s-h?' he asked.

Jimmy nodded.

'Oh, good, that should make things easier for once.' He spoke as if reading a script. 'James Michael Sullivan?'

Jimmy nodded again.

The man ticked his piece of paper and continued. 'Confirm your date of birth?'

Jimmy attempted to speak, but his throat was dry, and it cracked. The optometrist rolled his eyes in annoyance, the thick lenses magnifying them. Jimmy thought he looked like an odd sort of manga character.

Jimmy tried again, croaking his date of birth in a hoarse voice. The man ticked his clipboard, scribbled something, and then set it aside on the counter behind him.

'Right, wheel yourself closer to that,' the optometrist instructed, indicating the large device. It rested on a table in the middle of the room, connected to a refurbished laptop. It had a chin rest and forehead bracket, which Jimmy supposed was for his use. Two circular lenses protruded outwards.

'Okay, that's correct, now place your chin on the rest, and steady your head as best as you can against this bracket.'

The man touched each part of the instrument in explanation. He then slipped a face mask on and wheeled his stool into position opposite Jimmy. A tiny screen and finger-controlled joystick sat on the operator's side of the instrument.

'Now, just stare into the lenses.'

Jimmy obeyed.

'That's correct,' the man said. 'You should see a bright dot of light. Do you see this?'

'Yes.'

'Now, close your left eye, and keep staring at the light.' Jimmy followed the instructions. 'Your left eye, not your right eye.' The optometrist sighed. Jimmy obliged, feeling foolish. 'That's correct. Do not blink. Good.' There was no sound or change to Jimmy's field of vision, but the optometrist said, 'Okay, now the other eye, same as before.' Jimmy opened his left eye and shut his right eye, staring at the dot of light and waiting. 'All done, you can sit back.'

The man rotated to face the laptop. 'Let's take a look at what these images of your inner eye tell us, shall we.' The man was talking to himself, so Jimmy didn't respond.

The optometrist typed on the worn keyboard and then clicked his mouse. As he waited a few moments, he stared blankly at the wall behind Jimmy, tapping the heels of his smart leather shoes. Jimmy found this disconcerting. The optometrist then re-lowered his eyes back to the laptop screen. He appeared baffled and shook his head. 'Damn, I must have entered incorrect parameters.' He typed quickly again on the keyboard, double-checked what he had entered, then clicked the mouse once more. He didn't take his eyes off the screen. Jimmy waited, anxious in the event of a grim diagnosis. The optometrist was puffing out his cheeks as he waited. Leaning back, he blew the air out.

'That's crazy, that can't be correct,' he said, sitting forwards again and squinting intently at the screen. 'Okay, we need to take the images again and then re-run the algorithm; just to be certain. Back you get.'

He directed Jimmy with a wave of his finger. Jimmy obliged, following the instructions as before. The optometrist hung over his laptop in rapt anticipation as the circuit board hummed. 'Good Lord! Well, aren't you something.' He sat upright and ogled Jimmy with wide round eyes. 'You have a CPU ratio of 11:1. That's pure madness. I've seen nothing like it!'

'Excuse me?' Jimmy said, feeling alarmed.

'Your CPU ratio.' Then he realised Jimmy wouldn't know what the acronym meant, and elaborated. 'Your consumption per use ratio of occudorphin is off the charts!'

Whatever that is, Jimmy thought, *it doesn't sound good.* He didn't have long to dwell.

———◎———

'Jimmy, Jimmy,' Jessica placed her hand on his chest and soothingly roused him. The assessor had already processed Jimmy. His results weren't in, but she expected him to be allocated to a forced-labour facility soon. She hoped for the best, perhaps an agricultural assignment in the countryside. Horrible, tough, but potentially survivable. A place in which he could have time to recover. He was still weak.

Jimmy opened his eyes sluggishly and blinked in the bright light. Someone had replaced the malfunctioning fluorescent tube.

'How are you feeling, Jimmy? I see you finished your dinner tonight,' she said, looking pleased.

Jimmy pushed himself into a half-sitting position with the aid of his elbows as Jessica leant forwards to rearrange the pillows behind him. He spotted a familiar heart-shaped mole on her neck. 'Much better, I think,' he said groggily, smacking his dry lips together.

'Here you go,' Jessica said, passing him a glass of water that sat beside his bunk. It left a wet, round ring on the floor.

He drank deeply, regarding her. 'You know, I've had a few dark moments in my life, and quite a few recently.'

'Yes, but they're over now.' Jessica positioned her body to block the view of anonymous eyes peering through the unblinking surveillance camera. Then, she took his hand where it rested and gave it a supportive squeeze. Her reassurance was false, but she wanted him to feel safe, if only for the moment.

'No, that's not what I mean,' Jimmy said, searching for the words. 'What I mean to say, what I want you to know, is that each time when I felt most alone, most desperate, something or someone always pitched up to give me hope.'

'That's good, Jimmy. Hope is important.' Jessica still held his hand and knelt beside him. Hope was one of the few things that had kept her sane under Kilgore's abuse. And Jimmy would need every ounce of it where he was going.

'The thing is, when I lay here, in and out of consciousness, I thought I was going to die. In fact, I was certain of it. Strangely enough, it didn't scare me. But I was called back. Something bright, brilliant and shining called me back and told me it wasn't my time.'

'Oh, Jimmy, I'm really pleased. I also thought you might not pull through. And just look how far you've come.'

'You're still not understanding me, Jess,' Jimmy said. 'The something bright, brilliant and shining—well, it was you. In the darkness, you shone through all the pain and misery and called me back. Do you see?'

Jessica's eyes brimmed with tears, and she held back the urge to cry. She took a deep breath, but couldn't bring herself to answer him. What it was to be needed, loved. She had carved out her own space where she was in power and in control. She clasped his hand, and then she let go to pull a silver chain and pendant from her pocket. 'I think this is yours,' she said, holding it out, but hidden before her body.

Jimmy grinned and took it in his hand. 'Yes,' he said softly, 'I believe it is.' The chain hung from his hand as he brought the pendant closer. It was circular and shaped in the Earth's image. He traced its smooth surface with his finger. 'It was my aunt's. It's all I have left of her,' he said. He moved to place the chain over his head, but Jessica stopped him.

'No, Jimmy, you can't do that! That symbol is banned. It's lucky that I found it on you before anybody else did. They would have executed you had they seen it!' Jessica swiped to retrieve it from him, but missed.

'Let's be honest, Jess, I don't think the odds of my making it out of this mess alive are strong,' Jimmy said.

Jessica caught her breath, surprised at how calmly he understood his predicament.

'Tell you what, Jimmy, hand it over, and I'll make certain you get it back when it's safe? I promise,' Jessica said, holding out her hand.

Jimmy studied Jessica's thoughtful eyes and delicate skin. He smiled and dropped the chain into her palm. As she clasped her slim fingers around it and deposited it into her trouser pocket, Jimmy leant forwards and placed his hand on her cheek. Jessica jerked back in surprise. The CCTV camera nestled in the room's corner watched coolly, with infinite patience. But this was her space—a place where she could be who she wanted to be. The fear of discovery only made her want Jimmy's love more.

'What I wanted to say, before you purposefully changed the subject,' he whispered, 'is, I'm forever in your debt.'

Jimmy lured her eyes to meet his. She didn't answer, but placed her hand over his and sat, looking into his blue-grey kind eyes.

Jimmy spoke first. 'You know, you remind me of someone,' he said. And then he choked up.

'What is it?' Jessica said, sitting back on her haunches, letting go of his hand. 'Was it a girl?' she asked carefully. She hoped the answer would be 'no'. 'Your girlfriend?'

'No. No, not my girlfriend. Just my best friend. I'd known her since childhood. But she's dead, so it doesn't matter anymore,' Jimmy said in a detached voice. He stared down at his hands resting in his lap.

Words failed her. She felt a silly stab of jealousy but forced it aside. 'Do you know how she died?'

'An accident. The van that was bringing us here turned over on the motorway. She must have died instantly, though. I guess that's something.' Jimmy continued to stare at his hands.

'Yes, I'm sorry, Jimmy; I heard about the accident. Do you mind my asking what her name was?' It was good to give people a name. It made them real.

Jimmy shook his head, bitterness welling up inside him.

'It's okay, you don't have to,' she said, taking hold of one of his hands and squeezing it comfortingly again.

'Anouk. Anouk Walker.'

Jessica's breath caught in her throat. She released his hand and thought back to the report she'd filed. 'Who did you say she was?'

The urgency in her voice made Jimmy look up. 'Anouk Walker. But why? What's wrong?'

Jessica didn't answer. She was already on her feet. She clumsily entered the code into the touchpad to release the door. It beeped in error, and she fumbled to enter the code again. As the gate swung open, she dashed out, slamming it shut and calling back, 'I just need to check on something, Jimmy. I'll be back soon!'

The tiny light at the base of the camera, in the corner of the cell block, blinked green.

———————◉———————

One floor above the cell block and a few moments before, Kilgore glowered at the CCTV monitors. He had dismissed the attendant red jacket from the observation room so that he could be with Jessica and Jimmy alone. Horizontal lines travelled from one side of the screen to the other. But the image was still clear for

Kilgore to discern detail. Jimmy's hand was on Jessica's cheek and, despite a clumsy effort to conceal, her hand clasped in his. They gazed into each other's eyes.

Kilgore felt a flush of anger and betrayal. 'Well, well, puppy-dog,' he said. He imagined crushing Jimmy's eyes with his thumbs in their sockets. 'And as for you, Jessica, you treacherous little whore...'

9

The filing cabinet's key was stuck. 'Come on, come on.' Jessica jiggled it from side to side. Jimmy would be taken soon, and little time remained. She pulled the key out, and after inserting it again in the keyhole, twisted it to the left while pushing on the drawer. The cabinet bolt caught and pulled downwards as the key turned.

'Oh, thank you.' The drawer squeaked open. It slid backwards on its runners and came to a clanging stop. A musky smell of old paper wafted from the open drawer. Apprehensively, she glanced over her shoulder at the office door. Her father was out but could return at any moment.

Despite her rush, she dexterously fingered through the suspension files. The folder that she needed was filed under the name of the unfortunate squad who had ended on the motorway a few weeks ago. She tried under 'S' for Sigma, but the file was empty. 'Think, Jessica, think.' And then—'Kappa Squad, that's it!' Moving over alphabetised tags to the letter 'K', she opened the file to find two folders suspended within. She removed the second—the most recently added—and placed it on top of the cabinet.

Jessica opened the brown folder: a thick wad of pages; reports concerning the squad's activities. Her report would be last, so she skipped ahead to the final pages. *That's the one*, she thought, reciting the report's title. Report #63: Motor Vehicle Accident. She skimmed through the material, searching for the relevant information. The applicable section stuck out in a summary table: Occupants: 10; Injuries: 2; Fatalities: 5. The list below named the fatalities. Two were female: Makwetu, Thozoma Elizabeth and Michael, Georgina Grace.

'I knew it!' The report did not list an Anouk Walker.

'Knew what?'

Jessica half-turned; her heart in her throat. Kilgore's voice seeped like bitter treacle. He was standing in his office doorway, observing her. His black, deep-set eyes regarded her with icy contempt. 'My pet.' He glided towards her. 'You seem perturbed?' His bony fingers unfurled on one hand as he extended a palm gesture towards her as if to help. Long stained fingernails were prominent from the white of his veined hands. The door shut behind him, seemingly independently of his touch.

Jessica turned fully to face him, pushing the cabinet door closed with her stomach and pulling the key out with one hand. She was vulnerable, recognising his demeanour. Her skin crawled. It was the stalking of a calculated predator who had cornered its prey—measured and deliberate. It held no sympathy, no remorse. 'Just, just some filing work, Father. I'm a little behind.'

Kilgore stood uncomfortably close to her. She could smell and feel his warm, stale breath on her face. He unhurriedly leaned over her shoulder and peered down at the file resting open on the cabinet. His cheek brushed hers, sending a shudder down her back. 'Have you enjoyed your reading?' he said into her ear, pressing his body against hers.

Jessica tried to move out of his way, but Kilgore pushed

her leisurely back with his left arm across her chest. He made a mild tutting sound and shook his head subtly. His body pressed more firmly against hers; the steel handles of the cabinet pressed unpleasantly against her spine. 'You have been a naughty little girl, haven't you?' Kilgore moved his face an inch from Jessica's. 'A naughty little trollop...'

Jessica tried again to move from his grip, but he thumped her forcefully back into place. The steel cabinet now bit into her ribs, causing her to gasp in pain. She turned the key over in her hand. Kilgore carried on. 'I have been patient with you, Jessica. I have, haven't I?' He invited her agreement by nodding. She drew her head back and aside, trying to put distance between them. He pressed harder on her. It hurt.

'Yes, Father, yes, you have.' Her jaw tightened.

'And I have waited too long while you played your silly games, teasing me, flirting.' Kilgore moved his free right hand between their bodies and downward.

'No, Father, please! I'll do anything.' Her voice was trembling now, and moisture gathered in her eyes. But resolve swelled up. She held the key tighter, ready to strike.

'Yes, yes, you will.' Kilgore grappled at the waistband of her trousers. He bared a string of coffee-stained teeth through tight lips.

'No, no, please!' She grabbed the wrist of the offending hand, raising her right arm behind him, about to slash into his neck with the key.

There was a loud knock on the door. Kilgore's hand stopped and glided out from between their bodies. Jessica eagerly let go of his wrist and lowered her unseen arm.

'Yes! What the hell is it!' Kilgore shouted.

'It's Marge, Senior Superintendent.' There was a pause. 'Marge from Accounts.'

'Yes, Marge, what is it?' Spittle flew from his mouth and onto Jessica's face. He loosened his grip but still kept Jessica in place with his arm.

'You asked me to bring the figures to you as soon as they were available,' Marge said from behind the closed door.

Kilgore didn't respond as he tried to remember.

'I'm afraid they don't look good, sir,' Marge said, anticipating a fractious meeting.

Kilgore sighed and released Jessica. Moving back, he hissed, pointing a finger at her. 'We're not done, my girl. We're not nearly done.'

Jessica dipped her quavering head, showing that she understood. *If you touch me again, you filthy pig, I'll kill you.*

Kilgore turned and dusted his clothing. 'Yes, fine, come in, Marge.' His tone evened.

Marge entered with a bundle of folders tucked under her arm. One poked out and appeared as though it might fall. She was a round woman and bustled towards Kilgore's desk without taking in her surroundings. She placed the folders trimly on his desk, patted their sides into line, and said, 'I know you'll be disappointed, sir, but...' Until now, she hadn't noticed Jessica, distraught, standing rigid against the cabinet. 'My goodness me, are you alright, dear?' she asked, taking a step towards her.

'She's fine! I'm afraid that Jessica has been ill-behaved, and I have found it necessary to reprimand her,' Kilgore said. Before Marge could respond, he addressed Jessica. 'Off you go now, pet. Think carefully about what we talked about, and we'll resume our discussion this evening.' Then, only just remembering, he stepped to Jessica's side. He whispered so that only she could hear. 'And there's something about your new boyfriend you should know. I would have killed him already, but it turns out he's special. He's off to the Factory.'

Jessica inhaled sharply.

'When they are done with him, what's left will be picked apart and dissected. And I do hope that he is still alive when they get to the last slice.' Kilgore elongated the last consonant between his tongue and palate.

Jessica closed her eyes and breathed as Kilgore melted backwards. She gathered herself and walked haltingly to the door. Adrenaline made it difficult to move her muscles.

Marge dabbed Jessica's arm in concern as she passed. She wanted to say something, brow furrowed in worry. Her mouth was moving, but no words escaped. The office door shut behind Jessica.

Jimmy's time had run out. The Bureau's underground parking facility led from the basement corridor, where the holding cells were also located. A red jacket was walking on either side of Jimmy. One guided him by his lower arm. He wore the Factory's black jumpsuit, with its trademark golden eye embroidered into the nylon garment, resting over his right shoulder blade.

'Stop.' Jessica ran to catch up. Her heart was still galloping from her encounter with Kilgore. She weaved between cars and concrete pillars. The transport van's rear two doors were already open. The red jackets didn't heed her call.

'I said, stop!'

The men turned around with Jimmy. To her relief, he was unharmed.

'That's close enough, young lady.' One of the red jackets took a step forwards.

Jessica ignored him at a brisk walk.

'I said,' the red jacket unclipped a baton from his belt,

'stand aside!'

Jessica stopped. After a wild few seconds of thought, she pulled herself upright, and mustered as haughty a tone as possible. 'Excuse me! Have you any idea who I am?' She drew her slight frame up as though offended.

'Miss, I have no idea who the bleeding hell you are. And frankly, I don't give a shit. Move on your way.' He used his baton to show that she should return. She didn't move. 'Interfering with red jacket business is an indictable offence, punishable with a minimum sentence of public whipping.'

'Yours or mine?' Jessica asked with mock arrogance. She put a scornful smile on her face. 'My name, young man, is Jessica Kilgore. Recognise it, by any chance?' She sniggered mirthlessly. She was used to assuming a role when she had to.

The man's face fell as if slapped. He swallowed hard. 'Sorry, ma'am, I didn't know.' He lowered his baton and stepped aside with his head bowed. 'Please accept my sincere apologies.'

'That all depends, squaddie,' Jessica said, sweeping past him. 'My father wanted me to give this degenerate a little message.' Stopping and swivelling around to face the red jacket, she added, 'I imagine you don't mind giving me a minute to deliver it, do you?'

'Not at all, ma'am,' the red jacket said, indicating with a subdued wave that his colleague should release Jimmy.

The red jacket holding Jimmy's arm released him and moved aside to stand respectfully alongside his partner.

Jessica stifled her racing respiration. She approached Jimmy with an indifferent expression, risking a half-smile and a fleeting wink once she had turned her back to the red jackets. 'Jimmy, I'm so sorry,' she said in a lowered voice. Her arms itched with the urge to hug him and hold him tight.

'There's nothing for you to be sorry about. I'm more worried about you.'

Jessica's head jerked back. 'Me?'

'I've seen how your father looks at you,' Jimmy said with disquiet. 'It's...'

'Please don't worry about me, Jimmy, I've got it under control.' She lied skilfully but appeared needlessly ashamed, her mind flashing back to her recent experience.

'Are you absolutely certain?' Jimmy studied her face for any betraying hint.

'Yes, totally certain.'

Jimmy seemed satisfied, and his shoulders relaxed.

'It's you that I'm worried about; they're taking you to the Factory!' Jimmy's CPU ratio result had condemned him to this fate rather than the precarious reality of forced labour.

'I know,' Jimmy said. The optometrist had mentioned the Factory before departing on the day of his assessment, but didn't say more.

'You know?'

'Yes.'

His calm disposition disconcerted Jessica. 'How...'

The red jacket coughed lightly.

'Is there something I can help you with?' Jessica asked over her shoulder.

'Again, apologies, ma'am, but we do have a tight schedule. It's monitored.'

Jessica resumed. 'Jimmy, we don't have time, but I need to tell you something important.'

Jimmy nodded for her to continue.

'Anouk. Anouk Walker; she's alive.'

Jimmy's mouth dropped open comically. The red jackets moved towards them. And one last thing: 'I will come to find you,' Jessica said. 'Do you trust me?'

'Of course I do,' Jimmy said, smiling softly. 'Now hit me.'

'What?' Jessica asked. He cast his eyes to the approaching red jackets. Jessica followed his gaze. The penny dropped. She launched a proficient fist into his solar plexus. Jimmy doubled down, wheezing.

The red jackets traded an approving glance, then hauled him up by the arms. 'Come on, no malingering here.' They dragged him backwards to the van and bundled him in. The doors slammed shut, and the red jacket who had spoken to Jessica approached her. 'I'd just like to say sorry again for my behaviour back there, ma'am. You see, we often get upset people…'

'That's alright, officer.' She wanted to scream.

'Well, okay, then.' He hoped the matter was closed. 'We'll be off then. Good day, ma'am.'

Jessica raised her hand in token farewell as the red jacket made his way back to the van and settled into the passenger seat. His door closed, the engine rumbled, and the van pulled away. The overhead strip lighting threw an optical distortion across the golden serpent on the side of the vehicle. It appeared to slither sideways for a moment.

For Higher Virtue. What a damn joke!

The van carried the words away, trundling up the ramp to street level until it was gone.

Jessica didn't have time to collect any of her belongings. She took the elevator situated close to the holding cells to the building's foyer. Once there, she crossed the black granite floor. Golden radiating geometric shapes spread from its centre, representing the rising sun. She took a complimentary umbrella from a stand next to the turnstiles, pulled up her sweater's sleeve, and scanned the underside of her wrist on the chip reader. A small keloid marked where the State had, in her childhood, inserted the chip. The red light surrounding the reader, which sat on top of the turnstile, turned green and the glass panels swung automatically open.

'Good afternoon, Ms Kilgore!' the officer at the reception called keenly after her, as she exited from the Bureau's two large black iron doors onto the busy street. She did not respond. He thought nothing of her rudeness. She was a Kilgore, after all.

It was a little after midday. Relatively affluent shoppers were common in the government district. The constant drizzle and threat of downpour did little to dampen their enthusiasm for foreign-made goods. Yet, despite their pretences, the lack of new products was clear. Global trade had shrunk to a tenth of its previous size. New Albion's roaring international trade in shimmer could not compensate. Raw commodities were scarce, let alone manufactured goods. Re-heeled shoes clattered and darned woollen coats wove in among the throng of pedestrians.

Jessica dodged between people to reach the side of the road. She glanced both ways and waited for an old car spewing dark exhaust fumes to pass. She opened her umbrella. It was black, with the serpent emblem of the Bureau on it in gold. She skipped across the road, trying to avoid the largest puddles, but one foot landed squarely in a deceptively deep pothole. Her foot disappeared ankle-deep. 'Sod it!' She extracted a saturated ballerina shoe and trouser leg, and continued with an arhythmic squelching sound as she made her way to the opposite pavement.

Walking a few hundred yards down the road, she took shelter under a covered tram stop. She was alone. No other travellers were waiting. Public transport was unreliable. She removed her mobile phone from her back trouser pocket. The screen lit up and sprang to life when recognising her face. She swiped through her contact list and came across the name of the person she was searching for. She pressed call and waited, imagining the receiver's mobile phone shining on their desk and vibrating between scattered stationery. There was no answer. *Damn*, Jessica thought, and tried again.

'Hello, Marge speaking.'

'Marge, this is Jessica,' she said in a hushed tone.

A bus rolled past. 'Sorry, I'm having difficulty hearing you. Who is this?' Marge raised her voice. Her office colleagues glanced up and then went back to their keyboards.

'It's Jessica,' she said more forcefully.

'Jessica, oh my gosh, I didn't know it was you. I only got "No Caller ID" on the screen. Where are you, dear?' Marge covered her mouth with her hand. 'I was concerned about you. Are you okay?'

'I'm fine, I'm fine,' Jessica responded truthfully, feeling increasingly in control. 'But I need to ask you a favour, Marge?'

'Yes?' Marge asked. 'What is it?' She reached for a pad and pen to take notes.

'I need contact details for someone,' Jessica said, and swiftly added, 'But Marge, you can't use your computer.'

Marge replied, 'Okaaay, but is that a good idea?' She pushed the pad and pen away.

'No, Marge, it's not; it could get you into a lot of trouble. But I do need this,' Jessica said. There was a long pause again, so Jessica continued. 'Allan from maintenance is ill today. I know because I processed his absence request. If you go to his storeroom, you'll find an old PC. You can use that.' A car drove close to the pavement, hitting a pool of water that arced and sprayed a few feet from Jessica.

Jessica was almost at the point of giving up when Marge replied. 'Okay, dear, I'll go down to the storeroom now. But you must promise me something first?'

'What, Marge?'

'Wherever you are, you are not to come back here. Run, my girl. It's not safe for you here anymore.' Marge had seen the look in Kilgore's eyes, and it spoke of cruel retribution.

'Yes, I promise,' Jessica said, though she had already decided this. Marge's concern moved her. 'I'll call you back in five minutes. Don't call me, though.' She stood huddled in one corner of the shelter, avoiding any further spray from passing vehicles.

Marge flushed as she scurried as fast as possible on her short legs without drawing attention to herself. She let herself into the storeroom and turned the computer on as Jessica called her back.

'Hello, dear, is that you?' She was moving a collection of tools—screwdrivers, wrenches and a hammer—in order to access the keyboard.

'Yes, Marge, it's me. Are you by the PC?'

'Yes,' Marge said.

Jessica gave her login details over the racket of traffic. She knew their use would be traced, but now that she was on the run, this was of little concern, so long as Marge's involvement remained hidden.

'Okay, we're in.'

'Alright, great. I need the contact details of an Anouk Walker; her last known residential address.' Jessica spelt out Anouk's first name and could hear Marge typing.

'Yes, there's only one that appears and...' there was a brief pause as Marge continued to read, 'she's in this city. Address of No. 20 Jervis Gardens.'

'No. 20 Jervis Gardens,' Jessica repeated. She didn't recognise the address. As she tried to memorise it, she glimpsed red jackets on the opposite side of the road. She didn't know whether anyone had detected her absence, but she wouldn't take the chance.

'Sorry, Marge, I need to go.'

'But...' Marge said. Jessica had already hung up. Marge held her phone back to confirm the blank screen. She'd wanted to say the records showed Anouk no longer lived there.

Jessica stood on the driveway of an old council estate. It appeared deserted. Water flow had worn the asphalt, leaving loose aggregate gathered in small transverse ridges. Apartment blocks surrounded her in a U-shape, and exterior stairs clung their way down to the driveway with small signs at their entrance showing which numbered apartments they led to. Concrete frontages loomed above. *Grim.*

She had found Jervis Gardens through an app. Once she located it, she turned off her mobile phone and discarded it in a public rubbish bin, knowing it could track her movements. She took public transport to the apartment through the use of Alba credits. Like all citizens, her credits were loaded onto the ID chip in her wrist on the last day of each month. Catching public transport was a necessary trade-off between speed and her whereabouts being traced.

Rain was pattering on her open umbrella, where she had taken refuge. The first flight of stairs at the end of the closest block showed apartment numbers 1–30. She made her way up, being careful not to slip on the wet steps. Once she reached the top, a sign with an arrow pointing left read 1–10. An arrow pointing horizontally upward to the next flight of stairs read 11–20. She continued to climb until she reached the second storey. The weathered door to apartment number 20 lay to her right. It was a darker shade of grey and called for a fresh coat of paint. A chipped plastic house sign with brightly painted yellow flowers, which had no reason to flourish in the surrounds, hung askew alongside.

Jessica knocked on the door with nervous excitement. There was no answer. She knocked again. The sun was not yet setting, but the dense cloud cover had prematurely brought an evening dullness. There were no lights on inside. She peered through the barred kitchen window. A small round table with four chairs sat in the gloom.

'May I help you?' a voice asked.

Jessica jumped in fright. She put a hand over her chest, holding the umbrella in the other, and turned, catching her breath. An older man had emerged from the apartment further down the walkway. He supported himself with one hand holding the rail.

'Oh, heavens!' Jessica said, exhaling. 'You startled me!'

'I'm sorry, I didn't intend to.' The man then noticed the Bureau's emblem on the umbrella. His face hardened.

Jessica had followed his gaze and closed the umbrella. 'It's not mine. It's, um, borrowed.'

The man waited patiently. His silence was as much resistance as it was self-preservation. Water dripped down over the ledge of the walkway from above as Jessica considered how best to proceed. 'I'm looking for someone; perhaps you can help?' There was still no response, so she continued, 'Anouk Walker. Do you know her?'

The man was unwilling to talk again, but then he asked, 'What do you want from Anouk?' He sounded protective.

'You know her?' she asked. The man had reverted to silence again. She hadn't answered his question yet. 'A friend—a good friend—suggested that I find her here.' She embellished the truth.

'Does the friend have a name?'

Jessica was getting somewhere. 'Yes, of course. James

Sullivan; Jimmy.'

The old man's suspicion lessened. 'I suppose you can't be one of them,' he said, pointing to the umbrella. 'They were already here.'

'They were!'

'A couple of weeks ago. Took her.'

His answer was unvarnished and to the point. It plunged Jessica into despair. Where did she go from here? 'Was there anyone else living with her?' she asked.

The man didn't respond. Instead, he regarded Jessica for a while. 'Yes, her mother, Janice,' he said.

'And...'

'She's dead.' He spared her question. 'Slit her wrists in the bath when they took Anouk.' Jessica froze. He abandoned his usual reserve and added, 'She got into a warm bath dressed, in her best, apart from shoes. Put the record player on. When they found her, the stylus was still tracking the spinning record.'

'But that can't be.' Jessica sank into her own body.

The old man walked up to her and rested his hand on her shoulder. 'Chin up, lass. You can't be one of them. You care too much.'

The rain was falling heavier now, and a coil of water was making its way to Jessica's shoes from where it had pooled alongside the walkway's edge.

'There's one other thing,' he said. 'The first lot who took her were not red jackets after all.'

That took a moment to settle in. Jessica looked up. 'What?' Embryonic hope grew.

'They were Resistance, it turns out. Caused an almighty stink, I can tell you!' He knitted his brow in reflection. 'They thought we were all in on it.'

Reinvigorated, Jessica straightened her posture. Dizziness

washed over her. 'And where can I find them?' she asked, already knowing the answer.

'The industrial quarter, of course,' the man said. 'But you can't go with that.' He pointed to the umbrella that she had dropped unnoticed, lying at her feet. 'Wait here,' he said, and disappeared with a shuffle into his apartment. This was two doors further down the walkway, and it took him some time. He reappeared holding a rainbow-coloured umbrella. 'Here, take this, and be sure to dump that one,' he said, pointing to the black umbrella, 'when nobody is around.'

Jessica met him halfway. 'Thank you; that's very kind.' She took the bright umbrella from him. She nodded her thanks again before making to leave. Help from strangers was scarce.

'Oh. If you find Anouk, tell her that her Valentine sends his love,' he said with a cryptic smile.

———◎———

As Jessica got her new umbrella, Kilgore learned she'd left the Bureau at noon and hadn't returned by evening. He was talking to the foyer desk officer. 'Yes, I heard you say that she left early afternoon, but where did she go?' he said down the receiver. It was a pointless question. The officer had merely logged her departure.

The man tried to answer the impossible. 'All I can tell you, sir, is that she checked out at 12:13 pm.'

'Imbecile!' Kilgore slammed the handset down on its holder.

He stood seething, hands flat on his desk. A ping alerted him to an email, and it refocused his attention. He sat down in his chair and spun to face his PC. Jessica's recent computer activity would provide a clue as to her whereabouts. Kilgore had access to employee computer records. His thin fingers sped to enter his access code. He hammered the keys, and they rattled ominously. Activity entries started early at 7:16 am. He scrolled down the list to the last entry, recorded at 12:32 p.m. That was impossible. The front desk had confirmed that she had checked out at 12:13 pm.

He clicked on the dropdown icon for the 12:32 pm entry for further information. It read, 'Contact details >> Anouk Walker >> Last known address.' Kilgore was an intelligent man. He processed information quickly. But he remained frozen, staring, struggling to comprehend the words on the screen.

The single line, glaring at him from the backlit illumination of the flat screen, had radically altered the routine of his life. He let out a guttural howl of rage and took hold of the screen. He ripped it from its heavy pedestal and hurled it against his office door. The wires attached to its rear pulled the PC tower off his desk with it, landing with a smashing thud on the scuffed parquet floor. The frosted pane in the top half of his office door disintegrated into falling shards of glass, along with his stencilled name in gold lettering.

Kilgore stood again. His hands were flat on his desk, but he was now hunched and panting. His lips were wet with bubbling saliva when the first brave employee dared peek through the shattered pane. Kilgore kept his head down, eyes rolling up to show only their whites to the employee.

'Mobilise all squads.'

10

Officers transported Jimmy and five other detainees. Not all were spritters, but all were undesirables, in black jumpsuits, hands manacled. The journey had taken about an hour, and Jimmy shifted restlessly on his seat. His anxiety arose less from anticipating their destination and more from his recent motor vehicle accident; his flashbacks continued to haunt him. He sat in the same location at the van's rear as he had done that fateful morning.

His fellow detainees displayed a variety of emotions, from dejected to vigilant. One detainee kept mechanically tapping imaginary pockets on his jumpsuit. *There's no shimmer there, mate.* Nothing here to settle your nerves.

The van came to a stop. As the rear doors swung open, light streamed in from their sides, framing a black, depthless portrait. Jimmy's eyes acclimatised. The van had backed onto the entrance of a building. No trace of light emitted from the darkness within, but the musty smell of damp gave a clue to its interior. There was a banging of hands on both sides of the van.

'Out you all get.' 'Move along.' 'Go on,' sang a chorus of voices amid the din of battered metal panels. There was a single red jacket in the rear with them. He was standing bent, and he was uncuffing them before ardently ushering them out. His urgency spoke of his unease. The muted light fitted to the van's roof shone on him as he worked beneath it. His shadowed movements exhorted the detainees along. Fear crossed the red jacket's face.

Once all detainees disembarked, jumping two by two, they entered the building. A rolling steel door rumbled, extinguishing the sunlight spilling around the rear of the van as it dropped shut. It closed with a clang that left no doubt of its finality, stranding them in disconsolate limbo. A detainee let out a long, mournful wail in the darkness—it crawled across Jimmy's flesh. The wailing stopped with the sound of another rolling steel door from within.

The comforting warmth of fellow detainees surrounded Jimmy—he was, despite everything, not alone—jostling together, attempting to seek refuge in numbers. In the distance, they appeared in the rudimentary light. They approached as guards in two disciplined lines but scuffling with their bodies slouched. LED motion lights intermittently lit their path towards the detainees: dull white glows that flickered awake and died again, punctuated by darkness. The guards too wore black jumpsuits that greedily absorbed any available light around them.

Silence descended on the group of clustered detainees. The surreal sight of the newcomers transfixed them. Their shuffling drew closer. They disappeared between a LED light, which slowly faded, then reappeared a few yards from the group under another. Their emaciated frames were distinguishable in the ghostly hue. They carried long black staves that were clasped with both hands. Each guard rested their staff lightly against the hips of those in front of them. This formed a barrier on the outer side of both lines. The foremost pair held their staves differently. The first grasped his across the stomach of the other, and the second used hers in the fashion of a guide cane, running it forwards along the floor. Some had long thin hair, while others had only wispy tufts remaining.

As the two rows split to encircle the group, their eyes drew a fearful moan from the detainees. They were sightless and milky white.

The same detainee resumed his wailing. Three guards positioned themselves at the rear and three on either side of the group. One stood at the front. There was no sign they heard the wailing detainee. They shuffled again in a speechless but co-ordinated march, and the wailing stopped. The detainees, still huddled together, moved forwards, driven by a shared desire to avoid touching their guides, who marched with purpose. Despite taking a winding route under partial illumination, they gave the impression of knowing where they were going. Their horned and calloused bare feet scratched and scraped across the filthy concrete floor as they went.

They passed features in the pitch darkness. Corners, bends and curves seemed to take shape. The pale light emanating every so often from above didn't reach far. Flickers of movement pierced the curtain of darkness. Then, without warning, an apparition sprang into momentary light. Jimmy jumped. It appeared human, but he couldn't be certain. It undeniably had appendages. The guide to his right swung his staff. It connected to the creature, which let out a blood-curdling screech. Its white, hairless flesh dissolved into the dark, and the guide rested his staff against the hip of his colleague again.

The wailing began once more. Other detainees muttered, and some sobbed. But the march continued for a few minutes longer. A white glow materialised into view. Unlike the other lighting, it was constant. It was difficult to judge distance in the dark, but as they approached the light, it appeared it was hovering over a metal structure with steps descending on either side. An ancient-looking man hovered in the spectral illumination on a platform. One knotted, arthritic hand hung by his side; the other grasped what resembled a shepherd's crook. He also stared through clouded eyes. Despite his wraithlike build, his countenance was one of complete serenity. He wore a white robe.

The guards steered Jimmy and others to stand below the structure. They formed a protective semicircle around them. Silence had fallen again. The detainees gazed up in apprehensive awe.

The man began, 'You, Lord, keep my lamp burning; my God turns my darkness into light.' To Jimmy's surprise, their guides spoke in answer. 'Amen,' they intoned in unison. Their voices echoed, revealing their location as a large space.

'Welcome to the Factory, my friends,' the white-robed man said in an unexpectedly powerful voice. 'I am the Master.' He stared blankly into the darkness, unsettling Jimmy. 'You have, I sense, met my Sibylline.' He opened his arms to show their surrounding guides. The Sibylline made a purring sound at their mention. 'It would be to your great advantage to perceive them as guides, as friends and protectors in this place, rather than guards.' He lingered, letting his advice embed. 'Many of you will struggle with this. I understand. But you will soon come to realise that there are far worse things in here than blind guides.'

The wailing detainee began his doleful lament for the fourth time. One guide would surely silence him. But all remained still, as did the Master. No action was needed; the oppressive silence clawed his mouth shut.

'This is a prison. There is no escape. It will be the place

where we all find our deaths. This is certain,' the Master said. 'But the manner in which you journey to your death is, under God's grace, yours to decide. The Almighty offers you a choice, even in this place of darkness.'

A detainee abruptly burst from the group and broke through the line of Sibylline. As before, they did nothing to stop the person, who ran mindlessly into the dark seeking an alternative salvation. There was a rushing sound, a gliding movement, and then the thumping of bodies colliding. An agonising scream issued from the obscurity. It ended almost as soon as it began, with a sharp crack that echoed across the walls. A creature screeched as before, and the sound of a limp body being dragged faded out of hearing.

The detainees began whimpering again. Shaking bodies pressed against Jimmy. And then the besieging silence threw a thick veil over their murmuring until all were quiet.

The Master resumed. 'As I said, the choice is yours. There is freedom of sorts at the Factory.' Another long pause followed. 'You will now be taken to your rooms. They have bars, and they have gates. But they are unlocked. You may choose to lock them or not. You may leave your room or not. The option is yours. Each of you will share his or her room with a mentor. They will guide you through your first days and weeks in this place.' He then concluded, 'The Lord bless you and keep you. The Lord make His face shine upon you, and be gracious to you. The Lord lift up His countenance upon you, and give you peace.'

'Peace...' echoed as he disappeared from the light.

Sibylline escorted Jimmy and his four remaining fellow detainees to their accommodation. Between shadows and transitory light, their lodgings seemed to be a conventional prison wing. A narrow metal staircase climbed three flights, hemmed in by ascending rows of barred cells and open-mesh steel walkways on either side. Unlike other areas of the Factory, this one throbbed with the sounds of torment. Sounds of delusion, pain and suffering ricocheted off hard surfaces. There was a loud whacking sound. A voice repeated the same words, 'flapping high, flapping high, flapping high...' on endless playback. Some giggled coyly; others hooted like owls. But the incessant keening and cries for help disturbed Jimmy the most. And there were the others. Those who sat in the dark, watching and waiting.

Jimmy's cell was on the second level. The Sibylline unlocked the gate and let him in. They departed as quietly as they had arrived. He stood in a small space, walled on three sides, with a barred gate at his back.

'Methinks you should close and lock the gate.' The voice was nasal. Jimmy twitched in response. The pale overhead LED light came to life, revealing a small, thin man sitting on the lower bunk. His arm was outstretched, and he held a dangling key in front of his face. 'Go on, have it?' He gave the key a little shake.

Jimmy took a few cautious steps forwards and reached to take the key. The man moved faster than he had guessed. He locked tight with his free hand onto Jimmy's injured wrist and pulled it towards him. Jimmy stumbled forwards and let out a yelp. The injury, although healed with stitches, was still tender to the touch.

The man's nose tickled across Jimmy's skin as he sniffed from his scarred wrist, moving up his sleeved arm. 'Mm, fresh, methinks.' He rubbed his face against Jimmy's clothing as if it were a perfume stick. Jimmy pulled his hand away and stepped back in horror. 'Well, that's not nice, not nice at all. Methinks you'll be wanting advice soon. Won't you? Yes, you will. Better be nice then, methinks.' He held out the key again, and Jimmy snatched it from him.

Jimmy turned and closed the gate with a clang. Feeling for the keyhole with his fingers, he inserted the key. He twisted it free, then gave the gate a hard yank to ensure it was locked. He turned back, his hand outstretched with the key, but the man was no longer sitting on the bed. Jimmy spun. He was now squatting in the corner of the room over a pit latrine. He had removed his jumpsuit from his upper body to facilitate defecation. It lay bunched at his knees. Jimmy looked away, but the man didn't care.

'Are you my mentor?' Jimmy asked, still looking in the opposite direction.

'Mm, questions, so many questions. Methinks, we should both get questions. One question buys one question. Fair, methinks?' He strained to dislodge a dry stool, and Jimmy studied him. His clouded eyes showed in the insipid light. Though sightless, he wore square, heavy-rimmed spectacles—one lens missing, the other cracked. The spectacles sat lopsided on his nose because of the uneven weight distribution. Jimmy's crawling skin and tension subsided. The man crouched, absorbed in his bodily functions, wretched and abandoned.

'Alright then, one question for one question. It's a deal,' Jimmy said. He scanned his surroundings but couldn't make out much.

The man's head lifted eagerly. 'Me first? I did give you the key.'

'Okay, you go first,' Jimmy said. He moved carefully and leant against the wall opposite the man, finding comfort in the protection it offered from behind. The disturbing surroundings failed to curb his intrigue. What could the man possibly want to know from him?

'Mm, tricky, tricky, methinks.' The man assessed his options so as not to waste the question. 'Remind me, what does marmalade taste and look like? Smell like too?'

Jimmy almost laughed in disbelief but contained himself—it was not a question he was expecting. He paused. 'Well, it's orange...'

'Yes, yes...'

The encouragement worked. Jimmy tried harder. 'It's not only orange; it has many colours. There are shades of orange and yellow. Hints of red and pink.'

The man had fallen silent. He squatted with rapt attention. Jimmy understood what the man needed. 'It's sticky and glistens in the light. Runs slowly off a spoon and falls in syrupy lumps. It's sweet with undertones of honey, citrus and pepper. And it smells like a field of orange blossoms on a warm summer afternoon.'

Jimmy scrutinised the man closely. Still crouching, he seemed transported elsewhere. His mouth hung ajar, and his breathing was hushed as if he were sleeping—looking more familiar, less alien. He inhabited a world of nothingness. His sensory deprivation fuelled an addiction to stimulus. Remembering was his drug.

Jimmy roused the man from his dreamlike state. 'Can you tell me who you are and why you're here?'

The man snapped out of his trance. He stood up and pulled his arms through the sleeves of his jumpsuit. 'That's two questions, methinks.' He began zipping the front of the suit closed. An impatient prickle ran through Jimmy. He was about to protest when the man continued. 'I'm your mentor, and I'm here to teach you.'

Jimmy had already found out this much. It wasn't the sort of detailed response he had hoped for. He realised he would have to be more direct in his inquiry. The cacophony of sounds from other inmates didn't lend itself to searching questions.

The mentor had crossed confidently to the lower bunk. Despite his blindness, he moved fast. His jumpsuit was worn and shabby in places. He assumed his original position, balanced cross-legged at the edge of his bed. His bare toes wiggled as he spoke. 'Let me think.' He swayed backwards and forwards. 'Tell me about the last time you walked through damp grass. Did it touch you? Did it tickle you?'

It was during his escape from the accident scene. Jimmy described the sound of grass sweeping against his legs and the feel of its sleek florets over his fingers; the rare, indulgent late-summer light falling across swaying stalks and drifting pollen stirred by his steps. His mentor again listened intently and in peace. Jimmy, too, found solace in the memory.

The contracted conversation continued in this fashion for some time. Jimmy couldn't tell how long. The passage of time was inconsistent in the darkness. He learned that the man had seen many generations of mentees arrive and leave the Factory. Jimmy had yet to discover where these people went and what became of them. He came to understand that darkness was perpetual but played an essential part in the Factory's production process. But he did not know what product was manufactured. And he figured out, by observing the man, that maintaining a semblance of sanity meant finding refuge in imagination. Jimmy thought of Jessica. Her blonde hair lifted in the imaginary breeze.

'Do you trust me?' she asked again.

'Of course I do,' Jimmy said.

———◉———

Several sleeps passed before the Sibylline came for Jimmy. He was sleeping again. The top bunk was more comfortable than he had expected. Still, there was no pillow, and the mattress was hard. He dared not think what stains covered its surface. A threadbare blanket was his only luxury. But exhaustion had driven him into deep slumber. Even the sounds of distress failed to penetrate his sporadic dreams. He had been dreaming before awaking—the Master was standing in a halo of light. He was holding both arms aloft with his shepherd's crook in one hand. In a thunderous voice he called out, 'The light shines in the darkness, and the darkness has not overcome it!' And then his voice changed, and the light faded behind the clouds. 'Get up now. Get up now,' he repeated in a high pitch. His mentor's voice slipped into his dream. He was jogging Jimmy awake.

The mentor was lying on his back. He placed both feet flat against the mattress slats above him and pumped his legs up and down until he heard resentful groaning. 'Get up now,' he said. 'You're off to earn our dinner, methinks.'

Jimmy rolled out of the bunk but misjudged the height. His ankles and knees took the strain of the fall, landing with a thud and shooting pain as he encountered the floor. He rolled awkwardly to his side. Had he twisted an ankle? Adopting a sitting position, he massaged the ankle with his fingers until the spasm subsided. He pursed his lips and breathed out, hobbling to his feet. His eyes had adjusted to the dark over the intervening hours-days. Where there had once been blackness, he now saw shapes within the gloom. The double bunk was the only piece of furniture in the cell. He had already identified the pit latrine. He could also make out a drinking fountain. A ceramic basin was half-embedded in the wall. It was the only reflective white surface in the vicinity, and this created the illusion of its eerily floating.

Four Sibylline waited patiently outside his cell. His mentor had unlocked the gate and held it open, motivating Jimmy through with an energetic wave of his hands. Jimmy moved through the gate and stood between the Sibylline, two on either side. His mentor had placed a lingering hand on his shoulder as he passed. He had receded into the shadows by the time Jimmy turned to say goodbye.

The footsteps of the Sibylline clanked on the mesh walkway in accompaniment to the chorus of night noises. He was in a forest with fantasy beasts. The bars of the cells were tree trunks, moving shadows as he walked, the forest beyond. They slid over enigmatic figures in the erratic pallid light. Some moved; others sat still. The Sibylline reliably surrounded him as they descended the stairs and made their way away from the cells. They crossed into silence as the wild sounds dissipated behind them.

Jimmy had envisioned that the spaces they travelled through were vast empty halls. In reality, they were interlinking rooms, some larger and some smaller. All contained what appeared to be light industrial machinery or stacked manufacturing supplies. Steel tanks, pipes and valves. Crates, barrels and boxes. To Jimmy's astonishment, they were not alone. People moved deliberately but silently as they worked. Sibylline stood sentry among them, their long staves held vertically and to the front. Now and then, the opaque glow of a LED light broke with a darting movement, and a screech shattered the quiet.

Jimmy's escort had come to a standstill. The Sibylline to his front and sides peeled away and then all four withdrew behind him. They scuffled, and a door closed. They had entered a room without his being aware. His surrounds pressed in—more frightening now that the Sibylline had gone. Jimmy had fast come to rely on them.

'Sit down.' The voice was hoarse.

Jimmy squeaked, but not loudly; like a mouse tapped unexpectedly on the back. He hesitantly sat on the floor.

'Not there—on the chair.' The room lacked a motion-detecting light. Jimmy sat where he was. He felt paralysed by indecision.

'If you do not sit yourself in the chair, you will be helped to do so.'

He had few options but to comply. In an awkward stoop, Jimmy stood and took a few uncertain shuffles. Using his fingertips as antennae, he made out what resembled a dentist's chair. He clambered in and slid down into position. The sleeve of his jumpsuit pushed upward as he reclined, and the plastic chair cover stuck against his exposed skin. It squeaked, sounding embarrassingly like a fart. He considered an apology when an overhead lamp exploded into light. Jimmy scrunched his face, his body driven back into the seat, the air punched from him. Before he could orient himself, manacles attached to the armrest were clamped around his wrists. A restraining belt was then forcefully tightened around his midriff and arms, expelling any remaining air from his lungs. In quick succession, clamps secured his ankles to the leg rest, and a strap pinned his forehead. The concentrated glare blinded him. But as his eyes adjusted, he saw the lamp mounted to the ceiling on an adjustable arm. A shadowy figure moved into the lamp's glare. There was a metallic clatter of instruments being arranged on a tray. Despite his fierce treatment, he felt obliged to open his mouth wide, as he did as a young child when visiting the dentist.

'Hello, I'm Doctor Mildmay.' The man introduced himself with rehearsed geniality.

This reminded Jimmy of automated public announcements in government buildings. 'Welcome to the Department of Homeland Registration'; 'Please remember to take your belongings with you when you leave'; or 'Have a nice day. And remember, a good citizen is an alert citizen'. It was meant to be calming and reassuring but was in fact facile. Jimmy tried to move in his restraints but found himself immobilised.

'I'll be seeing to your procedure today,' the doctor said. Jimmy was about to ask what procedure when the doctor continued, 'I understand you're a special case. A remarkable CPU ratio.' The doctor was leaning closer to Jimmy. He sat wearing a blue surgical mask and clear protective eyewear, a single magnifying loupe protruding from the frame above one eye. A strong-smelling latex glove rested on his temple as the man cleaned around Jimmy's left eye with a cotton swab. A substance imbued in the cotton seeped over his eyelid and stung, causing it to water.

'Apologies, apologies,' the doctor said affably, drying the resulting tears away with a new cotton swab. 'Professor Brougham at the Institute is fascinated. He's even expressed an interest in examining you himself.'

'Fancy that!' Jimmy thought. Was he to feel flattered?

The doctor twisted in his seat and collected a metal instrument from the tray with a scraping sound. He held it close to Jimmy's left eye. It was the size of a hand and had two thin metal arms that were sprung apart in a V-shape. Each end held a semicircular wire with hooked edges. 'Now,' the doctor said, 'this little instrument is called a speculum. It holds your eyelids open so that I can get a better look.' He said this while pulling Jimmy's upper eyelid up and inserting one hooked wire under its pink sac-like underside. He then repeated the procedure on the lower eyelid so that the whites of Jimmy's eye were visible on its globe. The cold arms of the instrument rested to the side of his face, and its spring kept his eyelids apart.

'Easy-peasy.' The doctor sat back beyond the glare of the lamp. He appraised his work. 'Now, the next part is likely to be a little uncomfortable, and you'll feel a sharp prick,' he said.

A falling sensation overwhelmed Jimmy. The image of milky white eyes in the dark assailed him. Why had it not occurred to him earlier? But the thought of them now caused him terror. 'You won't hurt it, will you?' Jimmy spurted. 'My eye, it will be fine. It won't be damaged?' He tried to nod, but his head didn't move.

'No,' the doctor said, 'you'll lose the sight in the eye.'

Jimmy screamed. 'No, please, please!' He pulled against his restraints, and his veins bulged, but he could not move. His soaring blood pressure and increased heart rate turned his neck and face bright red.

'Now, now. It will all be over very quickly.'

Did he mean the procedure or Jimmy's life—or did he care either way? Jimmy collapsed into sputtering wetness. Spittle bubbled from his mouth, mucus collected below his nose, and tears ran down his cheeks. He blinked moisture away with one eye, but the other remained open and mad, rolling in his skull. He sobbed as the doctor pressed on.

'This is called an occucanula,' he said, holding a small steel device that was connected to a head strap. 'It fits over your eyeball. I then tighten this screw to ensure these tiny clamps hold it in place. See.' He revolved a hollow half-ball device with protruding fixtures in his hand. The doctor then moved the device towards Jimmy's eye and with a quick rotating motion, slid it over and around his eyeball. A cold foreign object pressed against Jimmy's eye socket. The pressure increased as the doctor twisted the screw and the clamps pressed down on the sides of his eyeball. His vision blurred on the affected side.

'And now for the grand dénouement.' With a flourish, he produced a thin needle. Its blunt end was slightly larger and threaded like a screw. He held this between tweezers and lowered his face close to Jimmy's. His magnifying loupe hovered just above the now enclosed eyeball. Slowly and carefully, he eased the needle through a minuscule hole in the occucanula's midpoint. There was resistance and then a sharp pain as the needle slid in. The room muffled Jimmy's cry as he grieved the loss of his eye.

'All done. You can stop your crying now,' the doctor said. The hole the needle passed through was threaded as well. He incrementally tightened the blunt end of the needle into place with the tweezers. A few accessories were attached to the instrument and head strap. Jimmy couldn't see what these were. The doctor did not bother to inform him. His job was complete. He turned the lamp off, plunging the room into darkness again.

Jimmy couldn't say how the doctor worked in the dark. Whatever the answer, he performed his duties precisely. He loosened the strap across Jimmy's forehead first and then secured the occucanula into place around Jimmy's head with its accompanying strap. The restraints on his ankles, midriff, arms and wrists were released.

'Oh,' the doctor said, 'I almost forgot.'

Suddenly, a searing light turned on in front of Jimmy's covered eye; as if he were staring at the sun with this eye alone. From his other eye, in the darkness, he was cast aside in the remotest place imaginable. Nausea welled. His thoughts were his company.

———— ◎ ————

The four Sibylline were waiting for Jimmy under the glow of LED light when the door opened. He was sitting on the edge of the chair. He was shaking and jittery from adrenaline. The doctor had disappeared. Jimmy got to his feet, abruptly grew faint, and sat down again. After a pause, he tried again but now steadied himself, resting his hand on the chair's backrest.

He made his way towards the Sibylline, passing through the door like a listing ship. The light in one eye and near darkness in the other threw him off balance. He sought to regain bodily equilibrium but overcorrected and hit his shoulder hard against the doorframe.

When he was clear of the door, the Sibylline surrounded him in a protective embrace and began their passage back to his cell. Jimmy swerved, bumping against his guides. With resolute determination, they bore his stumbling weight and propelled him forwards.

A crashing noise startled Jimmy. An inmate, who had been quiet when Jimmy left, resumed his chant. 'Flapping high, flapping high…'

Jimmy's mentor was holding onto the bars of the gate when they drew near. He unlocked it and swung it backwards, hitching a ride by squeezing his bare feet between the bars and the lower gate frame. Jimmy entered the cell as the Sibylline vanished down the walkway.

'Is it bright? It's lovely, methinks.' The mentor tapped his eye to show the occucanula over Jimmy's.

'Why didn't you tell me?' Jimmy faced the bunk without turning towards the mentor. He shook and felt motion sick.

'Questions for questions. You didn't ask.' The mentor swung back on the gate with a clang. A clunk indicated the lock had fallen into place.

'I'm not playing any more of your silly games.' Jimmy knew that the man owed him nothing. He understood that this place had distorted his mentor beyond all recognition. But he still felt betrayed. Jimmy climbed to the top bunk and threw himself down, pulling the thin blanket over his body. He wished he were dead. He tried to close his eyes to find inner peace. But this was no longer possible. The light in his eye was inescapable.

It burned brightly and relentlessly. He considered tearing the occucanula out. The temptation was near and growing. It was an itch he had to scratch.

'Don't pull it out.' The mentor had also lain on the bunk below Jimmy. 'Plenty of people pull it out, methinks, but you'll just pop your eyeball. Nasty that; no point.' He was biting his fingernails, grinding the keratin between his teeth and swallowing. 'You get that one for nothing.' He rapidly added so as not to introduce a precedent, 'But only because you'll get us dinner soon.'

What did he mean, 'dinner soon'? Jimmy turned onto his side, staring where he knew the wall running alongside the bed was. Whatever adjustment to the dark he'd gained over hours or days was lost after his visit to the doctor. Light burned on one side; darkness lay on the other. He thought of Jessica but couldn't remember her face. What had she meant by 'Anouk. Anouk Walker; she's alive'. Surely this was just a lie. A joke at his expense between Kilgore and his pathological daughter. Yes, it was all hilarious. They laughed together in his mind. The laughter grew louder and louder. Jimmy placed his hands over his ears. He craved the release of shimmer. The sweet fall into warm nothingness—shimmerfall.

By some unseen force, a yellow-greenish light flashed against the wall in front of him. A glow-worm had inexplicably broken into the Factory. From where it came was a mystery. It drew his attention away from unkind thoughts. Its twinkling bioluminescence carried a message. His arm lay tucked beneath him, his heartbeat slowing to match the pulsating light. A calmness returned. He felt ashamed to have thought ill of Jessica. He knew goodness when he saw it. And she was good; a pure soul. He trusted her. Anouk was alive, and Jessica would find him. And although Jimmy did not believe that God existed, he recited, 'where there is despair, hope; where there is darkness, light.'

Shimmer? No—shadow, gloom, shade.

Somewhere in the eternal midnight of the Factory, the Master was coming to see him.

11

The Allied Resistance—commonly called the Resistance—didn't look like much to Anouk. A ragtag collection of former community organisers, activists and change-makers who shared some political allegiances. As if reading her mind, Aidan said, 'They're not a bad bunch. They do what they can. And you know what?' He paused. 'I think they... we... are getting better at it every day.'

Aidan knew more than this. The Resistance had offered him a lifeline. A new supportive environment, away from shimmer's temptations, where he could rebuild trust and meaning.

'Better at what? Just look at them,' Anouk said, taking an unlabelled box from the rear of a truck. She slid it over the folded tailgate and let her arms fall to catch its weight.

'Misfits? Not going to argue with you there, Dimples. But that was always the problem, wasn't it?' Aidan leaned against the corner of the truck over its rear lights. 'It was all protest in the past. We argued over little things and lost sight of the big thing before it was too late. Before the Change, that is. We believed there was still time...'. His voice trailed off.

It was early morning, and fog surrounded them, signalling a new season. Anouk staggered with the box of supplies and stacked it on top of a pile that she had already unloaded. 'Yeah, seriously, Aidan. That doesn't answer my question.' None of it made sense to her. 'Why do you think this lot are anything special?' she asked in a hushed voice, shrugging with raised eyebrows. Resistance members worked in the immediate vicinity, and people didn't appreciate careless banter.

Aidan carried on philosophising as though he hadn't heard her. 'It wasn't good enough that we all agreed on stuff like justice and freedom, equality or respect for the environment. No!' He wagged his finger. 'It was all the tiny ways we differed that consumed us—individual freedom versus collective responsibility? Equality or equity? Carbon reduction versus offset? Techno-optimism or scepticism. Blah, blah! All privileged nonsense. People's lives got worse, and we squabbled. And extreme nationalism grew and grew. Fascism fed off our discontent...'

'Oi, professor!' Anouk rolled her eyes. 'Would you mind speaking English for a moment?' Stopping, she flung her arms up in exasperation. 'And if it's not too much to ask, your Royal Highness, a hand with these boxes would also be quite nice!'

Fred grunted as she moved boxes from the back of a truck within arm's reach of Anouk. 'Fat chance! You're having a laugh.' She grinned at Anouk. 'This one will take any opportunity to skive. Besides, he loves to pontificate about politics. Reminds him of his university days.'

A large smirk grew on Anouk's face.

'Oh, jeez,' Aidan sighed. 'Why did you have to go and tell her that. I'll never hear the bloody end of it!'

'Oo-la-la,' Anouk snickered, placing her hands on her hips and swaying. 'Well, well, Professor Aidan Bekker! Should I bow, should I scrape?'

'Hilarious!' Aidan stared daggers at Fred. 'Anyway, it was a long time ago. The Change put an end to it, like everything else. I never got to finish my studies...'

Anouk was sensitive enough not to press the issue.

'The point I was trying to make,' he said, steering the discussion back, 'is that we didn't take them seriously—the nationalist fascist nutjobs.'

'Maybe you were talking so much, nobody had a chance to.' Anouk put her hand over her mouth and pretended to yawn.

Aidan was on a roll. 'We were so smug and certain that democracy was here to stay that we fought among ourselves. We didn't recognise who the real enemy was until it was too late.'

There was a moment of uncomfortable silence. Things grew too serious for Anouk, so she tried to change the subject. 'So, how does a fancy professor...'

'Student,' Aidan said.

'Get to graduate to become a drug dealer?' She meant it in good humour. 'That seems like a big career move. Ambitious, even.'

Aidan pulled himself up from reclining against the truck. He took the box that was already in Anouk's hands and stacked it onto the existing pile. His fingers touched hers, sending a conscious tingling up her arm.

'You'll have to blame me for that,' Fred said. 'This one,' tipping her head towards Aidan, 'was in a bad way with shimmer. I brought him here to straighten him out. Although I must say, Mother was not too pleased with that. I got a right old bollocking!' She flicked her fingers together. 'But what could I do? He's my cuz.' She shrugged. Aidan had done the same for Anouk.

'Yip.' Aidan picked up the story's thread. 'So, the Resistance let me stay when I was straight, but on condition I made myself useful. I already knew the streets. Drug dealing was a logical contribution. It was in my blood, so to speak.' He attempted a smile.

Anouk stopped unpacking boxes. She scratched her head. 'That's never made sense to me. Why did you sell drugs?'

It was Aidan's turn to tease. 'You know, Fred, she's cute.' He paused in mock thought. 'Sometimes even sharp. But do you think the naivety's real, or is it just a show?' He winked at Anouk. Fred shook her head and cast her eyes heavenward.

'Piss off,' Anouk said. 'Just tell me, alright?' Didn't he trust her? She sat down on the pile of stacked boxes, crossed one leg over the other and folded her arms, waiting.

'Okay, fine.' Aidan resumed his leaning position. Fred rolled her eyes again. 'Put very simply, the Resistance sells drugs for money: how else could we afford this stuff?' He pointed to the boxes of supplies.

'No?' Anouk glanced at Fred for confirmation. 'You mean the Resistance is actually drug dealing!'

Fred nodded.

'Crazy, right?' Aidan said, 'But that's not half of it. We're just the middleman. Who do you think the drug lords are?'

Anouk scrunched up her face. She had never thought about it.

'The good ol' Governing Council! The Government themselves!' Aidan revealed with jazz hands. 'For Higher Virtue.'

'But New Albion...' Anouk said, trying to fit the pieces together.

'Is a fascist narco-state,' Fred finished for her. She had also stopped working and was resting in a seated position, legs dangling over the tailgate. 'Around the same time as the Change, when most liberal democracies in the world were crumbling. You remember what it was like...'

Both Aidan and Anouk stared down—they remembered.

'The climate crisis and calamity, AI disruption and unemployment, economic collapse...'

'The fighting, the starving,' Anouk said, staring blankly at her feet.

Fred nodded. 'And the nationalist fascists blamed all the shit on others—foreigners, immigrants, gays, Black people—the list grew and is still growing.'

'Yes, I get this, but...'

Fred interrupted Anouk. 'Countries had to find new ways of raising revenue. Shimmer was ours.' She raised her shoulders and hands. 'Thing is, it turned out to be far more successful than they expected. Some even say it's the only thing still traded globally.'

Anouk paused, considering. 'So, the State makes the drugs, we sell the drugs, and the profits are shared?' The double standard baffled her.

'Sort of,' Aidan responded. 'But you make it sound like an equal partnership.'

'It sounds pretty much like a partnership to me!' The sudden turn of events bruised Anouk's growing faith in the Resistance.

Fred intervened. 'No, not really. Think of it more like a patriarchal forced marriage where the husband is abusive.'

Anouk didn't think the analogy was good but kept on listening.

'We're forced to sell shimmer to get by. It earns the State a huge amount of money while they can blame degenerate spritters and others for the problem. We earn a tiny fraction for our role.' She emphasised this by holding her index finger and thumb a touch apart. 'We then support all those who can't get by: people deemed undesirable. The State shunts us to derelict corners, cut us off, and pretends its problem is solved.'

'But it isn't,' Anouk said. The bigger picture unsettled her, and she shifted on the pile of stacked boxes.

'No, it isn't,' Fred said. 'There's a truce of sorts. We sell their drugs, and they leave us, mostly, to care for those that they despise. They can blame us for the world that they've created, out of sight. It's a political win for them.'

'Or so they think,' Aidan said.

'Indeed.' Fred bobbed her head. 'Or so they think. We're biding our time. And time is the most important thing that shimmer buys. We have plans.'

Anouk sat listening. A man approached and spoke before she realised he was there.

'Apologies, Fred. Mother sent me.' The man was average-looking, the type who wouldn't stand out in a crowd. But he was soft-spoken and had a natural courtesy about him. He was the third dealer from the nightclub. He had stayed behind, talking to the bartender, when Anouk had left with the others.

'Hello, Sam. All good with you?' Fred asked.

'Yeah, I guess. Same ol', same ol', you know,' he said, tilting his head to greet Anouk and Aidan.

'Aren't you right,' Fred said, still sitting and swinging her legs. 'What's up?'

Sam became more serious. 'There's unusual movement of red jackets on our boundaries. They're not scheduled patrols or the usual Free Fliers. It's something else, looks co-ordinated, and Mother's concerned.'

'Not a raid, surely?' Fred asked, jumping down to stand. She appeared worried.

'No, we don't think so. Their formation is unfamiliar. They've closed some routes to the boundary but not others. It's odd.' Sam paused, reflecting. 'Anyway, Mother would like you to lead a team to check it out. We're already assembled.'

'No worries, Sam, I'll be over in a minute,' Fred said.

'Righty-ho.' Sam gave an untrained salute and left.

Aidan cast Fred a quizzical look. 'A salute? Really?' He hid a laugh behind a smile. 'To you?'

Fred reddened. 'Well, we'll need to professionalise. Anyway, you two finish off here before the ceremony while I take a look at what the red jackets want.'

'Yes, sir, er, ma'am,' Aidan snapped to attention. He and Anouk both doubled over in laughter, clutching their sides in pleasurable pain.

'You're both prats, you know that!' Fred said, stalking off.

———◎———

Somewhere beyond the boundaries of the industrial quarter, Jessica had spent the previous night in a commercial recycling bin. Temperatures were falling now that autumn had arrived. Although no one had collected recycling for many years, by chance the bin was full of waste paper. Not all the paper was unsullied. She removed a wrapper stuck in her hair during the early hours. An impossibly gummy clump now bulged to the side. Jessica was fastidious because she was meticulous in all that she did. This time she was just thankful for the bin's warmth and cushioning. Others had likely inhabited it before—spritters, perhaps. Yet no one saw them in public; society pushed them to the margins, underground. Officials highlighted their presence when propaganda demanded it. Her only other companion was the uppermost half of a Jack, a basic humanoid robot from before the Change, slumped in one corner. Wires dangled like entrails from its midriff, and it stared at her through hollow sockets; scavengers had long since appropriated its eyes for more useful purposes.

It had rained steadily throughout the night. She was safe in her accommodation. Heavy showers had beaten on the plastic container but could find no entry. Even with the near-constant drumming of falling rain, an unusual amount of traffic passed on the adjacent road. Given the curfew, these would be red jackets. And they were travelling towards the old industrial quarter.

Morning had dawned. A slit of light filtered through the container's lid. Her leg was cramping from lying in the same position for many hours. She pressed her foot to the far side of the bin, stretching against the pain. The sound of footsteps on wet paving stones made her stop. Her breathing slowed, and she dragged a loose piece of cardboard over a visible thigh.

A woman flung the bin's lid open. Too late, Jessica exposed her face. The woman let out a yelp in dismay and tottered backwards, clutching her chest. She had opened the bin to deposit household scrap when she saw a face without a body. After collecting herself, she moved forwards to peek over the bin's rim. Jessica strained not to move. Her leg was cramping again. She kept her blue eyes open, trying not to blink. But the life in Jessica's eyes startled the woman even more. She expected a dead body—one discarded in the bin. She teetered backwards for a second time.

The woman stood regaining her breath on the street until an oncoming vehicle forced her to move. It was a red jacket patrol. They passed without stopping. The image of a dishevelled woman discarding a black bin bag was no cause for concern. She crept back to the rim of the bin. Two eyes and then a nose appeared over the edge. 'Are you alive?' The woman whispered.

'Yes,' Jessica squeaked; she couldn't think of anything better to say and burrowed further down into the wastepaper.

More of the woman's face emerged; she was middle-aged, her hair peppered with grey. 'Are you running from them?' Her voice was soft.

'Yes.' After the events of the previous day, Jessica was vulnerable. It was the best she could muster.

The woman extended a hand. 'Alright, love. You had best come with me.'

Jessica didn't respond.

'Come on now,' she said, 'we don't have much time. There'll be another patrol.'

Jessica surrendered to the stranger. She took the woman's hand and was half hoisted and half stood to her feet. As she lifted, she pressed the black Bureau umbrella deeper into the surrounding paper with her other hand. It would only have invited suspicion. She had opened the bin to get rid of the umbrella, but had sought refuge within its inviting contents. With the woman's support, Jessica scissored over the bin's edge and hopped onto the pavement. Fog muffled her landing. The rainbow-coloured umbrella was within reach, and she snatched it.

'Come on,' the woman said, tossing her household waste into the bin. She let the lid clatter shut, and disappeared within the haze.

———— ◎ ————

Kilgore stood behind the filthy, streaked window with his hands clasped behind him. The street beyond was empty. All was quiet save for the irritating breath of the red jacket standing too close. 'Do you mind?' he said, turning to the disconcerted man. 'A little space would be appreciated.'

The man stood back without delay. Kilgore recommenced his surveillance of the street.

Red jacket squads stationed themselves along the entire boundary of the industrial quarter. Every known crossing, from barricade to tunnel, was now closed. Every crossing, apart from the one he scanned. *That's right, my pet. Walk directly into Daddy's snare.* He imagined the expression on Jessica's face when she saw him. It was deliciously terrifying.

'Sir, Iota Squad reports that another group of people are gathering to cross into the quarter,' the squad leader said. 'Should we stop them?'

'No, we wait. Tell them to hold back. Under no circumstances are they to make their presence known. Is that understood?'

'Perfectly, sir.' The squad leader relayed the order via portable two-way radio to the squaddies in hiding.

The fog that had hung in the air all morning was dissipating. Across the street, the warehouse door appeared barred with nailed timber. But it was a ruse. It had opened twice that morning as undesirables flocked for the safety of the quarter.

A group of refugees hurried across the street. There were five frightened-looking people. Two were women and three were children. Probably lesbians. *Foul.* Jessica was not among them. No harm in letting a few enter. It matched the spirit of the deal between the Resistance and the Council. *Besides, it's inevitable that we'll round them up, eventually.* The Governing Council was becoming frustrated with the increased number of terrorist incidents. Authorities would liquidate every quarter in every town and city. An alternative to shimmer sales would need finding, new dealers—but this was a detail. The Guild or the Cartel, rival criminal networks, were likely alternatives. They already ran the drug dens and underground clubs where shimmer was consumed. Their businesses could easily extend to sales.

'Another group is gathering to cross, sir.'

Kilgore focused his attention back on the street.

———◉———

Jessica had made good progress towards the quarter in search of Anouk the previous afternoon. The woman who had salvaged her from the recycling bin led her to an abandoned pottery. It was an elegant old brick building. They entered through a side door into a cavernous workshop. It was empty apart from a small group of people crowded a few yards away. Light strained through large grille window panes set high above them. Many were broken, causing rays of light to scatter in the dust-filled air.

Jessica's companion nodded to another woman standing apart from the group. She nodded back. 'Off you go. They'll help you.' The woman standing beside Jessica pointed towards the group. 'Good luck, lovely.' She was gone before Jessica could thank her.

Jessica crossed the concrete floor to the group. The young woman standing slightly apart was addressing them. She stopped when Jessica arrived. 'Hello, my name is Ann.' She was lean and of medium height. 'And you are?'

'Jessica.'

'Hello, Jessica. I was just telling everyone that there's been strange movement of red jackets over the last while. We don't yet know what they're up to. And we're a little worried.' She paused, thinking how best to frame her advice. 'It looks like there is only one route left open to the quarter. That's suspicious, to say the least.' She shook her head and sighed. 'But we're still guiding people through.'

Jessica's gut wrenched: all entrances but one were closed because Kilgore had come looking for her.

'So we're advising people to think carefully about crossing today. But the choice is yours.'

There was silence and then concerned muttering between group members. Jessica knew there was no option but to risk the crossing. The longer she stayed outside the safety of the quarter, the longer she gave Kilgore time to tighten his noose. Hiding among the refugees would provide camouflage. 'I'm in,' she said, stepping forwards.

'Good. Anyone else?' Ann asked.

To Jessica's surprise, nobody else came forwards. She had hoped to blend into a larger group; the risk of crossing alone was much higher. But she couldn't pull out now. A knot sat in the pit of her stomach.

Ann waited for a few moments. 'Fine, that's absolutely fine. If you choose to cross on another day, please check in with your local organiser to confirm the assembly point.'

The small group of people dispersed mutely. Some seemed disappointed, others anxious.

'Right, it looks like it's you and me,' Ann said. She gave Jessica a reassuring wink. 'You'll be fine. We'll be there in a flash. Others have crossed safely today.'

A sense of foreboding crept up Jessica's body like sinking sand.

———◎———

The squad leader was about to offer Kilgore lunch when his handheld receiver crackled into life. 'Another group, sir,' he said, passing the message on.

Kilgore didn't answer. He continued to scrutinise the street for movement. And then he saw her. She was a couple of feet from his window, pressed against the wall, waiting to cross. She was oblivious to his presence. Kilgore's lips rounded over his gums into a smile. 'Tell the men to move in.'

Jessica was halfway towards the boarded door on the opposite side of the street when Kilgore emerged from his lair. He walked out, following a stream of red jackets to the left of where she stood. Another squad of red jackets spilled onto the street to her right. She and Ann stopped in their tracks. They were cornered.

'Hello, pet.' It was too easy, and Kilgore felt disappointed. 'Daddy has missed you.'

Ann viewed her with bewilderment. Guilt surged through Jessica. She should have told her! Why didn't she tell her beforehand? She turned to face Kilgore.

It was the second time in just a few minutes he felt disappointed. He had rehearsed her horror and fear. But in its place—nothing. Her face was impassive and cold.

'Father,' Jessica said. She was still holding the rainbow umbrella.

'Why, you don't look pleased to see me?' Kilgore's mouth dropped in mock surprise. 'And I see you've already met new, um, diverse friends.' He cast his eyes down at the umbrella. 'I knew I should have broken you in earlier. Never leave a filly free from its bit too long, eh?'

'You disgust me. You always have!' Jessica's tongue clipped the words as they left her mouth. 'You are not my father and never will be! You are nothing more than a sick and twisted animal.'

'Sweetheart!' Kilgore clutched at his heart. 'You shouldn't.' He removed his nickel-plated pistol from the inside pocket of his jacket and leisurely raised it level with Jessica's head. Cocking his head to one side, he grinned toothily.

Jessica closed her eyes, expecting Kilgore to pull the trigger. Shadows fell from the top of the building to which she was heading. They threw elongated pillars of shade across the street and caused all below to look up. Dark figures were indistinguishable from the cloud-streaked sun behind them. But the rifles pointing down at them were unmistakable.

Kilgore was the first to speak. 'Don't be damn fools!' he called out derisively. 'This doesn't concern you. Turn around and go play heroes elsewhere.'

'Oh, but it does, Senior Superintendent,' Fred called back. 'You see, she is one of us.' Her rifle tilted towards Ann.

'I have no need for this pile of shit.' Kilgore jabbed in Ann's general direction. 'Take her! But this one,' he said, pointing to Jessica, 'she's mine.'

'Mm. I don't think so, Kilgore. She doesn't seem to think she belongs to you.'

Kilgore bristled at the use of his name. 'Well, what do stupid little girls know?' He raised his pistol only to be blinded by an escaping ray of sun as a cloud moved. A single shot rang out, and the bullet struck. It rebounded on the asphalt inches from Kilgore's feet. All those on the street below crouched instinctively.

'Ann, move!' Fred shouted. Ann grabbed Jessica by the arm and hauled her to the door. It opened as if expecting their arrival, as Kilgore and the red jackets straightened from their crouching positions. Jessica glanced over her shoulder before the door slammed shut. Kilgore's face twisted with rage, his true inhuman self laid bare.

———◈———

Near the unfolding spectacle, Aidan's head sagged. 'Please tell me you're ready?' He drummed his fingers against the wall in boredom. 'It's just an induction ceremony. Nobody will care what you look like.' He had been outside the door for close to an hour. 'We're going to be late if...'

The door swung open, and steam billowed out. Anouk stood with damp hair in the doorway. 'I will care, Aidan.'

She's gorgeous. He leant against the wall and slipped.

'Besides, I was starting to think that you cared too.' She ambled past and pinched his bottom playfully.

Do something, you idiot! She's going to think you're a total loser.

'Anouk?'

She turned with an expert brush through her hair. 'Yes?'

Aidan's stomach clenched, and he stepped forwards and put his hands on her hips. Her green eyes stared back. She didn't pull away, and as he drew her tenderly closer, her warm body pressed against his.

'I must say, it's taken you quite a while. Thought I was going to have to take matters into my own hands.' She slid them onto his rear.

'I would never have objected.' Aidan leant forwards and kissed Anouk on her parted lips. It was warm, intimate and inviting. *Is she wearing perfume? Whatever it is, it's lovely.*

'Ahem.'

Aidan and Anouk pushed away from each other, looking bashful.

'I don't mean to interrupt,' a man standing behind them said, 'but I have been waiting for a century to get into the shower.' He said this with such conviction that Aidan almost replied in astonishment, 'A century, really?'

'Sorry.' Anouk stepped to the side to allow him to pass.

Aidan and the man entered a step-and-slide, as they kept moving in the same direction while trying to pass each other.

'Young man, are you planning to let me through or is this your way of asking me to dance? Either way, you won't be getting a kiss.' Aidan stopped and reset. He wound his shoulder to the right, showing his direction of travel, and freed himself of further humiliation as he circled around the man.

'Come on.' Anouk grinned and, taking his hand, pulled him on a jog through double swinging doors into the mess hall. They weaved between tables and chairs to reach the far end, and another set of double doors. These struck Anouk and Aidan as a perfect finish line, and they simultaneously sped up into competition. They scattered chairs in their wake. Aidan slid over the last table, and Anouk catapulted herself over another on two hands and landed on her feet. In a tie, they each burst through adjacent doors, laughing.

People filled the old conference hall. Quiet fell over the audience as they twisted in their seats to see the cause of the commotion. Mother looked livid. She stood on a slightly raised platform and glared in their direction. The swinging doors found their equilibrium and came to a shuddering close.

'As I was saying.' Mother continued giving the pair dirty looks. 'It is one of my greatest privileges to welcome new members to our Resistance.' She addressed the audience as Anouk and Aidan sheepishly found seats in the back row.

'Do you know which one you'll choose?' Aidan spoke behind his hand. Anouk shrugged and widened her eyes. He tried again, but louder. 'Which civic? Which civic will you align with?'

A woman in the row ahead turned and shushed them.

'No.' Anouk mouthed the word. It was the truth. The three civic movement symbols alternated in her mind. These movements first joined in the Unity Marches, protesting against the increased political influence of the nationalist fascist Blood Martyrs. Later, after the Change, they unified to form the Resistance. The choice was only symbolic, but it was important; saying something about who she was and who she wanted to become.

'I would like to welcome you to our family. You are joining at an exciting time; we are working on new solutions for a new world—a spark of hope, if you will,' Mother said. She called the first new member onto the platform. He was a young man, still in his late teens; gawky and failing spectacularly in growing his first beard.

He stood in front of Mother, who cupped three round lapel pins in the palm of her hands. They were black apart from the silver detailing in the centre. The first depicted the three downward-facing diagonal arrows of the Anti-Fascist Civic. The second, the outline of Earth for the Environmental Civic. And the last, a mathematical equal sign for the Equality Civic. The young man plucked the equality pin from Mother's hands without hesitation. The audience erupted into a collective chant of 'equality, freedom, environment,' then clapped and cheered. The young man beamed as Mother pinned the symbol to his T-shirt.

He then took a seat at a long table behind her. It had a rectangular wooden board and mallet resting on top. The young man rested his right forearm on the table with the palm of his hand facing upward. His fingers were trembling. Anouk knew what was about to happen and cringed, closing her eyes. A Resistance member was already waiting with a surgical scalpel. She swabbed the young man's wrist with alcohol disinfectant and then cut a tiny incision alongside a small pre-existing scar. Apart from inhaling sharply, the man made no further sound. The woman slid the round-tipped tweezers into the incision and, in a blink, pulled out a microchip. She then dipped the microchip in a steel bowl of water to wash off the blood, dried it, and placed it in the centre of the wooden board. After having his minor wound cleaned and dressed, the young man raised the wooden mallet to the sound of rhythmic clapping and brought it down with a loud thud on the microchip. A cheer erupted from the audience in ultimate recognition of the man freeing himself from State surveillance and control.

The audience chanted, cheered and clapped as three new members joined. Anouk was the last. She muttered to Aidan, 'Where are Fred and Ann?' He looked around the hall and showed that he didn't know. Anouk scanned the hall a final time to make certain they weren't there. She had grown fond of them over the intervening weeks.

'Anouk Scarlett Walker,' Mother announced. Anouk touched her forehead with her head down as she rose to her feet—hating being the centre of attention. She passed Rachel, who ignored her, as she walked up the middle aisle. She tripped on the step to the platform, steadied herself to audience chuckles, and stopped before Mother.

It was the first time that Anouk had stood close to Mother. Her face, although austere, was easy. It communicated discipline and determination but also humanity. Mother spoke only to her. 'I must admit, I'm pleased to see you here. I had my doubts when you first arrived. But others were—how best to describe?' She paused and thought. 'Persuasive in their belief of you.' She smiled, looking back towards Aidan. 'I hope their trust was not misplaced.'

She extended her palms outward with three pins to choose from. Anouk swallowed hard. Mother didn't understand the shame she carried, made worse by the often implied judgement and stigma of her past. Anouk stared through her embarrassment, down at the pins. All eyes were on her. She struggled to make a choice, her hand hovering over Mother's. And then, a certainty came to her. She took the anti-fascist pin and returned it to Mother, who fastened it to the front of her hoodie. Anouk had chosen freedom.

Giddiness filled her as she made her way to join the other new members seated at the elevated table. The crowd cheered, and she saw Aidan getting to his feet and clapping. The microchip removal was less painful than expected. For once, she felt the master of her own destiny. The microchip did more than track her movements and store her personal information. Its banal use during everyday life—to pay, to access, to identify—hid its coercive function. It was a device to mark and constrain who she was, against the State's idea of normal. She could now decide her own identities—who she was in all her beautiful complexity, contradictions and messiness.

As Mother quieted the audience and signalled them to sit, Fred and Ann came in through the double side door. They were escorting a young and petite blonde woman. She appeared tousled but was standing with decorum. Audience members near the door fell silent. The silence spread little by little across the hall until uneven muttering filled the void. Some people, having worked close to the Bureau, recognised her. And then shouting erupted—'traitor!', 'scum!', 'fascist trash!' Some members rose to their feet to get a better look at what the fuss was about; others did so in outrage.

Mother bellowed for silence, and the audience grudgingly fell quiet.

'Jessica Kilgore!' a woman screamed from one corner.

Anouk stood trembling in shock. 'No!' she called out in a shaking but authoritative voice, and the audience turned from looking at the woman to her. 'This is Jessica Amber Walker. She's my sister!'

12

The Master stood above Jimmy, who was kneeling at his feet. Sibylline positioned themselves at the Master's side and at the entrance to the cell's gate. They purred imperceptibly as he spoke. It was as if his words stroked their souls, and they rippled in gratitude. The nebulous glow of the cell's single light reflected from his white robe, creating the impression of an aura.

The Master administered Jimmy's last rites. He performed them for all new inmates once they were fitted with an occucanula. Death was a certainty thereafter. Jimmy's knees hurt on the cold concrete, but he bowed his head as directed. The Master recited the Bible from heart. 'And Jesus said unto Martha, "I am the resurrection and the life. The one who believes in me will live, even though they die; and whoever lives by believing in me will never die".'

Jimmy's mind wandered as the Master continued. His aunt came to mind. Like him, she wasn't religious either. The closest she ever got to religion was her commitment to, and love of, nature. The thought of her bedtime stories brought a rare smile to his lips. She used to read him passages from Lovelock. *Not the best bedtime stories,* but they comforted him in much the same way as the Master found succour in the Bible. All living things worked synchronously together with their surrounding environment to reproduce the potential for life on Earth—Gaia. The Master was correct, but not in the way he thought. Death was not the end, but the beginning of new life that sprang from the old in perpetual harmony. At that moment, Jimmy found true peace, feeling one with the world around him.

The Master finished with a last verse: 'The people who were sitting in darkness have seen a great light, and for those who were sitting in the land and shadow of death, upon them a light has dawned.' He touched Jimmy lightly on the top of his head and then left.

The gate clanged shut, and the Master disappeared from view with his slouching escort. Jimmy creaked to his feet on stiff joints. 'It's time to check your yield,' the mentor said, jumping and gliding to the gate. He had listened to Jimmy receive his last rites, but not with a great deal of interest. He had heard them many times before and was growing bored. As the key turned in the lock and Jimmy pushed himself into a standing position, an apparition darted in front of the cell's bars. He'd imagined it—until it returned.

The glow of the cell light cast a ghastly pallor as the creature hung with white hands and swollen knuckles onto the cell bars. Its nails curled long, apart from one that something had ripped off, leaving a mushy stump in its place. A sickly wheeze issued from its mouth, followed by a deep rattling in its chest. Like the Sibylline, only thin, long tufts of hair remained on its scalp, and white clouded eyes stared vacantly from its face. But unlike the Sibylline, weeping sores infested its skin. In between the tattered remains of its black jumpsuit, improbably bloated legs with indistinct discoloured patches supported its gaunt body.

It sniffed at Jimmy by pressing its face between two bars. He could see its inflamed and bleeding gums. Many of its teeth had fallen out. The mentor moved rapidly. He had withdrawn the key and stabbed down with it at the creature's closest hand. The key didn't seem to make contact, but a familiar shrieking filled the air and reverberated through the cell block and into the darkness as the creature fled. It descended the metal stairs in a series of large leaps.

'What the hell was that!' Jimmy said.

'Methinks you must have heard them before.' His mentor assumed an oddly carefree manner, wiping the key clean against the front of his jumpsuit. 'Them be Screechers. Nasty-nasties, they are.'

'But what are they?' Jimmy's pounding heart had yet to settle.

The mentor looked as though he were thinking about how best to explain. 'They're you, they're me. They were guests of the Factory that didn't pass the test. They are the leftovers.' He grew agitated and hopped on the spot. 'Now, sit down on my bed and let me take a closer feel of you.'

Jimmy's mentor was strange and often incomprehensible, but not threatening. Jimmy had developed trust in him. He obeyed and sat on the lower bunk while his mentor squatted beside him, fingertips pattering as he inspected the occucanula and head strap. 'I'm sorry, I still don't understand?' Jimmy remained still while the mentor finished his bizarre examination.

'Always so many questions. It's my turn, methinks?'

'Yes, yes,' Jimmy said. 'I swear I'll answer any of your questions. But can you please just answer this one first?'

The mentor scowled but offered additional detail as requested. 'When they are finished with our eyes, when there's nothing more to harvest, the Master decides what duties we have. If you haven't died or killed yourself, you must work. Some become mentors, some become factory workers and some, the true believers in Him, join the Sibylline. But the leftovers, the bad or the mad, they must make their own way in the darkness. You can never be alone. They wait for you, they eat you, they drink you, they have you.'

Jimmy shuddered. In his mind's eye, the Screecher's scurvy-induced swollen gums and shattered teeth sank into his neck, blood oozing from their tight sucking lips. And yet, these monsters were people. Flesh and bone but withered. Some had always been bad, but all were driven insane. Flinging the vision from his mind, he asked, 'What do you mean by "harvest"? What do they harvest from our eyes?'

His mentor tutted disapprovingly.

'Sorry,' Jimmy said. 'It's your turn, go on.'

The mentor gladly accepted Jimmy's offer. He wanted Jimmy to describe breaking storm clouds on a humid summer day, a young child laughing, and the rich scent of beeswax. This was more than his fair share, but Jimmy did his best to enliven each description, drawing on his own sensory memory. The mottled greys and yellows in parting clouds, the unblemished skin of a baby and the irresistible invitation to join in its gummy giggle, and the sweet smell of grass and wildflower pollen in beeswax.

When the mentor first asked Jimmy to describe life beyond the Factory, he enjoyed this. He took part in the escapism. The darkness would recede, and colour would return. He slipped inexorably into fantasy, and it frightened him. One day he might rely on illusion as much as he had on shimmer. He could have succumbed to the allure of memories as a coping strategy for the trauma of the Factory and his urges for shimmer. But the price he had paid for a drug-free existence was too high to throw away. And so, after each description, he would tear his way to the bleakness of reality and be thankful for his sanity.

As he gasped, mouldy damp air pulled him back to the present. His mentor stood still in a daydream. 'So, harvest. What do you mean by harvest?'

There was a hiatus as the mentor collected himself. He went back to feeling Jimmy's head strap. He opened his mouth to repeat the question when the little man slid something from the strap's side and brought it forwards. 'This!' He held what looked like a test tube, fitted with a tapered silicone stopper. A small hole was visible in the stopper's top for the insertion or extraction of substances. 'Shine.'

Jimmy's hand followed the occucanula's outline. Until now, he hadn't dared. But curiosity won over his fear and revulsion. His inflamed eyelid, its puffy rim pressed against the device, gripped it in place along with the head strap. A small tube joined the focal point of the exposed metal, ran up over his ear, and fixed to the head strap. It seemed linked to the test tube. 'Excuse me; shine?'

'Yes, shine. They're harvesting shine. You know, glimmer or shimmer,' the mentor said.

The dawning revelation stunned Jimmy. 'Are you saying that shimmer comes from human beings? From us?' His mouth felt dry, and he struggled to swallow his thickening saliva.

The mentor sat back in surprise. 'Yes. Where did you think it comes from?' He listened attentively for Jimmy's response. None was forthcoming. 'Methinks sometimes people see what they want. It's purified and then crystallised. All those pretty crystals come from somewhere.'

Jimmy watched his mentor stand. Turmoil swam through his mind. Was shimmer really from people? How could that be? But the evidence lay in his mentor's hand as he made his way to the cell's one wall and pressed a small button that Jimmy had not yet detected in the gloom. The LED light in the cell throbbed.

A high-pitched sound accompanied it. It reminded Jimmy of a dog whistle. He was certain that there were frequencies he could not hear, calling for someone or something.

The Sibylline soon brought food and an empty test tube, exchanging it for the full one. They passed two large bowls of tepid, slushy oats under the bars. There were no spoons, and Jimmy and his mentor had to scoop the contents into their mouths with their hands. Jimmy hadn't eaten for days, but despite his hunger, he still found the food difficult to stomach. A greasy film of what tasted like pork fat covered the inside of his mouth. He had to scrape with his tongue to rid himself of the coating and its rancid aftertaste. His mentor didn't share his dislike. After licking the slop from its container, he retrieved Jimmy's abandoned bowl and lapped any vestiges out. He paused only to lick his lips.

They didn't speak while they ate. The cell block was unusually quiet apart from the sporadic grunting noise of satisfaction made by his mentor. A bang against the side of a metal staircase shattered the stillness, followed by the now-familiar refrain: 'flapping high, flapping high...' issuing from the cell on the third floor. The shrill shriek and sound of scuffling below barely registered as he climbed to his bed and fell asleep.

In his dream, Jimmy stood on a summit, gazing across a vast expanse of mountain peaks that stretched past the horizon. Most lay shrouded in cloud and mist. Ice and snow covered the highest exposed mountaintops, and the few discernible valleys appeared bottomless. The wind whistled around him, and snowflakes whipped up off the closest ridges in swirling flurries. But rather than bitter gusts, Jimmy experienced a cool breeze against his exposed arms and face. He shivered more in anticipation than cold.

His parents appeared. They looked unwell. Even though they had died when he was an infant, he remembered them effortlessly. They were standing a few feet beside him, the same age as he was now. They did not smile or move but stared at him, wanting to say something. His mother's long straw-coloured hair caught in a soft wind. Her eyes were of a similar shape and colour to Jimmy's—blue-grey. They had a twinkle in them. His father was taller, also with light hair, but he had curls. These ruffled at his forehead in an updraught. He looked gentle but vulnerable.

Jimmy spoke first. 'Why did you leave me?' It was a question he had asked, but no one knew the answer. They were drug addicts long before the Change, and they died with needles in their arms.

He knew the sound of his mother's voice was imagined, but it was lovely. Kind and safe. His lungs constricted with grief.

'This world is hard, Jimmy; it isn't made for us all.' The wind wailed. 'Please forgive us for failing you. We love you, baby boy, we love you.' They dissolved into an eddy of snow.

His aunt replaced them. She stood planted, her round frame resolute in the harsh surroundings. She wore a dark blue woollen pashmina over a grey dress, three keys hanging around her neck on a braided cord. She didn't need to say anything as she raised her arms towards Jimmy, inviting a tight hug—calling, calling. But he couldn't move even though he ached to be enveloped in her safe embrace. It wasn't time yet. He struggled, but his feet would not move. Sadness overwhelmed him, sobbing. 'Why, why did you leave me?'

'I never left you, sweet boy.' She smiled reassuringly, her arms still outstretched. 'Nothing truly leaves this world. I am with you every minute of every day, in all the nature's messages; I am here.' As she lowered her arms, the wind caught her pashmina, twisting it upward in a spiral. The keys chimed. As if by a flamboyant magician's trick, she was gone.

Anouk and Jessica stood in her place, hand in hand. Although their colouring was different, and Jessica was shorter than Anouk, their resemblance was striking. They both had a dash of freckles. Jimmy saw what he had not seen before. They were sisters. He adored them; one as his friend and the other as his soulmate. They looked happy and healthy. 'Come back to me?'

'Soon.' Anouk nodded.

Jessica looked towards Anouk, then back to Jimmy. 'I promise, Jimmy.'

The mountain range behind Anouk and Jessica grew. It rose against the horizon, blotting out light until its shadows obliterated all before it. The two young women disappeared into the darkness, and Kilgore took their place, hovering menacingly. 'Puppy-dog.'

A routine had taken hold of Jimmy's life. It was how he marked the passing of time. He slept as much as possible, calling upon happy thoughts to banish ensuing nightmares. His realisation that Anouk and Jessica were sisters comforted him. They had each other, and he was certain that they were safe and together.

He had stirred from frequent slumber and lay on his back, staring up at the ceiling. White dots floated across the darkness from his functioning eye, appearing as stars in the night sky while he listened to his mentor talk. The constant bright light in his left eye no longer bothered him; his brain had compartmentalised the stimulus outside of conscious awareness.

When he was not asleep, he and his mentor talked for

much of the remaining time. Between the howls and screeching, harvesting and eating, Jimmy learnt much about the Factory. Its horror and pain. His mentor explained the mystery of darkness and light.

It began with the Institute for Human Enhancement: a convenient cloak for the obscene. The Governing Council tasked the Institute to pacify individuals who represented a political threat to the State after the Change—later defined as undesirables. Terror alone didn't control them.

Existing proven techniques for reducing individual agency, such as lobotomy, proved inefficient. Newsflash: 'The Grand Failure of Lobotomy'. Who could guess that cutting frontal brain tissue through the eye socket wouldn't work at scale? After undergoing the procedure, many people were no better than vegetables—dribbling and apathetic. It was costly and unsustainable. The State lost a valuable pool of forced labour and gained dependents needing care.

'The Council even drew up plans for mass internment and execution,' the Mentor said.

Jimmy shuddered. 'Like the Nazis.'

Disused factories were the prisons. It didn't work: a simple solution for the lobotomised zombies, but still too costly.

Systematic mass murder was the logical next step. 'And then the discovery of a hormone called occudorphin.' The Mentor clapped his hands and snapped his fingers. In dissecting the eyes of lobotomy patients who had died, a junior doctor at the Institute found the answer. Brougham, now a professor, saved the State not only financial cost but discovered its key source of future revenue.

The Council needed more. Something politically elegant. People had known for years that sunlight enhanced mood and had a calming influence, encouraging the body to release hormones such as endorphins and serotonin. But only after the Change did the Institute stumble upon the remarkable properties of occudorphin. Specialised cells at the rear of the inner eye produced the hormone. Light also stimulated its production, but by ten times more than other hormones. When metabolised by humans in a purified form, it resulted in intense euphoria and a feeling of wellbeing, coupled with behavioural passivity and compliance.

'Finally, the perfect form of control,' the Mentor said.

'So, they ended up making money from it?'

'That's right. Factories don't cost much, methinks. They basically run themselves. Think of them as self-funding.' The mentor chuckled. 'The State takes the shine—that's shimmer to you,' he clarified, 'and sells it for a huge profit.'

'And they pacify a large proportion of the population who are otherwise likely to rebel?'

'Spot on!' his mentor said. He was enjoying himself, and his talking gathered pace. 'But it gets better still. They—the Governing Council—don't look like the bad guys. It's the spritters and all the other undesirables that are to blame.'

A sudden slowing of his account suggested admiration. 'Methinks it was not a great advertisement for the Council, slicing people's brains or locking them up and then killing them. It makes them look like the good guys when they can blame other people. "For Higher Virtue" and that rubbish! They're the ones supposedly fighting for a better world by rounding up all the spritters and other undesirables. But—and here's the genius—at the same time they don't solve any of the problems that they promised to. If anything, they create a more miserable world where people need an escape through shimmer! It's brilliant!' He leant back against the wall alongside his bed.

Jimmy shook his head in disbelief. 'They've created a virtuous cycle.'

'That's a good way to describe it.' His mentor shuffled off his bunk. 'It's time for lunch, methinks. Let's check your yield.'

Jimmy hung his head over the side of the top bunk so that his mentor could remove the test tube. He expertly weighed it in his hand. 'Oh, that's a good one. You're a prized milk cow, you are!' He chortled, and moved to press the button on the wall. The LED light in the cell pulsated, and the high-pitched whistle sounded.

They waited for a few minutes in silence for the Sibylline to arrive. Jimmy was brooding over what he'd learned. 'How do you know all this stuff?'

His mentor didn't answer, so he tried a different tack. 'Did someone tell you about how shimmer came about?' There was still no reply. He couldn't see his mentor's features in the murk, but sensed the topic made him uneasy.

The Sibylline had arrived and exchanged the test tube for the usual food. The mentor brought Jimmy his bowl but said nothing as he sat down on his bunk to eat. He slurped the fatty oats. *A treat today.* Thin strips of pulled pork lay in the gooey mess. It was an extravagance. His diet lacked variety—no fresh produce and meat only on rare occasions.

A predictable intermittent thud, followed by 'flapping high, flapping high…' began again. 'Jeez, what the bloody hell is that?' Jimmy moaned as he tried to extricate a piece of meat from between two teeth.

The mentor broke his silence. 'Someone jumping off the walkway. Methinks they have had enough. Poor soul. What did you think the man means by "flapping high" after they jump?'

'What!' Jimmy spluttered. The thought hadn't even crossed his mind. It made sense—there were no barriers apart from the walkway handrails. It was the only means of suicide available to inmates. The Master's words came back to him: 'The Almighty offers you a choice, even in this place of darkness.' Jimmy refocused. 'But what happens to their bodies? Where do they go?' He never saw corpses during his rare visits to and from the cell block. The walls of his cell closed in.

The mentor had not stopped munching throughout. He paused to answer. 'Screechers, most times.' He burped. 'Also a good source of protein for us.'

Jimmy vomited on the edge of his bed. He kept retching. Morsels of half-masticated oats and human meat trickled over his mattress and onto the floor. Only the sight of his mentor on all fours, licking his vomit, forced him upright and out of view. He sat in one corner, pressed against the wall as far as possible from the lapping sound, pretending that he was somewhere else; anywhere else. His mentor rose from the ground, his mouth ringed with the remains of his feast. The gagging reflex took hold again. Jimmy spluttered, but his stomach was empty and spasmed. He clutched at his sides and groaned in pain.

The mentor oriented towards the sound and faced Jimmy. The tips of his fingers came to rest on the wet edge of the top mattress. As much as he had become an animal, driven by the most basic instincts of survival, he remained human. The contradiction was palpable when he spoke.

'I know what you're thinking and I know how you feel, but you have a choice. Methinks the Master will have told you this. You can live, or you can die.'

Jimmy sensed the mentor could see him through his milky white eyes. They were staring intently at him through the thick rims of his broken and functionless spectacles.

'I'm not ready to die.' His confession was raw and honest. 'Those who have chosen to die have no need of their bodies.' He then lowered himself out of sight onto his bunk.

Jimmy didn't despise the mentor for his choice. It was rational, even if repugnant. The incongruity was morally reconcilable in the dread of the Midnight Factory.

———————◎———————

There was stillness.

'I was a research manager at the Institute.'

Jimmy sat up, his nausea dissipating.

'I worked for Professor Brougham. That's how I know these things.' His mentor spoke in a clipped, regretful tone.

They stayed silent for a time, each absorbed in their own thoughts, with their own demons to wrestle. Jimmy leant forwards and passed his half-full bowl of food down to his mentor. 'Here'.

It was lifted wordlessly from his hand, and the gulping resumed. When it ceased, Jimmy found his voice first. 'How did you end up in this place?'

'Mm, now that's a sad story, methinks,' the mentor said. 'In one word: synthetic.'

'Synthetic?' Jimmy asked.

'Synthetic. Yes.' The mentor stopped while he ruminated. 'The Institute found a way to produce shimmer synthetically, with no human harvesting.'

Jimmy sat back. 'But why not make it without us then?'

'Ah, two very good reasons if you're the Governing Council. First, the virtuous cycle, remember? And second, it's cheap and easy to produce.'

Jimmy understood the first point but not the second. *Surely if it's cheap and easy to produce without the need of human herds, why not do that?*

The mentor answered this question before Jimmy had time

to vocalise it. 'If it's cheap and easy to produce, other people can do it. The State makes a lot of money from it. It has a monopoly over the entire market. It would not be good if competitors got hold of the recipe.'

'And that's why you're here, isn't it?' Jimmy guessed, 'You were going to sell the recipe?'

'You're a smart one, methinks.' The mentor chuckled for the second time that day. 'There are many people in New Albion and beyond who would pay very good money to have that recipe. I would have been made. The problem is, I got caught.'

'And they brought you here as punishment.'

The mentor snorted. 'But you've got to give it to Professor Brougham. There's a certain poetry to it, methinks. I took his recipe, and he took my eyes.'

———◎———

Kilgore didn't know how Jessica had accessed Anouk's contact details. The front desk at the Bureau confirmed she had left the building before anyone retrieved the information. He had tracked the point of access to an old PC stationed in the caretaker's storeroom. Records confirmed that the caretaker had been ill that day. Jessica would have known this, as she had processed his absence request.

A rat was to blame. And Kilgore knew who this was, although he couldn't prove it. *That fat tub of lard, Marge.* Nothing could be done. A room full of co-workers confirmed she was present when the information was accessed. He couldn't kill them all. And so, instead, he had had the caretaker Allan's legs broken. Allan had been ill that day, but someone had to be made an example, and he hadn't secured the storeroom. It was a convenient excuse to administer punishment. Kilgore sat reminiscing at his desk. *He would walk again, even if with the aid of a crutch.*

But Jessica's betrayal still stung. He would make her pay, together with the rest of the wannabe Resistance. Their days were numbered. He hadn't put out an alert about Jessica. It was not sentimentality or affection. There was nothing he felt for her—never had been. She was one of several orbiting objects to manipulate and control. To feed his lust for power and dominance. She'd still be useful, still had a part to play, though how remained unclear.

Chief Superintendent Moran had blackened his mood even further. She had called in the morning to inform him that his presence would no longer be required for the Undersecretary of Industry's visit in two weeks. 'I am certain you have better things to do.' Yet Kilgore was not a fool. He was being screwed. Numbers were up, and the entire operation was running more efficiently than it ever had.

That cow! Stealing the credit that he was due. She would have to go, be got rid of. He was certain of that. No clear path presented itself, but opportunities to shaft colleagues always eventually did. Experience had taught him that. He would bide his time, exercise patience.

In the meantime, he would satisfy his urge for revenge elsewhere. He picked up the telephone handset and dialled. 'Hello, yes, is that Professor Brougham?'

13

The stormwater channel was permanently full. Predictions in days gone by of heavier rainfall and flooding were correct. Yet, those same predictions suggested summers would also be drier. Winter was drawing closer, and there had only been a few days without rain over the past year. The channel now contained a churning river.

Anouk and Aidan watched it flow through the old industrial quarter. It was mesmerising. They sat with their legs suspended over a culvert that bridged the water. A section of the pedestrian guardrail had collapsed, corroded, allowing for a convenient sitting spot. The culvert had once carried traffic, but few vehicles passed through the quarter now.

'Do you miss it?' Anouk asked. She flicked a rusty bottle top into the rolling water and watched it sink.

Aidan was lost in thought—how could he kiss her without looking like a muppet? 'Miss what?'

'Shimmer. I think about it all the time. But I wish I didn't.'

The moment was gone. 'Sometimes.' He paused. 'But it gets better.' This was partially truthful.

'I sure as shit hope so.' The pull of shimmer nagged her constantly.

Aidan reflected on his own experience. An autumn leaf, carried from a once salubrious district, spun in the current by the concrete wall. An undulation prodded the leaf into the rippling flow, washing it into the mouth of the culvert, where it vanished.

'The best way to describe it is like when someone close to you dies,' Aidan said. 'At first you think about it all the time. The loss comes in waves. But slowly, over a period, the waves get further apart.' He still secretly kept the glass end of his favourite pipette in his shirt pocket.

'How much further apart?' Anouk asked hopefully, still staring at the water.

'Well, just like when someone you loved, when they die, you never forget them. So sometimes.' He shrugged. 'But it gets easier.' He nudged her. 'Just keep busy. Learn new things. Keep active.'

'Like I have a choice!' Aidan's words made sense, but it didn't stop the yearning. Jessica's return had opened old wounds and insecurities. She was pleased—at least she thought she was—to see her sister again. Jessica reminded Anouk of a happier, more innocent, time when the family was together; a memory that she had hidden over the years following the disappearance of Jessica and their father. Concealing it in her subconscious was a defence mechanism. That, along with the fantasy of Jessica and her father escaping to a safer, happier place, helped her endure life's brutality in New Albion. And now she knew: Jessica wasn't saved—Kilgore had adopted her. The thought of learning further was frightening.

Aidan put his hand on Anouk's, which was resting at her side. 'Are you planning on visiting her?' he asked. Anouk hadn't spoken with Jessica yet. They had taken her, partly for her own safety, to secure accommodation. Questioning had followed, but she had not yet been released.

'Mother still doesn't trust her,' Anouk said. 'Does she?' Moss was growing underneath her hand, and the warmth of Aidan's hand over hers felt like a welcoming duvet.

'No, she doesn't. Do you?' It was a blunt but fair question.

'Honestly,' Anouk said, looking at Aidan's face, 'I don't know. But I'm not used to your being so serious. Come on.' She grabbed hold of a still-upright section of the pedestrian guardrail and hoisted herself up.

'Where are we going?' Aidan asked. They had skipped work allocation that morning and slipped out while the sun dared shine. Return would inevitably lead to some unpleasant manual or menial task—or both.

'We're going to find out who Jessica is.'

They found Fred outside the makeshift armoury. It had been a modest local bank branch serving nearby businesses before the quarter was abandoned. It had looked out of place even before the Change. Its brutalist design clashed with the local architecture. A rampant black horse was still visible but faded on the former bank's signage above the entrance door. The Resistance stored a collection of small firearms in the still functional vault.

Fred was pleased to see them. Aidan grimaced, suspecting it was because a thankless task awaited. But, to his surprise, upon hearing where they were heading, she offered to escort him and Anouk to Jessica's holding room. It was in the same old office block where Anouk had weened herself from shimmer. 'Good memories,' she said to Aidan as they climbed the familiar stairs. He chuckled in response.

'We've been hoping you would pay her a visit soon,' Fred said to Anouk. 'She's been asking after you.'

'Has she?' Anouk flushed hot, anticipating the meeting; her mind was drifting elsewhere. Her nervousness increased because of the sounds and smells of the building—silence, dust and disinfectant. They were strongly associated with coming clean.

They exited the stairwell and turned into the corridor where Jessica was held. Rachel and another man stood guard at a door twenty yards further along. Aidan had stopped to tie a loose shoelace when Fred surreptitiously whispered, 'A little bird told me they caught you and Aidan snogging the other day.' Anouk blushed. 'No, don't be embarrassed. Good on you. Let's face it, it took you long enough!' She winked.

'It must have been the perfume you loaned me. God knows I was running out of other ideas,' Anouk said, rolling her eyes.

'It's my pleasure. But the perfume wasn't actually mine.' Fred stopped to let Aidan catch up.

'No? Whose was it?' Anouk asked.

'Rachel's.' Fred inclined her head in Rachel's direction, and Anouk looked towards her in surprise. Rachel met her gaze with a reticent smile. 'Give her time; she's trying,' Fred said. Aidan jogged the final few yards to join them.

'It's okay, Rachel. Mother's fine with them visiting,' Fred said as they neared the door.

'Are they both going in?' Rachel asked. Fred looked at Anouk and Aidan, who nodded. 'You'd better be careful,' Rachel said. 'Your sister's pretty. And we know how much this one likes pretty girls.' She huffed dramatically, but with a small smile, waving in Aidan's general direction. It was backhanded, but Anouk received it for the compliment that it was.

The door swung open, and they entered the small room. It was like the one that Anouk had occupied several weeks previously. It had a larger, barred window and a proper bed instead of just a mattress. Jessica had folded the sheets precisely, with hospital corners. She must have heard them coming; she waited tidily in the room's centre. Anouk noticed how similarly Jessica and her mother carried themselves. She stood facing the door, hands clasped in front of her, legs neatly together. She was also blonde, as her mother once was, and petite. Her clothes were the same as when she arrived. She wore a navy V-neck sweater, tailored khaki trousers, and ballerina flats—all cleaned since her arrival. Jessica had also freshened up. Not a hair was out of place in her ponytail, sweeping flawlessly back off her face. *All she's missing is a pearl necklace.* Anouk felt scruffy in her hoodie, cargo trousers and hiking boots.

The door clicked behind them as it closed. Fred had left them to get reacquainted. Anouk and Jessica stood facing each other awkwardly—Anouk shuffled and Jessica bit her lower lip.

Aidan succumbed to the uneasiness first. 'Hello.' He stepped out from behind Anouk and extended his hand. 'My name's Aidan. I'm, um, a friend of Anouk's.'

Jessica's body relaxed. 'Hello, Aidan, a friend of Anouk's.' She also stepped forwards and took his hand lightly in hers. She shook it in an impossibly refined way. 'It's very nice to meet you.' She then turned to Anouk and said hesitantly but with poise, 'Would it be strange if I gave you a hug?'

Words stuck in the back of Anouk's throat. Instead of trying to force a garbled response, she enveloped Jessica in an embrace. They clung to each other. Both had been lonely for so long. It didn't matter to Anouk whether Jessica was a spy. What mattered was that she was back, close and real. Anouk had felt like an orphan after losing her father and sister. Her mother was never quite the same once they had gone.

Jessica drew from Anouk's hold. She had been crying, and

her eyes were puffy and pink. 'Sorry.' She wiped the tears away delicately with the back of her hand.

'You're sorry? Just look at me!' Anouk rummaged around in one of her trouser pockets for some folded toilet paper. Tissues were scarce. She blew her nose forcefully.

The sound must have been striking because Jessica laughed in amusement. It lacked the polish she was accustomed to. But she liked it. Anouk, she established, was an open book. What you saw was what you got.

Anouk finished by drying her eyes with the used toilet paper. It was damp, and she looked around, considering where best to dispose of it. Aidan took it from her and stepped into the background again. She loved him at that moment. She turned back to Jessica and caught sight of the rainbow umbrella in the room.

Jessica followed her gaze. 'Oh, I almost forgot.' A mischievous spark appeared in her eyes. 'Your Valentine sends his love.'

Anouk laughed in surprise and delight. Jessica was referring to Mr Cooke, who lived two apartments down from her own at Jervis Gardens. Aidan's eyes narrowed.

'You look so much like Mum,' Anouk said. Their mother had had sharper, more angular features, whereas Jessica was altogether softer-looking. Still, their colouring and physique were almost identical.

'Anouk, she's dead,' Jessica said. 'I'm sorry.'

'Sorry' seemed a strange word to use; she was also Jessica's mother, after all. But it had been a long time since Jessica had seen her.

Anouk cast her eyes down, not being able to hold Jessica's gaze. 'How?'

'She killed herself.' Jessica chose not to provide further details—there was no need. She took Anouk's hands into her own. She led Anouk to the bed, then sat beside her. Aidan positioned himself unobtrusively, cross-legged on the floor.

Anouk felt bizarrely little, as though a door had slammed shut on her emotions. Perhaps pity for her mother, guilty about her lack of emotion, but not much more. She would face up to the complexity of their relationship and find the strength to say goodbye in her own way, and grieve the relationship that was never fully reconciled, when the time was right. She sat in thought, staring at a withered and dry potted plant left to die years before in the room's corner.

Jessica mistook her silence for shock. 'But I have some great news. News that you need to know.' She tried to draw Anouk back. Anouk looked up from staring at her knees. 'Jimmy is alive!'

———◎———

They spoke for hours until it was evening. Jessica told them everything about Jimmy—how she met him and where he'd been taken. Anouk and Aidan struggled to comprehend the sheer dreadfulness of the Factory. Jessica lacked the details of its operation or how occudorphin was extracted, but enough about the inmates' fate induced visceral dismay. Their collusion with the State in the trade of shimmer hit Aidan hard. He kept repeating the same question. 'So, shimmer is made from people? You said they get shimmer from people somehow? To be clear, it's people that shimmer comes from?'

None of them were free from the stain of shimmer. They had all contributed to maintaining a brutal economy that traded in human misery. *It's s the logical extreme of a free market economy in a fascist state—the basic law of supply and demand rules,* Aidan thought. But in New Albion's case, a fascist ideology—

preaching a natural social hierarchy and subordinating individual rights—served as the economy's raw material.

'Mother needs to know,' Aidan said, shaking his head in disbelief. He had finally accepted what was described.

'What makes you think she doesn't know already?' Anouk stared at her hands, seeing blood.

He considered the possibility. 'Either way, I want to know what she has to say.' He rose to his feet. 'And besides, Jimmy needs saving. For fuck's sake, it's the least I can do.'

Anouk and Jessica understood how he felt. Redemption was a long road, and they needed to start somewhere. And Jimmy was not something; he was everything to them. 'It's a good start,' Anouk said, standing.

'Do you think they will let me help?' Jessica asked.

'I'll ask.' Aidan knocked on the door to be let out. 'I'll also get some food on my way back. The room service is appalling here,' he said as Rachel appeared from behind the opening door. She scowled.

———◎———

Aidan had found Fred and asked whether she could wangle a meeting with Mother. She returned with news after they finished eating dinner on their laps back in Jessica's holding room. The Resistance's local Administrative Committee would speak with them. They were already convening their weekly meeting, and Jessica's future was the last agenda item. Aidan and Anouk's attendance offered the committee a chance to gather additional testimony. If Jessica were exposed as a spy, she would face summary execution. The possibility was clear to all of them, yet Fred's uneasy revelation still shocked them.

'I knew it was a risk in coming here,' Jessica said. 'But what choice did I have? My sister is here, and Jimmy needs me. And I couldn't stay a second longer near that sicko Kilgore!'

They departed for the old conference hall, where Anouk had been inducted into the Resistance days earlier. The anti-fascist pin still clung to her hoodie. No one spoke as they walked. Anouk thought of her and Jessica's attempted escape with their father. The Resistance had already questioned Jessica extensively about how she had come under Kilgore's charge. But the sisters had pieced together a fuller picture of what had happened—it was a car accident. It was frightening, but nothing extraordinary. Yet it had had a profound impact on all of their lives. Her mind drifted back...

They drove north through the night to reach a safe route out by dawn. Both of the girls were scared. It was curfew, and their father was navigating a winding Highlands road without headlights to avoid unnecessary attention. Snow rather than rain was drifting down. Why he swerved they didn't know. It might have just been ice on the road. They broke through the stone wall of an ancient bridge and bobbed in a swollen river.

Her father yelled for them to get out as the interior filled with frigid water. As the eldest child, Anouk was in the front passenger seat and lowered her window to squeeze through. Her father had unbuckled her and was leaning backwards doing the same for Jessica when Anouk slipped out into the icy river. The current was strong; she clung to the window rim as long as she could. They were struggling inside—'Dad, Dad!' Anouk was swept away from the car, its brake lights flashing on and off, half-submerged, while her father fought to manoeuvre inside.

Anouk faded from view behind the car. Jessica screamed,

but no one heard her frantic cries. Her father hauled her over, between the two front seats, just as the car's nose dipped. He hadn't unbuckled himself as he attempted to lower his window. It had opened a crack when the lever broke from the door. He bellowed for Jessica to climb through the window that Anouk had used, but water streamed through the opening, forcing her backwards. He drove his window down with his hand. It had given way without warning, and he choked on water as it gushed through. His powerful arms pulled her towards him through the torrent and then pushed her out through the window. She didn't get to see him again. The car had sunk beyond view by the time she had spluttered to the river's wintry surface.

Anouk was fortunate. Disoriented, she paddled to the bank, and stumbled through frozen thickets back to the road. Dazed, soaked and with chattering teeth, she waved down a passing car. They were charitable and risked involvement, taking her to the closest village. They summoned the red jackets who, after scanning her details, transported her back south to her mother. They hadn't yet identified her father as one of the most wanted undesirables.

Jessica was less lucky; she had washed ashore. She had survived sub-zero temperatures during the remaining night. The hay bale left as grazing for the surrounding Highland cattle had kept her sufficiently warm. One especially curious cow inspected her condition several times over the night—she wished for a shaggy coat too.

Anouk's story alerted the red jackets and volunteer rescuers to the accident and the potential for further survivors. The volunteers found Jessica severely hypothermic. She was unconscious and they resuscitated her. Red jackets would not have bothered. But her luck had run out. By then, the authorities knew who her father was, and the State assigned her to its flagship Adoption and Re-Education Programme for the children of dissidents. They were under no legal obligation to notify her mother. Kilgore was her fate. He had placed his name on the adoption register as it seemed a clever move; one that showed his devotion to the State in entrenching its ideology. He didn't expect or want to be a father.

———— ◎ ————

Fred reached the double doors to the conference hall first. 'I'd better go in and see if they're ready for us. Is that okay?'

Fred's question jolted Anouk back to reality. She missed what Fred had asked.

'Yeah, that's fine,' Aidan said as Fred angled her way through the swinging doors. He led the others to a nearby table. They were in the mess hall after dinner, its only guests. Aidan leant towards Jessica from across the table. 'We can get you out now, if you want? Nobody's here to stop us; it would be easy enough.'

Jessica smiled wearily. 'Where would I go? Thank you, Aidan.' She touched his forearm. 'But it's here or nowhere.'

Fred returned to collect them. Inside the conference hall, the Administrative Committee was waiting, with Mother acting as Chair. They sat elevated on a raised platform at the far side of the hall, and they asked Jessica to sit before them. Anouk and Aidan sat in the middle of the row of chairs behind Jessica. Fred lingered by the entrance doors, at the rear of the hall, after she had called them in.

As elsewhere in the building, the hall had a nylon carpet. An undetected leak had spread from a corner, leaving a large stain. It resembled a Rorschach inkblot. Anouk peered over her shoulder. The stain caught her attention, resembling either a large, ominous insect with extended wings and salivating mandibles, or a guardian angel with arms raised to the heavens. Anouk hoped it represented an angel.

'Thank you all for attending our committee meeting,' Mother said. 'The attendance of Aidan Bekker, Fred Malone, Anouk Walker and Jessica Kilgore is noted.' She spoke to the Committee Secretary, indicating she should minute their presence. 'We only have one remaining agenda item this evening, and that is to consider the status of Jessica Kilgore.'

Anouk muttered, stifling a snort of derision—it was the second time Jessica had been called a Kilgore. Status! Now there was a euphemism if ever there was one. The last agenda item was better described as the verdict in a capital trial. She whispered in Aidan's ear. 'Are they kidding me?' He gently shushed her.

Mother glared sternly at Anouk. 'We have considered the evidence before us. We note,' she turned to Jessica, 'that your statement relies on the claim that you nursed a certain James Sullivan back to health before the Bureau for Virtue assigned him to the Factory. You stated it was he who alerted you to your sister, Anouk, being alive?'

Jessica cleared her throat with a cough and stood apprehensively. 'Yes.' She floated, uncertain whether to sit or stand. She sat again.

'And are we simply meant to take your word for this?' an officious-looking man seated to Mother's right asked. He wore a frown. 'You worked at the Bureau for years. You are Jerome Kilgore's daughter. You would have had easy access to information, allowing you to fabricate any story you chose?'

Anouk bristled at the repeated suggestion of Jessica being Kilgore's daughter. She was slouching in her chair. Her heels were resting on the floor and the toes of her boots against the legs of Jessica's chair. She tensed her legs and unintentionally pushed the chair forwards. It made a grating sound, and Mother cast

Anouk another disapproving look.

Jessica didn't notice. She shifted in her chair. The discussion was unpromising so far. It was agonising to watch Jessica stand hesitantly again to respond to the officious man's question. The proceedings had taken an inquisitorial turn. 'N-no,' Jessica stammered, 'that's incorrect. It's not easy at all to access that sort of information.'

Aidan shut his eyes and winced. 'Come on,' he said under his breath, clenching his fists. 'Stay focused.'

His eyes flashed open when Anouk spoke. She had risen and moved out from behind Jessica to see the panel members more clearly. She clasped her hands on the chair ahead of her. Her face had reddened, and her resentment was unmistakable.

'Can the committee explain why my sister is on trial when she escaped kidnapping? It is a trial, isn't it?'

Mother opened her mouth to reply, but Anouk charged on ahead. 'Because we would like to know,' Aidan sunk lower into his seat, 'what the committee knows of the Resistance's involvement in the selling of shimmer and its criminal production!'

Mother tried to speak again.

'That's correct!' Anouk's voice climbed, and she pointed an accusatory finger at the committee members. 'There are people right here who have been complicit in murder. Murder! Why are...'

'That's quite enough!' Mother bellowed, also rising to her feet. 'You will sit down, and not say another word, or we will have you removed.'

Anouk was still fuming, but Aidan had taken her hand and subtly guided her down to sit beside him.

There was a pregnant pause as Mother matched Anouk's glare. She shifted her eyes to Jessica without moving her head. 'Now,' she said more calmly as she sat back down, 'can you show me any evidence that you actually knew James Sullivan as you've described?' It would at least be a starting point—something that might recommend mercy.

'Jimmy,' Jessica said delicately.

'Pardon me?'

'Jimmy. His name is Jimmy. And I can describe him to you if that would help?' Jessica shrugged and glanced back at Anouk.

Mother conversed with the other committee members. 'No, I'm afraid that will be insufficient. That is the type of information that could easily be gleaned from the Bureau's records.'

Jessica's passive response made it clear she expected as much. 'Then, no, I have nothing further to add.' She lowered herself back down onto her seat. As her trousers tightened against her thighs, something hard pressed inside her pocket. It was Jimmy's chain. He had given this to her for safekeeping before being transported to the Factory. 'Wait.' She pulled herself straight and plunged her hand into the pocket to retrieve the silver chain and pendant. 'I have this.' She held the chain up for the panel to see. 'It's Jimmy's. He gave it to me to take care of before they took him.'

Mother peered up from the piece of paper that she was scribbling on. 'Bring it here.' She held her hand out, and Jessica walked onto the low platform, stepping up to the table. She coiled the chain and pendant in the palm of Mother's hand, who studied it closely for a while. The pendant resembled the Earth. After a while, Mother drifted from it, lost in thought. 'Maggie,' Mother murmured. Jimmy's aunt—smiling and stout—rose in her memory, and grief struck her.

'Sorry?' Jessica said.

'Maggie.' Mother emerged from contemplation. She addressed the room, holding the chain and pendant up. 'This was Maggie's.' Her voice trailed off. 'She was a dear friend.'

Mother pressed the chain to her chest. 'She was Jimmy's aunt and the leader of the Environmental Civic before...' She trailed off. 'You can sit down,' she said to Jessica, pulling herself together, then turned to discuss the development with her colleagues.

Fred came to sit beside Anouk and Aidan as Jessica returned to her chair. She raised her eyebrows: 'And now?' A judgement would follow. Anouk was holding her breath. Jessica's raised shoulders showed she was holding her breath too.

The panel had decided. Their huddle relaxed, and pages were being re-arranged on the table. Anouk was ready to object, since she and Aidan hadn't given testimony yet—she was clutching at straws; they had nothing to add.

'Based on this fresh evidence coming to light,' Mother said, still holding Jimmy's pendant and chain. 'We are unable at this stage to determine your status.'

The pendant proved little, but it was enough to give Jessica the reprieve Mother was looking for; her colleagues doubted Jessica hadn't turned traitor. Anouk let out an audible sigh. Mother ignored her. 'As such, you will be confined to the industrial quarter until we can make a determination. You will report to the duty officer every eight hours. If you fail to do this, we will restrict you to your secured accommodation. Is that understood?'

'Yes,' Jessica said, lowering her shoulders in relief as she breathed out. This appeared out of character, as she was so composed.

'Well, good then.' Mother stood as if to leave, prompting the other committee members to do the same. 'I believe you will need this back.' She held the chain and pendant out to Jessica. As Jessica mounted the platform for the second time to collect it, Mother spoke to her fellow committee members. 'I would like to speak with Anouk, Aidan and Fred alone, if you don't mind.'

To Jessica, she said in a less formal tone and with a kind smile, 'You may wait in the mess hall; they shouldn't be too long.'

———⟶⟨◎⟩———

Only those asked to stay remained. Mother invited them to sit with her at the table around which the panel had convened. She sat, collecting her thoughts, pressing her palms together, fingers resting against her lips as though in prayer. She spoke but addressed no one in particular. 'It is important that you understand we welcome differences of opinion here. It is what separates us from the Governing Council.' Mother turned her attention specifically to Anouk, fixing her gaze, concentrated and unyielding. She didn't appear angry, but delivered a final warning. 'In fact, we need people who are passionate and who have ideas.' A 'but' felt imminent. 'However, you should know, Anouk, that we will not tolerate outbursts like the one witnessed earlier.'

Anouk was combative, and bit words back. There were unanswered questions concerning the Resistance's part in selling shimmer. Her shaken faith must have shown.

'You need to show that you understand, Anouk? You will not receive a second chance.'

Although it took willpower, Anouk gave a curt nod. She didn't apologise.

'Your agreement is your word, and that is good enough for me,' Mother said. 'That being agreed, I must confess that you are correct. We are involved in the trade of shimmer.'

Anouk's head jerked back, unprepared for such honesty.

'There is a realpolitik to it that I and others in the Resistance have struggled with for a long time. Our accommodation with the regime has allowed us time to organise and prepare. We have saved countless innocent lives, including your own, but at a terrible cost.' Although Mother kept Anouk's gaze throughout, her voice was strained.

Aidan whispered something inaudibly to himself. 'Pardon me?' Mother asked. It was a genuine invitation for Aidan to contribute.

Aidan looked up. He had been deep in thought, staring at his hands. 'Whoever fights monsters should see to it that in the process he does not become a monster.' This time, his words came out clearly.

'Friedrich Nietzsche,' Mother said, her eyebrows raised. She hesitated, inclining her head towards Aidan. 'It is a moral burden I will have to carry for the rest of my life. And I ask your forgiveness and all those,' now turning pointedly towards him, 'who have been affected by the scourge of shimmer.' Mother waited for Anouk's response.

Anouk didn't offer forgiveness, and Mother didn't expect her to. Instead, Anouk said, 'It has to stop.'

'Again, yes, you're correct. We have plans. I asked Fred to join this meeting as I understand that your trust in us may not be fully restored.'

Mother was right. Anouk didn't trust the Resistance's motives.

'Fred, my love, would you please fill Aidan and Anouk in?'

Fred cocked her head, uncertain what to say.

'Apologies,' Mother said. 'Could you please let them in on our little secret concerning the pen drive that Aidan kindly delivered?'

'Sure. It contains detailed information about the Institute responsible for leading research into shimmer. We have full blueprints, logistical times and schedules, and the names and positions of all personnel.'

'In short, we intend to blow it up,' Mother said. 'Our arrangement with the Governing Council is ending.' She placed her hands on the table, emphasising the point.

There was stunned silence. 'But won't that mean open civil war?' Anouk said. 'They won't just let us carry on as normal, will they?'

Aidan was processing the information and sat with his mouth open.

'No, they won't,' Fred said. 'It won't be easy. Shimmer bought us time to plan. We've arranged what we can. They will hammer us.' She struck the table with a fist, and its trellised surface wobbled.

'But Jimmy!' Anouk couldn't control herself. 'You need to let us get Jimmy out before things kick off? There will be a complete lockdown once you start.'

'That's simply out of the question,' Mother said.

'But...'

Fred interrupted to save Anouk from herself. 'It's been a long evening. Aidan, why don't you and Anouk get some fresh air? Clear your heads. And I'll catch up with you later.' She gave Aidan a pointed look. She was up to something.

'Come on, Anouk, Fred's right. Let's see how Jessica's doing?' Aidan encouraged Anouk to her feet. She opened her mouth, but Mother's warning was fresh in her mind. She and Aidan nodded a tense farewell and made their way out of the hall.

Fred waited until the swinging doors had settled into place before speaking. 'You know, it might not be such a bad idea letting them try.' She leaned back in her chair.

'I'm not convinced.' Mother breathed in deeply. 'Are you sure you're not letting your feelings for them get in the way?' She also reclined in her chair, trying to read Fred's motives.

'No, not at all.'

Mother didn't look persuaded.

'Honestly, it offers an opportunity. We need to launch our plans, and this would provide a very useful diversion. One we've been looking for. They'd be occupied completely elsewhere.'

Mother tapped her chin.

'And...' Fred interrupted her thoughts. 'If they're successful using intel from Jessica, it would answer that question. Whose side is she really on?'

'Okay, fine,' Mother said, 'but they will have to do it on their own.'

Fred smiled, prompting Mother to add, 'And you're not going with them.'

Fred's face fell.

'You are too precious to me.' Mother's expression changed. She was no longer Fred's boss, slipping into the role of her wife.

'You know I can't let Aidan go alone,' Fred said. 'Sometimes he has difficulty tying his own shoelaces.'

They both chuckled. The mental image of Aidan fumbling at his shoe was fitting.

'We can discuss that later,' Mother said, offering a truce. Thinking out loud, she said: 'We will need to tell Brother, Sister and the Cousins that Operation Motion is being brought forwards. If they free Jimmy, it will set the cat among the pigeons.'

Fred bit the nail on one finger.

'It's not ideal, I know,' Mother said, 'but we knew this day would come. Oh, and can you please brief Father?' She hesitated. 'But tell him only what he needs to know.'

14

Professor Brougham was late. Kilgore paced back and forth across the Bureau's black and gold foyer floor. He did not meet and greet guests. It was politically expedient to have them brought to his office. He put others in their place from the start. But the Professor was important, and Kilgore was determined to keep the day's schedule.

The officer at the front desk glanced fretfully over the countertop. Kilgore tense and in proximity was an unwelcome hazard. 'Can I call anyone for you, sir?' He rose to a semi-standing position. This was a mistake.

Kilgore stopped in his tracks and considered him peevishly. 'Are you able to teleport someone to the foyer?' His eyes were lifeless, cold.

'No, sir.' The officer hoped this would suffice, and that Kilgore would resume his pacing. He sank below the countertop. He was fortunate; Kilgore was too distracted to spend additional energy intimidating him.

Kilgore stopped again. He raised his arm, pulled it straight to free his shirt from his wristwatch, and read the time. It was nine thirty-six in the morning. The professor was five minutes late, yet Kilgore had planned the day meticulously. It needed to run according to plan in order to maximise its effect. He resumed his pacing.

Chief Superintendent Moran had an important guest coming that day. The Undersecretary of State for Industry would make his long-awaited visit, touring the Bureau and then the Factory, in order to assess the adequacy of operations. It was shaping into a success, and Moran meant to take all the credit. She had excluded Kilgore from the visit.

Earlier that morning, the Undersecretary had arrived. He had been early. The day's itinerary no longer included Kilgore's brief introduction to the Undersecretary. It was a purposeful slight engineered by Moran. Images of Moran writhing in pain played in his mind. Recently, this, together with Jessica's imagined slow demise, had dominated his thoughts. Women were manipulative and controlling, and Moran and Jessica were exemplars of the breed. The image of his mother surfaced.

Kilgore had planned to meet the professor at the Factory, but at the last moment, the Professor asked to meet him at the Bureau instead. Kilgore broke the pencil he was holding. It was essential that they arrive at the Factory before Moran and the Undersecretary. Moran knew nothing about Kilgore's plans. He could not wait to see the look on her face as he appeared with Professor Brougham and Jimmy, a prized experimental subject. *What a coup! What a victory!* It would upstage Chief Superintendent Moran. The best part was that she could do nothing and say nothing. She could not claim that he had been insubordinate. *I am, after all, only doing my job. And doing it bloody well!* He smirked to himself.

Kilgore pulled his watch out from under his sleeve and inspected it again. *Where is Brougham?* 'Move along, you crusty old fart,' he said under his breath.

———————— ◎ ————————

Meanwhile, Moran's plans were running early. The black luxury saloon splashed through puddled water as it approached the hastily erected checkpoint. Plastic orange barriers spanned the width of the road. The checkpoint was on the outskirts of the city, near a slip road that would take the vehicle and its escort onto the motorway.

'That's strange,' the driver said. 'I didn't know we'd cordoned this sector off? Do you want to call it in?'

The red jacket in the passenger seat leant forwards, clutching the dashboard, and narrowed her eyes, making out detail. 'No, I wouldn't worry. There have been reports of greater activity around the industrial quarter.' The saloon and its chaperoning van were skirting around the quarter. 'The undesirables have been up to something. It's probably just a precaution. Let's ask the chaps what's going on when we stop.'

The saloon slowed as it neared the checkpoint barrier. Its wheels crunched through an icy puddle and loose gravel. Two red jackets were guarding the checkpoint. One had stepped before the barrier, his automatic rifle slung to the front, as he put his hand up, showing them to stop. The other guard waited at the verge, combat ready with her finger resting on the trigger.

There were uninhabited red brick buildings on either side of the checkpoint. An alley led off the road before the barriers. This location was sparsely populated. It was near the boundary of the old industrial quarter, and respectable citizens kept away.

The saloon's driver clicked a button down on the door armrest to lower the window. He glanced in the rearview mirror as the car ground to a halt. From nowhere, a rusty car hurtled from the side alley behind him. The car's restored diesel engine gave a smoky roar as it smashed into the side of the escorting squad van behind him. Its metal bumper crumpled with the impact and chewed into the van, pushing it towards the opposite curb with a smell of burning rubber. The van's tyres collided with the concrete verge with a bang as they burst and pitched the vehicle at a forty-five-degree angle. Only the weight of the entangled attacking car prevented it from tipping over entirely.

'Five minutes and counting,' the red jacket, who had stepped before the barrier, shouted. Besides the driver of the rusty car, a further three red jackets appeared at the ambush scene. They had hidden themselves until now. The saloon's driver and passenger had no time to react. Everything had happened fast. The two red jackets manning the barrier circled the saloon, a rifle aimed at the driver and passenger. They had trained well for this operation. 'Go on, Aidan', one said.

Aidan stepped forwards. 'Get out, hands where we can see them.'

A woman and a man sat stricken in the rear seat.

'You too, Undersecretary.' He waved the barrel of his rifle in their direction. 'Now!' he screamed as the occupants hesitated.

The red jackets in the driver and front passenger seats exited with their hands above their heads. The Undersecretary fumbled with his seat belt. Once he released it, he unceremoniously clambered from the car. His companion made to follow. 'Not you, Chief Superintendent. Keep your backside where it is.' Moran sat back obediently. Despite her seniority, she had never faced an armed confrontation, and the experience was bewildering.

With their hands held in the air, the three previous occupants of the saloon were now being shunted at gunpoint towards a nearby building. 'In you get,' Aidan said, directing them to the glass entrance door. Newspaper clad the inside. The door stood unlocked, and they stumbled in with Aidan close behind.

The remaining bogus red jacket from the checkpoint climbed into the saloon to sit on the black leather seat alongside the Chief Superintendent. She nuzzled the barrel of a rifle against the Chief Superintendent's ribs. 'Good morning, Chief Superintendent Moran,' Anouk said in a falsely jaunty tone. She steadied her shaking hands. 'We're not going to have any problems with you, are we?' She forced a smile.

The other assailants pulled three red jackets from the damaged van. They were dazed, but none suffered serious injuries. 'I'll take this lot to join Aidan,' Fred said. 'We only have about three minutes left, so get these vehicles off the road sharpish.' Fred was herding the captives to the glass door as she finished the last sentence. Red jacket patrols were scheduled every ten minutes, but the team cut that time in half to account for any ad hoc Free Fliers.

Ann jogged to the rusty car's driver's seat while Rachel pulled and threw herself up into the suspended van. The engine of the car started with a splutter, and Ann drew it backwards. Its bumper tore loose with a scraping sound, and the van collapsed back onto all four wheels with a crash. Falling broken glass chimed as it scattered on the road. As the van corrected itself, Rachel lost her balance and toppled headfirst onto its front passenger seat. Her face emerged at the window just as the rusty car's engine died.

'Leave it!' Sam yelled as he dismantled the temporary checkpoint. 'Nobody will worry about it. It won't stand out as unusual here. Get the other van.'

Ann heeded his advice and jumped from the car. She crossed the road and hastily made her way down the alley. Rachel turned on the ignition of the damaged van. The engine sprang to life; the collision hadn't damaged it. She rolled the steering wheel hard to the right and circled around the rusty car. The van's flat tyres flapped in complaint as she followed Ann down the alley.

Sam turned the swivel feet of the orange plastic barriers so they could stack. He then dragged them, walking backwards, over the road and towards the glass door through which Aidan and Fred had disappeared. Slithers of debris from the collision littered the road and caught under the barriers. He kicked them aside as he went. Once he reached the door, he pushed it open with his bottom and, using his one foot as a doorstop, he hauled them through. 'How are we doing?'

'Fine, almost done,' Fred said.

The three red jackets from the van, along with the Undersecretary, sat with their backs to the far wall of the neglected room. Cable ties secured their wrists and ankles, and silver duct tape sealed their mouths shut. One red jacket had a cut on his forehead and was woozy. Blood ran down the side of his face and stained his jacket collar in a richer shade of maroon. His companions had revived. They and the Undersecretary followed Sam's movements fearfully. He leaned the barriers against the entrance door and crossed to Aidan and Fred. 'Just one more,' Fred said.

Aidan was dressing the saloon driver's wrist with an adhesive bandage. He and his companion from the saloon were undergoing a minor surgical procedure a few feet from their bound colleagues. Moments earlier, Fred had made a small incision and pulled out his microchip with tweezers. This lay on a white cloth at her feet, and a red blot marked its resting place. Aidan had soon also tied the man's hands behind him. A second clean cloth lay beside the first as Fred extracted another microchip from the remaining red jacket's wrist.

Ann burst through the entrance door. 'Time's up.' She was panting. 'We need to get going.'

'All done,' Fred said, placing the second microchip onto the unused cloth. She folded the sterile cotton fabric and held one cloth in each hand. Aidan returned from depositing the driver to join his other colleagues against the wall and then, after dressing the wound on his wrist, collected the remaining red jacket to join them.

'You take these.' Fred handed the folded cotton bundles to Sam. 'This one,' she pressed a cloth into his right hand, 'is the woman's. This one,' passing another into his left hand, 'is the man's. Got it?'

'Think so.'

'No!' she barked, with a pointing finger. 'Repeat it to me.'

Her ferocity startled him. 'Right one, woman. Left one man.'

'It's okay, Fred. He's got it,' Aidan said.

'Okay.' Fred swallowed and lowered her finger, scanning the room. 'You're driving the saloon, Sam. Make certain you and Anouk fasten your microchips well.' He nodded. She then spun, looking around. 'Where's Rachel?'

'Just finished swapping the number plates of their van to ours,' Ann said. 'We're all good to go.'

'Excellent.' Fred's thumb tapped fingers as she counted off her to-dos. Mother had agreed to let her and the others join the operation. The mission's importance grew with the chance to capture both the Undersecretary and Moran. Ann, Rachel and Sam were keen to prove themselves. But Fred joining was conditional on her staying behind with the captives. It ate her alive. 'Aidan, Sam, Ann, off you go then. Quickly!' Fred grabbed hold of Aidan as he made to leave, hugging him tight. 'Stay safe, cuz?'

Some miles away, Jimmy was in conversation when the Sibylline came. Ever since the mentor revealed his past to Jimmy, a burden lifted. The damage done by the Factory to his mentor was irreparable. But the mentor's honesty had been self-soothing and cathartic. It had led to a release of tension and a renewal of his human self. He had lived increasingly in the present and relied less on Jimmy's descriptions of experiences outside of the Factory.

The Sibylline arrived silently; the mentor was the first to sense their presence. He had been telling Jimmy about his life as a boy. He had grown up in the West Country, among rolling green hills. His description of clotted cream and cider featured large—food always did. His father was a farmer, and he grew up certain that the farm would one day be his. Then, abruptly, he stopped talking and oriented towards the cell's gate. 'Methinks we have visitors.' The mentor seemed confused and didn't move. Their arrival was as unexpected to him as it was to Jimmy.

There was whooping from below. Inmates became excited by the Sibylline's presence. An orchestra of strange noises—hooting, howling, banging and bashing—built to a crescendo, only to be smothered by a screech from within the bowels of the cell block. The Sibylline waited for a few minutes. When there was no response from either the mentor or Jimmy, one produced a key and unlocked the cell gate. He scuffled into the cell with a characteristic slouch and lifted his staff to show Jimmy.

'No, I don't understand,' his mentor said. 'The yield in your eye is still good. Methinks it's too early to take the other. It can't be time.' At first, it appeared he was rationally trying to understand why the Sibylline were visiting earlier than expected. But the tone of his voice belied desperation. He had grown reliant on Jimmy in a way that he hadn't on previous mentees.

Jimmy rubbed his hands together and fidgeted with his head strap. His mentor had always provided guidance. Yet the

Sibylline's steady staff, pointing at him, offered little choice. Jimmy slid from the top bunk until his feet touched the cold floor. He stepped towards the Sibylline when he felt the mentor's hands clasp around the other leg. 'No, no, don't go!' he said, clawing his way up Jimmy's body from the bunk.

The LED light in the centre of the cell glowed down on Jimmy and his mentor in a frail beam. His mentor was facing him, his face cast up only a few inches from Jimmy's. It was the closest he had been in the light. Jimmy had imagined him as small, old and withered. He looked anaemic, certainly thin and short. But he was not old. At most, his mentor was five years older than him. His skin was grimy and his teeth were rotten, but he had no wrinkles. 'It's not right; they can't take you,' the mentor said, grasping Jimmy by the waist.

Jimmy gently prised his mentor's hands from his sides. 'It's okay, I'll be back soon.' The mentor shook his head. Jimmy turned to follow the Sibylline from the cell, leaving him alone under the ring of light. As the gate clanged shut, Jimmy glanced back at his mentor. His face twisted with anguish. He was alone and abandoned. It broke Jimmy's heart.

'There are darker things in the Factory than even I know about, Jimmy. Remember me.' These were the mentor's last words as he backed out of the light into the black void.

The saloon and accompanying squad van had made progress. They skirted around the industrial quarter and reached the motorway. It was a crisp morning. Outside the city's heat bubble, frost covered the surrounding fields. Sam observed a person trying to dig down into the frozen soil, searching for potatoes. It was an optimistic undertaking. The constant rain forced farmers to discard potato crops. But people still searched, hoping wet rot had not decimated every tuber. If something remained, they could eat it—even manky spuds, no matter how unappetising.

'Is it on?' Sam said, looking back in the rearview mirror at Anouk, who was sitting alongside the Chief Superintendent. She had taped the microchip removed from the red jacket to her right wrist. Sam had done the same with the other man's microchip. They had used skin-coloured plasters. Sam had grumbled when he put his on. 'We're not all pink,' he had said, rolling his eyes. He was ginger-haired and had snow white freckled skin.

'Yes, it's on.' Anouk was no longer pointing the rifle at Chief Superintendent Moran. It would have been awkward trying to apply the microchip and plaster while guarding her. But the Undersecretary being held hostage by Fred motivated her acquiescence. Moran understood she would comply or risk the Undersecretary's life.

'Remember, when we get there and are scanned, make certain your sleeve covers the plaster,' Sam said.

Anouk looked at the plaster's colour against his skin tone. 'I think that's more of a you problem than a me problem.' This prompted Sam to sigh and roll his eyes. 'If it helps,' Anouk said, 'think how pissed off Aidan would be with his complexion.'

'And rightly so!'

'More to the point,' Anouk said, speaking to Moran, 'is everything clear? You understand what we need of you?'

Moran stared back at her with a deadpan expression. 'There's no way that you will get away with this. Whether it's today or tomorrow, you will be found, and you will be brought to justice.'

'The only justice is the one that you and your fascist regime will face.' Anouk sought to obscure any visible self-doubt. 'To remind you: when we reach the Factory, you will inform the authorities that you have arrived before the Undersecretary to attend to additional preparation. You are to ask that a particular inmate, James Michael Sullivan, is brought to you.' Anouk drew breath. 'You explain he is of particular scientific interest to the Bureau and that he will leave with the accompanying squad of red jackets.'

'And what will become of me?' Moran's even tone had not changed. It was hard to read.

Anouk snorted. 'I thought that part was clear. You will accompany us. If we do not return within a specified time frame, the Undersecretary will die. If you alert anyone to the truth, you and the Undersecretary will die.'

Moran didn't respond. She turned her head, gazing out the window.

'No need to get into a strop.' Anouk knew it was childish but couldn't help herself. It was the first occasion she had held power over the regime, and it was dangerously intoxicating.

They were about midway to the Factory, and in half an hour they would arrive. If all went well, she would see Jimmy soon. She crossed her fingers. Jessica could not join them as she was still under close observation. The current operation was her idea. She had expert knowledge of the Undersecretary's visit, having drawn up the itinerary herself. The risk was that things had changed in the past weeks, but the plan held. *It will work.* Jimmy and Jessica's lives depended upon the operation's success.

———◉———

As Anouk absorbed herself in thought somewhere on the motorway, Jimmy walked in the dark with his guides, weaving through the Factory's intestines. He retraced many of the steps that he had taken upon his arrival. Factory workers soundlessly shifted in the shadows. He passed machinery and supplies again.

The steel tanks, pipes and valves. Crates, barrels and boxes. Yet after a while he sensed they were taking a different route. Jimmy had gained, as all inmates do, an acute sense of direction in darkness.

The Master stood waiting for them, and his constant white glow that grew progressively larger as they neared. The movement of Jimmy's head as he walked made it look as though the Master were floating in space. As always, Sibylline stood devoted guard around him. They shepherded Jimmy to stand in front of him. His guides and the Master's guard joined to form a protective circle around them both.

The Master regarded Jimmy's manifestation before him. His clouded eyes moved in their sockets, watching a scene no one else could see. He sagged, and he looked tired for the first time. His mature white beard quivered, and his long white hair lifted slightly. He then raised his shepherd's crook above his head with one hand. His white robe fell from a thin, wiry arm and hung in a loop. He made the sign of the cross with his other hand. 'And then there was light,' he said in a cracked voice. 'Light, light, light…' echoed, and a door slid mechanically open in a burst of brilliance.

The sudden glare blinded Jimmy's functioning eye for a few moments before dark curtains descended as it adjusted. These faded into mottled grey spots and then blurred vision. Silver-grey distorted shapes ushered him through the door, which glided shut afterwards. His vision remained blurred, and a headache built. He swayed, feeling dizzy, and backed to rest against the closed door.

He waited in bewildered silence and solitude. His eye attuned to the light. It was unpleasant, so he closed it. He felt the urge to brush away a phantom grain of sand—the imagined scratching on his healthy eyeball made his eye water. He was in a tiny room, its contours revealing themselves slowly—the polished steel reflected the fluorescent light tubes above him. Only the constant humming of the tubes filled the room. A second silver-white door revealed itself in the wall. It lay opposite Jimmy, and he fixed on it with an apprehensive stare. His fate lay beyond it. It too slid open as Jimmy had expected. Light reflected off the room's polished steel interior. Movement stirred beyond, where people were waiting for him.

With the unwilling aid of Chief Superintendent Moran, the team that volunteered to extract Jimmy had gained access to the Factory. Guards and dogs patrolled the perimeter—more to keep others out than inmates in. They passed through the guarded front gates, where security scanned Moran's microchip. The crew kept their faces down or turned, avoiding the glare of a prowling facial recognition camera. While Moran was unresponsive in her interactions with the guards, it was not uncommon for Bureau officials to be indifferent and offhand to subordinates. The barrier lifted as the licence plate reader completed its duty.

Anouk and Sam accompanied Moran into the Factory's reception area after parking the saloon. The others sought parking for the van near the entrance. They passed through a body scanner, depositing weapons on a side table, before collecting them from a bored guard. At the reception desk, they were all scanned. Anouk and Sam were careful not to reveal the plasters on their wrists, but the attendant red jacket wasn't paying attention. Anouk and Sam focused on the potential for behavioural monitoring. The omnipresent threat of algorithms whirring emotionlessly was hard to shake.

Moran followed her instructions, asking that Jimmy be brought to them. The desk officer appeared surprised. He had never received a request like this and had to think about how best to arrange it. Yet he did as he was asked.

Jimmy entered, and no one was prepared. The Chief Superintendent gasped as Jimmy felt his way out of the service elevator. Its double alternating doors, one at the rear and one to the front, allowed him to enter safely from the Factory floor into its lobby. He was unrecognisable since Anouk last saw him. His ashen skin stretched impossibly thin over his skeletal frame. The once-fitting black jumpsuit stank, hanging from him like a sheet that wrapped around him twice. Filth covered his bare feet, black dirt glued beneath his long, chipped toenails. Yet it was the occucanula that provoked the most horror among the onlookers. Its metal form stuck out of his one eye as though he were a science fiction cyborg. The tissue surrounding his eye was oozing and swollen. It had part engulfed the metal structure, claiming it as its own. A clear tube of yellow liquid ran from the focal point of the occucanula—where Jimmy's pupil should have been—into a test tube strapped to his head with leather.

'Good God!' Anouk reflexively raised a hand to her mouth. Sam was similarly clasping a hand over his mouth while Moran stood with hers agape. Jimmy rooted at the elevator door until it closed behind him with a merry ping. He spun around when it did and felt over its steel surface. He was likely blind in both eyes. Anouk wanted to run to him, but the charade needed to be maintained.

Thankfully, Moran couldn't bear the spectacle any longer. 'Well, aren't you going to get him?'

Anouk sprang into action. She crossed towards Jimmy from the reception desk. The Factory's emblem of a golden eye surveyed her movements, mounted above the reception desk.

It observed tirelessly and unwaveringly. The foyer showcased industrial chic, with Corten steel panels, polished concrete floors and gleaming aluminium ducting. It hid the terror of what lay behind it in architectural niceties. She reached Jimmy, and he spun to face her as a cornered animal might. His healthy eye moved over her, searching for substance. 'Who are you? What do you want from me?' His stance carved the image of a broken body.

Jimmy would recognise her voice; speak, and give the game away. Despite his ghastly appearance and near unbearable smell, Anouk longed to soothe him. To hold him, to comfort him and tell him it would be okay. Forcing the impulse down, she took hold of his arm and led him back towards the others. He relaxed at her gentle touch and sniffed at the air as though he recognised a scent.

'I wasn't expecting you, Chief Superintendent,' the desk officer said as Anouk returned, leading Jimmy beside her.

'No. I didn't call in before coming.' Moran stepped away from Jimmy in revulsion.

'No, it's not that, ma'am.' He was confused. 'I thought Senior Superintendent Kilgore was paying a visit with Professor Brougham this morning. In fact, he should have been here before you arrived.'

Jimmy's body tensed at the mention of Kilgore. Moran put her hands on her hips. 'Was he now?'

'Yes, ma'am, that's correct.' The desk officer was uncertain if she had asked a question. The telephone on his desk rang. 'Apologies, ma'am, I'll need to get that.' He trotted back to the reception counter.

'I think we had better get a move on,' Sam said—a masterclass in understatement. He prodded Moran in the ribs, and she hesitantly obliged. Anouk's heart was pounding as she tugged on Jimmy's arm to follow.

They reached the rotating entrance doors just as the desk officer put down the handset. He called after them. 'Ma'am, that was the front gate. They just called to say that Senior Superintendent Kilgore has arrived with his guest. He will be here any moment, if you would like to wait?'

They had exited the front lobby without responding to the desk officer's invitation. It was midday, and the crisp morning had turned grey and damp. It was drizzling. They stood under a modern rectangular steel portico, near the saloon parked in a visitor bay. There were no red jackets guarding the entrance. Anouk searched for the squad van. Aidan, Ann and Rachel were supposed to wait for them. 'Where are they?' Sam breathed in agitation just as the black van, with its golden serpent insignia on its side, rounded the building.

Thank fuck! Her tension subsided and then rose at the sight of a black luxury saloon driving behind it, followed by another squad van. 'Shit!'

'Anouk?' Jimmy's voice was fragile.

She hadn't meant to speak yet. They needed to get him safely into the van. 'Yes, Jimmy, it's me, it's Anouk.' She squeezed his arm. 'But we can't talk now, Jimmy; we've got to get you away.'

'I knew you would come,' he whispered. Those words were Jimmy—trusting and warm. But he exuded something new—a calmness and a peace, despite his brittle body.

'The first van will be Aidan,' Sam said. 'VIPs always have a tail escort.' The saloon that followed the front van had one.

A drop-off layby ran alongside the portico, and they moved close to the curb. A sharp prod to Moran's back shunted her forwards; she groaned in response. The front van drew alongside them, and its side door slid open. Aidan was driving. He had wanted to accompany Anouk inside the Factory, but his recent designation as an undesirable 'immigrant' hadn't recommended it; his skin colour would raise suspicion. Ann sat in the front row and waved them in without delay. Rachel had hopped out as the door slid open, the vehicles trailing behind, and ushered Anouk and Jimmy into the van. Her eyes widened in dismay as she glimpsed Jimmy.

Moran was being cajoled into the van when Kilgore spoke. He had disembarked and stood only a few yards from them. He was pleased with himself.

'Chief Superintendent Moran, what a surprise. I hadn't expected to see you here?' he drawled. His voice was chilling.

Anouk stared back at Moran from the seat she had taken inside the van. She pointed a rifle at Moran's chest and mouthed 'no', shaking her head slowly in warning from side to side.

Moran's lips arched into a smirk. 'It's over, my girl. I told you that you'd never get away with this.'

Rachel caught Moran's smirk too. Without further thought, she wheeled around and launched herself at Kilgore. She dug the nails of her hands into his face as he reeled back in shock. Professor Brougham had just alighted from the rear passenger seat of the saloon. He hurriedly re-entered and slammed the door shut. Kilgore let out a howl of bewilderment and pain. The red jackets in his escort were stunned into inaction. They hadn't foreseen one of their colleagues launching an attack on a superior.

Moran yelled out to them, 'Do something! Stop her!' This spurred them into action. They sought to pull Rachel off Kilgore. But she had unclipped her baton, swinging back at them, hitting down on Kilgore as he lay curled on the ground, whining and protecting his head. Sam pushed Moran into the van, and Rachel glanced back, screaming, 'Go!' The red jackets were too pre-occupied to notice Moran's abduction. A red jacket removed his pistol and fired a shot. It entered under Rachel's shoulder blade. The bullet ruptured from her chest and hit the windshield of Kilgore's saloon. The glass shattered as her body slumped to the ground, the bullet having pierced her heart.

———— ◎ ————

Time passed before Kilgore regained consciousness. He flinched as a paramedic dabbed the scratches on his face with a sterilising swab. The disinfectant stung. 'They'll leave scars, I'm afraid.'

'And they taught you this where? Night school for idiots?' Kilgore was sitting against the bonnet of his black saloon. Rachel had knocked him unconscious with a final parting blow of her baton.

The paramedic was unperturbed. Kilgore's reputation preceded him. But he had a job to do. He sloshed surgical spirits onto a clean swab, adding extra, and pressed it onto an untreated scratch. Kilgore winced, sucking in air. A large bump bulged on his forehead from where Rachel had landed an aimed swing. The skin had split, but the paramedic had already cleaned and dressed this.

The squad leader from Kilgore's escort loitered a few yards away. He waited for Kilgore to resume his questioning.

'And you say that Chief Superintendent Moran was with them when they passed through security at the front gate?' Kilgore ignored the latest discomfort inflicted by the paramedic.

'Yes, sir. She left with the other squad while we were pacifying *her*.' The squad leader pointed to Rachel's lifeless body. She knelt opposite the saloon's bumper, slumped forwards, her arms trailing backwards at her sides.

'They were not a squad, you fool. How many times do I need to explain this to you? They were terrorists.' Kilgore seethed. A pain penetrated one side of his head, behind an eye. His concussion made him feel nauseous. He prodded Rachel with his foot. 'Such a loss.' *But then, loyalty was so hard to come by these days.*

'Yes, sir, I understand, sir.' Beads of sweat gathered on the squad leader's upper lip. 'It's just that the Chief Superintendent appeared to leave with them willingly.' He wasn't certain. 'And she ordered passage at the front gate.'

Moran had not gone willingly. Yet the squad leader's account offered an unexpected opportunity. One Kilgore intended not to waste.

15

Ann looked out of the rear passenger window. Rain droplets pressed against the pane as the van drove down a country road. She followed a droplet with a finger as it wound its way backwards, leaving a transparent trail on the misted window. She was weeping. Rachel had been her best friend. How could she hear her voice as if she were sitting next to her? It made no sense. The words 'gone, gone, gone…' repeated cruelly and wouldn't let go.

Chief Superintendent Moran sat rigidly next to Ann, placing her hands on her knees and holding her arms and back straight. She stared dead ahead, expressionless. Sam sat in the same row but with his back pressed against the sliding side door. He faced Moran at an angle, holding a rifle across his lap and pointing it at her. He kept his eyes fixed on her, even as the van jolted over the rutted road.

After leaving the Factory compound, no one spoke for the first half an hour. They all expected swift pursuit, but none materialised. Rachel's handiwork with the baton had seen to that—a parting gift. The musty interior of the van, mixed with the lingering smell of the Factory exuding from Jimmy, made the journey feel oppressive. It was only after they had veered onto the country road, leading off the motorway from a rest area, that their apprehension eased. They processed Rachel's selfless act, each at a different pace.

Aidan sat alone in the vehicle's front, driving. He was concentrating on avoiding the worst obstacles on the road. His attentiveness might have been mistaken for a lack of emotion. Yet he was hollow and detached. He felt guilty. Rachel had fancied him for a long time, but his feelings for her were not reciprocal. He didn't know how to respond, how to manage her attentions—it was all too intense for him. So he'd just ignored things, pretending ignorance. And now she was dead, and he could never right that wrong. He glanced in the rearview mirror.

Anouk sat in the first row behind Aidan. Jimmy was asleep, lying across the seat with his head resting on her lap. Underneath his squalor and tortured physique, he was oddly content. He dreamed again of standing on the mountain summit, looking down across a vast range of peaks. But these now lay bare, free of cloud and mist. Rivers meandered through sunlit valleys; green and inviting.

A distant smile passed over Jimmy's lips as Anouk absently combed his greasy hair with her fingers, passing over the leather head strap. She didn't mind its oily feel, or the gunk from his traumatised eye seeping into the fabric of her trousers. She was protective of him and content. What would Jimmy say when he learnt of Rachel's sacrifice? Although Rachel was not her friend, and their mutual liking of Aidan complicated things, they could have grown close. Rachel had volunteered to free Jimmy. Whatever their differences in the past, she had turned out all right; she deserved peace from this wretched world.

Aidan had turned onto an untarred farm lane several miles back. He had stopped the van and disembarked to open a corroded field gate. It swung limply on its side hinges and dragged across the ground. The terrain worsened thereafter. It would ordinarily have been impassable for the van, but the last week had been unseasonably cold. The muddy earth had frozen, and recent drizzle had done little to soften the surface. At times the van's wheels spun on a slippery patch, only to regain their traction and lurch the vehicle erratically forwards. Jimmy slept uninterrupted.

'This looks like the spot.' Aidan came to a stop alongside a tree with three orange rings painted around its lower trunk. He pulled the handbrake up with a grating noise and turned off the engine. It was abruptly silent in the van as he wound down his window. Rain pattered against the remaining leaves of early winter, clinging stubbornly to their branches. Other trees also had painted rings to show that they were mature for felling. But the one alongside the van was distinctive in having three.

'What's up, Aidan?' Anouk asked. With the van's engine off, the internal fan no longer ran, and the windows misted further. Jimmy's smell was also more intense.

'Jeez, Anouk, he stinks! He smells like a wet dog that's rolled in shit.' Aidan's outburst was unnecessary and insensitive.

Jimmy stirred and opened his eye, remaining on the borderland of sleep. Aidan didn't need Anouk's reply. 'I'm sorry.' He turned with his elbow balanced on the top of his seat, looking back at Anouk. She was stone-faced. 'I really am.' He spoke to everyone apart from Moran. 'We need to wait for Fred. This is our meeting place. Let's get out of these rags while we wait.' He plucked at his red jacket. 'Anouk, I'll give you a hand with Jimmy.' This mollified Anouk sufficiently that she nodded in agreement.

Sam slid the side door open to allow the others out. He remained with Moran, while Aidan opened the van's rear liftgate and rummaged around for cable ties in his bag. 'Here you go, Sam.' He leant over the boot towards the back seat and offered a handful of ties. Sam instructed Moran to place her wrists together. He double fastened them, too tightly, and the veins in her hands swelled. He tied her ankles soon after. It was easier and safer to do now that the van was motionless.

Ann was watching over Moran as he did so, holding a pistol to her head.

Aidan looked up from unpacking. 'Steady now, Ann. We don't want to deprive the Chief Superintendent of her trial.'

It was easy to read Ann's thoughts. She lowered the pistol as Sam finished, wavered, then holstered it at her side. Her elbow met Moran's face with a smack as she climbed over towards the door.

'These should fit, Jimmy,' Aidan said, unpacking a bundle of clothes and trainers. Jimmy was standing hunched and shivering at the verge of the gravel lane. He had said nothing since leaving the Factory. A few yards from the van, he gazed into the woods. Drizzle droplets collected on branches and fell erratically into the undergrowth. In his imagination, he was descending the mountain. Ice gave way to brown grasses with a hint of fresh shoots. In reality, a droplet collected at his nose and then fell to a fern growing alongside the lane. A bold field mouse considered him, hidden beneath a frond.

'Did you pack these?' Anouk asked.

'Yes. I didn't remember him being so thin.' Aidan paused. 'I guess he wasn't.'

'No. It wasn't a criticism. I was thanking you. It was kind of you to think of him.' Anouk stepped closer, inviting intimacy.

Aidan shifted, then blurted, 'Look, I understand that now

Jimmy's back, things between us will have to change.' It was clumsy, and he stared at the ground.

Anouk didn't understand. And then she realised—he was jealous. 'I don't think of Jimmy like that, you daft prat.' She prodded him on the shoulder. 'I'll always be there for him. But you should know by now that I've got a bit of a thing for you.'

Aidan felt foolish. Anouk raised his head gently upward with her hand. She stood on tiptoes and kissed him delicately on the lips. 'Come on, let's finish dressing?'

'Alright, Dimples.' Aidan gave a sheepish but characteristic grin.

Anouk finished dressing, brushing over the anti-fascist pin that was fastened to her hoodie just below her collarbone. She had decided that she liked it. Aidan had worn his equality pin more conspicuously too; reclaiming his family's historical struggle. He was helping Jimmy out of his befouled jumpsuit. They were standing under the shelter of the van's rear liftgate as the jumpsuit dropped to the ground, its embroidered eye facing upward, coolly observing their disobedience.

Jimmy would need cleansing and medical treatment, and getting him into fresh clothes was a good first step. He stood in an unresponsive stupor. Anouk worked from the top down, and Aidan from the bottom up. They lifted and angled his withered limbs into garments. When they had dressed him, Anouk and Aidan stepped back together to evaluate their work. The clothes hung loosely, and Jimmy was patently ill.

But Jimmy's manner changed. He unfurled his back from its hunch, and the glazed look in his healthy eye cleared. In his mind, he had reached the bottom of a valley. Cold, clear water bubbled and churned. A river ran along a grassy green bank, healthy and hopeful with the promise of warmer days to come. And Anouk and Aidan beckoned towards him from the opposite side.

'Thank you.' He spoke to them in the present.

'Oh, Jimmy.' Anouk stepped into a hug, which he returned.

Jimmy had begun his long journey from ceaseless midnight.

———⟨◎⟩———

At his eager insistence, Professor Brougham went back to the main train station after the incident at the Factory. He scrambled into the transport, having claimed urgent business at the Institute.

Kilgore's eyes followed him with disdain. He would not launch a full-scale action to liberate Chief Superintendent Moran and apprehend her abductors. Jimmy's escape irked him, but there was a longer game, and he meant to win it. Rather than order the swift pursuit of the fleeing squad van, he directed resources to the last known whereabouts of Moran's convoy as it made its way to the Factory earlier that morning. This was close to the old industrial quarter. It was an easily justified decision—he was prioritising the rescue of the Undersecretary.

It had taken two days for Kilgore's red jackets to discover five of their colleagues in an abandoned building. They had been bound but provided with water the previous day. His red jackets were useless. A damaged, dented old car lay in the middle of the road that the terrorists had used in their ambush. Other than placing a flashing sign reading 'in here', the location of the hostages was obvious.

The Undersecretary was not with them—they had taken him as a prize. Kilgore didn't care. He was replaceable. Better still, Moran's role in the affair would come under greater scrutiny. Kilgore suspected Jessica had played a central role in freeing Jimmy. She knew the Undersecretary's itinerary and must have shared it with the terrorists. She just couldn't resist that puppy-dog. Still, a strange sense of pride stirred at her success. *My success*, he corrected himself. It was he who had raised such a deliciously devious whelp.

Kilgore had arranged a rare meeting. A white flag of truce fluttered from the black luxury saloon's bonnet. He made his way to the agreed location at the quarter's boundary. Since the incident at the Factory, red jackets had prevented any illicit movement between the city and the quarter. A cordon half a mile deep was in operation. If someone farted, he'd be able to hear them.

Kilgore reached his destination. The Change had destroyed the building. Its roof was gone, and any undamaged or loose materials had long since been requisitioned for other uses. Its jagged brick walls surrounded a large open floor space, mimicking an ancient amphitheatre. Mother waited for Kilgore. A handful of Resistance members, armed, were strategically located in elevated and covered positions around her. She stood near the heart of the destroyed building.

Kilgore swept through a ragged opening in the wall closest to his parked saloon. His black coat fanned out as he strode. An explosion had ripped through the original entrance, leaving a navigable gash. 'Pamela.' He walked, arms outstretched in greeting. 'It's been far too long.'

'Jerome,' Mother acknowledged. She didn't move, and Kilgore came to a stop three yards from her. His coat caught up with him and drifted around his legs.

He took a deep breath, smiling as he did so, and surveyed the well-positioned Resistance members. His entourage had spread out behind him, remaining on the lower ground, overlooked. There was something about Mother: he needed her respect and at the same time despised her. *Bitch.* 'Well, you certainly came well prepared.'

She didn't respond.

'I was hoping to meet your lovely new wife?' The harsh scratches left by Rachel on his face had scabbed over. His cheeks were not as sallow because of the swelling.

'You wanted to speak?'

'Indeed, I do.' Kilgore broke off for a moment, formulating his words. 'The Governing Council kindly requests the immediate release and return of the former Chief Superintendent of the Bureau for Virtue and the Undersecretary for Industry. We have reason to believe that they are currently enjoying your hospitality.' He said this as if rehearsed, in one breath, to get it over with as soon as possible.

'What gives you the impression that they are with us?' Unlike most people, Mother didn't fear Kilgore.

Kilgore slouched, bored. This was not the message that he had come to deliver. 'Come, come. Let's not play tedious games, Pamela. We old friends can be honest with each other, can we not?'

Mother collected her thoughts. 'Very well. We have them. They will not, however, be returning with you. They are to stand trial for crimes against humanity, including acts such as enslavement, torture and murder.'

Kilgore didn't negotiate. This surprised Mother. He had delivered the Council's demand, and there was no personal mileage in it for him to press the issue. He flexed his hands upward, long yellowed fingernails manicured. 'You must know that it is over.' He lowered his hands and flicked them towards the industrial quarter. 'By tomorrow evening, it will no longer exist. Every man, woman and child—gone, dead.' He was enjoying himself now.

'You are welcome to try, Senior Superintendent.'

Kilgore broke out into a whooping laugh. The hyena-like

squeal-groan lasted longer than anyone cared for. Even Mother lost her steely composure.

'Are we finished here, Kilgore?'

'Almost.' He pretended to wipe away tears of mirth. 'How hope will deceive.' He again cast a look at Mother's entourage, waiting a few moments before speaking again. 'Tell you what. You have a little something of mine. My daughter, Jessica.' He was now delivering his key message. 'Give her back to her loving father, and I personally guarantee that all children will be provided with safe passage and new homes before we flatten the quarter.'

'We will not hand her over to die,' Mother said without hesitation.

'My dear Pamela, what on earth do you think of me? I'm not a monster.' His stained teeth showed through a forced smile. 'I'm her father. Naturally, I will discipline her. Harshly, I can't lie. But I can assure you, nothing more serious than that.'

Mother opened her mouth to respond when he interjected. 'I haven't even flagged her as missing. If you don't believe me, ask Moran. She has no idea about Jessica's indiscretions.'

'The answer is no, Kilgore. It is what separates us from you—the right to choose; liberty. Jessica has chosen to remain with us, and we will defend her right to do so,' Mother said. There was finality in her voice. 'We don't traffic young women.'

Mother had pressed a nerve, and Kilgore visibly stiffened. 'Very well. I am disappointed; I can't lie. But the offer remains open for as long as it takes.' His eyes narrowed. 'I wish you well, Pamela. Let us hope no one close to you meets an unfortunate end, like that poor sweet girl who gave me these.' His hand went to an aggravated cut on his face. 'There wasn't much left of her once we had dragged her dead body back to the Bureau behind my car,' he said dreamily.

This finally needled Mother, and her face drained of colour. Kilgore didn't wait for a response. Turning, he strode back towards the opening beyond which his car was waiting. He was smiling. 'Oh, and it's Chief Superintendent Kilgore now.' He waved backwards over his head in farewell.

A single snowflake drifted down to the ground and settled in the muddy tyre tracks left by Kilgore's departure.

------◎------

It was dusk, and the sun was setting on the day they rescued Jimmy. There was no sunset, just a deepening gloom as the clouds darkened.

Fred arrived, and she was relieved they were waiting. 'I'm sorry that I'm late.' She panted, moisture blooming from her mouth as she pushed through the last few yards of undergrowth. Still wearing a red jacket, she was drenched, and her wet hair was plastered over her face. She stepped over the narrow berm running the length of the lane.

'The idiot Undersecretary made a run for it. He bolted after I ditched the car near the motorway. He was bloody fast too, even with his wrists tied.' Fred skimmed over the assembled group, bunched under the rear liftgate. She ignored both Jimmy's strange appearance and Rachel's absence, still agitated by her recent experience.

She went to the rear of the van, shuffled between her colleagues, and unpacked a change of clothes. 'Damn fool ran onto the motorway, straight in front of an articulated lorry. There was nothing I could do. Not much left of him.' She shook her head and shrugged. The scene had upset her. Then, her head jerked up and around. 'Where's Rachel?' A moment afterwards, she took in Jimmy fully. 'Sweet Lord!'

Fred was fond of Rachel, but she took the news of her death in her stride. She was becoming a professional soldier. Loss was inevitable in war, and Fred had already prepared herself for this. Rachel's death affected her, but she pushed this aside. Grieving would have to wait.

Aidan and Fred drove the van down a woodsman's track and left it a few hundred yards from the lane. They cut branches from a nearby yew tree and laid these over the vehicle to offer camouflage. The others were waiting for them on the lane when they returned. It was deep dusk now, and the temperature was falling. It was no longer raining, but everything felt damp, including their new set of clothes. Sam unbound Moran's ankles and taped her mouth shut.

'I think we're all set.' Fred counted the rucksacks that they were lugging. These were squeezed into the rear of the van. No one knew what they contained, apart from her. Only Moran and Jimmy had nothing to carry. Aidan had found a fallen branch, and he had fashioned it into a walking stick for Jimmy. A penknife clipped to the side of one rucksack proved useful for this. Anouk remained at Jimmy's side to offer support if needed. 'Off to the east we go.' Fred took the first step.

Nobody followed. 'East?' Anouk asked. The others were puzzled too. 'Aren't we heading back to the city, to the quarter?'

Fred stopped mid-step and turned. She forgot only she had been briefed on the next stage of their escape. Operation Motion was a controlled secret; only a handful of key Resistance members knew its full scope. 'You don't want to return to the quarter any time soon.' Fred was ahead of the group. She hooked her thumbs under the shoulder straps of her rucksack. 'It won't be pretty there for a while. I barely got out—the entire boundary with the city is cut off. Red jackets are crawling everywhere.'

Sam looked at Ann and shrugged. Aidan cast an uncertain

glance towards Anouk. She spoke for them all. 'But what of the others? Everyone still stuck in the quarter?' She wouldn't abandon them. The quarter had become her home. The vibrant mix of its inhabitants and its idiosyncratic functioning felt familiar and safe.

'Mother's there; she has it in hand.' Mother exuded gravitas and competence. And although she was most often serious, she also displayed empathy and warmth. She was a leader who inspired trust.

Buoyed by this information, the group pressed on. Their destination was a mystery, but one that could wait. They had tarried too long at the meeting point, and Fred led them from the lane onto a woodland path.

Near the path they reached a mass grave. It pre-dated the Change by a year or two. Instead of human remains lay the charred skeletons of Jacks, or Hijacks, as they had commonly been called. As the world descended into chaos, this first generation of humanoid robots bore the ire of a frightened population. Angry mobs blamed them for job losses they had supposedly 'hijacked', rounded them up, and destroyed them en masse. They lay dismembered in a shallow grave. The group stood silently before the grand spectacle of scapegoating, then pressed on. Only Aidan lingered thinking of *Heinrich Heine's* prophetic words: '...they will also ultimately burn people.'. He shook his head.

The dense trees and low-lying vegetation in the dingy surrounds forced the group to stop after an hour as plotting a safe route proved too difficult. Night fell; the icy conditions of the past weeks returned. Sam made a small fire close to the base of an ancient oak. The smoke was invisible at night, and by morning any residual smouldering would travel up the trunk and dissipate among the tree's branches. After collecting a supply of dead wood, they huddled together as close as the flames would allow. The fire hissed and spat from the wet, but provided some relief from the biting cold. Moran sat exiled and bound to a neighbouring tree. She refused to speak, which was a blessing. She had accepted a spare sleeping bag, in which she was wrapped.

There were only basic rations, waterproofs, sleeping bags, a first aid kit, and a few essential tools. But they found comfort sitting next to each other, pressed together in a semicircle, and tucked into their sleeping bags. Ann's teeth chattered. Fred took pity on them. 'Bugger it!' She produced an old bottle of whiskey. She had brought it from the quarter and was saving it for a special occasion. They took turns passing the bottle around, taking one sip at a time. It burnt warmly down their throats and into their chests.

The light of the flames shapeshifted against the knotted bark of the old oak. It was cold, and their situation was perilous. Yet they entered a different world. A world where the Change hadn't happened—where people hadn't surrendered hope over despair. They sat, as the young and carefree had done since time immemorial, sharing stories and laughing well beyond what was sensible. Anouk took another sip of whiskey, and her gaze moved over her friends. Jimmy sat by her side. He said nothing but seemed peaceful. Aidan had finished imitating Kilgore and was laughing hardest at his own joke. Fred, Ann and Sam were laughing at Aidan. Anouk knew what she was fighting for, and it was a future worth any sacrifice. Rachel had believed it too.

Nobody slept much. They kept one another company until the chilly dawn broke. A few rays of sunlight shone through the naked canopy, luring them under false pretences to leave their sleeping bags. Once out, only movement kept them warm. They packed the few items that they had removed from their rucksacks the evening before and pushed on along their path. Fred's handheld compass served as their guide.

They stayed under woodland cover, crossing fallow farmland once. Other people were few. They stumbled upon a group of wretched spritters who had melted silently away, red-eyed and hopeless, reclaiming their invisibility. They also found a farmer and son working a small patch of ground, having faith that a winter crop would take root. The pair's eyes followed the travellers as they walked on by. They offered no greeting and resumed their thankless work once they were certain danger had passed. The group stopped for a few rest breaks over the course of the day, drinking fresh stream water now and then. Jimmy tired often and needed help. Aidan looped Jimmy's arm around his neck and supported him where he could. Moran dragged her feet, Sam encouraging her once with a hard whack across the back of her legs. She kept up after that.

By evening they had reached the last leg of their journey. Someone had left an estate car at the junction of two gravel roads for them. A World War Two pillbox stood a few yards to the side, smothered in dense ivy. The car was parked out of immediate sight, tucked behind the pillbox on a stony slope where struggling grass grew in patches. Fred got into the driving seat with Ann sitting beside her. Anouk and Aidan sat in the rear seat, Jimmy between them. Sam volunteered to sit in the large boot with Moran and the backpacks. He constructed a comfortable seat with them and watched over her. They perfected the art of glowering at each other. Two plain loaves of bread waited for them in the boot. They all tucked into them as soon as the car's engine started. Displaced gravel shot out from under the tyres as the car fought its way back up the slope and onto the road.

They drove all night, creeping along country back lanes. Fred knew where she was going, having frequently left the relative safety of the quarter and travelled around the country on secret business for Mother. She had trekked this route before.

They travelled with the car's headlights off. Anouk clenched the seat in front of her, nails biting into its upholstery. It brought back frightening memories of her and Jessica fleeing with their father. But on this occasion, their escape was successful. In the early morning, they approached their destination. The town, renamed Free Port by the Resistance, was the easternmost settlement in the country. It was on low-lying ground, leading to the coast. Hills rose in the north, and marshland stretched to the west. They met no red jacket patrols. There was no one in sight. But they sensed that eyes watched them from the town. She and Fred were awake as it started to snow.

Two days later, and an inch of snow covered the old industrial quarter. It crunched under Kilgore's feet as he stepped from his car. Apart from the tracks made by armoured personnel carriers and two tanks, the white blanket of ice crystals lay undisturbed.

The Bureau had assembled a small army to subdue the quarter. As they moved through barricades and stormed strategically important outlying buildings, they realised that the Resistance and the inhabitants had evacuated. There was nobody and nothing left. People had stripped the place, taking anything of value.

Kilgore shook his head in disbelief. *How did they do it?* Swivelling on his heel, he studied the old brick buildings. An office block stood prominently ahead. Intelligence reports showed Mother had used it as her command centre. He walked towards it, all sounds dampened by the snow.

It was quiet as he pushed the revolving door. It was oiled

and rotated without a sound. The entrance was clean but empty. There were five doors. Signs indicated that the double doors on his right led to the 'cafeteria', three doors on his left led to the 'ladies', 'gentlemen' and 'stairs'. 'Conference hall' doors lay in front of him. Kilgore approached them. The heels of his black polished shoes clipped on grey ceramic tiles. He swung the doors open with both hands and saw the white card. It was upright on the table at the far end of the hall. Chairs were stacked to the sides so that the table on a raised platform and the card stood out. It drew Kilgore forwards. As a black-clothed spectre, he glided across the hall and stepped up onto the platform. He leant over the table and picked up the card with thin, pale fingers. It was addressed to him—'Kilgore'. He recognised Jessica's handwriting. He opened it and read:

None of us knows how this will end. But all of us know it will end. The only certainty in life is that it is better to live in hope than in despair, in unity rather than division; to love rather than hate. There is more good in us than bad; of this I am certain. And when we meet the end, whatever that may be, may we hold our heads high and say that it was a life worth living for all of Earth's creatures.

~ Maggie Sullivan ~

It was an extract from Jimmy's aunt's last speech, given the day the Blood Martyrs killed her. Kilgore recognised it. He had been at the Unity Marches undercover. He crumpled the card in his hand and let it fall to the floor. Operation Motion was drawing to a close across the country. War would soon follow.

16

A gust of freezing night air pushed the window open, banging it against the adjacent wall. The curtains billowed as Mother stood up to force the window closed, holding a blanket draped across her shoulders tight at her neck. She bolted it closed, returning to a gate-leg writing table, and sat on a wooden chair that squeaked. She stared at the flickering candle flame, deep in thought, before turning back to the letter she had finished composing. Her handwriting was elegant, with flowing refined lettering.

Dear Father,

I am sorry that it's been so long since I put pen to paper. I trust all of our official updates have reached you in good health.

You will no doubt have already received news that Operation Motion was a success. Thank goodness! All those years of doubt and your stubbornness seem to have paid off.

I remember my scepticism that the scale of our—your— ambition was possible. Why did I believe that the Governing

Council's order to abandon swathes of our country and its people to the fate of the rising sea was justifiable? I can only think the dreadful recent events of the Change clouded my judgement. Thank you for telling me otherwise. How we learn through our mistakes!

The Council's judgement that it was too costly to renew and extend coastal defences when only a few places could be saved was wrong. Their misjudgment has been our gain.

The water came, but we persevered against all odds. We extended coastal defences where they failed, and we brought back law and order in the vacuum of their cowardice. We should be proud.

It pains me we couldn't save it all, but a few beautiful villages and towns of Suffolk, Norfolk and Cambridgeshire survive, offering sanctuary to the people. When I feel low, I think of all the lives we have saved rather than those lost, and I hear Maggie reminding us of Victor Hugo—'To love, or to have loved, is enough. Demand nothing further. There is no other pearl to be found in the shadowy folds of life.' We inhabit those shadowy folds, you and I.

Yet, for all our faults and failures, I still believe our cause is just, reflected in the actions of our enemy. In their foolishness, the Council treated our new home like all other dumping grounds for undesirables. How naïve to surrender Free Port to us—their most important hub for the export of shimmer. Only their arrogance led them to believe our running operations provided them with a timeless alibi. From today it is ours and ours alone—well done!

I will write again soon, I promise. There are important things I must tell you, but they will have to wait.

With all my warmest wishes,
Mother

Mother leant back in her chair and sighed, picking up the pages, reflecting on their contents. She folded them, running her thumb and index finger along the crease, before sliding them into an envelope. 'Forgive me, Arthur.' She placed the letter on the table and blew the candle out.

———— ◎ ————

The next morning, Anouk leant against a thick metal rail. Snow had accumulated on the wind-bearing side. She was standing on top of an enormous concrete sea wall. It stretched to the south of the harbour and to its north. The Resistance had likewise fortified the harbour wall. The reason they had involved themselves in the trade of shimmer was clear. Fred suggested the small income accrued through sales was used to support the destitute and undesirable. This was partially true. Mother's explanation that the funds allowed the Resistance time to organise and prepare was also an understatement. The Resistance had funded the wide development of thriving and increasingly self-sufficient communities nestled within the growing expanse of marshland. They had achieved energy independence from the vast floating offshore wind farms in the east.

Anouk had wrapped herself in a parka from the starter kit for new arrivals. She zipped the faux fur-lined hood under her chin, fastening it in place over her head, shivering as an icy blast of wind from the North Sea found its way through seams. It was snowing heavily as sea spray stung her eyes. Anouk and the others had arrived at Free Port in time before blizzard conditions arrived. They were one of the last groups to enter the town before the weather deteriorated. There were over three feet of snow already.

Operation Motion had been triggered two weeks prior to

their arrival. It signalled the Resistance's final strategic retreat from all major centres. The slow relocation of people and resources to the east had taken place over many years. Authorities either failed to notice it or dismissed it as irrelevant. As long as red jackets met quotas during scheduled pickings, the Bureau paid little attention to undesirables crossing the countryside to a long-abandoned watery wasteland.

Operation Motion had raised the risk of alerting the Bureau to potential trouble—that something bigger was afoot. It evacuated most of those who remained in urban quarters. Many people travelled east over a short period. Sometimes, local Bureau superintendents became suspicious of the greater than usual movement of people and hampered their progress. But most times, small groups travelling at night, across remote routes, had evaded suspicion and harassment. The scale of the operation had escaped notice; it had been a success.

Not all people had come to the east. A few remained where they were. Some were old or infirm; others were tired of running. They were now at the mercy of the Bureau. Some had yet to arrive, the weather hindering their withdrawal. Most of them had taken shelter in rural safe houses and would make their way when they could. The large majority of those who remained did so clear-eyed and consciously. They were the army of sleeper cells planted throughout the country—in cities, towns, villages and hamlets—awaiting orders.

Anouk made her way down a steep flight of slippery steps, leading from the top of the sea wall to a street below. The biting wind eased behind the shelter of the wall. She had become restless within the confines of the accommodation that she and Aidan were now sharing. He had suggested that she get fresh air. *There's fresh and then there's frigging freezing*, she thought sullenly, pushing her ungloved hands deeper into the pockets of her parka. The view from the wall was impressive, but she didn't need to see it twice.

She reached street level and walked down the road abutting the harbour, slipping on compacted ice. Her arms flung out, but she remained on her feet. Snow had been an increasingly rare event in New Albion, replaced by even further rain. The novelty delighted Anouk, but it wore off quickly. She continued down the road and turned right, passing rows of Georgian terraces painted in soft pinks, blues and yellows, before heading back to the studio apartment allocated to them upon arrival. It was located above an old shoe store on the high street. Although the original sign remained, the red-painted '70% discount' stencilled on the window had faded; officials now used the space as a registration office for newcomers. Anouk and Aidan had been helping at the office for the two weeks since reaching Free Port. Compared with accommodation in the industrial quarter, their new apartment was comfortable. It felt light, and someone had painted the walls. It was sparsely but adequately furnished. She reached their door on the high street. Her fingers were numb with cold, and she struggled to manipulate the key into place. The door banged open onto a narrow corridor, aided by a blast of polar air and a flurry of snowflakes.

Anouk grumbled as she entered the studio apartment from a short and curved flight of stairs, winding from the corridor. 'Lazy bugger.' Aidan was still tucked up in bed, and he had fallen asleep again. They had both slept an unusual amount since arriving. The cold weather and long winter nights didn't help, making everyone feel like hibernating. The expedition to free Jimmy had also taken a greater toll than expected. They were all tired.

Anouk unzipped her parka and hung it over one of the two chairs at a small table. She unlaced her boots—they still had snow caught in the ribbed soles. She thumped them onto the mat and left them there to dry, stripping out of her remaining clothes and letting them drop to the floor. It was too cold to fold them neatly. She slipped naked into bed beside Aidan, who was lying on his side.

Anouk pressed herself against his warm body. He moaned as she snuck an icy hand under his T-shirt and over his toned stomach. She wove a leg over his and snuggled against his back. Anouk adored Aidan's smell. Nestling her face into the nape of his neck, she breathed in his scent. She felt aroused and pressed her pelvis against his thigh. She waited a moment, hoping that he might read the signs, and when he didn't move, she reached down into his underwear.

'So you're not that fast asleep.' Anouk sat up and turned Aidan over. He smiled with his eyes still closed. Anouk enjoyed having sex with Aidan. He was a considerate lover, always letting her finish first. *It helps that he can keep stiff*, she thought, as she removed his boxer shorts and straddled over him. She guided him in with a hand behind her back and moved down. Aidan opened his eyes, gazing at her face, and traced Anouk's spine with his middle finger from the nape downward. She shivered and arched her lower back in response, applying satisfying pressure. Leaning backwards, she took hold of the duvet with one hand, the fingertips of the other resting on his flat stomach. Anouk covered her shoulders with the duvet and then slid forwards to lie on top of Aidan's warm and inviting body, savouring the feeling of his legs between hers as she moved them backwards.

Their sex was energetic and intense. They were new to each other, and everything they tried carried anticipatory excitement and a shared thrill in exploring the borderlands of taboo. It was the same thrill that had led them both to shimmer.

When they had finished, they lay on their backs breathing

heavily, staring at the ceiling. 'It's kind of funny, isn't it?'

'What is, Dimples?'

'Sex. It's weird. Two people rubbing their bits together until, well, they get a muscle spasm.'

Aidan mulled over Anouk's observation for a while. 'I see what you mean, but I don't like to overthink it.' He placed an arm behind his head. 'It feels good. Does it need to be anything more than that?'

'Guess not.' Anouk pulled the duvet over her exposed shoulders. She wanted to add, 'Well, it can mean something more if it's with someone special.' But she knew Aidan wasn't commenting on their relationship specifically. There was no point in arguing. She was falling for Aidan, and he seemed to feel the same. Her mind wandered to Jimmy and Jessica.

Anouk hadn't put two and two together. More than civic duty motivated Jessica's concern and interest in Jimmy when she first appeared at the quarter. She had fallen madly in love with him. Aidan had laughed at first when Anouk had mentioned her hunch. 'You don't say!' In hindsight, Jessica's feelings for Jimmy were obvious back then, and even more so now.

They had admitted Jimmy to a small but surprisingly well-equipped medical clinic as soon as they reached Free Port. Jessica had barely left his side since. Doctors successfully removed his occucanula and quelled the eye infection with antibiotics. There was some talk of having to remove the eye entirely. Thankfully, they didn't have to, though he would never see from it again. It was already turning an opaque white. But Jessica's doting on Jimmy seemed to work. He was putting on weight, and a healthy flush had returned to his skin. His mind would take longer to heal than his body, if ever it did. Yet he talked when necessary and smiled at jokes. His dry sense of humour was gone, and Anouk missed it.

At first, Anouk had felt jealous. She had just got her best friend back and her sister appeared from the dead. But Jimmy and Jessica engrossed themselves in each other and spent more time together than with her. It seemed unfair to begin with. She had learnt of the Factory's horror and trauma, and Jessica's fight for survival. Kilgore's harsh disciplinary regime and increasing sexual interest in her had left hidden scars. She was grateful they had found each other. It couldn't have been better if she'd tried. Her sister, her best friend—*perfect. It's perfect.*

'We'd better get up.' Aidan threw the duvet aside and let cold air in. 'It's lunchtime.'

The chill disturbed Anouk's reverie. 'Oi, it's bloody freezing.' Anouk tried to grab the duvet back.

Aidan snatched it from her reach. 'Mm...' he rumbled appreciatively, assessing her naked form.

'Yeah, you'll be lucky to get any again after that, mister.' Anouk begrudgingly stood to look for her clothes; she remembered dropping them somewhere.

'I would say keep your panties on, but you seem to have permanently lost them.'

Anouk grabbed a pillow and flung it in his direction. It missed and hit a mug off the table. 'Take that grin off your face immediately, Aidan Bekker!' She pointed an impish warning finger at him.

Aidan farted by mistake. 'Oops.' He covered his mouth in mock surprise, still grinning. It was nice to laugh despite everything.

———— ◎ ————

Across the icy marshes and further south, Kilgore entered an establishment for the well-heeled. It was his first official meeting as Chief Superintendent of the Bureau for Virtue since displacing Moran. It was a rare occasion on which he deemed the colleagues with whom he was meeting worthy. The Governing Council had scheduled a full emergency meeting for later that afternoon. He, together with his counterpart, the Chief Superintendent of the Bureau Against Vice, had been called for a pre-meeting at the Savoy. By the time Kilgore arrived, their bosses and ministerial appointees—the Secretaries of State—were already ensconced in high wingback chairs in the Beaufort Bar. Its jet-black and gold décor reminded him of his Bureau's headquarters, although the bar was more lavishly appointed. To Kilgore's great satisfaction, the corresponding Undersecretaries of State, one of whom was his direct line manager, had not been invited to attend. He was meeting the big players.

The Chief Superintendent of the Bureau Against Vice, Mortimer Ulysses, was speaking. He had ordered cognac on the rocks, as the Secretaries of State had already done, and was swirling it in his glass as he spoke. The ice cubes chimed against the crystal. 'Gentlemen, give me a week and I'll flush the terrorists from their swamp.' He raised a cigar to his lips and puffed on it with an assured smile between pink round cheeks. Kilgore didn't like him. It wasn't his naked ambition or his mediocrity, but the propensity to overstep his remit. While Kilgore's Bureau for Virtue co-ordinated efforts across local law enforcement agencies, the Bureau Against Vice handled national enforcement. The responsibilities of each Bureau were purposefully ambiguous, leading to competition between them; a technique of control adopted by the Governing Council for all State apparatus. Mortimer had assumed that the unexpected mass movement across counties, of undesirables to the east, fell within his responsibilities. Kilgore sat and listened. He waited to hear more before correcting him.

'The policy thus far endorsed by the Governing Council is clear.' Giles McGovern was the Secretary of State for Virtue—Kilgore's boss. He was a thin, pale man, similar to Kilgore, but with piercing, perceptive blue eyes. 'It will never be possible to subdue all dissent. We therefore control it, mould it to our purposes. Visible discipline and punishment discourage, shimmer dulls and dilutes, and any remaining resistance justifies the status quo. We provide security and relative peace for the citizenry's acquiescence.'

Ogilvy Preston, the Secretary of State Against Vice, leaned in. 'It is a policy that has served your Ministry extremely well, Giles.' He pointed with his glowing cigar. 'But it is time for a change of direction.'

Mortimer nodded in agreement with his boss.

Ogilvy continued, 'The terrorists are organising, and they pose an increased threat. The botched affair at the Factory and the capture of two senior party members and subsequent death of one testify amply to this.' Looking at Kilgore, he ran a finger over his cheek, suggestively mirroring the site of the red scabbed welts on his face. Kilgore shifted in his seat. He took a sip from his freshly served glass of cognac—a helpful distraction. The implied criticism of his Bureau's handling of the Factory affair was unsettling. He had shifted blame onto Moran, but the stain of failure lingered—he had brought none of the perpetrators to justice.

Mortimer sensed Kilgore's vulnerability and sought to exploit it. 'I agree fully, Secretary.' He nodded sycophantically. 'It is a great shame that the Bureau for Virtue could not apprehend the suspects who were involved in the abduction of party members and the escape of the inmate from the Factory.' He paused and stared at Kilgore. 'If achieved, it may have reassured the Council that their existing policy towards terrorists was sound.

But now...'

Kilgore interjected in a sibilant and crisp voice that muzzled argument. 'Yes, Moran's involvement was quite unfortunate. Who would have known?' He displayed a tight smile as he continued. 'But I am not one to disown responsibility. Far from it.' He raised his hands in feigned capitulation. 'We have learnt from our mistakes; we are pivoting.' Kilgore itemised additional measures undertaken on his fingers. 'Public disciplinary spectacles have increased fourfold. You may have seen the flogging taking place in Trafalgar on your way here. And we are close to coming to an agreement with the Smugglers' Guild in assuming responsibility for shimmer sales now that the terrorists have reneged on our arrangement.'

Mortimer appeared ready to counter, but Kilgore pressed on. The conversation needed redirecting. 'But this is surely all old news to you, gentlemen. I would hate to bore you,' Kilgore said with a slow wave of his hand. 'The Chief Superintendent is correct.' He cast a triumphant smirk at Mortimer. 'Attention must now fall on national priorities—how the terrorists could group in such numbers in the east and what on earth will be done about it?!'

Mortimer realised Kilgore had outplayed him. He eased out of his belligerence and leaned back in his chair. 'Kilgore, my dear fellow, there is no need to be defensive. We are, after all, on the same side, one team.' He drew deeply on his cigar and blew a plume of smoke to obscure his visible irritation.

'It would seem that we are agreed,' Ogilvy, the Secretary of State Against Vice, said. 'At least mostly.' He deferred to Giles' differing opinion over national policy by inclining his head. 'I will recommend to the Governing Council that a battalion of red jackets be sent to liberate the east. Free Port is the most accessible town, and we have reports that the terrorists' current leadership is gathered there. We need to get this thing under control, gentlemen. Our markets on the Continent are getting jittery. We have until now represented a paragon of stability to our neighbours.' He stood with his hands on his portly stomach. 'And under no circumstances are you to use bombardment. It will have to be a ground assault, Mortimer. I don't care how many red jackets you lose. They are holding scientists from Project Spark hostage. We need them alive.'

⎯⎯⎯◎⎯⎯⎯

Jessica and Mother left the old police station where the Resistance headquartered in Free Port. It was busy inside, as were all indoor spaces in the town. People congregated away from the cold. Free Port had had a population of seventy thousand people prior to the Change. It now accommodated a hundred and forty thousand refugees and Resistance members. The cold made congestion obvious; indoors, in overcrowded, sweaty spaces. A woman bumped into Jessica as they walked to the entrance. She half-turned and apologised before wedging towards the reception counter.

'Don't mind her. She's one of our scientist guests; always in a flap.' Bodies pushed and thronged. 'It will get better.' Mother twisted her shoulder to avoid another collision. 'We're still struggling to allocate accommodation. People will have to share, but there will be enough for all.'

Jessica frowned, eyes distant. Mother's words drifted. 'She had no idea that I was here.'

'Sorry, dear?'

'Moran. She didn't know that I'd deserted.' Jessica hesitated, correcting herself. 'She hadn't a clue that I'd escaped.'

Mother had requested that Jessica meet with Moran that

morning. She had explained that they hoped to extract additional information from her. In reality, Mother wanted to find out whether Moran knew of Jessica's escape. Kilgore's words came back to her. 'If you don't believe me, ask Moran. She has no idea...'

'Yes. I must say that I was surprised too.' Kilgore had claimed not to have officially flagged Jessica's desertion, but Mother hadn't believed him. Yet it was true—*Moran knows nothing. Kilgore's pride is dented, and he believes only Jessica's capture and subjugation will suffice.* An official record of her desertion would disallow this. *What a fragile little man.*

They exited the police station and walked along a cleared path, snow heaped on either side. 'What will become of her?' Jessica asked, but she knew the answer already.

'Well, she has been fairly tried.' Mother sighed. 'She was found guilty of a range of capital crimes. So, she'll hang.' It was not snowing, but the air was heavy, expecting more.

Moran was guilty of the crimes she was accused of. *All the pain, all the killing*—it was enough to last a lifetime, and Moran swinging from a rope was repugnant. 'Will it be done in public?'

Mother stopped walking and turned towards Jessica. 'No, we don't do that, dear.' Jessica's recent conversation with Moran from behind a one-way mirror said enough. Moran had provided Jessica with some protection from Kilgore's worst excesses. 'Hilary Moran will be offered some dignity in death. It will be done behind closed doors.' Mother regarded Jessica. 'You don't owe her anything, you know. She stood by and allowed Kilgore to adopt you. She knew what sort of man he is.'

Jessica's throat tightened. She moved on, spurring Mother back into a walk. 'I understand that. But it will be nice to live in a world without hanging.'

Mother didn't respond. She agreed. It was yet another

compromise she had to make along the Resistance's path to victory. Jessica understood the idea of resistance. She had perfected the art through minor acts of defiance while under Kilgore's control—a deleted file here, silently mocking him there. It taught her how to survive and gave her strength. But the Resistance's need to have justice done and seen was different. It called for moral concessions.

Jessica and Mother walked. They were meeting the others shortly. Mother had waited until Jimmy was well enough to join the meeting. Jessica's conversation with Moran was the ultimate piece of the puzzle before this could proceed. The streets were empty apart from the odd volunteer who was shovelling snow off pavements. There was no grit, and constant clearing was necessary. 'Here we are,' Mother said as they reached the library. It was one of the few public buildings still in its original use. Mother had selected this venue as it had some comfortable meeting rooms and was less threatening than the police station.

It was full but quiet. Despite the changed reality of New Albion, the library still commanded hushed voices. Mother led Jessica in through a solid oak door. The meeting room had blinds drawn across its glass-panelled frontage. Jessica saw Jimmy first as she entered through the doorway. He was wearing his silver chain and pendant again. She crossed over to sit beside him behind a large conference table. Smiling as she passed Anouk, she squeezed her shoulder in greeting. Aidan was sitting next to Anouk. 'Why is it that the Walker sisters are always late?' He rolled his eyes. Fred was sitting opposite him and gave his ankle a sharp kick. 'Ow!' He doubled over to assess the damage.

Mother gave them both a jaded expression from the door. 'Aidan, Fred, a far more sensible question is why do you two both revert into silly teenagers every time that you're together?'

'Because he's my cuz. And, being his elder and intellectual

superior, it's my duty to keep him in line.' Fred winked at Aidan. The others, apart from Aidan and Mother, laughed. He was still grimacing and rubbing his ankle.

Mother took her seat at the head of the table and waited until the laughter died. Aidan was still fussing, bent over, when she spoke. 'Thank you all for coming.' She sounded formal given the context, and Fred picked up that Mother was apprehensive. This was uncommon, and it worried her. 'I've caught up with all of you since you returned, including Ann and Sam, who aren't with us today. First, let me begin by saying again: well done! You all displayed the most incredible bravery. We will, of course, also never forget Rachel's sacrifice.' She paused, offering a moment for reflection. The room was silent. 'Her sacrifice and your bravery saved two lives.' She glanced at Jimmy and Jessica. 'Jimmy, welcome again. We have had very interesting, if not disturbing, conversations about your time at the Factory. You are a remarkable young man. Your aunt, my friend Maggie, would have been very proud of you.' Jimmy was sitting closest to Mother, and she leant forwards and placed her hand over his as she spoke. 'Jessica, you have proven yourself over the last few weeks, and I hope you'll consider being inducted into the Resistance.' Jessica nodded. She hoped so too.

Mother sat for a moment, considering Jessica and Jimmy. She weighed continuing. 'I have a favour to ask. And I don't ask it lightly.' She then addressed Anouk and Aidan. 'You'll remember that Fred and I told you of our plans to destroy the Institute for Human Enhancement.' They nodded. 'We thought until recently that this alone would be a victory. It is, as you know, responsible for leading research into shimmer. Its destruction, together with our no longer selling shimmer for the Governing Council, would send a powerful signal that we intend to disrupt the State's primary source of income and control.' Anouk and

Aidan nodded again. 'And there's no use pretending that they haven't told you this already.' Mother cast a glance towards Jimmy and Jessica. Their smiles were confirmation enough.

Mother would have chastised Anouk and Aidan for their imprudence. But now was not the time. 'My conversations with Jimmy revealed an extraordinary secret that the State has been at pains to hide. The Institute discovered how to produce shimmer synthetically. It is, according to Jimmy's source, both cheap and easy to produce and does not require human subjects.' She stopped to gauge everyone's reaction to this information. They looked astonished, but they had not understood its full significance. 'The importance of this cannot be understated. If we can get our hands on the formula for, let's call it synthetic, we could not only disrupt the Governing Council's strangle hold on the shimmer trade, but also destroy it!'

No one spoke at first. They thought through what Mother had said. A few people walked past the meeting room. Aidan's lips twitched. He pushed his seat backwards, and it scraped on the floor. 'Are you suggesting that we, the Resistance, steal the secret of how to make shimmer synthetically, produce it, and then sell it ourselves?'

Mother gave a qualified nod. She guessed what the next question would be.

It came from Anouk. 'But how would we be better than the Governing Council? We would just replace them as both the producers and sellers of a fucked-up drug? Why would we do that?'

'I'll answer your question, Anouk. However, before I do, let me finish in asking my favour?'

'Go on,' Anouk said. She hadn't realised that there was more to Mother's request. Her mouth felt dry.

'I won't beat around the bush. There is no easy way to ask

this.' Mother winced. 'We need Jessica to deliver Jimmy to the Institute.'

Air exploded from Jessica as if someone had punched her in the gut.

'We have learnt that Professor Brougham, who heads the Institute, would do almost anything to examine Jimmy's high productive potential of occudorphin. We also know that Kilgore has not logged Jessica as a deserter. She could legitimately deliver Jimmy to Brougham. He wouldn't expect a thing. This would provide an opportunity to steal the formula for synthetic.'

'Absolutely not!' Jessica rose to her feet. 'How could you ask anything more of Jimmy? Shame on you, after all that he has gone through.'

'Hold on,' Jimmy said. He softly took hold of Jessica's hand. She regarded him in astonishment but trusted him completely, sitting down gradually again. Mother shifted in her seat, and the others sat aghast. Jessica's unfamiliar outburst and Jimmy's calm intervention were difficult to absorb alongside Mother's request. 'Please finish.'

'Thank you, Jimmy.' The conversation would have ended then and there if it were not for him. 'You have been asked to attend this meeting because I know that if Jimmy and Jessica agreed to my request, you would all insist upon going too.' Mother regarded Fred with concerned eyes. Her personal sacrifice in making the request was putting Fred's life in potential danger. She knew Fred would never leave Aidan's side.

'And there is one last thing.' Mother closed her eyes. 'If you're successful, you will need to take the formula to Iceland.'

'Iceland! Are you crazy? Why the hell would we go to Iceland? There's nothing there. It's even colder there than here!' Anouk's eyes widened, staring at Mother as though she had lost her mind.

'Because, Anouk,' Mother opened her eyes, 'it is the only democratic country left in Europe. It is also where we have the means to decipher the formula, and Father already leads our efforts there.'

'Well, then, tell him to bloody well come and get it himself.'

'I could do that.' Mother tapped the table. 'But he's not just the Father of the Resistance, Anouk. He's your and Jessica's father too.'

The stunned silence gave way to a deeper, frozen shock.

———◎———

Against Kilgore's advice, Mortimer, the Chief Superintendent of the Bureau Against Vice, ordered his red jackets to lay siege to Free Port. It was mid-winter, and snow and ice prevented any significant offensive manoeuvre. Kilgore's colleague and rival was in charge of the operation. He was keen to show his burning patriotism by committing his forces as soon as possible.

'Bloody fool,' Kilgore said aloud, as he surveyed Free Port from their encampment. The narrow strip lay west of the land that allowed road access to the town. It was folly. The road was impassable because of the thick snow, and it would be until spring. Nobody came or went from the town. Patrols going out in the icy cold was a meaningless exercise. It served no purpose other than for show. He didn't care about the freezing red jackets or about his fellow Chief Superintendent. They could go to hell for all he cared. He did, however, care about what the town concealed.

Kilgore stared into the distance. The outlines of buildings emerged from the winter cheerlessness. A wind turbine was visible against the horizon. Its blades chased the strong coastal gale. Jessica and Jimmy had found sanctuary in the town. He knew more than that—their shared address, the work they had been allocated, and that Jessica was no longer a virgin.

'You've got to give it to puppy-dog; even with one eye, he makes a bloody nuisance of himself, pissing all over the place. And how much do you want for all this information?' Kilgore asked, turning away from the town to face the informant, who was curiously looking over their shoulder.

'Only one thing,' she said. 'I want them both dead.' Ann had bet her life on revenge.

17

The Family gathered at their headquarters in the High Town, sitting on the cliffs above the sea. Despite the five-metre increase in sea level, it was safe. Centuries of draining the fens had been reversed, and many inhabited towns and villages in the old fenlands were now islands, accessible by boat. The surrounding washes, salt marshes and fens were slowly a recovering and expanding ecosystem. Marshland mostly cut off Free Port, and a string of east coast settlements, from the rest of the country. A narrow strip of land gave road access to the town, thanks to the massive tidal barriers at the harbour mouth. These tidal barriers would have been a feat of engineering before the Change. That the Resistance had constructed them with limited resources was a miracle.

The Family were stooped around the table; the report delivered earlier that day hung like a leaden weight around their necks.

'So, it's confirmed? Beyond any doubt?' Mother asked. Each key member of the leadership was given a family codename.

'I'm afraid so,' Brother said. He was younger than Mother.

Tall and broad-shouldered, he exuded physical confidence without being overbearing. 'Father has just sent conclusive evidence from the observatory in Iceland. It has stopped. Completely.' There was no room for ambiguity in his delivery.

It was early spring in Free Port but still unseasonably cold. The winter had been long and harsh—no records existed of such sustained snow and sub-zero temperatures. On average, it had been ten degrees Celsius lower than normal. Snow and ice had covered everything until two weeks ago, when the thaw began.

Cousin spoke after a while; a frisson filled the room. He drummed his fingers on the table. 'It wasn't supposed to happen for a few more years. We thought we had longer.' Cousin was leaning over the table, resting on folded arms. Although he was standing, his short stature gave the impression that he might be sitting. Niece was not in attendance. She had left Free Port for the fens.

Uncle was sitting alongside Mother. His codename was misleading. He was the youngest in the room by many years. While he was closer in age to Anouk, he commanded enormous respect from the other Family members. He had assumed the leadership of the Environmental Civic only a year ago. Where Brother displayed self-assured physicality, Uncle conveyed intellect. He pored over the details of the report. Shortsighted, he held the document absurdly close to his nose. 'They think it is a massive subglacial lake in the Arctic. The glacial ice shield collapsed.' He looked at the others with wide eyes. 'It's been dumping more the two million cubic metres per second of fresh water into the North Atlantic since late summer. That's equivalent to the amount of water in eight hundred Olympic size swimming pools every second!'

Cousin whistled in disbelief.

'Well, that would account for the unexplained two-metre rise in sea level over autumn and winter.' Mother frowned. 'What further can we expect?'

Uncle put his head down and scanned the report, sucking in air and holding his breath as he did so. He shook his head in dismay, summarising the main points as he read. 'Four additional months of freshwater flow into the ocean. That'll take us to June this year until the sea level stabilises. So, best-case scenario, we're looking at a four-to-six-metre rise in total from this event alone.'

'Can our defences withstand that, given the rises that we've experienced?' Brother asked. He shifted his weight to his other foot. The blackout blinds in the room remained permanently drawn, offering privacy. A light pendant hung over the table and obscured his face.

Mother's response was tepid. 'Maybe. We factored in a ten-metre rise. But that was based on the slow melting of the ice caps.' She faced Uncle. 'This sounds like a catastrophic release of water?'

'That's correct.' Uncle stared at Cousin, willing him to stop drumming his fingers. It was distracting. 'At the upper end of the projections, the water will breach our defences. We have already had a four-to-five-metre rise since measurements began.'

No one spoke. A clock on the wall ticked in the background, reminding them that time continued.

'And don't forget, if Father's report is correct, and the AMOC has stopped, then the winter that we have just experienced will be the new normal. Summers will be colder by the same degree too.'

'And it can't be reversed?' Cousin already knew that once the Atlantic Meridional Overturning Circulation, or AMOC for short, had stopped, the warm water brought from the equator would cease. The Northern Hemisphere would get colder and drier without warm moisture in the air.

He clung to false hope, but any good news would do. They

had remained in the room for a long time, with the windows and doors closed. The stale air didn't lend itself to optimism.

'Oh, the current will start again,' Uncle said.

Cousin straightened, appearing more hopeful.

'In about one and a half thousand years, when the effects of all that fresh water have dissipated.'

Cousin's face fell into dejection.

'The fresh water being released from the subglacial lake in the Arctic acts as a barrier to warm water travelling north from the equator.'

Mother sensed that the discussion was reaching a dead end. She pushed her chair back from the table, scraping it along the wooden floorboards. The room pressed claustrophobically around her. 'We must not forget that we've been preparing for this for a long time. We don't yet know whether sea levels will breach our defences. And we have developed our indoor vertical farming techniques specifically for this sort of event.' Cousin opened his mouth to speak, but Mother raised her hand. 'It is essential now more than ever that we remain upbeat. Our people need hope.' She surveyed the room, ensuring that the Family agreed on this point. 'We safeguarded an abundant supply of independent energy, and Father's work in Iceland has proven more beneficial in preparing us for a colder future than even I thought possible.'

A knock rattled the door. 'Come in.'

The door opened, and Fred poked her head into view. 'Apologies for the interruption.' She had been running. Her flushed face was sweaty, and she caught her breath. 'Sister asked that I come. It's started. The red jackets are attacking.'

'Secure the scientists,' Mother said.

From outside Free Port, Kilgore watched as a squadron of heavy armour smashed through the first of three lines of defence. The crashing carried even at a distance. Wire dragged behind a tank before lassoing around a shrub, releasing and snapping backwards with a twang. The Resistance had set their defensive line across five hundred yards of solid ground. It lay leading to the access road that bridged reeded marshland to the town. From his vantage point, Kilgore saw tanks churn the muddy ground. Lumps of sodden earth flew upward as they broke over the shallow trenches the defenders had abandoned at the sight of oncoming armour. *They must have known we would use armour?* Why had the terrorists not placed anti-tank obstacles at their first line of defence? *Perhaps they didn't have enough?*

The position consisted only of large coils of barbed concertina wire stretched out in front of a few trench lines. *Maybe it served as a temporary defensive position against infantry over the winter?* The position had withstood a few red jacket sorties to test its strength, but it collapsed immediately when the armour advanced. Shell fire from artillery and tanks had not been used to weaken the terrorists' positions prior to the attack. The Chief Superintendent of the Bureau Against Vice was adamant. Mortimer's superior, the Secretary of State, had been explicit: there was to be no bombardment, for fear of harming the valuable scientists held hostage by the Resistance. He followed Ogilvy's order to the letter, even though the defenders were outside the town's boundaries, uneasy about the consequences should anything go wrong.

The terrorists retreated, scattering. They fled in panic, screaming as distant gunfire popped. Dashing disorderly and untrained to the second line of defence, they traversed the uneven terrain and crossed between overlapping gaps in the wire fortification. They sought refuge in a trench from tank machine-gun fire that was now within range, rattling behind them. Brrrrrrt—a spurt of bullets mowed down a few of their comrades at the rear. One cried out in anguish, eviscerated and lying on the wet ground, clutching at his abdomen. The assault was proving all too easy.

The second defensive position stood at the beginning of the strip of land that gave direct access to the town. Plant-filled marshland spread out from its sides. It was a strategically challenging position that would force the armour into single file. Engineers had placed a few concrete pyramid-shaped structures, known as dragon's teeth, beside barbed wire before a line of trenches. Snow still capped them, refusing to melt. The fortifications offered improvement but fell short of a formidable defence.

Kilgore squinted into the distance, trying to identify what he had overlooked. What were they playing at? The most exposed point of the red jacket attack would cross the narrow access road. It was at least a mile long and vulnerable to counterattack. The breadth of the frontal assault would remain limited. Yet intelligence suggested that the terrorists didn't possess anti-tank weaponry. They concentrated the dragon's teeth at the third and final line of defence. It stood at the end of the access road, blocking entry into the town. Yet even this fortification was insubstantial and easy to overcome. One tank carried bulldozer blades. It would lead the last assault, clearing the way for the remaining armour and infantry.

Small arms burst into rattling along the second defensive line. Voices cried out. No time—the tanks trundled forwards. Defender bullets twanged ineffectively. They bounced off the armoured tanks with a metallic twist. Thick machine-gun fire clattered, filling the air with the sharp smell of sulphur. The defender's light weaponry was no match. It died out under a hail of whirring lead. People ran; the tanks rumbled on. A flash, and muffled screaming. The tanks lacked coordination. One attempted to wind between two concrete obstacles. A scraping crunch—it collided with another, forcing it towards a dragon's tooth. Whack—it hit. The tooth grated along the ground until leaning backwards. It dug under the tank with a creak. The tank's tracks spun. Another fitted with bulldozer blades tore forwards, clearing a path for those behind.

Kilgore pulled his eyes from the unfolding battle. The battled riveted and exhilarated him, yet uninterested senior officers dotted the immediate vicinity, complacent and bored. The largest group clustered around Kilgore's colleague, the Chief Superintendent for the Bureau Against Vice, convinced the battle was won before it had even begun. Champagne was already being served on a grassy rise, while no one attended to the fighting. One officer slapped Mortimer jovially on the back, leading to uproarious laughter.

Despite the terrorists' amateurish performance, Kilgore felt certain a surprise awaited the already committed squadron and the two additional companies of red jackets ordered into armoured personnel carriers. It was not his problem. He was there as an observer. Besides, his informant had been in contact with news. Unobserved, he stole into the background. Kilgore had business elsewhere.

—————⟨◎⟩—————

Fighting broke out before Ann and Sam came for them. Anouk and Aidan were preparing lunch, but were packed and ready for action. Their intense combat training had stretched over the gruelling winter months. They had already pulled on their camouflage fatigues and were lacing their boots when Sam rushed through the door unannounced. 'It's time. We're to muster.'

Aidan had grabbed his rucksack and was following Sam out through the doorway as Anouk finished double-knotting her remaining shoelace. She spun around, seizing her rucksack in full movement and dashed after them, leaving the door open. Their lunch, prized fried eggs, lay warm in the pan.

Ann was waiting for them at the front door, her trusty hunting knife at her side. A few civilians were darting into the presumed safety of surrounding buildings. Otherwise, the high street was empty. 'Are you both good to go?' Ann asked as they began jogging down the street to the pre-determined meeting point, their boots slapping rhythmically against cobbled stones.

'Yip, think so.' Aidan's voice wavered with nervous excitement. A tight knot formed in the pit of his stomach. Other combatants exited houses. A few joined Anouk and her friends, but the majority peeled away in the opposite direction, down the street, towards the distant sound of fighting.

Jimmy's decision that had brought them to this point had not been easy. He would act as bait, travelling to the Institute to steal the synthetic formula. Jessica had pleaded with him to reconsider:

'I won't let them do it to you!' Jessica paced the floor; Jimmy sat silent, eyes fixed on her. Her words slipped through a thin silver veil, as though he lived in a space between worlds. 'Just look at you. Look what they've done to you! It doesn't even feel that you're fully with me...'

'I am, Jess.' He reached out from where he was sitting and invited her closer. Jessica moved towards him, then stopped.

'Then prove it? Stay.' Jessica glared and put her hands on her hips. There was silence. 'You can't, can you!' With tears in her eyes, she crossed and knelt in front of Jimmy. 'Can't you see what that place did?' She rested her hand on his knee. 'It hurt you, so that you're no longer really here; so you don't have to feel anymore.' A tear collected on her chin.

'That's not true, Jess, I am here. It's just...' he brushed a strand of hair from her face and swept the tear up before it fell. He was with her but somewhere else too. 'I feel calm, unhurried. And certain.' The mentor's last words echoed in Jimmy's mind—'Remember me'. 'I remember,' he said, gazing into the distance. His gaze shifted and met Jessica's wet eyes. They were so kind.

A white owl shattered their peace. They sat up, startled. It flew clattering against the nearby window, clawed at it, beat its wings while looking in, then glided away.

That was then. Now, as they jogged, the mission was set in motion. Jessica had reluctantly agreed to Mother's plan. Mother had played her hand well. The last card hit the poker table, and Anouk, Aidan and Fred threw in theirs—of course they would. Jimmy was Mother's primary target from the start, and she had judged him correctly. His sense of loyalty was his weakness. Ann and Sam had also volunteered to join the team as soon as they learnt of the mission—they now saw themselves and acted as a team.

Anouk and Aidan were uneasy with a plan that led to the Resistance assuming control of the shimmer trade from the Governing Council. They argued the issue repeatedly, searching for a solution. No matter how pure the Resistance's intentions, or how sincere their benevolence, they were certain power would ultimately corrupt. But they hadn't experienced the dreadfulness of the Factory. Jimmy had. Synthetic would save innumerable people from torment. They understood who the primary enemy was—the Governing Council. Dreams of utopia were for another day.

They ran past The Oak Tavern and around the old leisure centre. Cutting across the common, they reached the meeting point in fifteen minutes. The church was in a community park in the town's north. They gathered with twenty-five others under the observation of the church's round tower. Anouk bent down, hanging her arms forwards. She had a stitch and gasped for breath.

'You're going to have to do better than that, Dimples,' Aidan said, struggling to control his own rapid breathing.

'Whatever, hero.' His jibe wasn't worth further response, not until Anouk's heart rate slowed.

Jimmy, Jessica and Fred had arrived before them. 'How the hell did you get here before us?' Anouk raised her red, sweaty face and supported her body with her hands on her knees.

'Magic.' Fred winked and tilted her head towards Mother's vintage Land Rover. It was the envy of the townspeople. Ann and Sam sauntered over to inspect it, their faces pressed against the front passenger window. Jimmy plucked at the ivy on the church wall. He turned the leaves intently in his hand, shading his healthy eye from the glare—the season's first cloudless day.

Mother appeared at Anouk's side as she stood upright with her hands on her hips. 'Are you alright? You look damn awful.'

'Cheers.' Anouk wheezed and straightened. 'The compliments keep coming today.'

Mother had approached them for a purpose, and it wasn't small talk. The battle raged on, and time was running out. 'Anouk, Jessica; can I please have a brief word in private?'

Mother turned to lead them a short distance from the others. Anouk glanced at Jessica, who shrugged. They followed Mother to stand among gravestones—not a positive sign. 'There's one last thing I need to tell you before you head off.'

'Jeez, not again!' Anouk hadn't meant to say this so forcefully. Mother looked enquiringly at her. 'It's just like, well, you're the gift that never stops giving—there's always another nasty surprise around the corner.' Anouk unzipped the top of her fatigues and fluffed air inside to cool down.

Mother didn't take offence. 'Yes, you're right. It's an occupational hazard, I'm afraid. I'm a keeper of secrets. And I have one more to share with you before you go.'

Anouk and Jessica waited apprehensively.

'Do you want to hear it?'

'Okay,' Jessica squeaked. She answered without convincing herself. Her petite figure assumed its distinctive controlled posture.

'Your father doesn't know that you're both alive and well. And that's of my doing.' Mother's delivery was uncompromising and blunt.

The sisters froze. Anouk's jaw dropped; Jessica inhaled sharply. Anouk had stopped fluffing her fatigues. 'Yip, that pretty much meets my expectations for the next instalment of "welcome to my fucked-up life",' she said, half-laughing.

She and Jessica had been distressed after learning their father was alive. Their hurt was twofold: that he might have abandoned them when they were young, and that, although they were now safe among the Resistance, he hadn't contacted them. They had agreed not to reach out to him—he needed to come to them.

'Let me explain, and hopefully you will understand why,' Mother said.

Neither Anouk nor Jessica responded. They were due an explanation. Jessica remained frozen—rigid, unreadable and perpendicular.

'After your car crashed into the river, your father survived, but just. Local folk sympathetic to our cause took him in. Once he recovered, he learned that you, Anouk, had been returned to your mother. However, Jessica's kidnapping under the State's Adoption and Re-Education Programme left no record of her having survived the accident. He, and all of us, assumed that you had died, Jessica.'

Anouk and Jessica still didn't respond.

'Your father was devastated when he thought he'd lost you both. He blamed himself. He considered trying to recover you from your mother, Anouk, but had lost confidence in himself. Your mother seemed like a better, safer, option. The State thought he was dead, and we, the Family, saw benefit in keeping it that way. We sent him in secret to Iceland to lead our operations there. He had originally planned to take you both there with him.'

'But he could have come for me. He chose not to,' Anouk said, with a familiar tightening in her throat. Jessica's body softened, and she wove a comforting arm around her waist.

'He was a mess, Anouk. He was a liability here. The decision was as much the Family's as it was his. If you want to blame anyone, blame us.' Mother could remain reasonable and calm no matter the circumstance.

Jessica was still consoling Anouk who was inhaling shakily. Aidan was looking on concerned from a distance. Something was afoot; Jimmy started towards them. Anouk mouthed, 'It's okay.'

'Why didn't you tell him we were here with you?' Jessica asked quietly.

'I almost did twice,' Mother said. 'Understand that your father is, um, a passionate man. Tempestuous, even. He's a fantastic leader, but he is prone, in my opinion, to acting impulsively. A little like one of his daughters.' The direction of Mother's look left no doubt whom she meant—Anouk. 'I needed to know that Anouk was going to clean up from her addiction before contacting him. He would have been over in a flash, putting us all at risk for, I'm sorry to say, a potential dead end.'

Anouk groaned, throwing her arms up. 'And it keeps on getting better.'

Mother was determined to finish, and she needed to leave to get back to the fighting. 'I was going to contact him after your induction, and then Jessica appeared, throwing a spanner in the works. I then had to wait to find out Jessica's loyalties. And to be truthful,' she wagged her finger and tilted her head towards Jessica, 'the coincidence of you showing up seemed far too lucky.'

Jessica responded in time to suppress Anouk's wounded protestations. 'And then, when you had satisfied yourself that Anouk and I weren't spies, Jimmy turned up with the secret about synthetic.' She uncoupled her arm from Anouk and sat down on an ancient headstone, careful not to stand where the body had been laid to rest.

'Correct. There's too much riding on this. We need to get the formula for synthetic. Your father, Arthur, would have dissuaded your involvement.'

Anouk was about to argue, but Mother cut her off. 'He would have, Anouk, and I would not blame him. It's what any loving father would do. And he loves you; this I know for a fact. Yet war is bigger than us. Arthur will be furious with me, but he will understand my reasoning.'

Anouk and Jessica also understood Mother's reasoning—it made sense. But she filtered all her decisions through the logic of ultimate victory. This came at a cost to real, living people. Mother was about to leave when she asked, 'Do you know why your father and Jimmy's aunt's codename in the Resistance are Father and Aunt?' The sisters hadn't given this much thought. 'Because you girls and Jimmy were the most important things to them. We named Arthur and Maggie after the relationships that meant the most to them.'

Sister led the Resistance's armed activities, observing the battle below. She was stocky, standing square on the north hill of the town, charting the progress of the battle through a pair of binoculars. Mother had just returned. 'How is it going?' She took a last large stride to stand beside Sister.

'Fine.' Sister didn't lower the binoculars. 'All is going according to plan. They didn't bombard our positions, just as you predicted.' She turned her head, glanced at Mother, then resumed gazing through the binoculars. 'It shouldn't be too long now.'

'They won't use artillery,' Mother said. 'The team working on Spark is potentially worth more to them than shimmer.'

A boom rolled up towards them as the battle continued to unfold below. Tanks had broken through the second line of defence and were lunging towards the final fortification at the access road's end. A mechanical vibration buzzed through the air. The defenders had small motored boats moored in the marsh just behind the second defensive line. They abandoned their position with minimal loss of life and slipped stealthily into the tall reeds just before the remaining dragon's teeth ground aside. 'It's important that we strike at the correct time.'

'I'm aware of that, ma'am.' Sister's military training was slow to wear off, and she preferred this salutation to 'Mother'. 'We just need to wait for the remaining personnel carriers to enter the strip road.'

A company of red jackets was holding back beyond the already breached second line of defence. The tanks had now reached the final defensive line. Confusion arose because the tank with the bulldozer blade hadn't been allowed, by mistake, to take the access road first. The tank blocking its path was backing up close to the bank that dropped steeply to marshland. The saturated ground suddenly gave way under the tank's weight. It slid seamlessly, sinking half-submerged, but irretrievably, into water and sludgy mud.

Sister winced. 'They're remarkably useless. Ah, there we go. The others are on the move.' She lowered her binoculars and pointed towards the remaining personnel carriers as they drove onto the access road.

The tank fitted with bulldozer blades made swift work of the last dragon's teeth that blocked a direct path into town. Small arms rattled in unconvincing defence.

'Now?' Mother asked impatiently.

'No, give it a little while longer.' Sister's voice was calm, with a trained coolness. Seconds dragged on painfully. The rear personnel carrier was halfway to the end of the access road. Eleven tanks still operated, lined in single file behind the bulldozer. Twenty personnel carriers ground to a halt behind them.

'Now!' Sister barked. A junior officer standing forwards, and at the ready, raised a flare gun and pulled the trigger. A red flare arched up into the sky, and immediately hell broke loose on the plain below.

Contrary to Mortimer's intelligence reports, the Resistance had gained a small cache of light anti-armour weapons. They used these to deadly effect from their hidden positions among the reeds. A punching blast issued from behind the last defensive position. The tank with bulldozer blades exploded in a flash of light and smoke, followed by a shower of descending sparks. Shortly afterwards, another boom reverberated, emanating from within the marshland to the east of the access road. The assailants remained hidden while the rearmost armoured personnel carrier shattered into flame. There was pandemonium as tanks and armoured personnel carriers manoeuvred around each other to flee—but there was no room. Red jackets feared being targeted by anti-armour weaponry and exited the safety of their vehicles. Resistance fighters were lying in ambush between the reeds, hidden in flat-bottomed boats. It was a massacre.

'Send the order,' Sister said. 'All units to preserve remaining anti-armour. They're to finish them with light weapons only. And confirm that the barriers are open?' The red flare had prompted not only the use of anti-armour weaponry to close off further advance or retreat of red jackets, but also signalled for the massive tidal barriers to be opened. It was peak tide. A wall of sea water, six metres high, was gushing through the mouth of the harbour and onto the adjoining marshland. There were no places for the red jackets to escape. Water drowned them in their vehicles, or gunmen shot them as they tried to flee. They sat petrified as the water rose around them.

'It's done.' The junior officer lowered the radio handset. He joined Mother and Sister to stare at the rising water and the flotsam of obedient corpses.

'We will lose the lower reaches of the town,' Sister muttered. She knew the plan, and it was well prepared. An unfortunate necessity.

'We knew that. It's been evacuated. Our moat is complete. They'll have to find a different way in now.'

Mother saw scores of red jackets seeking refuge. A large red and white New Albion flag hung limply from its pole attached to the top of a personnel carrier. The flag's fly end dangled in the rising water, pulling it downward as it soaked. Some red jackets dashed into the surrounding marsh; others clambered onto the roofs of the carriers. Snipers methodically picked them off, one by one. A spiralling plume of black smoke caught in the wind and bent double, blowing in their direction. The acrid smell of burning rubber wafted over Mother. 'What a God damn waste.'

In the rear positions, the Bureau command must have been viewing the carnage in dismay.

'I think it's time we lit the green flare.'

They were waiting for the signal showing when best to attempt an undetected departure from Free Port. Hiking to the north-eastern edge of the town where marshland began, they had passed time. The sky was still clear, and in their sheltered position, away from the onshore wind, they had stretched out in the sunshine and absorbed the warmth as though they were cold-blooded. The dull thud of explosions kept them alert; apart from Aidan, who had fallen asleep.

A green flare curved in the afternoon sky. Fred sat up—her legs crossed with her arms clasped around them. The flare had faded into a smoky trail. The ensuing battle would distract the red jackets guarding the town's perimeter.

'I guess this is where we say *auf Wiedersehen?*' Fred was sitting with the team who would attempt to steal the formula for synthetic from the Institute. But she would soon depart with a platoon of Resistance fighters, leading them on an independent mission to attack and destroy the Institute.

'*Au revoir.*' Aidan had woken and got to his feet. He dusted dead grass off his fatigues.

'He never speaks French to me.' Anouk had been inattentively drilling a small hole with her finger in the ground as she lay on the grass, staring up at the sky. Soil jammed under her fingernails, and she picked it out absentmindedly as she rolled to her feet.

Aidan's face transformed into a smooth and winning grin.

'That's because, *ma chéri*, we already speak the language of love.'

Anouk stepped back, screwing up her face. 'You can be creepy sometimes, do you know that?'

'Agreed,' Fred said. She turned her attention to Aidan. '*Dis 'n wonderwerk dat jy ooit 'n vriendin gekry het!*'

Jessica rubbed her neck and then offered Jimmy a hand, dragging him up. She put her arms around his waist, staring lovingly up at him. 'I didn't understand a word of that! Did you?'

Aidan smiled smugly. 'Luckily for me, neither did I. She's been trying to speak Afrikaans to me for years. I just ignore it.' He laughed and waved Fred away.

'Okay, enough showing off.' Sam folded his arms. 'Blah, blah, we get it. Ann and I are the only dullards who can just speak English.'

'Nope, me too.' Even Jessica stopped, surprised at Jimmy. He rarely talked after his return.

'You're right, Sam. We all need to head off.' Fred got to her feet and grabbed Aidan in one of her bear hugs. 'You all stay alive, you hear me.' She let go of him and walked backwards before turning towards her awaiting platoon.

The small team that had rescued Jimmy watched as Fred and her fighters gathered their things and headed further north alongside the edge of the marshland. The timing of the operation was crucial. Jimmy and his escort needed to reach the Institute first. It was on the boundary of the fens as part of a historic university. Fred would travel north and then loop back south. This would give the others time to steal the formula before the Institute attack, which would then create a diversion for their escape.

'Do you think it will work?' Sam asked Ann. They would cross the marshland until it merged with the river. Reaching the river by the evening, they would then travel along its course under the cover of night. The trek overland to the fens would be the most dangerous leg of their journey.

Sam tried again. 'Ann?'

She didn't answer.

It was the same day, but the sun was setting in the west. Kilgore was standing on a wooden jetty that had seen better days. Its pillars were rotting at their foundations. His thin body produced an elongated shadow, crossing darkly over a patch of open water then splintering between reeds. The informant's directions had led him straight to the timeworn jetty. She gave a detailed description of how to find where Jessica and Jimmy would alight. Kilgore reached it. He did not hide himself. Not yet. Time was on his side.

18

The punt carried six Resistance fighters. It had left after the battle at Free Port and stole clandestinely through the marshland. The crew took turns poling the boat down the river and through reeded stretches. The pole caught often in the viscid mud, causing someone to steady the punter as they wriggled it free. They were novice punters, and their progress was slow.

The night was cold but bright. The crew didn't talk. They nestled together, hooded under cloaks to keep warm. A shooting star streaked across the skyline, its light gleaming in the mysterious depths of the placid water. Its distant burning prompted a secret wish or two among them. Not all was quiet. Nature had inexorably reclaimed what people had abandoned. A vixen screamed forlornly, calling to her mate, only to be answered by the twoo of a tawny owl. The mellow splashing of the pole, sliding smoothly between the hands of the punter, marked time as they glided to their destination—an old jetty. It awaited their arrival, and beyond, so too eyes from the night's shadows.

Night passed, and the sun was pushing through the pink Belt of Venus in the east. Movement stirred in the reeds; their smooth shifting was confounding. They passed in front of the morning's first light, tantalisingly suggesting the appearance of Kilgore's quarry. He had been duped more than once into believing they had arrived, but this time he was certain. 'They are here,' Kilgore said.

He was crouched on one side of the jetty, hidden in the shrubs alongside the marsh. His joints ached from the long, frigid, sedentary night. An insect crawled over his collar and down his neck. He strained to make out further detail in the increasing glare, pinched it, squashed, and then rubbed. It crunched and popped. He strung his thumb and finger along a blade of grass, ridding himself of the insect's remains.

The red jackets hid in an arch around the jetty. Some pressed flat among the shrubs at the marsh's edge, while others took cover in the undergrowth below the surrounding woodland. They were damp and disgruntled. The punt was visible, although the crew lacked definition against the gleaming sun. Their irresolute bodies wavered as dark moving lines over an orange canvas. The closer they drew, the more definition they assumed.

Kilgore counted six terrorists. He distinguished their forms, but hooded cloaks wrapped around their crowded bodies obscured their features. Only the punter, a tall man, had his hood and cloak thrown back. He was the sole crew member who was not cold—pushing the boat forwards provided ample body heat. The man's features were indistinct with the sun at his back, but it wasn't Jimmy. He was, by comparison, broad-shouldered and strapping. He gave one final push, then lifted the pole as the punt coasted the last few yards before bumping into the rickety jetty.

Muscles tensed in anticipation among the ranks of the red jackets. Their trap would soon be sprung. Kilgore was waiting for all the passengers to disembark before giving the order to seize the terrorists. He would not risk their escaping. The punter was the last to alight. He sprang to join the others on the jetty as a colleague tied the boat to a pillar. His landing caused the already crooked frame to groan and judder.

'Set them loose,' Kilgore said to a squad leader crouching nearby. He got to one knee as the squad leader whistled shrilly between two fingers. The red jackets sprang into action, and Kilgore followed. But he froze and lowered himself down again. Jessica wasn't among the crew that came ashore. The sun had risen, revealing their features. Hers were easy to recognise. 'Blast.' He scowled, pressing himself even further down on the ground, jagged stones gnawing into his bony chest.

The terrorists were not taken by surprise. Unhurried and untroubled, they flung their hoods back over their heads, turning to face the charging red jackets.

'Good morning,' Sister said with a broad smile.

The encircling red jackets ground to a halt as predators do when their prey do not run. They regarded each other with uncertainty, anticipating further orders. But Kilgore was nowhere to be seen. As Resistance fighters appeared out of the woodland, armed and poised to fire, Kilgore slipped soundlessly into the marsh. His silk suit, already sullied from a rough night outdoors, broadened on the surface of the water before sinking with his body. His nostrils poked just above the surface as he snaked his way through the reeds and out of sight. The red jackets surrendered almost immediately, dropping their firearms.

Ann was a double agent: Mother's idea. She had risked everything to avenge Rachel. Kilgore had been her target in a well-orchestrated deception. She wanted him to pay—to be captured and suffer the indignity of a public trial. She had fed Kilgore trivial information all winter in order to gain his trust. Although the red jackets had taken prisoners, the plan failed. Kilgore evaded capture and would not be fooled twice.

———— ◈ ————

By the time Kilgore limped with blistered heels into the moribund encampment on the outskirts of Free Port, it was evening. He had hidden in the cold water for over two hours until Sister gave up her hunt for him. The terrorists only had a single boat to search for him in the immediate vicinity. He evaded their combing of the dense reeds, but could hardly walk when he first emerged. Mud dulled his leather shoes, ordinarily so shiny. One sole had broken free, and flip-flopped as he walked. His only consolation was that Mortimer Ulysses, Chief Superintendent for the Bureau Against Vice, had been executed that morning for gross negligence. His body hung limply from a firing post, and crows perched on his shoulders and pecked at his eyes. The Governing Council was unforgiving of failure. Kilgore's return, much to his relief, was unnoticed in the ensuing chaos of defeat.

———— ◈ ————

Jimmy's small escort, tasked with stealing the synthetic formula, reached their destination in the fens as Kilgore hobbled into the red jacket camp. They had crossed the marshland from Free Port overnight and landed a mile further north from where Kilgore had lain in wait. Fred had suggested they scout a nearby dilapidated barn—she had once sought refuge from the biting cold in an old van parked within. She didn't know whether it still worked, but it was in good nick. Many of the barn's dark cladding boards had fallen off or hung askew. The lower walls remained intact, painted in the region's traditional pink-wash. Passersby would struggle to spot the van, and the flat countryside around it was deserted. A rusty wind vane squeaked in protest at its abandonment.

'Fred must have been too freezing to notice', Aidan said. The van sat unhealthily and hunched. Cobwebs and dust choked it, and a family of rodents had nested in the rear seat. The barn doors clattered against the wind. Ann and Sam were hobby mechanics—they had restored the car used in the ambush for Jimmy's rescue. They got to work immediately. The tyres were bald, edges cracked, yet they expanded promisingly when pumped. Sam sourced diesel from a well-sealed outside storage tank, treated with protective biocide years earlier. He scanned the flat horizon for telltale signs of rising dust. Ann loosened the drain bolt under the van's tank. Her hands were sweaty and shaking. Degraded fuel sploshed out, dark black through oxidation, with slimy clumps of diesel bug. She bent over the hood checking oil, coolant and plugs. Sam wobble-ran with a jerrycan to fill the van with new fuel. The others were anxious. Time passed.

An hour later, the van rolled outside. The battery was dead, and the wheels whined. Aidan had found the van's keys on a nearby shelf, fumbling them out of a jar of nails. He hurtled into the driving seat and grated the gear into second, sticking his head out the window. 'Now!' The others heaved from behind, gathering speed on the gravel country road. Tyres crunched as Aidan released the clutch and applied pressure to the accelerator—but the van stuttered and burped. Failure. 'Shit!' No—the engine caught and a plume of black smoke exited the exhaust with an elated bang.

They didn't need to travel far. With the van, time was on their side. Would it get them there? Every mile was a gift. It was open countryside—rifles lurked at every bend. They expected trouble and prepared for it, cold steel in their hands. The Resistance didn't wield full control outside of the marshland and fens. They drove slowly, avoiding major routes. The chaotic red jacket defeat at Free Port and Kilgore's ambush in the morning had drawn resources from the countryside. They met with no opposition. But the van hit an angular pothole, bursting the tyre. They stood guard for twenty minutes while Sam and Ann changed it. The wind worked its way through an open window, and a crystal strung over the rearview mirror chimed time as it hit against the windscreen. Changing the tyre took longer than expected—a wheel nut had seized because of rust.

The van's brakes squealed as they ground to a halt, the engine spluttering for the last time.

They reached the watery border of the fens in the late afternoon. Niece, who had left Free Port to take administrative control of the area, had travelled personally to meet them. She and two armed colleagues had travelled by bayou boat. 'Thank goodness,' Jessica said. One rusty van was enough. The large, flat-bottomed craft, made of aluminium, looked fancifully elegant. Its rear-mounted and caged propellor roared as a column of air thrust the boat over the water's surface. The boat's noise testified to the Resistance's confident dominance over the fens.

Their journey took less than half an hour. The tension of the night before, travelling as silently as possible through untamed marshland with nothing more than a handheld compass as a guide, faded from memory as air swept their hair back and their faces blushed from the crisp surrounds. Anouk sat next to Aidan. The clean oxygen filled her lungs, energising her. Taking hold of his hand, she raised it as though they were flying—free.

She laughed as she twisted in her seat to look back at Jimmy and Jessica. Hair blew backwards and caught in her eyes. But she saw they were smiling too. Jessica burrowed under Jimmy's arm, seeking refuge from the chill wind. Anouk faced forwards again to see Ann and Sam. They were sitting at the front of the boat. Ann was pointing to something in the distance and talking loudly to Sam. He peered ahead, one arm hanging over the side of the boat, letting spray hit his hand. Anouk couldn't hear what Ann was saying over the din of the giant fan, but she saw what they were looking at.

A majestic cathedral rose on an island, and a stained-glass lantern crowned its central octagonal tower. It was lit, and the coloured glass was visible, but lacking in detail. The engine of the boat cut out, and its fan slowed as they neared a small marina. Several bayou boats and large longboats were moored there. One had coal smoke billowing from its chimney, acrid and earthy. A curious face peered from behind a porthole, disappearing to leave only a flickering candle visible on a table within.

'There are no lights on in the town,' Anouk said to Aidan. She spoke louder than intended, the thumping propellers still in her ears. Niece overheard her. 'Yes, the bastards cut our electricity supply over the winter.' She leapt onto the dock to oversee the boat's fastening to a bollard, pulling on the rope to ensure that it was secure before continuing. 'We get our energy straight from Free Port and its offshore wind generation. We God damn nearly froze this winter without it!'

Ann pointed to the glowing tower lantern. 'What about that then?' She remained unusually reserved; something weighed on her mind.

'That?' Niece pointed up. Ann nodded. 'Oh, we always keep that alight. To remind ourselves and anyone peeking in that we're still here, alive and kicking.' She grinned puckishly. Niece was middle-aged and looked remarkably like Sam. She had coarse ginger hair and a distinct horsey feel about her. She bent down to inspect that the second rope was secure. 'It's a little bit of hope in our isolation, you see. We'll get by with wood heating. But fingers crossed that Project Spark bears fruit soon.'

Nobody responded. The project didn't ring any bells for those gathered, apart from Aidan. He placed a finger over his mouth, trying to recall. 'I'm certain I've heard of that. Perhaps Fred...'

Niece interrupted him. 'Ah, I probably shouldn't have said anything about that.' She wagged her finger in self-admonishment. While a competent organiser and loyal compatriot, Niece was not politically astute. It was one reason Mother had sent her to administer an important but isolated population centre. 'Let's just say that life will be a lot easier if we pull it off.' The others understood that the conversation had ended.

Without further word, Niece crossed the dock and set off at a fast pace. When no one followed, she turned and beckoned them along. 'Come on, I'm sure you're starving. We've got the best eel stew in these parts.' Jessica mimicked retching to Jimmy. He didn't respond. He had had far worse. But Anouk patted her sympathetically on the shoulder. Aidan didn't care; he was hungry.

They walked past a corroded steel boat hoist and crossed over a bridge from the marina into the town. Determined water rose, forcing the abandonment of some of the town's lower reaches, but most stood above the waterline. When they stopped to survey where they had come from, Anouk could see that larger engineered flood defences were protecting part of the town, including the marina.

Niece showed them to a tatty pub. As they passed through the hefty oak entrance door, they stepped back in time. A fire blazed in a large stone aperture that originally facilitated open-hearth cooking. The lack of electricity had forced a return to tried and tested methods. A cast-iron pot hung on one side over glowing embers from a trammel chain with a hook. Seated at a table close to the fire, Jessica murmured to Anouk. 'Eel stew!'

The landlord was a stout lady with stereotypically rosy cheeks. Before leaving, Niece requested she see to the needs of the small group. The landlord wiped her hands on her dirty apron before she bustled over with local ale, chunks of freshly baked bread and stew. Chatting non-stop, she asked questions without waiting for a response, merrily moving on to the next set of guests.

Aidan happily tucked into his meal, but only after instinctively taking a taster mouthful of Anouk's food. He couldn't shake the shimmer ritual of sampling a tester hit to ensure that she was safe to continue. She didn't comment. She watched him gulp down mouthfuls of bread and stew between slurps of ale and smiled. The others also hesitated first to examine the stew, when a young girl of around eight shyly approached the table. She said nothing but stood staring at Anouk in awe. Without taking his eyes from his meal, Aidan grunted, 'You have an admirer.' Anouk's reputation following Jimmy's rescue from the Factory had blossomed. Unbeknownst to her, she had a young fan club from the old industrial quarter that recognised her and that was now dispersed across the East.

Anouk sat at the end of a bench and twisted around. 'Oh, hello.' She found the girl gawking and paralysed only a few yards away. The girl was horror-struck at being addressed, glancing fretfully at a group of friends standing at the other end of the hearth, egging her on. Anouk smiled. 'Can I help with anything?'

'You, you're…'. The girl stammered, her cheeks turning bright red.

'Anouk.'

The girl, toeing the ground, with her arms held behind her back, writhed awkwardly. 'You're brilliant.' With this blurt, the cat was out of the bag, and so she added, 'and brave and beautiful.' Her friends giggled.

'Well, thank you.' Anouk was astonished. 'But if you think I'm brave and beautiful, meet my sister.' She cocked her head in Jessica's direction, across the table. Jessica was grinning broadly during the interaction.

The girl's eyes darted in the direction Anouk was showing. Her mouth fell open. 'There are two of you!' She reeled back in disbelief to share the news with her friends.

Aidan snorted, still not taking his eyes off his food. Jessica blew Anouk a kiss. Sam was speaking. 'Well, King of England or not, they strung him up with the rest of them.'

Ann rolled her eyes and sighed. 'Why should we be worried about a posh, entitled git?'

'For no other reason, I suppose,' Sam said calmly, 'that he was prepared to die like everyone else. He didn't have to.'

Ann huffed and pulled at her collar; the weave pulled too tight. 'And now his useless little son is a puppet for the regime. Fat lot of use that sacrifice did him!' She was losing her cool—she didn't always agree with Sam on politics.

Jimmy spoke. 'To be right isn't always about having an answer.' If said by anyone else, it might have come across as patronising. But Jimmy spoke simple truths without an agenda. He had traversed hell to find honesty.

Ann sat back. 'True, Jimmy, true.'

The animated life of the pub continued—vivid and vital. Waterfowl hung looped alongside the hearth, soon to be added to a new pot over the fire. The low ceiling absorbed the warmth of the fire as the friends finished their meal. It was better than Jessica had imagined—hot and nourishing.

They sat, enjoying each other's company. The landlord returned to let them know where they could find their rooms. They would get up early to travel to the Institute. Jessica rose first, leading Jimmy across the room and up a flight of uneven stairs. 'I guess someone's getting lucky tonight,' Aidan chortled.

'He's not the only one,' Anouk said, raising her eyebrows suggestively. If this were her last night, she would make it count.

⬤◎⬤

Elsewhere, Mother had been busy ensuring the mission's success.

Chen Bai had a penchant for gold jewellery; every finger was stacked with rings. Mother had brought him a gift: a heavy gold chain with a matching pendant in the shape of a C. It was encrusted with diamonds.

'Pam, you shouldn't have.' He took the gift enthusiastically from her hands. 'But you should know, you can't buy my love.' His fur coat ruffled flamboyantly in the light wind.

They were meeting on an isolated country road somewhere in the Midlands. The road ran between two hills, where their cars pulled alongside each other, facing in opposite directions. Each had a pre-agreed escort of three armed guards, who stood to the side. Mother and Chen met precisely in the middle of the gravel road, between the cars.

'It's the least I could do,' Mother said. 'Thank you for agreeing to meet me at such short notice.' A horse had wandered over the adjacent sloping field and peered over the fence, trying to eavesdrop. It whinnied.

'Now, tell me you're not mad at me, Pam, for stealing your

business from the Governing Council?' Chen was the boss of the Smugglers' Guild. He hoped she was angry—he enjoyed winning.

Mother's response disappointed him. 'Not at all, Chen. "All is fair in love and war".' He stiffened, the armed men accompanying him incorrectly interpreting this as danger. They stepped forwards with their hands on their holstered pistols. He waved them irritably back. Mother sought to ease the tension. 'I know when I am beaten, that's all.' The Resistance had in truth strategically withdrawn from facilitating shimmer sales. Chen relaxed. He liked what he heard. 'I do, however, come with an intriguing business opportunity.' She waited.

Chen flinched first. 'Will it make me rich? Will I be able to buy a lot of pretty things?' He wriggled his gold-laden fingers. The sale of shimmer would soon make him more wealthy than he could ever have imagined.

'Filthy rich.' His eau de cologne was too intense.

Chen smiled, raising an eyebrow. 'Don't let me stop you.'

Mother launched her pitch. 'We are moving into direct competition with the Governing Council. How should I put it?' She rubbed her fingers together. 'It fits our general business model. We will produce shimmer but not undertake direct sales.'

'I see.' Chen adopted a more serious posture. 'You are correct; I am intrigued. And do you envisage a partnership with the Guild?' His voice dropped.

'We do.' Mother nodded and paused. 'At a fifty per cent reduction to current wholesale prices. We will let you set your own retail prices, of course.'

Chen spluttered. 'Fifty per cent! And your operating margin...'

'Is entirely protected through increasingly efficient production methods.' Mother knew it was a risk to offer such good terms. The Guild would suspect her motives. But it was a balancing act between their suspicion and their support.

'I see. Well, it goes without saying that we would be interested in learning more. When could we expect first delivery?' Chen was considering the minutiae. He was hooked; Mother could tell.

'Within six months. But there is a proviso.'

His shoulders squared. 'And what might that be?' He folded his arms.

'That you show your good faith, nothing more. We have an important package that needs to be delivered to Iceland. It must reach its destination.'

Chen forced a laugh. 'Come now, Pam. You know as well as I do that this isn't something that we can guarantee. Customs officials have been more eager since your recent activities.' The Resistance had increased smuggling costs for the Guild through their escalating conflict with the State. It was a sore point for Chen.

Mother nodded sagely. 'Yes, I understand. That is why you will combine it with an assignment being sent from the Governing Council. We know they use your courier services too. They won't interfere with their own flight.'

'Pah!' Spittle escaped Chen's mouth. 'That's a massive risk. If they discovered our duplicity, our sales agreement with them would be all but over.'

'Understood, understood...' Mother held her chin in her hand. 'But before we approach your competition, the Cartel, do consider the fifty per cent wholesale reduction we're offering.' She knew it was a done deal. Chen's eyes betrayed greed.

———◎———

'Are you ready?' Jessica was standing behind Jimmy with her hand placed flat on his back. He wore the Factory's black jumpsuit with the golden eye embroidered over his shoulder blade—new but authentic.

Jimmy didn't answer at first. He stood gazing, encased within the dormer window of their bedroom, situated under the eaves of the old pub. Jessica shuddered—he stood in a coffin dressed in funeral black

'Jimmy?'

'Have you ever wondered how geese know it's time to migrate?' A flock of pink-footed geese waddled to the water's reeded bank.

His warmth radiated through the jumpsuit. 'How?'

'When the seasons change and the flock decide it's time to move. Isn't that amazing? They just know.' He remained still, observing. His back expanded rhythmically as he breathed under Jessica's hand.

'You don't have to do this, Jimmy.' They had had this conversation before, but Jessica carried on anyway. She placed a hand on each of his shoulders and nestled her cheek against his back. His heart beat against her face.

When she first saw Jimmy lying stricken in the Bureau, she saw herself in him—alone and vulnerable to Kilgore's brutality. In nursing him back to health, she had saved him as much as she had saved herself. She rejected her father, his sadism, and defined who she was. But she had fallen in love with Jimmy. He was the opposite of Kilgore—tender, giving and safe.

'Stay, Jimmy. You don't have to go.' The last word was almost inaudible.

He was still staring out the window. 'The seasons are changing, Jess—it's time.'

'But I promised you I would come, that I would save you.' Jessica pulled Jimmy's shoulder around so that he faced her. She stroked her palm over his disfigured eye, tilting her head with tears welling.

His brow furrowed. 'You did save me?' He bent forwards, placing his forehead against hers and stared into her eyes.

———◉———

It was later that morning, and nobody had slept well. Niece and two Resistance fighters had ferried them within a few miles of the Institute. They had received word en route that Mother had secured safe passage for them to Iceland. *Cutting it fine*, Anouk thought. They had changed into red jacket uniforms and taped microchips to their wrists. Sister had sent these across the fens by punt overnight, extracted from red jackets captured at Kilgore's ambush. They had a limited shelf-life as microchips were re-validated every twenty-four hours. They hoped that the chaos following the battle at Free Port may have extended their use, as it was unlikely that troops were being accurately accounted for yet. Only Jessica and Jimmy would play themselves in the charade to follow. They had formally been inducted into the Resistance a few weeks prior but had not had their microchips removed to ensure that the mission could go ahead.

A squad van had been arranged for them. *It's certainly easier having help this time.* Anouk remembered their expedition to free Jimmy. Mother allowed them to go, but offered a bare minimum of support. Handcuffed, Jimmy sat between Sam and Anouk in the row of seats behind the driver. It was chilling seeing him dressed like that again, but he wore the outfit without complaint and with complete composure. Aidan was driving. Jessica, dressed in a smart suit, sat in the seat beside him—drawn and depressed. Ann sat alone in the second row, fidgeting with her hunting knife, picking under her fingernails. She glanced over her shoulder, again and again.

The Institute for Human Enhancement stood on the edge of the ancient university city, now hemmed in by fenland. A well-maintained road led in a straight line to an impressive building. Almost entirely glass, it was once the state-of-the-art headquarters of a biomedical company. Built on a triangular footprint with rounded edges, its vertically stepped façade merged with a saw-tooth roof. Its glass mirrored the surroundings as if under perpetual surveillance.

The van slowed in front of a guardhouse and a barrier. A red jacket exited and walked to the driver's window with a clipboard. If someone of mixed heritage in uniform surprised him, he didn't show it. He appeared bored and disengaged. 'Your business?'

'Jessica Kilgore to see Professor Brougham.' Aidan didn't elaborate further. The less said, the better.

'Ah.' The guard appeared more engaged and peered in to look closely at Jessica in the front seat. 'Would you mind my scanning you in, ma'am? You see, you're not on my list.' He prodded his clipboard with a finger.

'Certainly.' Jessica leant over Aidan to present her wrist, eager to get beyond the barrier. The guard pressed the handheld microchip reader to her skin. It bleeped an error sound. Aidan subtly reached down for his pistol.

'Oh, bugger, it's been temperamental all week.'

The guard whacked the reader with the palm of his other hand and tried again. It worked. The LED screen flashed 'Jessica Kilgore. Access Approved'.

'You're good to go.' He signalled his colleague in the guardhouse to lift the barrier.

'Thank you, officer.' Jessica sat back and, on further reflection, sat up. 'One thing, though.' She extracted lipstick from her purse, pulling down the vanity mirror. 'Could my men make a quick call from the guardhouse to let my father know that I've arrived safely?' Staring into the mirror, she applied a thin coating of lipstick and rubbed her lips together. She turned her head to the guard. 'He's such a worrier.'

'Certainly, ma'am.' The request was unorthodox, but the guard would not refuse Kilgore's daughter. The back door slid open, and Sam and Ann stepped out of the van. Sam headed into the guardhouse, striking up small talk with the man inside. Meanwhile, Ann lingered casually by the driver's window, standing just behind the guard, while Aidan kept him occupied by asking where in the country he was from. Sam picked up the telephone receiver, and when the red jacket in the guardhouse turned to attend to something else, he dipped his head, signalling to Ann. They simultaneously hit the two red jackets hard over their heads. Ann used the handle of her pistol, and Sam the telephone receiver. Both red jackets crumpled to the ground.

'Christ, I think I killed mine,' Ann cursed as Aidan got out to help her drag the body into the guardhouse.

'Just keep them tied up.' Aidan got back into the van. 'The exit needs to remain clear, remember, just in case we come running.'

The van drove under the open barrier and towards the Institute. It closed behind them. Anouk glanced at her wristwatch. It was after midday. They had two hours left before Fred and her platoon would attack. 'It's not going to be enough time!'

───── ◎ ─────

As the team entered the grounds of the Institute, Kilgore was in transit back to the Bureau. He had spent the night at the encampment in Mortimer's former quarters. The place was well stocked with luxuries. Kilgore had tottered out to see him later that night, after a warm bath, and offered him a single malt whiskey. A cigar dangled from his mouth, and he wore a borrowed satin bathrobe. Mortimer didn't respond. His corpse stared at the offering with eyeless sockets. 'Well, there's no need to sulk.' Kilgore had cackled inebriated before turning in for the night—humour and liquor a fragile shield to death.

Kilgore now sat in his black saloon, being chauffeured back to civilisation. He was recovered from the previous day's disappointments. More positive, more able to shape the narrative. He had survived a well-planned capture attempt. Losing men under his command would hardly be noticed given the massacre experienced at Free Port. 'The Battle of Free Port', it was informally being called. What a gift to the Resistance! It mattered little to the Governing Council, but it served as an enormous symbolic victory for the Resistance in a war that would grow larger, with higher stakes. There must be ways he could work these events to his favour.

The car phone next to him rang. He picked it up. 'Yes. Kilgore here.' The caller was his new assistant, replacing Jessica. She was assertive—it stirred hidden resentments. He wouldn't make the same mistake he had made with his daughter. He intended to saddle her sooner.

'Sir, you asked me to contact you immediately if your daughter appeared in scan logs.'

Kilgore's face broke into a rictus-like grin. 'Yes, that's correct.'

'She was logged entering the grounds of the Institute for Human Advancement only five minutes ago.'

Kilgore put the phone down without thanking his assistant. Mother could not resist using Jessica against him. She had fallen for his lie. He had not officially reported Jessica's absconding, but not because he wished to have her back. Far from it. She could be dead for all he cared. He longed to witness her slow and distressing death, and he still hoped to capture her for that purpose. But his primary aim was to use her. She was the perfect tracking device. Her 'approved access' status would tempt the Resistance to exploit her. It was enough to alert him to her whereabouts and the Resistance's next big move.

'Change of plans,' Kilgore said to his driver. 'Take me to the Institute for Human Advancement. And notify Central I'll need a company of red jackets to meet us there in an hour and a half. The Institute is under attack.'

19

Aidan had insisted on accompanying Anouk, Jessica and Jimmy into the Institute. 'I'm not just a bloody driver.' He still smarted from being relegated to that role at the Factory; segregation was his past and present. It was a risk to both him and the mission. Decree 1833 meant that it was uncommon to find anyone of mixed race among the red jackets—their presence was vanishingly rare. This had not raised suspicions at the guardhouse as they entered the grounds of the Institute, so he walked confidently as they approached the front desk in the reception area.

The space was light and airy, suggesting psychological and emotional wellbeing. The interior of the building comprised smooth curves and clean lines. Light oak spiralled and twisted around grey concrete to form working counters, stairs and meeting pods. The sinister work of the Institute took place in aesthetic sterility. The sickeningly sweet smell of vanilla permeated the air, seeking to cleanse the corruption of science.

'Your wrists,' the receptionist said as they arrived. Anouk cast Aidan a fretful glance. They had assumed that Jessica's being scanned at the guardhouse would exempt them from further scrutiny.

None of the four moved. The receptionist gave a high-pitched cough. 'Wrists, please.' Her tone was petulant as she shook the scanner. Jessica's performance had slipped. She hastily stepped forwards and presented hers first. The scanner bleeped approvingly. The receptionist showed no recognition of Jessica's surname. 'Next.' Jimmy was standing, cuffed, between Anouk and Aidan. They manhandled him forwards to be scanned. 'The subject last.' She sighed and rolled her eyes, expecting them to be familiar with the procedure.

Anouk stepped forwards. She closed her eyes as the scanner moved to her wrist, holding her arm bent to ensure that her shirt masked the plaster that attached the chip in place. A long bleeping sound and 'access denied' flashed in her mind, and the muscles in her torso tightened. Plan B was to fight their way in—not an attractive option. A short bleep signalled all was well. In the confusion of Free Port, the microchips hadn't undergone revalidation. Had they done so, the red jackets from which they were taken would have been officially listed as missing in action, and the chips would be worse than worthless—they would be exposed. They were lucky for now.

Aidan had to prod Anouk aside to present his wrist. She hadn't regained equanimity. A recognisable short bleep welcomed both Aidan and Jimmy to the Institute.

'I understand you have come to see Professor Brougham?' The gatehouse guard had informed the receptionist of this before his incapacitation. Jessica nodded and began to elaborate before being cut short. 'The Professor is a busy man. You do not have an appointment. You may sit there.' The receptionist's elbow was resting on the counter, and her hand flopped forwards with her fingers extended. She would not spend energy in directing them to a seating booth. 'The Professor may see you sometime later today.' She returned to her glossy magazine—*New Albion Today*: painted art featuring a happy suburban family on the cover. Her caustic attitude clashed with the background meditation music drifting through the reception area.

Jessica played her role well. 'Could you please let the good Professor know that Jessica Kilgore is here to see him?' Her voice was stony as she slid the magazine sideways from under the receptionist's nose. 'I bring a gift from my father, the Chief Superintendent. Tell him it has a CPU ratio of 11:1. He will understand.' The receptionist was about to respond, but Jessica's attitude was one of icy contempt. Authority at the Institute operated on this basis, and the receptionist responded accordingly.

'Certainly, ma'am.' Her manner transformed from sour to affectedly sweet. She placed the magazine down with her lips pursed. Jessica swivelled imperiously. She ushered the others to the booth but didn't sit with them. Such fraternisation would have appeared unconvincing. They didn't have long to wait. Professor Brougham descended the central stairs in hurried excitement.

'Miss Kilgore, what a surprise.' He scuttled across the reception area, approaching with his hand extended. 'I was unaware that you would pay a visit today.' His white laboratory coat was pristine and pressed, apart from a recent tea stain. He wore brown corduroy trousers and a checked red, blue and white shirt underneath. 'I don't believe that we've met.' He grasped Jessica's hand as she rose to meet him. He blinked his eyes and twitched his nose. His tics had worsened since witnessing Jimmy's escape from the Factory. He stole a quick look at Jimmy. His response was both tinged with craving and conditioned anxiety. He tried to stifle a tic, but the discomfort grew too great. His eyes blinked and his nose twitched again.

'Yes, very nice to meet you, Professor.' Jessica reclaimed her hand from his and let it fall to her side, yearning to wipe off Brougham's dealings with death. Instead, she clasped her hands courteously to her front. 'My father was simply mortified by the events at the Factory. We have recently apprehended the subject.' Jessica let her eyes flick towards Jimmy. 'My father is currently detained elsewhere—in the east.'

Brougham nodded, shaking his head in shared annoyance. He was clearly aware of the unfolding events.

'But he wished for me to bring the subject to you, by way of amends, as an apology for the inconvenience you have been caused.'

'Your father is a rare gentleman.' Brougham reached again for Jessica's hand. She didn't reciprocate. An awkward moment passed before he lowered his hand. He coughed, blinked his eyes, and wiped a non-existent speck off the front of one thick spectacle lens, leaving a greasy finger mark to join the others. 'Well, I imagine you'll be keen to get back to your doting father.'

'Actually, Professor.' Jessica fluttered her eyelashes. 'I was rather hoping, given the distance that I've travelled, to have a tour of your laboratory. It is world renowned.' Flattery would work on a man like Brougham. 'Perhaps I could even observe your initial examination of the subject. It would be such a thrill.' She tittered, bending her knees, squeezing them together.

'Well...' Brougham considered his wristwatch, hesitating.

'Please.'

'Oh, very well then.' Brougham's appetite for the fawning of others was limitless. 'I can't spare much time, though.'

'We're banking on that,' Anouk hissed to Aidan and Jimmy out of the corner of her mouth.

———◉———

Red jackets mobilised immediately after Kilgore's request for back-up, drawn from reserves still stationed at the encampment outside Free Port. Rather than meet the convoy of armoured and regular personnel carriers at the Institute, Kilgore's saloon met with it on the motorway. The driver slipped behind the lead armoured vehicle. Kilgore turned in his seat and looked through the rear window. *Three armoured personnel carriers, of say fifteen troops in each. Five transports of approximately ten in each.* A full company of red jackets was present. *Not bad. Not bad at all.*

The journey to the Institute took thirty minutes. The convoy was on the last stretch of road leading to the guardhouse. An avenue of birch trees lined the road, planted to project grandeur. The species was chosen for its fast growth. Like all things in New Albion, parsimony and quick fixes resulted in a disappointing result. They didn't offer the timeless splendour of oak or ash. Their branches were bare in the cold spring, presaging a portentous permanent change in flora because of the altered weather.

'Let the front transport know that they should pull aside to let us through when we arrive,' Kilgore said to his driver. The gatehouse had come into view, and a red jacket had exited, standing before the barrier. 'Also tell them to alight in case of trouble.'

The driver radioed ahead, and the armoured personnel carrier pulled to the side of the road as instructed. Its heavy tyres stamped grooves in the muddy verge. The red jacket from the gatehouse came to stand at the driver's window. She moved down to the passenger side as the window wound down. The privacy glass concealed Kilgore's face until the last moment.

'Well, hello, Ann. Fancy meeting you here.' Kilgore's inelastic scars on his face struggled to accommodate his smirk.

Fred watched Kilgore's arrival. 'Sweet arsing hell.' She and her platoon had concealed themselves behind an old earthen embankment in a field beside the Institute's fenced grounds. Years earlier, workers had hastily deposited and compacted mounds of soil and rock aggregate as a flood defence. But, as was characteristic of the deterioration in public services before the Change, engineers had miscalculated its required location. The embankment stood as testimony of a failed social and political order.

'What's on your mind?' Fred's lieutenant asked. His pointed beard poked out from under his helmet. They were lying on the embankment ridge, studying the red jackets. Fred's platoon had been in place since before sunrise. After Jimmy and his escort arrived at the Institute, they bided their time. Their attack was due to begin in another half hour. Any earlier, and the team might lack the time to get the synthetic formula.

'Shit, shit, shit,' Fred said. The red jackets had surrounded the gatehouse. Sam and Ann were kneeling opposite the barrier. A gaunt official dressed in a black suit stood over them. It looked like Kilgore, though the distance made it impossible to be sure. Every minute that passed made things worse. 'If we attack now, we can't be confident that the team will have achieved its aim.' She studied her lieutenant, hoping for an alternative. 'But if we wait any longer, the red jackets will have secured the perimeter. The team will never get out.' Her lieutenant's eyes were barely visible below the rim of his helmet, his expression unreadable. It was a perfect paradox.

Fred was in command; it was her call. The options spun like pinballs. 'We attack. We're easily outnumbered by five to one. But

we're lying on their flank, and we have the element of surprise.'
The embankment ran parallel to the convoy of vehicles halted
behind the barrier. 'Have the squadron form a hollow wedge.'
She pointed to the middle of the convoy. 'We aim for the centre.
If we can divide their forces, we can sow panic with small arms
and grenades. We can pick them off one by one from then on.'

'Yes, ma'am.' The lieutenant slid backwards and down the
slope to issue orders. He wore a ring embossed with the Earth
Civic symbol. He rubbed it superstitiously three times as he
departed.

———— ◎ ————

Anouk and Aidan had strapped Jimmy to a reclining treatment
chair under the instruction of Professor Brougham. They and
Jessica were not alone in Laboratory 1A. It was a large space with
ten other scientists in white laboratory coats. Their workstations
were along the room's edge. They worked industriously, cloaked
in personal protective equipment. The paraphernalia leant false
respectability to their work. Face masks, latex gloves, goggles
and plastic aprons. One scientist wore a hazmat suit and a
respirator. She was sealed inside a glass-controlled environmental
chamber, her actions difficult to discern. The others were peering
down microscopes, spinning liquid-filled test tubes within a
centrifuge, and freezing samples of human tissue in a liquid
nitrogen storage tank.

A digital keypad restricted access to and from the laboratory.
Jessica strained to see Professor Brougham enter the code, but he
was taller than her and had blocked her view. They had raised
a reclining operating chair, sporting arm and leg restraints, in
the centre of the room. It allowed for spectators and followed
a long, although recently resurrected, tradition in Europe of

public human cadaveric dissection. Brougham needed funding, and funding needed a show. Unlike his forebears, however, his theatre worked mostly on the living.

The audience would be spared a live dissection that day. Professor Brougham was merely humouring Jessica's interest. Jimmy recognised the device that was wheeled in front of his face on an adjustable overbed table: it was like the apparatus used by the optometrist to measure his CPU ratio at the Bureau. Brougham intended to confirm Jimmy's high production of occudorphin in his remaining functioning eye.

He leant over Jimmy, adjusting the position of his head relative to the device's chin rest. Brougham did not instruct his subjects, as the optometrist did, but physically manipulated their bodies as required. They were not human to him. Jessica stood beside Jimmy, and appeared fascinated by his work. Anouk knew the opposite. Jessica had no interest in Brougham's work. Rather, she was standing protective guard over Jimmy.

Brougham was making a great show of the simple procedure when an explosion vibrated through the building. Glass tremored; the lights flickered. The rapid gunfire was muffled by the glass, steel and concrete surrounds. Aidan instinctively checked the time. The assault on the Institute was half an hour early. An emergency signal blared, and the colour-changing LED lighting of the laboratory dimmed, replaced by throbbing red warning lights. He glared at Anouk, who was standing on the opposite side of Jimmy's reclining chair, and mouthed, 'Too early,' tapping his wristwatch.

Early or not, Anouk knew they needed to act decisively. They only had a matter of minutes to get the formula. 'Out! Get out!' she said to the laboratory scientists. They were motionless and resembled waxwork figures in a horror amusement park. She ran over to the nearest, grabbing him by the scruff of his neck and hurling him towards the door. The other scientists took their cue and scrambled for the exit too. Even the scientist in the controlled environmental chamber had begun decontamination procedures in the antechamber.

Professor Brougham appeared stricken. This was the second occasion in a short period that violence had found him. He blinked his eyes and twitched his nose. He vacillated between seeking refuge in an under-counter cupboard and making a dash for the exit.

Aidan decided for him. 'Not that way, Professor.' He stood in front of him, blocking any potential escape. The scientist in the hazmat suit surged from the environmental antechamber. With her respirator removed, she waddled in an ungainly run towards the exit. She entered the code into the keypad and, as the door unlocked, flung it open. Her foot caught on a stool, and she tumbled, landing sprawled in the adjoining corridor. Peeling from the floor, she first waddled one way in comic disarray and then the other. The pulled-forwards stool blocked the door from closing. 'Wha…' the Professor stopped. Aidan aimed his pistol at his chest while Jessica and Anouk unstrapped Jimmy.

'Brougham, you need to listen very carefully.' Aidan spoke to avoid any doubt or confusion, raising his voice to be heard over the blaring emergency signal. 'We need the formula for synthetic. You have two minutes to download it and hand it to us. If you fail, I will kill you.'

Brougham dithered—the Governing Council could also kill him.

'You have one minute and fifty seconds.' Aidan raised the pistol to his forehead.

Kilgore stood with Ann as a hostage in the reception area. Ann's cherished hunting knife was in one of his hands and a pistol in the other. He had instructed two red jackets to guard the entrance to the building. 'No one is to enter.' They had provided cover for his retreat into the building as a battle raged outside.

The receptionist scurried over to him, her high heels clicking urgently as she approached. She wobbled in her hurry, tripping, but corrected her balance before stopping in front of them. 'What the dickens is going on?' Her expression was tight; then, seeing Kilgore's pistol pointed at Ann, she flinched—wide-eyed and open-mouthed, she took a step backwards.

'Where is everyone?' Kilgore asked. The receptionist was alone. He had expected to find fleeing workers.

The brusqueness of the question took her aback. 'Th-they will have gone to the safe rooms in the basement. It's protocol.'

'And my daughter?' he asked without emotion. 'Jessica Kilgore?'

'Um...' The receptionist worked through her muddled thoughts. 'She delivered the subject to Professor Brougham. They went to Laboratory 1A.' She pointed to the curved central staircase. Kilgore had already shunted Ann forwards with the barrel of his pistol, and was heading to the staircase, when she added, 'But they are with the others, in the safe rooms.'

Kilgore left her standing alone in the empty reception area. *No, they blooming well aren't.* He motivated Ann to keep moving by skewering the barrel between her ribs.

They entered the first-floor corridor from a galleried landing. The red flashing light altered visible colours to either white or a dark green-blue. A corridor sign showed that the laboratory was on the left. The seat of a stool protruded from a doorway. Ann glanced over her shoulder at him. He breathed, 'Shh,' tapping the pistol with the hunting knife in warning. He moved the wrist of his knife-wielding hand to show that she should lead the way towards the door.

Brougham was standing at the outer edge of the laboratory, typing on a computer. The screen was holographic. Only well-funded State bodies gained modern technology. He pressed 'enter' and stepped back as a bar on the screen showed files were being downloaded wirelessly onto a pen drive. This was resting next to the keyboard. Aidan stood alongside him with a pistol while Anouk, Jimmy and Jessica observed from a few yards back. It had taken longer than two minutes to log in to the PC and begin the download. The sound of fighting continued but had slowed to a periodic rattle of gunfire.

Kilgore slipped into the laboratory behind them, pressing his pistol hard against Ann's right side. He held her left shoulder and pressed the hunting knife's blade against the back of her neck. He steered her around to stand beside the same counter where the others clustered. The noise of the alarm and eerie red light masked their movement. A flash of movement flickered in the corner of Jessica's eye.

'Hello darling, puppy-dog and friends,' Kilgore said as Jessica gasped and swayed. The others followed her afflicted gaze and also stepped backwards in disbelief. Apart from Aidan. He grabbed Brougham and pressed a pistol to his side. 'Oh, deary me, we seem to find ourselves in a stalemate of sorts.'

'I'm sorry.' Ann's voice was thick with emotion. She would rather have died than place them all in danger, but she had hoped for a way out. Kilgore grinned and leant close to her shoulder. 'Now, now, pussy-cat.' He traced the rim of her ear with the tip of his tongue.

Brougham stammered. 'Kilgore, my dear fellow, thank God...'

'Shut it!' Kilgore said. 'You fucking useless imbecile.'

Brougham's face fell. Until now, his dealings with Kilgore had rested on assumed mutual admiration. His nose twitched, his mouth slack. Dumbstruck.

'Shoot me.' Ann had found a way out. It was the only means of breaking the stalemate. Kilgore knew it too. But unlike the others, he was prepared to act. He tilted his pistol forwards and pulled the trigger. It was a perfect shot. It entered Brougham's forehead, between his eyes. There was no exit wound as his head snapped back. The bullet must have lodged somewhere in his skull. Aidan let go of Broughman as his dead weight brought him crashing to the floor.

'Well, that solves that!' Kilgore was pleased: the thrill of killing a celebrity—he would blame it on the terrorists. 'Now, it's time that you all put your weapons down and move to that glass box.' He showed the environmental chamber with Brougham's body, splayed, twitching involuntarily.

They slowly placed their weapons on the floor and walked backwards with their hands in the air. Their backs were now pressed against the wall, close to where the chamber was located. 'Father!' Jessica said.

'Not now, pet. We will have plenty of time to make up.'

Jimmy brushed his hand along the wall behind him. His fingertips caught the switch he was searching for. 'Get ready,' he whispered to Jessica. He pressed the light switch, and the LED lights turned off. His time at the Factory had provided him with an unusual talent—he could manoeuvre confidently in the pitch dark. Apart from the residual red light filtering around the half-closed door from the corridor, the laboratory was black as night.

Jimmy moved with lightning speed. The emergency alarm continued but was joined by sounds of struggling, erratic footfall, Ann screaming, and a white bang and flash of light as a pistol fired, clattering to the ground. Jessica groped frantically along the wall to where Jimmy had been standing. To her relief, her hand closed on the light switch, and she pressed it.

Ann was free of Kilgore's grasp. She stood back with her hands pressed against her mouth, staring. Aidan had stumbled blindly in the dark, towards the sound of struggle. Anouk trailed close behind him. He raised a chair over his head, positioning himself behind Kilgore. Jimmy had wrestled Kilgore's pistol from his hand. It was on the floor. But Ann's hunting knife had done its work. Jimmy slumped against Kilgore, hanging; a piece of meat. Kilgore had plunged the knife under his ribcage. It had passed through his clothing and pierced one lung. Jimmy coughed and splattered bloodied spittle across Kilgore's face. Kilgore's dark eyes shone with ecstasy. He twisted the blade, and Jimmy cried out in agony.

Aidan brought the chair down as hard as he could across Kilgore's back. The seat broke from its brackets, and skidded across the room, hitting a counter. Aidan dropped the backrest as Jessica and Anouk rushed to Jimmy's aid, kneeling beside him. Kilgore flopped to the floor like a rag doll, pulling the knife out as he fell. It still lay in his hand, which was covered in blood. Jimmy's wound gushed.

Aidan stooped, fingers pressing Kilgore's neck—nothing.

A ping sounded from the computer. 'Aidan, the pen drive!' Anouk pointed to the countertop.

He blinked and refocused on the 3D screen. A green bar was rotating in its centre. The download was complete. Making his way to the computer, he snatched the pen drive up.

Ann sourced the laboratory's obligatory first aid kit, mounted to a nearby wall over a sink. She ran over to Jessica and Anouk, opening the small box to find padding and bandages. Jimmy was in pain; lying on his back as they zipped his jumpsuit down to reveal the wound. He held his shaking hands limply above his chest as they pressed down hard to stem the bleeding; groaning as Anouk wrapped bandages tightly around his torso, holding the padding in place. Jessica was cradling his head in her lap. Her hair fell over his face; a flutter of private words.

'We need to leave,' Aidan said urgently, squatting down beside Anouk and gently squeezing her hand.

'Yes.' Anouk tied the last bandage into place. Her hands were sticky with blood. 'Jessica, did you hear we have to leave? We have to get him up.'

'You will be alright, my love. We will get you help.' Jessica rested his head on the floor.

Anouk and Aidan were the strongest in the group. They hauled Jimmy up, with his arms over their shoulders, and drag-lifted him across the room and over the stool propping the exit door open. Jessica and Ann were following close behind them when Kilgore stirred. They believed he was dead. Aidan had struck with force, and he had had no pulse. He looked up drunkenly and smiled when he saw Jessica. As he staggered to his feet, he lunged towards the door. She slipped through after Ann, grabbed a white lab coat hanging by the door, and kicked the stool back into the room. The door slammed shut and locked automatically just as Kilgore reached it. He stared at Jessica through the single glass pane. She stared back. His gaze was dark. It sucked all light and energy from the world around him, like a black hole. Grinning, he raised his blood-covered hand and drew the lines of a heart on the pane between them. He then pressed his finger against his face and smeared Jimmy's blood along the length of one scar.

———— ◎ ————

The reception area was empty as they descended the stairs.

It exuded a false tranquillity. The receptionist was no longer there. She had hastened to join the other Institute workers in the basement safe rooms. There weren't alarms in the reception as meditation music continued to play; the sound of flowing water overlaid by ambient tones. All explosions and gunfire had ceased. Jimmy wore the white laboratory coat Jessica had taken from the laboratory over his black jumpsuit. He drooped between Anouk and Aidan, his wound bleeding through the bandages and penetrating the fibres of the coat.

Automated glass doors slid open as they approached. Two red jackets stood guard on either side. They turned to the exiting party. A wounded scientist, three fellow red jackets, and a smartly dressed official led the way. Kilgore had ordered them not to let anyone enter. He had said nothing of those exiting. They accepted Jessica's authoritative instructions without question as she exited. 'Thank you. As you were. The Chief Superintendent has everything under control. We need to evacuate this injured man.' Her colleagues passed through the doors behind her and made their way to the squad van they had parked in an adjacent visitor bay. The red jackets resumed their guard. One narrowed his eyes, observing the group.

The Resistance's assault had failed. An armoured personnel carrier burned, crackling with leaping flames and belching oily smoke. The bodies of red jackets and Resistance fighters littered the field. Only five Resistance fighters appeared to be alive. Fred and Sam were among them. They stood in a line, pressed against the perimeter fence with their hands on their heads.

Aidan rounded the corner of the van. He stopped in his tracks. 'Oh, sweet Jesus.' Anouk followed his gaze. Fred was facing them, a hundred yards away. She was expressionless. Slowly, she shook her head, showing that they should not attempt a foolish rescue.

'Aidan, don't you dare,' Anouk warned. Jimmy was still hanging limply between them. Ann hadn't taken in the scene and opened the sliding side door for them to get in. She waited. Jessica had been trailing behind them to sit beside Jimmy, but Ann had already hissed that she should get in the front passenger seat to avoid suspicion.

Aidan didn't move.

'Don't be stupid. Fred is right; there's nothing we can do now. Get the fuck in.' Indecision paralysed Aidan, and Anouk tried a different approach to break the deadlock. 'Ann, take Jimmy from Aidan and let's get him in.'

Ann hesitated, then did as Anouk said. She unwrapped Jimmy's arm from over Aidan's shoulder and flopped it over hers by backing into Aidan's frozen form. They hoisted Jimmy's semi-conscious body onto the first row of rear passenger seats, and Ann sat beside him, pulling him upright and providing support. His head lolled onto her shoulder as he groaned in pain.

Anouk turned to Aidan, still frozen, staring at Fred and the other captives. One of the red jackets stood guard over the remaining Resistance fighters, with his rifle raised. He noticed Aidan's interest, stepped forwards and stared back. Anouk pinched Aidan hard under his arm, twisting a lump of soft flesh. 'You are going to kill us all, Aidan Bekker, do you hear?' The stinging under his arm and the urgency in Anouk's voice worked. He forced his gaze away from Fred.

'Y-yes.' He looked at Anouk. She waited a moment to satisfy herself that he had understood and shoved him towards the van's driver side. She climbed in next to Jimmy and slid the door shut with a thump. Aidan climbed in and slowly pulled the van out of the parking bay. He glanced at Fred as the van passed below the raised barrier. She didn't meet his gaze. The red jacket at the entrance to the building reached for his radio.

It was late afternoon, and the temperature had fallen below freezing. There was a cloudless sky. Fred's legs were cramping, and she was cold. She, Sam and three others had been standing motionless for two hours, facing the perimeter fence. The red jackets had left her dead compatriots where they had fallen. She shivered. But not because of the cold. Kilgore was standing behind her.

'Frederica Malone,' he said. She and the others had had their images processed, and the Bureau's facial recognition software had correctly identified them all. 'Pamela's new young bride.' He smiled, twisting his face around her shoulder. 'She will be so very distraught to learn of your capture. I wonder what she will give me to have you back?' He placed his thin hand on her buttocks. 'We can start by sending a finger and negotiating from there.' He paused, running his hand down her thigh. 'But before we do, I have a little question.' He stopped and squeezed, raising his stage voice. 'Are you a lesbian by choice or because you haven't had a proper man?'

20

The single-engine turboprop aircraft had clearance for take-off. Exhaust fumes formed a mirage behind the turbine as the propeller gathered speed. The pilot could have stepped out of *Treasure Island*—his single gold hooped earring and scar above his right eye sufficed. But he also had long black hair tied into a ponytail, and a devil's beard with a single beaded tassel. Jago Swaggart was not a pirate; he was a smuggler and worked for the Guild.

Chen, the boss of the Guild, had been precise in his instructions. The Resistance fighters would have to arrive before their scheduled evening departure. If they failed to do so, Jago had to leave immediately. They were already a few minutes late as the plane pulled from its ramp and taxied to the runway.

A black Bureau transport van swung onto the taxiway from an unguarded side entrance to the airport. The Guild paid well and bribed the guards to be elsewhere. The golden serpent caught the last rays of the setting sun, glinting. 'Should we be worried?' The first officer removed his braided cap and wiped his forehead with a handkerchief. He couldn't have been more different in appearance from Jago. He wore his brown hair neatly cut, and he kept his face clean-shaven. His uniform was standard—black trousers and shoes, and a white shirt sported a pair of black epaulette shoulder boards with three golden stripes showing his rank.

'No. Our cargo is listed as State property. There shouldn't be a problem.' The Bureau was fickle, and Jago wasn't certain. 'I'll go and see what they want.' He brought the plane to a standstill but kept the engine running. The rear of the plane seated nine passengers besides cargo, but stacked boxes had claimed four of the seats. Jago opened the cabin door. It swung down with stairs, letting in the whirring growl of the engine.

The side door of the van slid open. Two red jackets helped an injured man in a white coat and with a ghostly appearance from the rear seat. The colour of his skin matched his coat apart from where blood had caked. It was red-black, suggesting he had been bleeding intermittently for some time. A petite young blonde woman hopped from the front passenger seat as the driver also alighted. She ran over to the plane's steps, her hair tousled by the propellor's wash, and yelled above the noise of the engine. 'Mother sent us!'

Jago nodded and beckoned them to board, glancing up to check they weren't being followed. The young woman thumbed-up and ran back to the two red jackets. She pointed to the plane, encouraging her companions along, and hovered protectively as they made their way to its steps. Jago grabbed the injured man's arm as soon as he was within reach and pulled him upward as the two red jackets pushed. The man was standing but had little strength. He stumbled up the steps and nearly lost his footing. The blonde woman and one of the red jackets boarded close behind him. The remaining two red jackets were arguing at the foot of the steps.

'Get on the damn plane, Aidan.' Anouk's hair was flapping wildly around her head. The smell of aviation fuel was overpowering. She was standing on the second step, closer to Aidan in height.

'I'm not coming, Dimples. I can't,' Aidan shouted back. 'Fred's never left me, and I'm not about to desert her.'

'Then I'm bloody well not leaving either.' Anouk moved down to the first step, trying to push past him.

Aidan grabbed her shoulders with both hands. 'You can't. Jimmy and Jessica need you.' She started to object when he added, 'He's seriously injured, Anouk; you know that. Don't let him go without you.' He dug into the breast pocket of his jacket and withdrew the pen drive. 'Here, take it. It's our future. Synthetic will be the beginning of the end for the Governing Council. Make it count!' He put his other hand on her check and gave her a soft kiss. As his lips touched hers, the sound of the engine faded from consciousness. 'You're mine, Anouk Walker, and we will be together again.'

Anouk pulled back and regarded him in their private bubble of time and space. *This thoughtful, generous man, who only half a year ago was nothing more to me than a pain-in-the-arse dealer. He's now everything.* How far they had both come from self-doubt to purpose together.

Anouk didn't take her eyes off Aidan as she plucked the pen drive from his hand. She climbed backwards up the steps, still fixing her eyes upon his face. The plane's door wound up and closed like a camera shutter lens. Anouk carried the image of Aidan standing on the taxiway in her mind. He stood tall, dependable and brave. But the van was travelling towards the gated entrance when Anouk clambered over the seat to look out the window. A convoy of Bureau vehicles, lights flashing, threw dust into the distant crisp evening air.

The small plane shuddered as it carried them into the sky. New Albion's once green and pleasant land faded into the distance as the plane crossed unhindered over the North Sea and left the setting sun behind it. The harsh winter had bequeathed a brown and broken landscape in place of rolling emerald hills.

Jimmy slumped in the first row of seats, unconscious. His head rested against the oval passenger window. Anouk sat beside him in a seat separated by a central aisle. She rotated to sit sidewards, holding his one hand. Jessica knelt in front of Jimmy, with her head on his lap, holding his other hand. Ann had seated herself in the fourth row, among the boxes at the back of the cabin. She provided them with as much privacy as possible.

Jimmy was dreaming. He was back in the green valley. Snow-covered mountain peaks surrounded him, but the sun was bright with renewed hope. Warmer days had arrived, and the river effervesced with life along its wildflower-covered banks. A wooden cabin stood in the near distance, built in a blessed field. A spiral of grey smoke twirled upward from its stone chimney and promised simple pleasures in the years to come.

Jimmy stirred into consciousness. Anouk and Jessica had been sitting with him for over an hour and a half. There was nothing much they could do to stem his slow loss of blood. Pressure on the wound only seemed to aggravate things. His jumpsuit legs were sodden and sticky. It was dark outside, and his eyes opened. At that moment, the Northern Lights danced on the horizon. The swirling arcs and currents of greenish-blue light faded in and out of view. 'Look, Jimmy, look at them shine.' Anouk stood crouched and whispered into his ear. 'Isn't it lovely?' She was still holding his hand.

'Anouk, remember, all that glitters is not gold,' he said. She smiled in recognition. It was the old joke that they shared, reminding one another of shimmer's false promise. 'But,' he continued to her surprise, 'sometimes there are light, bright and beautiful things that offer hope.' He squeezed her hand gently, and his gaze shifted to Jessica. 'My darling.' He closed his eyes again.

Jimmy's aunt, Maggie, was striding out of the cabin towards him. She was beaming with joy as she reached his side. On this occasion, unlike when he first met her on the mountain, she didn't disappear. He reached out, and as he did so, she enveloped him in a tight embrace. 'You're here? You're really here?' he said, not wanting to believe.

'My sweet boy.' She smiled, cradling him to her chest. 'Nothing truly leaves this world. I was with you then, and I am with you now.' She released him from her tight grip to lead him towards the cabin. She h   ad taken the keys hanging around her neck and held the brightest in her hand. Jimmy turned. Anouk and Jessica stood on the opposite bank of the river. They were waving, and Jessica called, 'I love you, Jimmy, I always will…'

Jimmy was motionless. Jessica whispered into his ear, 'I love you Jimmy, I always will.' She was weeping. She pressed her face against his, her tears rolling down his cheek. Jimmy was dead. Yet she smelt his comforting and familiar scent as she burrowed her face closer to his. She pushed her body against his, willing her life for his. But Jimmy had left.

Jessica sat up, letting go of his hand. It slid down to rest against her abdomen, as if knowing the secret she had yet to tell him—it was too soon, she was too young, and the world was too cruel. She lifted his head gently with one hand and looped his silver chain and pendant over his ruffled hair with the other. Bringing it to her head, she let it fall to hang around her neck.

Anouk was crying silently. She clasped his other hand. It was still warm.

Ann offered her silent goodbyes to Jimmy from the back of the plane as it banked on its approach to the airport. His kind smile and gentle ways passed into memory. The Reykjavík peninsula was carved into a moonscape by millennia of volcanic activity. It was covered in snow and ice as the plane landed under the verdant heavens. The war in New Albion had only just begun, but Anouk held the pen drive in her hand. An army of Resistance fighters was rising, and she and Jessica had joined their ranks. Their father would be waiting for them. Their story had just begun. Hope was rekindled under the enchanted sky, and a tiny part of Jimmy lived on inside of Jessica.

About the author

Russell Luyt grew up in South Africa before moving to the United Kingdom, where he built a career in social psychology and academic writing. Now based in Paris, he has swapped lecture halls for quiet cafés, bringing his eye for detail and understanding of human behaviour to the world of fiction. He enjoys exploring stories that speak to both the heart and the mind, blending emotional intensity with social insight.

The Midnight Factory is the first book in *The Shimmerfall Trilogy*—a series exploring addiction, complicity, and fragile human connection in worlds pushed to their breaking point.

A Soundtrack to the Story

The bleak, rain-soaked world of *The Midnight Factory* doesn't end on the page—it reverberates in sound. In collaboration with redlane, a rising British indie rock band known for their raw energy and introspective edge, their single "Say You Want Me" serves as the official soundtrack to the novel.

With lyrics steeped in alienation, identity, and defiance, redlane's music captures the pulse of Anouk's struggle against shimmer and the Bureau—the fight to stay human when everything feels engineered to break you. Their songs move between raw energy and irony, echoing the same tension that runs through the story: the search for connection in a fractured world, and the cost of holding on when escape feels easier.

Like *The Midnight Factory*, redlane's sound walks the line between the real and the surreal—gritty yet dreamlike, furious yet fragile. *"Say You Want Me"* isn't just a companion track; it's an emotional mirror to the book's world, a fever dream of resistance, identity, and survival.

Discover more about redlane and listen to *"Say You Want Me"* at www.redlaneband.com or by scanning the QR code below.

In collaboration with redlane—featuring the track 'Say You Want Me'. Used with permission of Goldun Egg Ltd.

Synthetic State
Book Two of The Shimmerfall Trilogy

The fight that began in *The Midnight Factory* was only the beginning.

'When history is made, things happen fast; even over long winters, when time ticks backwards. I still hear the voices: Do you remember how certain everyone was, but nobody agreed? It was the end of the Governing Council, they said. And then they fought back.'

In this next chapter, Anouk faces shifting alliances, crushing betrayals, and the devastating truths shimmer was created to hide. As the Bureau's grip tightens and loyalties fracture, survival will demand choices that blur the line between hope and despair.

See www.shimmerfall.net or scan the QR code below to visit the official Shimmerfall Trilogy website and continue the journey.

Printed in Dunstable, United Kingdom

71032797R00184